GHOSTS OF LAMAR

RODGER ELLA

PROVERBS 24:27

Prepare thy work without and make it fit for thyself in the field;
and afterwards build thine house.

This is a work of fiction. Names, characters, businesses, places, events and incidents are either the products of the author's imagination or used in a fictitious manner. Any resemblance to actual persons, living or dead, or actual events is purely coincidental.

"There's good people and there's bad people in this world. There's good things and there's bad things in this world. Keep the good."

Love you always.

June 10, 1930 – February 5, 2026

THANK YOU:

Anh

Bryan Moss @boxingfitboss (Best boxing coach in Austin)

Marcus @gymfloetry (best boxing coach in NC)

Mom

Misty

Joci

Grandma

Marquese

Judy @audiencegranted

Rose @forwardlitconsulting

Round Rock Noble Inksters

Mitchell Gauvin (editor)

Milica Stankovic (cover design/interior design)

Tracey

Tom

Milan

Mary

Austin

And above all,

God.

PART 1: NEEDLE

CHAPTER 1:
WHO'S GOT MONEY FOR IODINE

July 2005

I crouched low in the wood-line behind the Chili's off 45th and Lamar Boulevard. The sun was high and biting through the trees. Roadkill cooked somewhere in the shade. I'd thrown up a honey bun and some bile already. It wasn't the heat or the roadkill, though; I was on the edge of withdrawals: the dope flu. It hit me in nauseating waves. I cradled my stomach with one hand and squinted at the cars pulling in through the leaves. I scanned for: Color. Model. Make. Occupants.

I patted my empty pockets hoping to feel some kind of money; I got nothing. I wiped my mouth with the hem of my shirt. An electric pang shot up from my elbow. I looked down at an abscess that had sprouted. I'd been bad about rotating veins and woke up one morning with an abscess blooming like a barnacle. It bulged with pus and smelled sour.

I gritted my teeth and put my palm over it as gently as I could.

A beat-up Chevy rolled in and then I started scanning the pine needles around me. I'd gotten lucky in landscaping and found 10s and 20s before. It was something I'd learned being on the street: if you ever need money, look down at your feet. It was the closest thing I had to prayer. If I looked long enough, I'd usually come across something.

And I didn't need much, just enough to settle the flu for the night and make it through the next morning without getting delirious.

I kicked a pinecone over and the pain in my arm came back in a tsunami. I tasted bile and swallowed hard.

An engine hummed as it slowed and I looked at the entrance.

A blue, freshly waxed '98 Lexus rolled in and backed into a spot a few cars away; Mom was the first to arrive.

I crept out of the foliage, staying low, and popped my head up twice to eyeball the Lexus as I crept. I got to her back bumper and checked her sideview mirror. She turned to the center console, and I saw a flash of blonde. I crept low to her window and jumped up screaming like a chimp.

Mom whipped around with a lit cigarette dangling from her lips and a tiny pink canister of pepper spray pointed at me.

I didn't duck; the window was still closed.

"Mom, that ain't gonna do nothing with the window up," I said.

"Well, *Jesus, Go'bay*," she said as she rolled her window down. The cabin smelled like a mix of spiced vanilla and tarry tobacco, "Fuck are you doing running up on me like that?"

"Little game of hide and seek. Lighten up."

I put my hand over my abscess as another jolt shot through me.

"You're lucky I didn't catch you with my .22," Mom murmured.

"You're a horrible shot, Mom. Would've missed even at this distance."

She rolled her eyes and leaned forward, primping herself using her sideview mirror, bouncing her curls with her palm. She pursed her pick think lips and scrunched her angular nose. The smoke from the cigarette in her other hand drifted lazily out the window.

"So, you back to the death sticks?" I asked.

She cut her eyes. "It's either that or jump off a bridge."

She took a deep pull on her cigarette, sucking her cheeks in.

"I get credit for showing up, don't I?"

She took her cigarette from her lips as she blew out. "Well, you *want* something," she said.

I once-overed Mom's polished dash and vacuumed back seat. There was a bag from T.J. Maxx, and a cake with white frosting for Dewey. It read in golden cursive: CONGRATULATIONS ON YOUR RESIDENCY!

"Dad just cleaned your car?"

"Yup," Mom said.

"Major Payne strikes again."

"You know how Daddy is," Mom said, "'Dress right, dress.'"

Mom dashed her ashes. They rolled down the door panel like tumbleweeds.

"So where is he?"

I glanced around the parking lot.

She nodded past me. I turned and scanned for the Ranger on the other side of the parking lot but didn't see the white gleam.

"Where?" I asked.

"Over there." She pointed her cigarette. "At the Garden."

I turned around, and sitting under an oak tree at the Olive Garden, there he was, idling in his jewel: '98 White Ranger. Manual. Deluxe crew cab. Not a streak on the windshield.

"Why do you think we took separate cars?" she said.

She waved at him.

He had his window open. A mahogany arm hung out the side of it. He waved at her.

I nodded at him.

He tapped his fist against the side of the Ranger. "Here we go," I said, as the butterflies in my belly burned.

"--don't start with him," Mom chided.

"I'm not starting. But you know how he is."

"You ain't even giving it a chance, Thom."

I turned back to her, my abscess fully exposed. Mom blew out a plume and her eyes zoomed in on it. Her shoulders dropped and her mouth slackened with despair.

"Go'bay, you're ruining yourself," she said as her nose curled and she caught a whiff. "It smells like a dumpster. You need some iodine."

"Don't worry about it, I'll go to CVS after."

"I know a lie when I hear one," she said, pulling hard on her cigarette, still staring.

"I'm gonna take care of it, Mom, let it go."

We were at a stalemate. She wanted me to stay. I needed money.

"Fine."

She chucked the cigarette out the window.

War averted.

"I've got something for you," she said, "get in."

She rolled up the window and turned to the backseat.

I circled the car, glancing at Dad. He bumped his fist against the Ranger once more. Earth, Wind and Fire, played faintly in his cabin.

I could feel his eyes on me like he was scouting the enemy.

Still, I was optimistic. I'd stoked Mom's compassion. I was at least getting forty dollars. And from the wretched look on her face, maybe fifty.

"Doesn't it look nice?" she said as she held out a blue paisley long-sleeve.

"Mom, it's ninety degrees out."

She shook it at me.

"We'll be inside. C'mon Go'bay, it'll look nice on you."

"It's not my style."

She dropped it in her lap like a tattered flag.

"You can't do it for me?"

I exhaled deeply at the windshield. I caught a glimpse of myself in the rearview. I had dark circles around my eyes and sunken cheeks. My skin had gone from golden brown to a dingy beige. But I also caught something else: Mom's purse in the back seat.

I looked at her, lifted my eyebrow, and shot a glance back at her purse.

Her eyes sank.

"Okay, I'll wear it, but I'm rolling the sleeves."

Mom sighed. "For the love of God, one of you has to let it go."

"What do you mean?"

"You think I was born yesterday?" she said, "I know what you're playing at."

"I'm not playing at anything."

"C'mon, Thom, I ask you to wear the shirt. You say no. And you say no, because you want to roll the sleeves. But really you just want Daddy to see how shitty you look."

"I'm just saying, Mom, you want the family photo more than

I do."

Mom blinked. Her eyes narrowed and looked ready for battle.

Either I caved and got what I wanted, or Mom would have a nervous breakdown in the parking lot.

"Fine, I'll wear it," I said.

I've done it enough to know two things about conning her: Don't overplay her sympathy, even mothers have limits. Some just have more flex than others. And two: it's slimy. Even the dope couldn't cut through the ick on my skin all the way; the residue lingered.

But love couldn't heal withdrawals; I needed the antidote. I was staring down the barrel of a night with a knotted stomach and the kind of sweats that could turn a sleeping bag into a wet cocoon.

I grabbed the shirt. Mom took out her soft pack and tapped out another Newport.

I peeled off my rancid T-shirt and pulled over the long sleeve.

"Looks pretty damn good," Mom said, flashing a grin.

I started rolling the sleeves.

"Thom," she said, lighting up and taking a pull, "no."

"You know what I need," I said.

She turned to the window and dropped her elbow on the sill and perched her mouth on her palm. The car hummed.

My abscess throbbed.

"How much?" she muttered as she stared at the Ranger.

"Forty."

"Twenty," she said firmly.

"Forty," I started *the beg*, "you know I *need* it."

Mom's shoulders shook, and she bit her palm. Tears rolled down her cheeks, catching the sun in bright orbs. She sucked in and sniffed deeply. Her neck, cheeks, and ears flushed deep crimson.

"Goddammitt, Go'bay," she said.

There's no sin greater than breaking your mother's heart just to steal from it, but some sins you have to talk yourself into; they become a matter of survival.

So, I waited.

Mom wiped her face and sucked in.

"You stay until Dewey gets here."

She turned and grabbed her purse out of the backseat, dropped it on the center console and fished out two crisp twenties.

She handed one to me. I took it and folded it once on itself. Then twice, doubled over. I shoved the square into my pocket.

"And play nice with Dad," she said.

She puffed on her cigarette and blew a billow out through her nose.

She held the other twenty in her other hand, away from me.

"I'll be a church mouse as long as he is." I reached for the twenty.

She pulled it away.

"Tonight, we're a family that can pretend. Play nice, and I'll give you the rest," she shook the twenty, "and then you can go waste it in your arm."

"You remember what he said?"

"You hurt him, too."

"Shit was fucked up," I said.

"Two things can be right, Go'bay."

I scratched my triceps. The sick was starting to hit me: the worms in my skin, the roaches crawling on my cheeks.

I looked up at the Ranger.

The fist pounded the panel.

Mom teetered on a stool putting up a banner for Dewey. She'd reserved a cluster of tables in the back corner. Dewey's cake sat sweating on the middle table. Tiny droplets ran down the edges picking up icing.

I gripped the folded square of the twenty in my pocket.

My nails stung my palm.

The clock above the entrance read 7:45.

"Thom!" Mom nudged my shoulder with her boot.

I turned around. "Yea?"

"I need a piece of tape!" She held out her hand.

"I gotchu."

I pulled a piece, and she took it with her thumb. I turned and watched the second-hand on the clock tick: slow and heinous.

"You're not leaving 'till Dewey gets here," she said behind me.

"I got it," I said, staring at the clock, praying for warp speed.

She sighed heavily in a waft of wintergreen and tobacco.

"All right, coming down," she said.

I turned and held the stool as she squatted down.

The banner read: CONGRATULATIONS DEWEY!

"Chivalry isn't dead," she said.

Her foot touched the floor, and I let go.

"Looks good, doesn't it?" she said, smiling.

"Yea. Nice. When's Dew supposed to be here again?"

I looked at the entrance. The clock read 7:46.

"Go'bay, we made a deal. Don't renege."

"I'm not renegging. Just asking."

"Eight."

Out of the corner of my eye I watched as the banner skittered along the brick wall and fell. It hung by a single piece of tape on the corner.

"Dammit," she said, "I need ya, Go'bay."

"Sure."

I turned and walked to the wall, grabbed the fallen banner, and handed the corner up to her.

The A/C blared at the entrance as someone opened the door. A car honked on the street and a semi roared downshifting. Sweat trickled from the top of my head all the way to my Adam's apple. I didn't have to turn. I knew who it was.

The hostess exclaimed, "Good evening, sir!"

"Hello love. I'm here for her," a baritone voice said.

"Go right ahead," the hostess chirped.

"Thank you, honey."

Mom wobbled on the stool.

His cologne was thick, nostril-filling, and spicey: Acqua di Giò.

I was a step too slow to help her step down.

"You just gonna stand there while your mother breaks her neck?"

He dropped his laptop-bag and shoulder checked me as he rushed to the stool.

"I helped her earlier," I said.

His head glistened with sweat as he extended his hand to Mom.

"Sure you did," he growled.

Mom took his hand and hopped down.

"Mom, this is what I was talking about."

"Play nice, both of you," Mom urged.

Dad took a napkin off the table and swept it across his head, his back to me.

"Where's Dew?" he asked Mom.

"On the way," she said.

He bent down and kissed her.

"I'll be glad when you quit smoking." He paused, and then smiled, "again."

Mom waved him off as his sweat dripped on her brow.

"Jesus, Arn, you're a swimming pool."

She wiped his forehead with the back of her hand and turned to look at the banner. She planted her hands on her hips and arched her back.

"Doesn't it look good?"

Dad tapped the seat of her pants.

"Work of art," he said.

I clocked the entrance again: 7:50.

"You know your son's here," she said.

"I saw him."

I didn't turn around. Time was ticking.

"You gonna say hello?" she said.

"Hello, son," he said, with grit.

"Hello, father." I kept my back to him.

"You decided to show up, huh? Five minutes in and you're already trying to skip out."

"If you want me to leave, just say the word, Arnold."

I turned on him and took my hands out of my pockets. He glanced at my sleeve. A small wet spot had emerged as the pus bled through. His eyes shook, bloodshot and hazel.

"You need to take care of yourself. It's a damn shame for your mother to see you like this," he said.

"Heard it. You got any other pearls of wisdom?"

I curled my fists.

"Both of you, please," Mom urged.

"No, Deb, he needs to hear it," Dad fumed, his mahogany cheeks twitching, "You're pissing your life away, son. And once it's down the drain it's gone. No second chances."

"Why're you so worried what I do?" I said, "I'm just Thomas, right? No last name? Remember that?"

Mom gripped Dad's shoulder.

"You're yelling at a wall, Arn. Let it go," she said softly.

Dad clenched his jaw and his fists became vices. He wheezed through a flaring nose. The veins in his knuckles twitched like nooses strangling kicking bodies.

I stepped my right foot back and off center.

Dad stepped forward.

Mom pulled him back.

"Arnie. Don't. We're in a Chili's for God's sake."

A waitress walked by carrying a massive, steaming tray of wings. She kept her eyes low and turned robotically as she dropped the tray off at a table of a small family: The mother and father watched us as a toddler kicked fat feet in a highchair between them and screamed, pawing at the wings.

Dad's shoulders slumped and he un-curled his fist. His shoulders heaved, He wheezed. Sweat dripped from his bushy silver and black mustache to the corners of his lips.

He opened his mouth to say something.

Mom gripped his shoulder tighter.

He softened.

"He's living his karma. I'm not wasting my breath talking about it," he said. He turned away from me and looked at the bathroom. "I need to go pee."

"Take your inhaler, Arn," Mom said.

Dad nodded, pulled his inhaler form his pocket, took two deep breaths in, and then strode to the bathroom.

"Fuck does he know about karma?" I said as soon as the door closed behind him.

"Thom, you promised not to make a big deal," she said.

"Twenty's enough," I said.

"You've gotta be fucking kidding me," she said. Her shoulders slumped.

Mom stared at me with brown eyes blurred by rage and tears. She turned and buried her face in her shirt.

I turned and made my way to the entrance. It was eight o'clock. I was only a few blocks from the drop-off spot. As I pulled my phone out of my pocket, the A/C blasted down on the double doors.

The hostess greeted Dewey. "Hello...doctor."

"Hello beautiful," Dewey said.

Dewey's high-yellow skin burned red as he wiped his head with his sleeve.

He stood in the doorway sporting a pair of ostrich-hide boots and a white lab coat slung over his arm that looked like he'd gotten it from the kid's department. His stethoscope hung from his back pocket like a plastic snake.

The hostess smirked.

"He just wants everyone to know he's a doctor," I said. "But really, he's got his hand up someone's ass all day."

Dewey gave me the finger and said, "At your service, fucker."

The hostess rolled her eyes.

"Do they make that lab coat in adult sizes?" I asked.

"You off to suck dicks for money?"

"Eat my ass."

I gave him my own finger.

He walked up to me, and once he was close, he threw a few soft punches to my abdomen and then grabbed me for a hug.

"Fuck, Go'bay, what's that smell?"

"Nothing. Just a cut," I said.

"Smells infected."

"I'm gonna get some iodine," I said.

We stepped back and I put my hand in my pocket where my phone and the twenty was.

I patted him on the shoulder with my free hand and pulled my phone out of my pocket as I walked past him. I typed in my dealer's number by memory. Some numbers you don't forget.

Dewey's hand landed on my shoulder when I was a step away from the door.

"You're really not staying?" he asked, his voice plaintive.

I turned around.

"You know the answer," I said, looking at the bathroom.

"Him?" he asked.

I nodded.

Dewey's shoulders dropped and he shook his head.

"You can't let it go, just for today?" he said, his eyes pleading.

"You already know what it's going to be."

"C'mon, Go'bay, at least stay for the cake. Some of my friends are coming."

"Dew, it'll be a fight. You want it to be the Middlecamp Brawl part two? In a Chili's?"

Dewey sighed and took his hand off my shoulder and let his arms hang limp at his sides. His lab coat nearly fell to the floor.

"It is what it is, I guess...Text me later."

"Later."

I was out the door and hitting send. My sweat fed the pavement. A zap of pain shot up my arm. I'd get some iodine after.

CHAPTER 2:
THE OWL'S ALWAYS WATCHING

April 2015

I stood on the wall of the Shell station off Lamar smoking a Marlboro, waiting for Ball.

I held my True Religion bag and tapped it against the wall. My rig was inside. It was a hot, spring afternoon. In the 90s. But close and sticky. The dumpster stunk beside me, its lid was flipped open like a massive black tongue sticking out of its mouth. Its breath was a mix of concentrated ammonia and decomposing corn dogs. I glanced up the street at the line of cars stuck behind the Cap Metro zipping by on the train tracks. The air above the traffic boiled. The sun was relentless, and even through my straw hat, my scalp burned. I'd been crawling around on a patio all day: new job laying patio bricks. I got paid ten dollars an hour, but landscaping's a cash business and that's what I needed. I'd thought I would make it to mid-summer, but I felt the itch to quit already. My palms burned through my work gloves. My hands were covered in white brick dust.

For ten years I'd ducked and dodged every punch that most users suffer. I'd seen people become tombstones. or so strung out they didn't even look recognizable.

Saw one guy steal his mother's retirement money that she was using to pay for her cancer treatment.

Even I wasn't that low.

They were stupid.

They were careless.

I'd mastered it. I'd developed a God-given system. I knew just how much dope I could use. I could get right to the edge without dumping myself over.

But I forgot the law: there's always a debt to pay when it comes to heroin. Either it happens early or it happens late, but the fee will get paid.

The gas station attendant walked by carrying a bag of trash over his shoulder. He glanced at me quickly and tossed the bag into the dumpster. He had a big, black, burly mustache, like Dad's.

I scanned the cars on the street for Ball. But, no telling what kind of car he'd be in; He was always in a different shitty car.

Ball was fat and full of rolls, had buckteeth, smelled like a pig and was always looking for a friend and, most importantly, he always managed to get his hands on the best dope. His newest batch was rumored to be liquid gold.

I'd called him the moment I got off the Cap Metro.

I was surprised when he'd picked up on the second ring. He'd had to be getting calls on the minute at that point.

"What's up?" He answered.

Ball had hacked a spit-wad on the other end.

"You got a package?" I'd asked.

"How much?"

"Forty."

"Where you at?" He'd asked.

"Shell. Off Lamar."

Ball snorted. He yelled "Shut up!" In the background.

"Huh?" I asked.

He snorted like he hadn't heard me.

"That place? Fucking cops crawling all over that place."

Two guys walked by with cold tall boys sweating in their hands. Traffic inch-wormed on Lamar.

"It's busy. Ain't seen a single cop since I been here. Not even an ambulance."

"All right," Ball grunted, "Be there in twenty. But we gotta be quick. Cash in hand. In and out."

"Got it."

Ball came twenty-one minutes past the twenty. He pulled up

in a Buick with a rattling engine and all of its hubcaps missing. His brakes squealed as he stopped. He backed into a spot in front of the dumpster.

"What up?" he said, rolling the passenger window down as I walked up.

"Hey," I said.

I stepped off the curb and pulled the door handle, then yanked my hand back: the metal was boiling.

"Doesn't work," Ball said, "Gotta pull from the inside."

I hooked my hand around the inside door handle, opened it, and hopped in. A few empty Coronas tinkled at my feet. Ball sweat madly even though he had the A/C blasting. I hit the button to roll the window up. I didn't want him passing out and then have to go digging through his pockets beside a pair of sweaty balls.

"What up man." Ball was so fat he spoke in breaths. "Long time—No see."

"You know how it is, got a new job," I said.

"Really?"

I put my hands up and clapped the white dust off my palms. "Layin' bricks."

Ball nodded and then scanned the pumps in front of us. I took my hat off and put it on my knee. I wiped the sweat off my burning and growing bald spot. People pulled in, got out quickly, and pumped their gas. They were too busy burning and in a hurry to notice a morbidly obese man dealing drugs in a piece of shit by a dumpster. I didn't see a cop anywhere. Not even the blacked outs.

Satisfied with the relative safety, Ball reached into the pocket of his grey cloth shorts and pulled out a package in aluminum foil. It crinkled in his hands and snatched sun rays as it shimmered. "You wanted forty, right?"

His voice was colored with paranoia. We knew each other, but we didn't really know each other. Just enough to know not to trust each other.

Then again, nobody knows anybody when dope's involved. I barely knew myself.

"I got it." I pulled forty crumpled dollars out of my pocket and smoothed them on the dash, the A/C blowing in my face. The cold stung my sunburn. As I put the final smoothing touches on my dusty twenties, there was movement on my periphery. I reached for the door handle to make a quick escape. Cops could've rolled up. I looked over at Ball. He was relaxed and stared out his window, waiting for me, as he tapped the package on his thigh. I took my hand off the door handle and relaxed. Again, there was movement, but it was behind me. I looked in the rearview and sitting in the backseat, as quiet as a prisoner, was a kid shoved into a car seat two sizes too small. He had a potbelly. His chunky arms and legs burst out of the crisscrossed seatbelt. His feet nearly touched the floor. He had the same piggish nose as Ball. The kid twitched in his dreams. And then farted.

"Hey," I nodded at the rearview, "who's...that?"

Ball didn't even turn, just picked a booger, and rolled his window down, flicking it out. "That's my kid—His mom's being a bitch—so I got him."

I took my bag out of my lap and set it on the floor. A few more regulars emerged at the corner of the building, drinking sweating Coors and swaying slightly as they watched us during lulls in their conversation.

I handed Ball the un-crumpled twenties. He handed me the aluminum foil. It stunk of vinegar. I unraveled it as slowly and quietly as I could and saw my prize: a yellow, fine powder. My heart tap-danced. It *was* good, not cakey like over-cooked shit.

"Now—be careful," Ball warned.

"Rumors are true, huh?" I said.

Ball smiled proudly. "Knocking niggas out—like Wilder."

"Who's that?"

He laughed and shook his head. "My brother—tested it." He pinched his fingers together, holding a molecule of truth between them. "His tester's fucking sensitive—checks for all kinds of shit—impurities, cutting agents, everything."

"And?"

"Came back—pure," Ball said.

"Blessings."

"Take it—slow," he said.

"I gotchu."

I looked at the powder in the foil as Ball's kid snored and Ball grunted. Saliva pooled under my tongue. I'd been waiting all day: bent down on my knees, laying crushed rocks, then a small white brick on top of it, then hammering it in with a rubber mallet: a thousand times over and over again. And with each strike of that mallet, the only thing I thought of more than the sun was that powder. My salvation. Salvation smelled like shit. I grabbed my bag at my feet and tucked my package in gently like it was a newborn.

A few of the empty Coronas clinked as I moved them out of the way.

Ball's kid coughed in the backseat.

"We're going to McDonald's—want to come?" he asked.

"I can't man. I've been waiting all day for this shit,"

"I'll get you a Mcdouble—you can cook—on the way."

I glanced in the backseat, Ball's kid's eyes flickered.

"Nah, can't."

Ball looked genuinely disappointed. His lips hung low like a curtain, and his buck teeth held them up in a sorrowful frown. Any other day, I would've taken him up on it, but it felt wrong for a kid to see what life really was. It wasn't college degrees, a wife, and two kids. It was leveraging your soul for something you could cook on a stove. Me and Ball were trapped like chimps in a zoo.

"Don't you have drops to make? I know your phone won't stop ringing with this shit," I said.

I zipped my bag shut.

"It won't—fucking—stop."

On cue, it rang. He reached down into the center console.

He put it to his ear. He waited, nodded, then said, "Yea--I'm up." Then, Ball looked in the rearview and yelled, "Wake up!--we're going to McDonald's."

The kid whined awake.

"See ya," I said. I opened the door and pushed out into the heat. I turned and closed his door quickly. He nodded at me. I looked back and saw my reflection in the window: Dope skinny. Eyes bulging out of thin sockets. Cheeks pulled in. Biege skin hanging on a skeleton. Clear snot ran down my nose.

Ball pulled off quickly, and as he did, a pair of fat arms flailed in the back seat. Then, a pair of fat shins kicked wildly in the air. Ball turned around and yelled, with the phone still to his ear, as the car bounced through the pump stations towards the street. How many drug deals had that kid seen and pretended to be asleep for? How many would he see that day or the rest of his life for that matter? People getting in and out of his dad's car just to talk about drugs and money. No pleasantries. Not regular people, just us.

I zoomed to the bathroom inside. The attendant looked at me and his nose curled. His bushy black eyebrows narrowed. I slunk inside and closed the door quickly. I double locked it and took my bag out to start cooking. As I sat down, I thought of Dad. As much as we were at war, he never would have had me in a spot like that.

Dope was a monkey I thought I'd tamed. It hadn't bit me yet. Ten years, and I hadn't seen the back of an ambulance once.

I'd never been so skinny—dope's also a weight loss program. In the snap of two fingers, I went from someone's son to living out of trash bags.

Dope's also an art—I'd painted my veins with junk until they hardened.

Dope's a form of karma—it always gives back as much you put in.

The bathroom stank as I cooked.

"Hey!" the attendant yelled from outside, "Don't do that shit in there!"

My phone buzzed in my pocket.

Dope's an ecstasy.

When the dope hit my veins—it was different. The purest orgasm I'd ever experienced. The whole world slid off me and I was euphoric down to my skin cells, drifting like a feather in the breeze.

Dope's gravity—and I stepped off a cliff, like a boulder: freefalling.

Truly amazing shit. But it felt different. Normally, there was a shelf I'd hit. Right before nodding I'd settle in. Like the feather gently touching earth. But I didn't hit it; I fell like a bomb.

Dope's a catastrophe—Death ain't an explosion. It's quiet and easy.

CHAPTER 3:
NOBODY'S EVER SAID SORRY IN THE MOMENT

I felt a slug at first, lodged deep in my throat. The second feeling was like trying to breathe through a straw filled with a milkshake. I coughed, and my skull ballooned and stung from the pressure.

Then came the orchestra: Beeping. Honking. Screeching. Then came a voice. Not Mom's, a man's:

"Don't try to pull it out!" he yelled.

I reached for it, but my hands were tied. I had a white sheet over my lower body. The slug snaked out of my mouth and split into two corrugated circuits ending in a machine. The machine barked and honked. Its screen flashed red and yellow. I reached for the slug again. I tried to rip my hands free. I yanked against the bed, shaking it. The man grabbed one hand. He had a white beard and small, blue eyes. Another hand grabbed my other wrist. It was Mom. Her face was stricken and tired. She shouted at someone behind her.

"He needs a bolus!"

"Working on it," a female voice replied, calmly.

I reached for the slug again.

"Calm down, son," the man urged. He tapped my hand and smiled bleakly.

"Bolus is in," the female voice said.

"Go'bay, it's okay, baby. Your nurse gave you some medicine. You're gonna go back to sleep, but we're getting that tube out soon. We just want you to be calm," Mom patted my hand gently.

"What the fuck?" I tried mouthing, but all I could taste was a disgusting sludge of mucus.

Mom gripped my hand vice-like.

And then the machine, the circuit, and the tube all faded.

Later that morning, Mom, Dewey, my nurse and the man who'd kept me from ripping out the tube stood around my bed. Their faces were grave.

Mom's arms were crossed and she tapped her foot nervously. Dewey chewed on a fingernail.

"My name is Terry," the man said, standing between me and the machine, "I'm your Respiratory Therapist. I'm going to be the one getting that tube out."

ASAP, please, I mouthed.

"Does he have a cuff leak?" Dewey asked behind him, his arms crossed. His lab coat thigh-length.

"Yes," Terry said quickly. I got the whiff of a Marlboro. "You a doc?"

"Neurologist."

"Brainiac. Great." Terry turned back to me. "Now on three, I need you to cough it out: One, two—" He yanked the slug out before three.

I coughed up wad after wad of saliva. My throat burned like I'd eaten a fistful of ghost peppers.

"Thank God," Mom said, sighing deeply as she uncrossed her arms and put her hands on her hips.

Terry wrapped the tube in a towel and tossed it in the trash can. Dewey was at my side rubbing my shoulder. His eyes: bloodshot.

"You good, Go'bay?" he asked.

I tried to speak, but all I got up was a mass of watery mucus.

"Suck all that up with this." My nurse handed me a blueish suction catheter that curved into a small bulb.

I put it in my mouth and spit the slime into it.

"Try not to talk, baby, you've had that tube in for a little while." Mom replaced the nurse and patted my hand as Dewey rubbed my shoulder.

"They almost had to trach you," Dewey said.

"Dewey!" Mom snapped. "Cut the shit."

"Why do you always protect him?"

Mom glared at him.

Dewey's shoulders dropped slightly.

"Sorry, Go'bay," he said.

More mucus, less watery though, welled in my mouth. I sucked on the bulb.

I looked out the window as the sun rose between the skyscrapers. Flashes of pink sunlight jumped from glass to glass. The Frost Bank building—affectionately known as the owl building, because it looks like an owl—glared at me.

The clock above the window ticked away from 7:15.

"Water," I rasped out to Mom.

"Not yet honey." She looked down at her watch, and let go of my hand.

"Dewey." She nodded towards the window.

Dewey's eyes got dark, and he stopped rubbing my shoulder. His lips trembled and a film of water appeared on his lower eyelids.

They left me and huddled at the window. The owl held watch as the sun rose higher. Dewey rubbed Mom's upper back and shoulders. She crossed her arms and shuddered as she put her face in her hands.

"What's going on?" I tried to ask, but a ball of saliva sat on my vocal cords like glue. I coughed it up and my nurse appeared at my side, rubbing my shoulder and smiling gently,

"I'm Ashley, your nurse. I'm going to give you something to keep you calm, okay? What do you go by, Go'bay?"

"It's a nickname," Dewey said, turning around quickly.

"Sorry," she said, leaning in, her hair smelled like vanilla.

"Thom," I rasped.

She patted my hand, and I turned to the window looking at Mom and Dewey. The sun pulled itself over the buildings and a white glow filled the room. Mom cried; Dewey trembled.

I woke up around nine that night. I could just make out the hour hand on the clock above the window. The owl was lit up, and his scowl looked permanent. My throat wasn't as sore. I could make out words, sentences. An ambulance strobed and screamed in the street below; red and white lights bounced around the glass façade of the hospital and the glass building beside it. The light over my bed glowed dim and green. Mom sat beside me talking quietly on her phone. She had on a black dress and no makeup; a box of tissues lay on her lap. And the bags under her eyes drooped heavily like over-filled water balloons.

"He's up, I'll call you back," she said.

She laid her phone down on my bedside table and blew her nose.

I pulled myself up in bed.

She grabbed my hand and held it tightly. My left arm burned from my IV; my right was too scarred.

"Hey, baby," she smiled weakly, "how you feeling?"

"Like hammered dog shit."

Ashley laughed beside me as she started more fluids.

"Sorry," I said.

Ashley smirked. "I feel like that on the drive home."

"How long have I slept?"

"Off and on all day," Ashley said, softly.

"Where's Dew?" I asked.

"He went home for a bit." Mom let go of my hand and blew her nose.

She looked completely empty.

"Why are you wearing black? Where's Dad?"

"I've got to go give report," Ashley said. She touched my shoulder. "I'll be back tomorrow morning, so don't go escaping."

"I'm jumping out the window," I said.

She smiled and then looked at Mom. "I'm sorry, Deb."

Mom nodded.

Ashley left and closed the door in a hush.

I turned to Mom. Her face looked ghoulish with all her makeup washed off. The red tint to her cheeks: erased. Her forehead was a worried formation of rolling hills. Her plump lips were pulled in.

"Are you okay?"

"Fine, Go'bay." Mom breathed in deeply.

I looked around the room. There was a couch under the window. Mom's purse lay sideways on the cushion like a wrecked ship. There was a blanket. A pillow.

Beside the couch, there was a door with photos taped on it and a small, amber overhead light above it.

One: Me and Dewey as chubby toddlers in a kiddie pool splashing butt-ass naked and smiling wildly. Dad's mahogany foot and crusted toenails stuck out of a sandal at the edge of the picture.

Another: A picture of me, in a Little League uniform. I was probably 10 or 11. I stopped playing rec at thirteen. The uniform was white with a cursive Red Sox logo stitched in it. I had a smearing of brown dirt at the bottom of my pants. My cleats were covered in red mud. Dad stood beside me in a baby blue button-down long-sleeve with the sleeves rolled up. His black slacks were splattered with dirt and his usually polished wingtips were dirt-crusted. His smile lifted his entire mustache.

Mom turned and looked at the photos. She blew out heavily.

"You remember that day?" she asked. She pointed to the Little League photo.

"Kind of."

She turned back to me. Tears ran down her cheeks.

"What do you remember?" She trembled and reached for more tissues.

"Where's Dad, Mom?" A lozenge of saliva lodged in my throat.

"What do you remember from that day, Go'bay?" Mom said as she slid her chair closer to me. I caught a glimpse of a single bat zigzagging through the street lights outside my window. Rolling purple clouds cloaked the night.

"I just want to hear it," Mom said softly as she reached for my hand.

I choked down the saliva like an ice cube. "I remember Dad got there late. It was the only game he was ever late for," I said.

"Mm hmm," Mom said holding my hand.

"But," tears welled in the corners of my eyes, "Dad walked into the dugout, and asked where I was. When I stood up, he walked over and hugged me. He said he was sorry he was late. He asked how I did. I told him I'd ground out twice."

Dad had hugged me firmly against his belly. I'd heard his heart-beat through his belly button.

I looked around the room. I didn't see his laptop bag. Or his hat.

I looked at Mom. She shook with tears. She gripped my hand harder.

"The coach tried to kick him out of the dugout. But he wouldn't move," I said.

"Stubborn as a mule," Mom laughed, but her eyes were focused on me.

"He said, 'Son.... you made contact...That's all that matters.'"

Mom put her chin on the bedrail. The bed shook and swayed. My vision got blurry.

After the game, Dad had thrown batting practice for me for two hours until the park staff turned off the lights.

"Mom, where's Dad?" I asked again.

"Thom, something happened," she said. The blood pressure cuff around my arm expanded. My heartbeat echoed like artillery in my ears.

Dad was at home when Mom called him and told him I'd been found. She said his voice cracked and he asked, "Is he alive?" Mom told him yes and his first words were, "Thank God." After that, she expected him to be spitting mad and yelling. But he wasn't. He moaned lowly like a beaten wolf.

On his way to the hospital, he came to an intersection. As he waited for the light to turn, his heart pumped against the pressure of four clogged arteries; and failed. They found him at the intersection, Ranger revving in park, his foot stuck on the gas pedal. He laid over the gear shift. Dead for ten minutes by the time EMS got there. They did CPR, but it was no use.

"There wasn't even a trickle of blood going to his brain when they did the CT," Mom said.

"When was the memorial?" I asked.

"Today."

"Is that what you and Dewey were talking about this morning?"

"Yes."

"Why didn't you tell me?"

"You'd just gotten extubated."

"So, he was never here?"

Mom sat up, grabbed a tissue, and shook her head. "He never—" she blew her nose deeply into the tissue— "made it."

My stomach twisted and contracted, and I threw up brownish vomit all over my sheets.

Mom waved frantically at the door. Ashley and the night nurse rushed in.

"He threw up. Can he get some Zofran and Ativan?" Mom's voice cracked.

"On the way," Ashley said. She rushed out of the room and returned with two syringes of clear fluid.

Mom put her hand on top of mine. The monitor behind me beeped. Mom glanced at it and bit her bottom lip.

"This is going to help you relax," Ashley said.

I woke up through the night in puddles of sweat. And when my eyes adjusted, I cried. I'd look at the picture of me and Dad at the Little League game and could just make out his smile.

CHAPTER 4:
THE GOOD DOCTOR

I woke up to a searing headache. When I tried opening my eyes my stomach twisted. I closed them tightly and sweat through my pillow. I felt every drop of sweat on my back like tiny freezing fingers.

"Thom," Mom said. "It's shift change. Ashley's coming in two seconds to give you your meds."

I pinched my eyes tighter. Every word boomed.

"What are they giving me?" I asked.

"Buprenorphine," Mom said.

"This is fucking hell."

"I know, baby."

The door opened softly, and Ashley whispered, "I've got something for you."

"Please."

A stinging sensation ran up my arm, not like heroin. It didn't spread nearly as quickly.

"Give it a moment, Thom."

"Mom?" I asked.

"Yea honey?"

"Where's my phone?"

The pain started to dip. I opened my eyes in slits and turned towards her. A car honked on the street. The sun rose in pink slices on the skyscrapers. Mom sat beside me with a Bible in her lap.

"No," she said. Her face was tight and her voice was sharp.

My eyes began to adjust, and I saw the features of her new face. The new bags. The new frown lines. The new worry lines. And a new anger in her brown eyes.

"What?" I asked.

"No, Thomas. Absolutely not," Mom said.

She sat back, crossed her legs and put her hands in her lap over her Bible.

"Why not?"

"You nearly died. You think you're just going to spring out of here and do it all over again?"

"You can't just hide my phone from me."

"I don't have it. Don't know where it is," Mom said. Her lips trembled, but she didn't break.

Her eyes were two pistols aimed at me.

I glanced at the bathroom door and closed my eyes. A spike hit my heart.

"I'm sorry, Mom."

"I know you are. But this has to be the last time Thom. You understand that right? There won't be a last time, next time. It'll just be a morgue and a headstone," she said.

I didn't want to be back in the hospital again, didn't want to see Ball again, didn't want to deal with more people who used drug deals as field trips, but I could already feel the urge. The hands around my neck. The voice in my ear. *Just a one-off.*

"I asked Ashley to get a psych consult for you," Mom said.

"I ain't crazy, Mom."

"It ain't about that, Thom," Mom said. "It's about rehab."

For ten years, I'd tip-toed around her about it. But Mom was worn thin. The bags under her eyes could drag the floor. Her hair was thin. And, as she gripped my hands, she tapped her foot on the ground like a piston.

I didn't have another parent left. She was it.

"Fuck," I said.

"Will you just listen to him? You want to leave AMA afterwards, fine. I won't try to stop you. But please, Go'bay, listen to him?"

The bed shook as she pumped her foot.

"Fine," I said.

Mom sighed and slumped back in her seat. She let go of my

hands and hugged the Bible.

The meds started to kick in.

"Who's the doc?" she asked Ashley.

Ashley smirked. "Dr. Heinz."

"Bad bedside manner?" Mom asked. Her face was quizzical as she leaned forward.

"No, he's just…unconventional," Ashley looked down at me, "He's got a story, too."

I laid back and looked up at the ceiling.

"Here he is," Mom said. She sat forward in her chair and patted my shin frantically.

A cup of half-finished chocolate pudding sat on the table in front of me. They'd finally pulled the feeding tube out of my nose and let me eat. The pudding was too sweet.

My door was cracked enough to get a full view of the good doctor talking to Ashley in sharp, quiet tones. He wasn't what I'd imagined. On a good day he was 5'3" in boots. His lab coat nearly dragged the floor. He had on thick circular glasses over a pair of wide, buggy eyes. He wore a blue linen button-down with the top button undone. White hair covered his small head in a frizzy and wild pattern as if he got his jolt in the morning by sticking forks in electrical sockets.

As he talked to Ashley, she shrunk. Each word out of his mouth was another inch off her spine. She was stooping by the time he finished. He turned to the open door and looked at me. His face was screwed tight. His eyes dark, blue, and penetrating. He crossed his arms and the sleeves of his lab-coat rolled up enough for me to see the greyish ink of tattoo circling his wrist.

"Ball-buster," Mom said, staring at him. Her mouth parted.

He stepped forward and opened the door. I swallowed a mix of phlegm and too-sweet chocolate. He stepped in, smiled quickly, and closed the door behind him.

"Hello, Thom," he said softly.

He pushed his lab coat back as he stuck his hands in his pockets.

His serious lips curled into a gentle smile. His bushy white eyebrows lifted. And his jaw softened.

"Hello," I said.

He strode over to Mom, his boots clacking on the floor and echoing. "Mrs. Middlecamp, may I take this chair beside you?" he asked.

"Of course," she said.

He pulled the chair to the side of my bed nearest the door. He laid his lab coat on the back and rolled his sleeves up and revealed two arms covered in tattoos.

One, on the left, was an assortment of skulls.

On the right, a massive cardinal. Its tiny feet grasped a branch and its wings lay tucked at its side. It perched on the top of his wrist and ran all the way up to the crook in his elbow. On both arms, underneath the ink, I saw tiny white marks of scar tissue. He sat down, crossed his legs and clasped his hands over his knees.

"I want to start off by saying to the both of you, I'm sorry for your loss," he said.

I nodded at him.

"Thank you," Mom said, wiping her nose.

He smiled at me and then looked at Mom with a curious grin. "So, the nurses say you call him Go'bay. Why's that?"

Mom's shoulders relaxed, and her lips softened into a smile as she looked at me and then him.

"When he came out, he looked almost gold. Golden Baby. Goldbay. Go'bay," Mom said. She leaned over the bedrail and put her hand on top of mine.

He smiled gently, then nodded at my pudding.

"Good to eat again?" he asked.

"It'll take some time," I said.

He nodded. "Good to have that tube out?"

"Never again."

"Well, that's up to you, isn't it?" He said.

Mom tapped her feet. Outside, a bell rang, sharp and high-pitched. I looked over his shoulder as a few nurses ran by my door pushing a massive cart with red drawers. Dr. Heinz didn't turn. Didn't blink. His lips slipped back into a tight place. His eyes shifted from soft to black and pointed behind his glasses.

He lifted two fingers.

"Two," he said.

"What?" I asked.

"Two."

I looked at Mom. She looked at him like he had a fungal growth.

He curled his two fingers back, clasped his hands over his knees and worked his knuckles. The cardinal moved on his wrist like it was ready for flight.

"Where are you friends?" he asked.

"Friends?" I asked.

"Yea, your friends. The people that you shoot with. People you buy from. You know, friends. Where are they?"

I clasped my hands in my lap.

"I don't know."

"They'll be in your bed soon enough. Probably the morgue. And so will she." He pointed at Mom. "In the bed you're in, or one just like it." He sighed and reached around to his jacket pocket. And pulled out a small, black device. "You wanted this right?"

He tossed the phone into my lap.

"Go ahead and call them. I'm the one hold-up to your discharge. I'll sign your papers. You can leave."

I held the phone in my hand. I could get Ball in ten minutes.

"But before you call whoever you're going to call, can I tell you about myself, first? Just a story."

The bell outside dinged frantically.

"Sure."

"I sat right where you did once," he said, "I woke up one morning with tubes coming out of every hole of my body and laid up in a hospital bed. I wasn't surprised. The moment it hits our veins; we all know the beginning and the end game. My focus was on getting out and getting high again. So, I waited. The more tubes they pulled, the more I plotted. First the breathing tube. Then the dick tube. Then the feeding tube. The only thing I had left was my IVs. I waited for shift change that day like a monk. I played nice with the nurse and waited until she started to give report. I hadn't caused any trouble, no need for her to worry. And she was new. She didn't know any better. So, as her and the other nurse joked, I had my shoes and bag already in the bed. I slipped my feet in, jumped out of the bed and ran as fast as I could. I followed the exit signs to the fire stairs and ducked out into the parking lot. Gone," he said, and snapped his fingers, "just like that."

He breathed heavily. He clenched his jaw and bit down on his bottom lip.

He put two fingers up again. "Two things happened that year. My mother got cancer. My girlfriend overdosed. And I was high at both of their funerals."

I laid back and stared at the ceiling, but I could still see him out of the corner of my eye. I felt as heavy as an anvil. The dinging outside my door rang frantically.

He looked at Mom. "I know you know that sound," he said, and then looked at me, "but do you?"

"No."

"It means somebody's dying...and you have no clue how little of a show it really is. Your heart misses a beat, just a misfire or two. Rhythm goes into the toilet. You close your eyes," he spoke low and snapped his fingers, "and you're gone. That's it. Lights out."

Mom shook as tears ran down her face.

"I lost a lot of people to dope and a lot of years. So, when I start talking my shit about rehab, I'm not talking about you getting out of here, or even going to school. I'm talking about living long enough to see the years that matter. The years that give life its definition.

"Another question for you: How many parents you got left, Thom?"

I swallowed deeply and stared into the green fluorescence above my bed. Fly carcasses lay scattered in its casing.

"Wife and kids? You want that?" he asked.

I stared into the green spots blinking in my vision.

"You keep going down this path and everything is collateral damage. The life you had and the life you thought you'd have." He paused, and then said sharply, "Look at me."

I looked at him.

He leaned forward, uncrossed his legs and planted his boots firm on the floor. He clasped his hands in front of him. No ring on his finger.

"So, this is the fork. I have a colleague who runs a very intensive rehab. Mostly individual one-on-one therapy. Extremely uncomfortable. You will go to dark places, Thom. But she's been highly effective."

I felt my phone in my hand.

"Or you go back out there. And maybe we do this again. Maybe I get to know your mother. Maybe she gets so worn down, she has a heart attack, too. Or a brain bleed. Then it's you, Thom. Maybe your brother buries the both of you. Maybe you get to be right about yourself; get to be right about the things you hide from yourself."

Hot tears filled my eyes.

"Thom," Mom's voice cracked. "Please, baby. You have to fight for your own life." She grabbed my hand and squeezed. "I can't keep putting myself through hell for you."

Her fingernails dug in.

"How long is it?" I asked.

"Eight weeks."

I couldn't look at Mom. I couldn't look at him. I focused on the carcasses in the light above me. Their bodies were being cooked into oblivion. They'd been drawn to the light and killed by it. Rehab was scary not because of what it was but what it meant. It was flying into a burning light looking for salvation. But, if I didn't go, how soon would I be back here? How many close calls does one person get? Dad didn't even get one.

Mom squeezed my hand so hard I felt pins and needles.

I nodded at the ceiling.

"I'll do it."

Mom and Dr. Heinz breathed out deeply. I smelled the coffee on his breath and the Newports on Mom's.

"So, Thom," Dr. Heinz continued, "I'm discharging you in a couple of days. I talked to Ashley about weaning your buprenorphine before then. We absolutely have to get it off before you start methadone."

"So, I'm going to go through withdrawals?" I asked.

"Not nearly as bad."

I swallowed.

His eyes narrowed and he put up one finger. "You get one day of freedom, in your mother and brother's care. But this is a deal of deals, my colleague doesn't usually allow any dwell time. It leads to bad decisions. But, in your case, with your recent loss, I think it imperative you spend time with your family and during treatment you're to have no contact. But, Thom, I must stress though, there is a caveat."

"What is it?"

"Time is of the essence. You miss show-time and you miss your spot. Her program is highly selective. You miss it and your chances of getting clean and staying clean go from slim, to near non-existent."

Mom nodded.

"And don't score anything off the street, it's just going to make *your* journey to recovery harder. You'll have to go through hell in real-time. You had the privilege of going on a sedation vacation throughout your withdrawals. You let a drop hit your veins now, and you're starting at the bottom of the mountain all over again."

I looked down at my phone in my lap. One day of freedom. A cold fear rushed through my veins.

"So, I'll start methadone?" I asked.

"Yup," Heinz said.

"Buprenorphine sucks."

"It does," he said.

CHAPTER 5:
YOU EVER BROKE A SPARROW'S HEART? GOD DON'T FORGIVE THAT

May 2015

Mom tapped her fingers on the steering wheel with a cigarette burning in her fingertips. She stared out the windshield of the Ranger. Her eyes had become a permanent film of post-tears. We idled outside the rehab as the sun began to cook the morning. The cabin was a pungent mix of tobacco tar and a burning clutch. Mom didn't drive stick. Dad did.

Dr. Heinz's colleague waved at us. Her long white lab coat billowed. She was younger than I'd expected. She had tan, wrinkle-free skin the color of a vidalia onion and plump-injected lips. Her blonde hair was permed and curled. She didn't look a day over thirty-five.

"She looks like a Barbie," Mom said.

The building was a façade of limestone and spotless tinted glass windows. Lining the front were bright ferns manicured into nearly perfect circles. The grass was cut in concentric squares. Mom had spent most of Dad's estate on the rehab. And it certainly didn't look like the kind of place where junkies went to get clean. It looked like a place where soccer moms went to get tummy-tucks.

"You think they'll know?" Mom asked.

I'd nodded off on the way over.

"That I'm high?"

"Yes," she said, blowing smoke out her open window.

"I'm sure they expect it," I said.

She looked at me and then down at her work badge. Her face flushed and her eyes narrowed to slits

"Your father was right about me. I'm too much of a warm blood for you, Go'bay."

"What's that supposed to mean?"

"It means...," she grabbed her badge and tossed it at the window. It clacked against the windshield. "... that I'm too soft. You con me every fucking time, and now I'm an accomplice!"

Tears ran down her cheeks. Her cigarette smoked in her left hand between her middle and ring finger.

My True Religion bag sat in my lap. The tag faded. The stitching was coming un-done. The zipper, rusted. If the world ended that moment, it was my time capsule. My life wasn't just in it; it was it.

Mom reached over and grabbed the bag out of my lap. "This is it, Thom." She shook it in my face. The spoon and pipe inside tinkled. She pointed at the rehab with the bag. "Either this works or I'm buying another tombstone. You get that?"

Mom tossed the bag at the back window, and the pipe inside shattered.

An icy shiver slithered down my spine and bounced around my pelvis.

Mom slumped in her chair as a warm wind blew through the Ranger. It lifted her hair and a strand got stuck to one of her tears.

"I'm sorry, Mom," I said, turning to the rehab.

The counsellor dug her hands in her lab coat. At the edge of her sleeve, I saw a grey sliver of ink.

"Do you think I'll make it?" I asked.

Mom sighed beside me. A fresh blast of tobacco perfumed the cabin.

"You don't have a choice," she said, "you just don't."

I grabbed Dad's green duffel bag out of the bed of the truck with all my clothes inside. My skin felt as gooey as bacon grease. The sun was cooking the last of my high. I walked up to the counselor as Mom turned the engine over. It bucked to life. She struggled with the clutch and took off in a sputter, looking at me once as she clenched her teeth around her cigarette. The Ranger fought with her down the street.

The counsellor stuck out a creamy white hand. Her lips parted into a bleached-white smile.

"My name is Elise," she said.

I shook her hand. Her palm was soft.

"Thom."

She smiled as she let go of my hand and put her hands in the pockets of her labcoat. She nodded at the disappearing Ranger.

"She must not drive stick shift that often," she said.

"It was my dad's."

She nodded. "I heard."

A kid screamed somewhere. The sun dipped behind a cloud and I felt the darkness in my bones.

"So, I have to warn you," she said as her mouth tightened and her eyes sharpened, "I know you're high."

I wiped my forehead as my high bottomed out and the sun peeked from behind the clouds. It felt like my soul was experiencing vertigo.

A school bus rolled by with squealing kids. It made a right. On the opposite street was an elementary school.

"For most people, that's an automatic disqualifier," she said, sharply. Her brow narrowed. "But, Heinz pulled a string for you."

I pulled the duffel bag higher.

"Still, You screwed yourself," she said, matter-of-factly.

My heart palpitated.

"You can't get full doses of methadone until you detox," she said.

The pores on my forehead opened and sweat ran freely.

"So, this is going to be hell," she said, her lips tight, "for a little while."

She took a hand out of her pocket and motioned for my duffel bag.

I let it roll off my shoulder and let it drop to the ground.

The bus squealed as kids screamed off of it.

I scratched my arm.

"In the meantime, we'll get you settled in," she said as she kicked the bag with her boot. "Security has to check this, but I'll get it back to you after dinner."

She smiled and turned and ushered me in. I started walking towards the door and looked at the placard above it: "New Life Rehabilitation Center."

Underneath it: "There are no shortcuts. The only way is through."

Elise grabbed my duffel and walked in behind me.

I turned and took one last time at the outside world through the glass door.

I saw my reflection:

My face was rounder, not as gaunt.

My hands weren't covered in brick dust.

But the holes in my pants were still there.

My shoes were still caked in a clay-colored residue.

My eyes were oversized black pupils.

The high was gone.

And I was alone, completely.

CHAPTER 6:
I GOT DOWN ON ONE KNEE

There were six of us seated in single-seater lemon-colored plush chairs. We sat in front of an empty fireplace. There weren't even fake logs or a fake fire in it. On the mantle above it was a single vase containing a tall green grass and a flower the color of a blazing peach: Indian Paintbrush. A single-paned glass window above the mantle reached high to the cornice of the ceiling. Sunlight entered through it and covered the entire room in a golden glow. A mahogany table sat in the middle of the room and on top of it, a small box of Kleenex.

We'd just finished dinner, in silence. We'd introduced ourselves to each other quickly, and dug in. As I ate, I felt a million needles under my skin. I picked at my chicken. A few of the people looked my age. A few were teenagers. Some were older than me. But our eyes were the same: tired with muted agitation, loaded with the shocked blankness of mortal desperation and starving for something to blunt the edge.

A ball of cold sweat rolled down the back of my ear.

A door opened to the left and Elise walked in, her boots clacking. Her white lab coat was gone. Her makeup was gone. The bags under her eyes, ubiquitous.

Her blonde hair was tied back. And she wore a blue polo, blue jeans, and cracked leather boots. Her arms were sinewed and covered in tattoos. Her triceps rippled as she walked. And her shoulders were round as domes.

She stood in front of us and glanced around the group like she was counting. She tightened her lips and turned to the Paintbrush on the mantle, pointing.

"Anybody know what that is?" she asked.

Everyone looked down. Some held their elbows and some bit their lips. One of the older men opened his mouth to speak, but thought better, and closed it. He crossed his legs and slumped down in his chair.

"It's Indian paintbrush," I said.

She turned around to me. A gold crucifix peaked out of from the top button of her polo.

"What do you know about it?" she asked, putting her hands in her pockets.

"It's native to Texas, I think," I said.

"And?"

"I don't know what else."

She smiled and looked at all of us.

"It's a parasite," she said as she sat down on the arm of an empty chair near the mantle and looked at us. Her face softened. "It finds a perfectly good host and as the host grows, so does the paintbrush," she said.

She clasped her hands in front of her and sat forward.

"A little about me. I sat where all of you sat once. I was sixteen, pregnant, and doing cocaine before school. I had a boyfriend who was eighteen, beautiful, and doped out of his mind." She sighed through her teeth and looked deeply at all of us.

Another ball of sweat rolled down the back of my neck, and I reached back and rubbed it with my sleeve.

"Suffice it to say, I lost the baby and kept the boyfriend. Fast forward a few years later and he OD'd. He was twenty-two years old. I'd nodded off and he'd finished off the rest; too much of the rest. When I woke up, his face was the color of ash, and his fingers were cold as popsicles. I called 9-1-1. They had me do CPR. And he survived, but there's a shit-ton of ways to survive and most of them aren't pretty. He had a massive brain injury. He was a vegetable in the bed, but we weren't married, so, his mother decided what happened to him. Instead of letting him go, she trach'd him. And he stared at a ceiling for the rest of his life. In and out of the hospital until an ulcer the size of a fist formed on his sacrum and cavitated straight through to the bone of his spinal column."

One of the young ones, a girl with brown hair and dark lipstick, cried into her palms. Elise reached for the Kleenex and handed it to her. And then continued.

"Anybody know why a mother would let her son rot in a bed like that?" Elise asked.

Everyone shook their heads.

"Shame," she said. "She was ashamed because of the things that happened to him when he was a kid that she couldn't protect him from." A pang shot through my sternum. "In her mind, the shame he felt was what drove him to drugs in the first place. A shame he never got to confront. And she felt that if she kept him alive long enough, he could survive to face it. She felt if she could keep him alive long enough, she could live down hers. But, he just ended up decaying in a bed. I remember the last time I saw him. I tried to lift his head off the pillow to kiss him and the back of his skull felt like mush."

She sat up straight and looked at all of us. In that moment, she looked much older. She'd lost her beauty. Lost her façade. She'd seen the inside of a black hole and it'd warped her. She sucked in deeply, a slight tremble on her lips.

"So," she said, "that's why this program focuses on adressing the shame. Wherever it's popped up in your life. And how to stop the cycle. Because it's attached itself to you and feeds on your life force." She put up one finger. "Shame is the first one," she put up another finger, "and that leads to hurt," she put up a third, "and hurt leads to anger. And if you listen to anger, you'll do something you regret. Which inevitably, leads back to shame. And that's all the cycle of addiction is, as it grows, it touches everything in your life. Every. Single. Thing."

She pointed at the Indian Paintbrush. "The flower is just the evidence of the addiction. The parasitism. But the shame, hurt, and anger. Those are the roots of it. So, as all of you grew in your addiction, the roots got stronger and took hold deeper and deeper. And the parasite bloomed."

Her lips closed around *bloomed* and a slimy feeling swept over my skin. The sunlight coming in through the window became mercurial and the room shimmered. I looked around and every face was vacant like they'd been embalmed. Elise looked at me, but her eyes were too immediate. Too pressing. She saw everything. She saw every crime I'd ever committed, everything I'd done to Mom. Dad. Dewey. Everything. A droplet of sweat crawled out from behind my ear again and rolled down my neck past my Adam's apple and settled at the notch in my sternum. I bent over and held my stomach, vomiting a brownish, yellow splatter of chicken chunks and bile. Elise rushed over to me and hooked me under my armpit, lifting me to my feet.

She tightened her lips. "This is why you gotta come clean. It makes it worse, Thomas."

I lay in a drenched bed. They handed me a plastic cup with two tiny white pills.

"It's not methadone. Your system hasn't cleared the buprenorphine," a voice said, "It's either this or nothing."

I swallowed the pills. The vertigo was endless, like a black hole had opened up in my navel and was sucking me in. I kept the lamp on near my bed and stared at the walls trying to keep calm. There was no oasis. Shadows split in the corners where the light couldn't reach and limbs began to emerge from the darkness. From those same shadows, hushing noises reverberated through the air like feet running over snow. I closed my eyes and felt a hand moving down my pelvis again. It moved past the perimeter of my waistband, going to a different hemisphere. As it travelled, I felt it breach something sacred and fragile; the breach was an ice bath. I crossed into a new world with a new calamity. "This'll be between us, Thom. It's just something adults and children do sometimes. There's nothing wrong with it. I promise," a soft and ugly voice said. A man's voice. I closed my eyes and tried to sleep, but I sweat through my sheets throughout the night. I got nothing but a cold glass of water and more empty promises from a woman's voice in the far distant atmosphere.

"Just need twenty-four more hours, Mr. Middlecamp."

Beneath my closed eyelids there was no silence, just the echoing of footsteps.

The male voice spoke again, "There's nothing wrong with it, I promise." A memory hit me with Menthol breath and a bath of Brut.

I opened my eyes as black spiders with white-knuckled fingers at the end of their legs crawled down the ceiling. They eased down on black silk using their deft fingers and licked the sweat from my cheeks. "Nothing wrong with it, Thom." Their limbs on my skin felt grotesque. I drowned in cold sweats. I saw my dad's last choking breaths as he sat in an intersection idling, fighting for his life while his Ranger hummed peacefully. I threw up again, emptying everything inside my stomach. Nurses rushed in. More pills. A bucket for a pillow. Vomit for the stuffing. More spiders crawling in the shadows.

Hell isn't buried or somewhere in a dark alley in space; it's in the here and now. Hell is a cold cauldron. A soup of ice. Hell whips the mind and makes the heart shiver. Each breath is at war with itself. What cracks first: the heart, the mind, or the soul? Hell's got its grip on all of those.

Another glass of water. More pills.

I heard Elise's soft voice cut through the furiousness at one point, *"If you never prayed, Thom, now is the time."*

The lights stayed on, and I shut my eyes. I swam in my bedsheets. I threw up mucus. At that point, I threw up spirits because there was nothing else left. There was no refuge. It didn't matter if my eyes were closed or open, my soul was being dragged away by its thin hair.

So, I crawled out of my bed and got down on my knees.

Trembling.

Sweating.

Paralyzed.

I started praying. I prayed to the God, a God, any God. Anyone who'd come to my rescue. Who'd let me live with a shred of soul left in me.

"God, if this is my punishment, I get it. I was a bad son. A bad brother. I chose this life and I knew it'd end up either here or in a cemetery. But, Lord, I'd rather be dead. I can't take this anymore. This is fucking hell. I never thought there was anything more than death, but this is it. Don't make me suffer like this. I can't take it. Please. God. Please, have mercy on me."

CHAPTER 7:
FUCK

The morning I started methadone, someone knocked gently on my door. It wasn't the mechanical one-two-three of my nurse. It was gentle, light. I'd managed to carve thirty minutes of sleep out of the night before.

"Come in." My throat was filled with spackle. I'd barely been able to keep down water. The door opened and a sliver of light ballooned into a silhouette. Elise stood in the glow with her hands in her lab coat.

"Hey, Thom," she said.

"You the Angel of Death?" I said.

She smirked and walked over slowly. She sat down heavily on the edge of the bed and patted my leg gently. Her hair was pulled back into a bun and her face had a light dusting of make-up. Still, her eyes were bloodshot.

"I've got some good news," she said.

"Yea?" I asked as a ray of sunlight entered the window and covered her face, it made her skin look as soft as milk.

She pulled out a small package of two pills. I sat up in the bed.

"You're starting your methadone, today," she said as she handed the package to me.

Her crucifix dangled and caught the beam of sunlight.

A pressure loosened behind my eyes, and for the first time after countless nights, I had a morning to look forward to. As I looked at the pills and then at Elise, a feeling came over me that I hadn't experienced in years: the humbling feeling of sobriety; it was the closest thing to clarity. It gave me a short and uncomfortable leash on the present moment.

"Take today to rest," she said, patting my leg. "We'll start one-on-ones tomorrow."

The morning our one-on-ones started, I sat on the couch facing Elise holding a cup of hot, black coffee. I blew ripples on its surface. The Styrofoam cup shook in my hands. The shadows had eventually stopped creeping. The voices were painful echoes. A few nights of withdrawals felt like slipping off the shelf of Time; it could've been years.

"So, Thom, do you remember anything you said to the nurses?" Elise asked.

I shivered and took a quick sip; it burned my uvula.

"No, not really," I coughed.

Elise nodded. She crossed her legs and clasped her hands around the peak of her highest knee.

"You said you remembered his cologne. Whose cologne was that, Thom?" Her voice was soft, not forceful.

I gulped and put my coffee in my lap, staring at the black surface. I went back into the recent memory. The ugliness crawled over my skin like a centipede. I sank back into the sofa. The buttons of the upholstery poked my shoulders and upper back. I looked around her office just to get a break from her stare. There were a few plaques from universities I'd never heard of. On the wall behind her sofa was a bookcase stocked with medical texts. On top of the bookshelf in a gold-plated picture frame was a photo of Elise and Dr. Heinz. Her hand dangled over his shoulder as he stood a foot shorter. Their faces were covered in neon paint and she wore a bikini and a green wreath around her head. Dr. Heinz had on a toga and a wreath of his own.

"You're a Chameleon," I said, nodding at the photo.

She turned around and looked at the photo. She chuckled.

"That's what rehab is. You get to see the sides of yourself that you never believed in. I never thought I'd make it to ten years sober. Never thought I'd be able to enjoy Tomorrowland without molly.

But, I wanted to give myself a shot at trying. I was finishing up my fellowship with Dr. Heinz and I asked him to go and can you fucking believe it? He went. Ten years sober. I celebrated it that day."

She turned back to me.

"But you have to be honest to get there. Honest with yourself, about yourself," she said, her voice slightly firmer.

I took the coffee to my lips and blew more ripples.

"So, whose cologne was it?" she asked again.

"He was my painting teacher. He was the best teacher I thought I'd ever had. He let me paint whatever I wanted. Always encouraging."

"So, what happened?" Elise asked.

"I don't remember exactly. I just remember bits and pieces. The ceiling fan was on in the classroom; it was one of those classrooms with the chairs with desks attached to them. We painted near the window during my afterschool program. For some reason it was just me and him that day."

"What do you remember most?" Elise asked.

"His hand, it was too smooth. I had a friend who had a pet snake. I held it one time and felt it's belly on my palm. It was too smooth. That's what his hand felt like. Too smooth," I said. I took a sip of my coffee.

"Nine, I think," I said.

"Did you tell anyone?"

I looked up. "My mother."

"What did she say?"

I stared into the black surface of my coffee.

Mom had looked at me with eyes as wide as saucers, hovering between rage and despair. She'd opened her mouth to say something and closed it again. She took my hand and kissed it and pulled me into her. Her belly was warm as she heaved in tears. There was a cold rock in my stomach since the moment he'd touched me. Mom held me and ran her fingers gently through my hair. Her fingers felt like they were unlocking a cage. I don't remember how long it was, but as Mom hugged and kissed me, I felt the knuckles of confusion relaxing and the fist inside my stomach unclenched. She'd whispered to me after some time, "Go'bay, I love you and you're safe here. It wasn't your fault. People are just shit sometimes. Real pieces of shit."

I rubbed my eyes and looked up at Elise. She smiled and leaned forward. No push. No command.

"I'm glad you heard yourself say that, Thom," she said.

She picked up a pen and notepad on her side of the coffee table and scribbled something on it. I rubbed my eyes again with my sleeve and when I opened them again, she was blurry.

"Can you see it, Thom?" she asked as she held up the notepad.

The scribbles took shape. She'd written three words. Each with its own period: Hurt. Anger. Shame.

"We're going to talk about these in depth, Thom, but think of this as your homework. I'm just a guide. You're the one that holds the key to unlocking your healing. But you have to be honest: brutally and uncomfortably. That's where the healing is. The devil's in the details but it's our job to go looking for him. We have to find his hiding spots so that you can know where they are for yourself; For your sobriety."

She put the pen on top of the notepad and slid it to my side of the table.

"What do you want me to do?" I asked.

"Write whatever comes to mind," Elise said, "Just like you did with telling me what you just told me. Engage that same level of honesty. You'll have more than enough time in the evenings to start working." I looked down at the notepad in front of me.

The pen laid heavily on it like it'd never move.

I sat at the desk near my window that night. The moon was riding high and blue. It was almost 8:00 pm. I'd been doodling on the notepad. I couldn't draw anything. Just cubes. Cubes on top of cubes. I was beginning a new one as the lamp flickered on my desk and then cut out. I sat in the darkness and as my eyes adjusted, a faint, bluish glow took over the room. I got up and walked to the window. Over the next few weeks, I saw the moon in all of its forms; from full, to sickle, to a whitish toenail. I counted its craters: all the moments of impact and destruction. I imagined all the cycles of cosmic debris hurling themselves against the solitary orb. I contemplated all of my own cycles of Hurt, Anger and Shame. The night I sat down to write about my Hurt, the moon glowed like a pearl and was as round as a pill.

CHAPTER 8:
HURT

March 2001

I was a senior in high school and had just graduated to cocaine and was rounding the corner on pills.

I was under the constant threat of drug-tests and permanent expulsion from the house.

I woke up that morning to the smell of burning bacon.

My door cracked open and Dad wheezed in the doorway.

"Arn, come get your inhaler baby," Mom said from the kitchen.

"Thomas, son, wake up," Dad said.

"Can I just sleep in?" I put my pillow over my face.

"Nope," Dad said curtly. "You, me and Dewey are going somewhere."

I pulled the pillow down as Dad cracked a smile. A mockingbird screeched outside my window.

"Where?" I asked and then looked over at my easel: on it sat a sketch of *Starry Night* on a canvas. My oils lay arranged on my desk, ready to paint.

"I was going to set some colors today."

Dad blinked.

"You'll have time for that when we get back," he said. "Now get up. Get a shirt on. Get some tennis shoes on and be out front." He paused and looked down at his watch. "In ten minutes."

Dad drummed his fingers on the steering wheel as we drove to whatever dimension of hell we were travelling to.

We passed a Whataburger with a white billowing exhaust tower. The buttery smell of biscuits was pungent.

"What about breakfast?" I asked as I laid my head on the glass. I was nursing a headache.

Dad took two puffs of his inhaler and looked in the rearview. "We'll have it after," Dad said.

The orange creamsicle A-frame disappeared behind us.

Suburbia morphed quickly as fescued, manicured lawns became brown plots of dead grass. Driveways with gleaming Mercedes and Toyotas morphed into driveways where rusted cars sat parked on cement blocks. The windows of the gas stations we passed became increasingly ornamented with security bars. Men my dad's age hung out front of the gas stations in tank tops with tall boys in their hands. We stopped at a light as a man in tattered Army fatigues and beat up Converses staggered towards us. He had a strawberry beard, cracked skin, and faded, grey eyes. He held a paper bag in one hand and in the other a cardboard sign written in crude black marker: *OEF Vet. Will do circus trix, or any trix, for money.*

I laughed as the light turned green.

"You think that's funny?" Dad said as he looked in the rearview. His eyes were sharp and accusing.

Dewey, who tried to stay out of everything, laid his head on his window and blew out a sputter.

"Kindof," I said.

"That's someone without discipline, Thomas. And that's the most important thing a man can possess in this world. Man has to have discipline in order to protect himself from himself. The world isn't your enemy, son; you are. And if you can't control yourself, you don't just become a victim, you become a casualty."

Dad nodded his head backwards towards the disappearing man. "That man's a casualty, Thom, nothing funny about it."

"Does that have something to do with where we're going?" Dewey piped up.

"That's part of it," Dad said.

Dewey glanced back at me and sat up in his seat.

Dad's eyes were glued to me in the rearview. My heart raced as we looked at each other. For once he didn't look angry or disappointed, just deeply concerned.

"How far away is it?" Dewey asked.

Dad took his eyes off of me and focused on the road. He drummed his fingers on the steering wheel slowly.

"We'll get there when we get there."

Dewey smirked and said, "I know where we're going."

"No, you don't," Dad said.

"Yea, I do."

"Ok, where we going then, Einstein?" Dad said.

"The third circle of hell," I said.

Dewey laughed, shook his head, and laid back down on the window as we bumped over a pothole.

Dad glanced back into the rearview. His eyes were almost soft. Almost.

"Be open, son."

I pointed out the window. "The liquor stores are open, can we pop into one of those?"

The softness evaporated as Dad frowned and gave me the heat again. This time with the intensity of a threat.

I laid my head back on the window and watched the laundromats, gas stations, and pawn shops pass by.

Dad turned down a dirt road. We kicked up a cloud of dust that snuck in through the cracked windows. Tiny pebbles got into my teeth and I could taste the grit for the rest of the day. Dad rolled up the windows as the main street disappeared behind us. Through short windows in the cloud of dust, we passed mechanic's shops with half-filled bays. The cars inside the bays were suspended in the air on hydraulic lifts, exposing the metal guts underneath. Dewey perked up as we rolled down the road. He planted his hands on his knees and craned his neck to see through the dusty billows. Pit bulls patrolled the chain-link fences and rusted tires were blanketed by hovering black clouds of mosquitoes; not a mechanic to be seen, though. As we travelled, Dad glanced at me and Dewey. A childlike smile creased his face.

Dad slowed to a stop outside one of the shops and cut the engine as the car was enveloped in a dusty brown shroud. A subwoofer bumped somewhere, rhythmic and heavy. As the dust cleared, I could make out two shadowy figures. They swung something over their heads. Dad wheezed heavily. He reached for his inhaler, took two puffs, relaxed back into his seat, and rolled the window down. As the cloud around us dissipated, a chain-link fence emerged. The two figures became two guys in shorts and tank tops heaving sledgehammers on tractor-trailer tires. They worked methodically, and effortlessly. In the open bays, giant black bags dangled and swayed as they caught sharp, thudding punches from more boxers. Some jump-roped and laughed. Some sat on milk crates undoing a fabric around their wrists. Others hit tiny bags attached to swivels that knocked like drumbeats to the rapid punches. Some guys threw punches at invisible opponents and then dodged invisible attacks. And each one of them hissed with every movement. Each one of them was focused. Their faces were sharp but not tight. Their movements were sandwiched between electric and smooth.

In the middle of the shop, where two bays had been, was a boxing ring. The ropes were frayed and drooped. Two boxers circled in the middle, bouncing like they had trampolines in their toes. They snapped quick punches at each other. One got hit clean. The shot made sweat zing off of his exposed head. I thought he'd drop. But, he didn't. Instead, he swam, bobbed and weaved, and pivoted on his feet like he hadn't felt a thing. Every punch was hissing music. I looked at Dad as he watched the fighters raptly. So did Dewey. I slid down even more in the backseat.

A coach hung over the ropes. He shouted instructions to the fighters in between puffs on his cigarette.

"That's a no-no," Dad said, shaking his head.

"What is, Pop?" Dewey chirped.

"They're not wearing headgear," Dad said.

"But isn't that what it is, two guys beating each other into brain damage?" I chirped from the backseat.

"No, Thomas, it's more than that." He sat forward and pulled the keys out of the ignition. "All right, you two. Let's go."

As we walked up, the coach hopped down from the ring and walked up to Dad with his hand outstretched. He and Dad shook hands and hugged, and then stepped back from each other. The coach took a drag on the cigarette that dangled from his lips. Dewey puffed out his shoulders and stood tall. I shoved my hands in my shorts and kicked around a rusted screw on the ground. I chewed a piece of grit from the dust cloud in my teeth.

"Arnie Middlecamp. How the fuck you been?" he said.

Beside the screw I was kicking around was a blood or oil stain. And then more crimson splotches spread out across the cement like islands of pain. I just wanted to kick the screw until it was time to leave.

Dew walked to the edge of the ring and watched the fighters circling each other. He had a mystic look on his face.

The bell rang.

The fighters tapped gloves and returned to their corners.

The coach turned. "All right, headgear!" he barked at them.

The coach took another drag of his cigarette.

Dad took his inhaler out of his pocket.

"You all right?" the coach asked.

"Irony," Dad chuckled. "Never smoked a day in my life."

Dad took a deep puff, coughed, then shoved his inhaler deep into his back pocket. He pointed at the fighters as they snapped on their headgear.

"Why didn't they have it on before?" he asked.

"Well," the coach said, "they've got pro debuts coming up. I like to have some hard, unprotected rounds before debuts."

Dad eyes widened. His mouth parted. "Pros, huh?"

The coach nodded.

"So what are these?" The coach said and pointed at me and Dewey.

"I want you to put *him* through some mitt work," Dad pointed at Dewey. "Tell me what you think."

The coach blew out at the ceiling and said, "Too easy."

He took his cigarette from his mouth and pointed at me with it. "What about him?"

Dad waved his hand at me.

"He's more of the artistic type, like Van Gogh. I'll work with him," he said.

"So was Tyson," the coach chuckled. "All right," he turned to Dewey, "let's see if you got the same pop."

Dewey did a quick calf raise.

"What are we doing, Pop?" I asked. I rolled the screw under my shoe.

Dad pointed to a bag in the corner in the back of the gym. It was far away from the ring and beyond a maze of boxers working at their stations.

"Meet me over there," he said. He turned to the coach, "Come here, Dewey," Dad said.

The three of them huddled together and talked in low voices. Dad slapped Dewey's back. Dewey stood straight and smiled. The coach smirked and dropped his cigarette on the ground as he grinded it into smithereens with his shoe. I turned and looked around to the back corner at the black heavy bag covered in silver duct tape. I hugged the wall and shrunk as I made my way towards it. I skirted a boxer shadow boxing. I danced out of the way of a swinging heavy bag as it was being pummeled by another boxer. The chain screeched with each blow. The bag itself thundered and moaned. I stepped over unchained heavy bags laying on the floor like beached whales. I kept my eyes low and my hands buried in my pockets. A few boxers looked out of the corners of their eyes at me, like I was a sheep in a wolf's den. That tiny screw was an island and an ocean away.

"All right son," Dad said as he gripped the bag around the waist. "Hit the bag, nice and easy."

Dad had quickly wrapped my hands. "I'm only gonna show you once," he said. He wrapped slowly, but I couldn't concentrate. The gym was an orchestra. Dinging. Thundering. Thwacking.

"Hey!" Dad said. His eyes were sharp and focused. "Pay attention."

"Sorry, Pop."

After he finished wrapping my hands, he handed me a pair of

black, cracked leather gloves. The foam inside peeked out of a hole in the thumb.

"Think of these as your paint brushes," Dad said.

I looked at them.

"What do you want me to do?" I said.

"Put them on, son," Dad said.

I tucked one into my armpit and shoved my hand in. The stuffing was shredded to bits inside. Tiny pieces of foam crawled in between my fingers. I finished putting them on and my gloved hands to my sides.

"Now," Dad said, standing in front of me, "Never drop your hands from your face. Keep them glued to your cheeks. This is your defense."

The bell rang. The gym grew quiet.

Dad put his hands up to the sides of his face and cupped his ears.

I lifted my gloves to my face; they smelled like fish.

They blocked Dad from my view.

Dad jerked the gloves down.

"Gotta see what you're fighting son. No use having gloves if you're fighting blind," he said.

"Sorry," I said and lowered my hands.

Dad softened. "It's okay, Go'bay, just focus. Now, put your hands up."

I put them up. My knees and legs felt like jelly.

Dad slapped the heavy bag.

"Think of this bag as your canvas. No need for big brush strokes at first. Just get the paint going."

"How do I punch?" I asked.

"Take your left hand and shoot it straight forward. It's called a jab. And it should all be from your stance." Dad took his right foot back and off center, squatted down, and bladed his torso.

I got into a similar awkward stance. Dad threw a zapping jab at the bag and recoiled his hand quickly. "Make sure you turn the wrist over," Dad said. He stepped back and looked up at the clock and quickly made his way to the back of the bag. "Okay, rest's almost over. Get ready. And make sure you turn the wrist over. Three minutes. All jabs. Wait for the bell."

The bell rang loudly throughout the gym. Where there was once silence the orchestra began anew.

"All right!" Dad said, "Go!"

I started throwing loose, flailing punches. Hitting the bag felt like swinging a pool noodle against a brick wall.

"You gotta snap it, Thom!" Dad said, his eyes urgent.

"I'm trying, Pop."

I tried making it snap, but my elbow burned.

Dad let go of the bag and marched around it. He grabbed both of my wrists and jerked my left hand towards his face and back.

"Like that!" he said. He stepped back and flailed his arm out girlishly. "It ain't no love tap, Son!"

Above the crinkle of the chains, the thudding of the heavy bags, and the howling, drumming beat of the speedbags, I heard the other boxers chuckling.

Dad shook his head sadly and looked over at Dewey working in the ring with the coach. The coach held up the mitts as Dewey threw some jabs. The mitts popped with each punch as Dewey danced light on his toes. The canvas thundered underneath him.

The cigarette dangling from the coach's mouth danced as he talked to Dewey. "Good snap on that jab. Natural motion."

"That's how you do it, Thom!" Dad said, pointing at the ring.

I kept flailing loosely as my arms started to burn with the sweat and exhaustion.

"How...long...Dad?"

Dad was still watching Dewey.

"How long, Pop?" I asked louder.

Dad turned on me and growled, "Till the bell tells you to stop."

I looked up at the clock, for a split second, and that was all it took.

Dad rushed towards me and slapped my face, hard. My cheek buzzed with hot and cold needles that echoed all the way to my brain. He stepped back and blinked at me. His face trembled with a deep fury.

"This is what I'm talking about!" he said. "You want to be the kind of man always looking at the clock. Seeing how little you can do? How much responsibility you can evade?"

I felt as tiny as the screw.

The bay doors were open, and I thought, I could just run from here. I could run, forever. I could disappear over the horizon and into the sun.

I looked around the gym. The other boxers turned away. Dewey glanced at me from the ring and shook his head.

"Pay attention," his coach said quickly. The coach playfully slapped Dewey with a mitt. "Back to it. Snap a jab."

The coach held up a mitt, and Dewey turned from me, back to the coach, back to the jab.

Dad's eyes were bulbous and deeply disappointed.

"You never listen," he said lowly. He stepped back and put his hands in his pockets. "You're soft like your grandad was."

The bell rang and hot tears greased my face. Every atom in me wanted to swing at Dad and crack his jaw so hard that he forgot his first name.

"What the fuck Dad?" I said.

Dad's lips trembled. "You want to end up like those guys on the street? You okay being a quitter? A casualty?"

My cheek squirmed with hot needles of pain. But the rest of me was a cold desolation. I'd never felt so alone.

"You fucking hit me," I said. I pulled the gloves off and tossed them on the ground.

"Better me than life, son! I hit you now, but life hits you at forty, and then what? Too late to change then. I'm trying to teach you something, Thomas. The road you choose now doesn't get bumpy until it's too late," Dad said, "you just don't get it."

He took his keys out of his pocket and tossed them at me.

"Go get the truck started. We'll be out in a minute."

I turned from Dad and walked quickly towards the open bay door and the Ranger.

The wind began whipping dirt and dust into a vortex and the boxers slung their sledgehammers inside of it. The canvas thundered in the ring behind me, and out of the corner of my eye, I saw Dewey as he jumped down and ran over to me.

"Go'bay," he said, putting a glove on my shoulder.

"Fuck off," I said as I shrugged him off and walked into the storm.

We sat in Elise's office the next morning and I looked up at her after I finished reading. She held her pen to her lip, thinking.

"So, after all that with your Dad at the gym, did things change?" she asked.

I plucked at my shirt. I'd gained weight, about twenty pounds so far. I weighed almost as much as I did when I graduated high school.

A heat rose in my belly.

"Thom?" Elise asked.

"There was a fight," I said. And I felt something that was completely new. A feeling that I'd been able to deaden for years: pure, unadulterated anxiety. It lifted like a mushroom cloud from my belly and ballooned in my head.

CHAPTER 9:
ANGER

June 2001

Six patties sizzled on a burning flat-top at the P. Terry's off Lamar boulevard. It was closing time. The smell of overly concentrated Pine-sol mixed with the cooking burgers. I was on mop duty, and Cruz was cooking up some patties for us. Cruz was my coworker and he was a short Venezuelan man in his early thirties. He had a black crew-cut fade, a big round nose, and excited brown eyes. He had a tribal tattoo running up his arm. He was having a baby with a white girl. He called her "Gringa."

Our manager was busy at the dumpster smoking a cigarette. I rung the mop out and laid it against the wall. Cruz flipped my two patties deftly with a wide spatula; their undersides were golden brown. He pressed the uncooked side down and the grease hissed. The smoke rose to my nose but couldn't clear the Pine-sol.

"Don't burn mine," I said.

"I gotchu," he said. "Fucking Gringa always burns mine, too." Cruz kept pressing but took a sniff to make sure.

I put my hands in my pockets and looked around. The manager was taking his time with his smoke.

"Hey, Cruz, you got any mota?"

"Yea," he said, raising his eyebrow lightly, "I thought your Dad was loco about that chit?"

"It ain't for me," I said.

Cruz eyed me cautiously. "Watch the patties," he said.

He handed me the spatula and went to his locker. He came back with a small bag of skunk.

"But it didn't come from me," he said. "Your dad is fucking El Silbón."

A few months after Dad took me to the gym and never took me back, he found my stash. Somehow. I thought I was slick; I'd cut out a hole into an old teddy bear's crotch—just big enough for a finger to fit through—and shoved baggy after baggy of pills into its fluffy stomach. But, somehow, Dad found it. That meant weekly home drug tests. Meant working full-time hours at P. Terry's after school. Then, he sold my car. It was a month before graduation. When I begged him not to, his answer was, "You want a mule truck, you work for it." I was riding the bus with ninth graders, as a senior. And last, but certainly not least, either Dad, Mom, or Dewey were on pick-up duty after I got off work. That night, it was Dewey, but he'd volunteered. He'd taken a beating earlier that morning in the first rounds of Golden Gloves.

In Dewey's three months, he'd advanced so quickly that he sparred high level amateurs. He did well enough in a smoker that his coach said he should do Golden Gloves; just to test the waters.

In his first fight, he punished the kid for three rounds, just short of a knockout. Still, the kid got lucky. He'd landed a few hard crackers on Dewey, too. Dewey's eyes were glazed as he came out of the ring. His cheeks swelled in a pink sheen. He looked like a carnival clown: shades of red, blue, and purple bruises and welts covered his face. We hugged once he got down to the stands and he whispered, "I need you to hook me up tonight."

That's why he volunteered, otherwise he'd be fucking his girlfriend in the back of his car at Zilker.

Dad was slightly suspicious; nobody ever just volunteered to be my chauffeur, especially not Dewey. But, it was Dewey, so Dad's only comment was, "Get him home quick so you can get a full eight."

Dewey was fighting in the 147 Championship the next day against a kid with nine amateur fights already.

Dewey crawled to the curb in his rusted Infiniti. It was Dad's graduation present to him. He was taking classes at ACC and planning to go pre-med. He put on his blinkers and rolled down the window. I dusted off the last of my two burgers and tossed the wrappers in the trashcan. P. Terry's glowed in a red neon behind me as I leaned in. Dewey had made himself a makeshift sauna suit which amounted to wrapping himself in garbage bags and duct tape. Beads of sweat rolled down his bruised face; he had to make weight every day.

I draped my apron over the windowsill.

"That thing smells like hamburger shit," he said. Every word was a grimace. He couldn't even turn his neck.

"You gotta stop letting the boys at the gym throat-fuck you," I said.

"Funny." A smile wrinkled his cheek. Purplish bruises circled his eye. A cut on his cheek glistened with Vaseline.

"You didn't keep your right hand up," I said.

Dewey was incredulous but didn't turn his head to face me. "I fucking pummeled that kid."

"That why you need this?" I asked. I pulled the baggy out of my pocket. It smelled like a cat's armpit.

"Fuck you," he said. "I can't sleep like this."

"You're welcome, Golden boy."

"Get in. Dad's probably counting the seconds."

I got in and slammed the door. Dewey grimaced.

"How's it feel?" I asked.

"Like I got hit trying to hug a freight train."

Dewey pulled off and I put the baggy in the cupholder. In front of it was a bottle of Febreze still encased in plastic.

"That's a dead giveaway," I said as we came to a red light.

"Dad will kill both of us if he finds out."

"No," I said, "Dad'll kill me. You'll get my room as a boxing gym."

I raised my eyebrow and looked at Dewey as his face buzzed green and he hit the gas.

Dewey mashed the button to roll the windows down and groaned. I grabbed the Febreeze and tossed it out the window. Dewey reached in his pocket and tossed a bowl in my lap.

"Fuck did you get this from?" I asked.

Dewey turned his neck one click at a time and smiled. "I have my ways," he said. "Now start packing Ms. Daisy."

We pulled to a stop at another red.

"I got some other stuff if you need it. It'll really knock you out," I said.

"Fuck that," Dewey said, "I'm not ending up a fucking junkie."

My heart twitched, "What, you think *I* am?"

"No," Dewey said wistfully.

The wind rippled through the cabin as Dewey wiped his forehead. The black plastic squeaked on his skin.

"This is another level of sore," he said. "Sleepless sore."

Dewey zoomed through a yellow light. The cabin howled. A siren wailed in the distance.

"Mom still at work?" I asked.

"Dad said a trauma came in. She's gonna be late," Dewey said.

We pulled to a stop at a light. The sirens were getting closer. Dewey glanced wide-eyed and paranoid in the rearview.

"Chill," I said. "They don't send the FBI to pull you over for weed. And they definitely ain't using sirens. Probably just a car wreck."

I handed him the bowl.

"Smoke up," I said.

"Don't make eye contact, I'll do the talking," I said to Dewey after I'd finished putting in some Clear Eyes. We'd made it home and were getting our story straight as Dewey's car sat parked in the gravel beside the Ranger. The forest behind our house was dark and impenetrable.

"Huh?" His eyes were a white glaze and he slid down in his seat. He turned to me.

"The pain's a memory," he said with a wistful smile.

I snapped my fingers. "You're going to fuck both of us. Get your shit together."

Dewey jumped up, gripped the steering wheel with both hands, and stared out into the darkness. An owl hooted. The crickets chirped like sprinklers. He bit his lip and looked at me with eyes like a hooked fish. He began to look frantically around the car.

"What?" I asked.

"We have to make sure we don't leave any. Anywhere!"

I laid my hand on his shoulder. The plastic of the garbage bag stuck to my palm.

"Fucker," I said softly, "I ditched it all out the window on I-35."

"What about the bowl?"

"In pieces on the side of the highway."

Dewey sat back, relieved.

"Give me the house keys," I said. "I'll do the talking."

I stood at the door as Dewey leaned on me. His breath smelled like iron.

"Brush your fucking teeth when you get upstairs, Dew. Your breath smells like ass," I said.

"Taste of victory, my nigga," he said.

As I turned the lock, I smelled black coffee. It was a canary in the coal mine in our house. If Mom had a bad night at work, she'd call ahead so Dad would make coffee.

"The trauma must've been bad," Dewey said.

We glanced at each other and bumped fists as I pushed the door open. The living room was black and the sofas looked like tombstones. The TV screen was a fixed, black pupil. There was a faint whistle upstairs coming from the kitchen. We tip-toed up and made the landing. Dad stood with his hands planted on the edge of the stove with his back to us. The light above the stove cast his shadow long and massive. He didn't even turn around.

"Dewey, I put a gallon of water by your bed. Finish it before you go to sleep," he said in a low, slow tone.

"Yes, sir." Dewey punched my shoulder with a doofus grin and turned quickly to go to his room.

"How was work, Thom?" Dad asked, and turned to me.

"Good," I said.

He crossed his arms and leaned back against the stove. He said with an abnormal calmness and an almost impossible tint of pride, "You're working hard lately."

I nodded.

Dad's phone buzzed on the counter. He stood up tall and tightened.

"You go to bed, too," he said curtly, walking to pick up his phone.

"On my way," I said.

I laid in bed for a while and stared at the popcorn ceiling letting the high wear off. I'd decided to put down some final touches on my first original piece before I went to bed: it was for Dewey when he won the championships the next day. I cracked the window as much as I could. Dad had installed a few fail-safes. Door alarms on the back and front doors. Sensitive floodlights. And the final touch, a bar that locked the window at a certain opening so I couldn't sneak out. In defiance, I painted it over in neon splatters. I finished laying down my paints around 12:00. Around 1:00, I woke up to the sound of Mom's car coming down the driveway. I closed my eyes and listened closely. Her door opened and closed. I looked at the clock on my bedside table: 1:30. I rolled out of bed and tip-toed to the window, peering outside. Mom's Lexus ticked to sleep behind Dewey's. Mom was nowhere to be seen. Then I heard the tell-tale squeak of Dewey's car door opening. Then, I smelled a skunk.

The next morning I woke up to a car door slamming. Then, the front door opened and slammed. Then, footsteps pounded the stairs. I ran the mental game quickly; I knew I'd cleaned out everything. I'd tossed the skunk out the window on I-35 a mile before our exit; If he'd been haunting the medians at night looking for the bones of our bowl, then he really was El Silbón.

Dad bellowed at the top of the stairs: "Dewitt. Thomas. Both of you. Up. Now!"

Dad rumbled down the hallway, his footsteps massive. He burst through my door. My easel nearly fell. Dad's face shook madly.

"Fuck is this?" he said.

He held up shaking hands: In one, the at-home test kits; In the other, a tiny, green nugget with red hairs.

"I don't know," I said. I'd learned one thing: even if you've got the hook in your mouth, don't jump. Dad was a master angler waiting for the slightest shiver of the line.

Dad glared at me trying to discern the truth. I focused on believing my image of the truth. The sun peeked through the slitted blinds and landed in bars on the floor.

"You're taking a test, then." He shook it at me.

"Dewey!" he shouted, his eyes still focused on me.

Behind Dad, Mom opened their bedroom door and stepped out cinching her robe.

"Arn, what the hell?" Mom looked down at her watch. "It's goddam seven in the morning."

Dad turned around, and held the evidence up to her face.

"I told you, Deb, the next time, He's out!" He shook the hand with the weed. "I found this in Dewey's car. He's getting his brother involved now, too."

"Dewey!" he shouted, again. A vein pulsed in his temple.

Mom's lips parted slightly, and she put her fingernail in her mouth. Her hair was cartoonishly wild and frizzy. And her eyes bloodshot.

"Baby, please," she said, putting her hand gently on Dad's shoulder. "You know the night I had."

Dad's jaw slackened, and his voice cracked as it softened.

"I'm sorry, baby. But, this is the last time. I've told him over and over again."

Mom shook her head.

Dad banged on Dewey's door with the tests still in his hand. They rattled inside the box. "Dewey!"

Mom glanced at me. Her eyes widened as she bit off a fingernail. I shrugged. I was certain I'd thrown that shit out the window.

Dewey opened his door and slowly peeked out. He blinked at Dad.

"What's going on?" he asked.

Dad shoved the nugget in his face.

Dewey's eyes ballooned.

Dewey didn't know not to let the hook set.

"Dad, I don't know what that is!" he said, pleading.

Dewey'd just fucked the both of us.

"You've got to be fucking kidding me," Dad said, dropping his shoulders sadly like he'd pulled in a dolphin. "Everybody downstairs."

He turned and marched down the hallway. The tests rattled in his hands like the far-off sounds of a shooting range.

Dewey looked at me, and then his eyes caught the painting in my room.

I closed my door quickly.

We all sat in the living room as Dad paced the center, he tapped the test against his thigh.

Mom crossed her legs and laid her arm on the armrest.

"For Christ's sake, Arn," she said.

But, Dad was too far away to hear her. His face was twisted and he moved his lips talking to himself. I knew my fate. I'd already started calculating: I had one friend, maybe two that I could call to couch surf. But after that, it got dark. Bridge under I-35 dark: The loosely put-up tents. The garbage everywhere. The stench of human shit, dog shit, lost shit.

Dad tapped his lip with the test and then turned to me, pointing at me with it.

"You," he said, "I could understand," he paused, "but you," he pointed at Dewey, "Championship's today. Fuck are you thinking?"

Dewey's face was brutal. The bruises around his eyes bulged like he had tiny plums beneath them. Especially his right side. And his busted lip looked too kissed.

"I don't know what that is, Pop!" he shouted a bit too loud.

Dad turned to me, smirking like a general catching a mutiny. "You teaching him the tricks of the trade?"

Mom spit out a fingernail and started chewing another.

"Neither of you fesses up, then Thom, you're out. And Dewey, no fight. No championship. No belt. All that work, for nothing."

I gulped down a rock of saliva. Dewey looked like he'd seen his final judgment.

"Dewey, be honest. Did you smoke this shit?" Dad asked.

Dewey shriveled.

Mom glanced at Dad.

All I wanted to do was get high and forget it all. I wanted to erase this moment as much as I could and make my real life a distant, painless memory. But, it'd kill Dewey if he couldn't compete. I was already in the net. Dewey still had a sliver of hope left.

"You're right, Dad. It was me," I said. I nearly choked on it. "I snuck into Dewey's room and took his keys. I guess I left some in the car."

"Dewey's the lightest sleeper in this house," Dad said incredulously.

"Not last night, we all saw that beating he took."

"How'd you get out the window?"

"The window-lock really ain't that hard to figure out, Pop."

Dad chewed on it. He glanced back and forth from me to Dewey. Dewey, in a stroke of profound wisdom, just looked forward. He didn't agree or disagree.

Mom ripped a nail off her pinky and sucked on the end of her finger as it started to bleed.

Dad pointed the tests at me. "You're out!"

"Dad, please," I said.

"You're going down the same road your grandad did," Dad said.

Dad's lips trembled, and his eyes glistened. A tear crept out of his eye and rolled down his cheek.

"Don't you know I'm trying to save you, son?"

Mom coughed and sat forward and said softly, "It's mine, Arn."

Dad was still laser-locked on me. He didn't hear her.

"Arnie!" Mom said as she slapped her thighs loudly.

Dad wheeled around, "Yes, Deb?"

"It's mine."

"Deb," Dad said, "you don't have to save him."

"I'm not lying, Arn. I got it from Cynthia."

"Cynthia?"

"We worked the trauma together last night," Mom said. Mom rubbed her hands together as her lips trembled and her eyes glossed over.

Dad wiped a tear from his cheek. His shoulders dropped. He shrunk.

"What the fuck, Deb?" he said, softly.

"Yup," Mom said, reaching for the test, now limp in Dad's hand. "Give it to me. I'll pop hot."

Dad's head swayed. His grip on the test loosened as it dropped out of his hand and fell to the carpet. They looked at each other, and then, the dam in Mom broke. Her shoulders shook and she burst into tears.

"It was hell, Arn," Mom said, "Four fatalities. The whole trauma bay was covered in blood: Mom, three kids." Mom put her head in her hands and started crying in broken fits. "We'd get one back and the other would code again. Over and over, Arn."

Dad melted as he walked to Mom. He placed his hand behind her head gently and she leaned into him weeping. She sobbed in clipped howls. He leaned down and whispered something softly into her ear.

Mom grabbed him around the waist and cried into his belly.

"I'm sorry Arnie..." she said.

He kissed her forehead.

"It's okay sweetheart," Dad said. He sat down beside her and she laid on him as he rubbed her shoulders.

He stiffened and turned to us.

"Both of you. Upstairs. Now."

I'd somehow gotten a stay of execution in the eleventh hour.

I popped up and slapped Dewey's knee. Dewey was frozen. He stared at the floor wide-eyed.

"Let's go," I said.

Dewey looked up at me blinking like he felt water on his gills again.

"Hey," I whispered quickly, "This is Planet Earth. Let's go."

"Hurry up!" Dad barked.

We rushed up the stairs.

Dewey punched my shoulder in the hallway.

"Man, you slipped a bullet," he said.

"*We* slipped a bullet," I said.

"Fuck," he said, "Almost lost it there."

Dewey looked down and rubbed his knuckles.

"Thank God for Mom," he said slowly.

"I smelled a skunk last night," I said, "but, Mom was actually smoking. The fuck."

"Stroke of fortune," Dewey said.

"For sure."

Downstairs, Mom talked quietly and slowly in between blowing her nose and sniffing. Dad didn't say a word.

"What was that painting you were working on?" he asked.

"Nothing," I said. I went into my room and closed the door quickly.

Mom was on pick-up duty the night of the Championship. Dewey was going on right after I got off work. Mom rolled to the curb as I took my apron off and slung it over my shoulder. I'd bought a couple of Percs off of Cruz and made sure the tiny baggy was deep in my front pocket. I was excited; Percs were a gentle music when they hit, every muscle and fiber inside me hummed like a plucked chord.

Mom rolled the window down.

"We ain't got much time," she said.

She lit a cigarette as I got in. I tossed my apron in the back.

"What time is he fighting, again?" I asked.

"7:30," Mom said.

The clock on the dash read 7:20.

"Did you bring it?" I asked.

Mom blew out a plume and motioned with her cigarette behind me.

"Backseat," she said.

She shifted into drive and we rolled into traffic.

I glanced in the rearview as we passed a green light. The light flashed through the cabin and illuminated the outline of the canvas under a white sheet.

"Shit, I forgot to sign it," I said.

"Language, Go'bay. And I brought some paint and a brush."

I turned and looked in the backseat. Beside the canvas was a small plastic container of white paint and a thin brush. I grabbed the container and the canvas and sat them in my lap.

"You think Dad's gonna like it?" I asked.

Mom smiled. "They both are."

"How far away are we?" I asked.

"Five minutes." Mom skirted through another yellow, just as it turned red. We were only a few minutes off.

We crested a hill and saw lights strobing blue, red, and white.

"Fuck me," Mom said. She flicked her cigarette out the window and we rolled to a stop.

She breathed in deeply and gripped the steering wheel with both hands. In front of us: a flashing gaggle of ambulances, police cars, and fire-trucks. Cops, paramedics, and firemen with distressed faces surrounded a flipped over pickup smashed like a soda can. It was sandwiched between a semi and a concrete girder. On the side of the road, lay a pink baby-seat.

"My god," Mom said as we inched forward, and each flash of light painted Mom's face in a shade of weariness and fear.

We came to a stop and she laid her hand limply on the gearshift.

I reached over slowly and laid my hand on top of hers.

She looked at me as a quiet tear ran down her cheek.

We pulled into the parking lot of the arena as families filtered out. They hugged their fighters with pride: win, lose, or draw.

Dad called Mom as soon as we put the car in park. Mom picked up the phone. I sunk in my seat as I heard his voice on the other end and touched my pocket full of euphoria.

"Hey, honey," Mom replied. Her face was wooden as she listened and then she let out a small burst of laughter.

"Then that would make you Chong," she said.

Dad's voice buzzed in her ear. Her smile faded quickly as she glanced at me and then the canvas. Her face sagged like candle wax.

"How's he doing?" Mom asked.

Mom nodded solemnly.

"Dewey lost?" I asked.

Mom put her finger up. I looked out the window and into the double doors. Dad stood behind them on the phone and rubbed his eyes as he talked to Mom. He had his Longhorns snap-back on and lifted it twice.

"Ok, bye," Mom said, and hung up.

Dad disappeared behind the dark glass.

"Your brother lost," Mom said, turning to me.

"I could tell."

As we waited for them to come out, I felt the weight of loss for Dewey. Dewey would wake up at four in the morning to go running. He'd come home from school, do his homework, and then go to the gym for two hours. And it was that way for months. He ate like a rabbit. He weighed himself constantly. Slept in a sauna suit. And all of that for six minutes of nothing. I held my canvas and fanned my signature. It felt grotesque and out of place now.

"Here they come!" Mom said, tapping my leg.

"You think he'll want it?" I asked, as Dad held the door open for Dewey.

"Bring it," Mom said.

Mom got out and rushed over to Dewey. Dewey was still in shock and hugged Mom limply. I walked over and held the canvas in my hands but it felt heavier by the second; full of wasted time and wasted energy.

"It's okay, baby," Mom said, kissing Dewey's head, "your Dad said you fought well."

"You did, son," Dad said. He patted Dewey's back gently.

"And your brother's got something for you."

Dewey looked at me plainly. Dad's eyes grew when he saw the back of the canvas.

"It's nothing," I said, as I hugged it close.

"Go ahead, Thom," Mom said. "It's beautiful."

I turned the canvas around as a family walked past. I tried to shield it from them.

Dad massaged Dewey's shoulders, but his eyes widened and he tapped the brim of his cap.

"Damn, son," he said.

Dewey looked like he'd been beaten with a baseball bat. His eyes were bruised all over. His lips were fat and pouchy, but even with all the bruising, I could see a glimmer of rage in his eyes. He wiped his nose.

"What the fuck is that?" he said, pointing.

"It's you," I said.

It was supposed to be Dew. I'd painted a portrait of him as a triumphant champion. He stood in the middle of a ring holding up two gloved hands covered in the crimson, dripping blood of his opponent. He was bloodied and bruised from scalp to clavicle but sported a wide, gap-toothed smile and his eyes were white as beacons. He wore a dazzling gold championship belt around his waist. His body shimmered on the canvas.

Dewey regarded it and then sucked in deeply and said, "It looks like shit."

I simmered. Dad shoved Dewey. "Watch it," he said. "I think it looks great."

Dew looked up at Dad, his puckered face even more hurt and crawling with rage.

Dew pointed at me and yelled, "It's his fault I lost!"

"How so?" Dad asked. "You just fought somebody better than you. It happens."

"I was gassed in the last round, you saw!" Dewey spat.

"How is that your brother's fault?" Dad asked pointedly.

"It was his weed, Dad. He convinced me to smoke it."

A jelly-like mix of fear and anger ran through me as Dad looked from Dewey, to me, to Mom, to me. Dad zeroed in on me. His hands twitched angrily at his side. His eyes burned. His lips trembled. His fists curled. A few people passed by and bent their heads.

"So, it *was* yours?" Dad asked, pointing at me harshly.

"Arnie, not here," Mom urged.

"Deb, he's my son too." Dad put his hand up at her.

"Arnie!" Mom hissed. "Don't talk to me like that."

"No, Deb," Dad said turning to Mom, "I'm not going soft on him."

He turned back to me and said, "You know how hard your brother worked, just to get here? And you jeopardize that, for what?"

"It's just a little weed. Mom had some," I said.

"This isn't your mother's problem. It's yours."

"Well, I'm sorry I ruined Golden Boy's chances."

A few bats chirped overhead.

Dewey cried on Mom's shoulder. She patted his head.

"It's always about you, isn't it?" Dad said. "Fuck your responsibilities. Fuck the consequences. Right, Thom? Do what you want. It's your life. You don't care what it does to your mother? Your brother?"

In that moment, I didn't want to just leave anymore. I didn't want to be a part of the fucking family. Fuck if I ended up under a bridge somewhere. I didn't want to know my father anymore.

"Fuck you!" I shouted.

Dad stepped to me. "What'd you say to me, boy?"

Dad lifted his fist. He was so close I could smell the coffee on his breath from that morning. A white paste of spit accumulated at the corner of his lip.

"You want to do something?" he growled.

I threw down my canvas.

Dad glanced down as it echoed and splintered on the pavement.

When he looked back up, I swung loose. Like a javelin. He wasn't ready. I was. It landed after a brief arc with a thud. His cheek and my knuckles subsumed each other.

"Oh my god!" Mom cried.

Dad stumbled back with his hand to his face.

Dewey lifted his head off of Mom's shoulder, his bruised eyes wide, and his bulbous mouth dropped.

Dad took his hand from his face and looked at it. His brow furrowed deeply as he thought. Then he looked up at me and his voice trembled with rage as he whispered, "Don't come back to my fucking house."

"Wasn't planning on it, Arnold," I said. Every atom in my bloodstream was zinging.

Dad pointed at my signature on the canvas. The paint still dripped. "And don't use my last fucking name," Dad growled.

"Arnie!" Mom said, rushing past him to me.

"Fuck it, Mom!"

Those three months I'd worked on it, I'd done two things: drugs and painting. I ran my miles on my canvas. I struggled with the sketching. Ruminated over the colors. Stared at the canvas for hours. All for Dewey. All for Dad. I bent down and lifted the canvas over my head and smashed it against the asphalt. With each splintering swing, my vision blurred with tears that came from a hot, hateful place inside of me. Every swing was a confirmation of my hurt and anger. Soon it lay in pieces at my feet, but the anger didn't wash away. The world was a dark blur.

The wood lay in splinters but pieces of Dewey remained: a single, gloved fist raised in the air; a smile on a broken cheek.

I stalked off into the darkness and put my hand on my pocket feeling for the baggie and the pills inside it. I had enough to worry about tomorrow, tomorrow.

The Indian Paintbrush from the dayroom sat on the coffee table between the two sofas in Elise's office. Its petals fluttered harmlessly as the A/C kicked on. The sun glowed through the two windows on either side of her desk opposite us.

"So," Elise said, as she ran her hand through her hair and crossed her legs, leaning towards me, "did you?"

I'd started the outline of a cube on my notepad and looked up. "Did I what?"

"Did you have enough pills?" she asked. She planted her chin on her palm and tapped her cheek with her fingers.

"I had enough to get me through a couple of hours," I said.

Elise narrowed her eyes and then nodded at the Indian Paintbrush.

"Thom, the drugs are just petals. Just window-dressing. I can take a pair of scissors and prune every leaf and bud that sprouts and still get nowhere. Now, why is that?"

I looked up from the cube.

"No wrong answers here, Thom," she said.

"You didn't get the root," I said.

"Boom," she said.

I looked down at my cube and began shading it in. I took away its dimension and made it two-dimensional again.

"What do you feel right now?" Elise asked.

I thought of Dad, the way he'd looked after I'd punched him: He wasn't just angry, or disappointed, or furious. He was hurt. I'd erased his idea of his youngest son. He was better off, I thought. Everyone was better off if I left. I was un-fixable. There was no coming back to the family, in my mind, after that. And then, the horror hit me. A gust of regret swept through me so deeply that it felt like it had always been there, hibernating for years and years, and it woke up to a spring-like despair: I never got to say sorry.

"I don't know," I said.

"Dig, Thom," she said, "give me three emotions. The first three that pop into your head."

I gripped my pen, hard. And a balloon of fire rose inside me.

"I feel fucking angry. And hurt. And I fucking hate myself for doing that."

"And?" Elise urged softly.

"I fucking regret it. I regret ever being fucking born."

Elise's foot shook and she wrung her hands. Green veins popped out of her knuckles like thick hoses, but her eyes were soft and warming.

"That's where we have to go next, Thom," she said.

Outside, the kids screamed like banshees at the elementary school. They screamed with all of themselves: complete wholes.

"What do you mean?" I asked.

"Your shame," Elise said.

"I can't," I said.

"Why not?" Elise asked. Her face was quizzical.

I couldn't open my mouth to it.

"Is it about your abuser?" she asked.

"No," I said.

"Your dad?" she asked.

"No," I said, "it's about my mom."

A cold root of embarrassment spread from back of my throat and rushed down my trachea like menthol. It passed my heart and sucked the courage from it. By the time it got to my stomach, I was so ashamed I couldn't draw a line if I'd wanted to.

"At some point you'll have to address it, Thom," Elise said, "if not inside these walls, then out there. But mark my words, the longer it lingers, the deeper the root grows."

CHAPTER 10:
YOU MEAN I'M LEAVING?

A week later I sat in front of Elise's desk. She drummed her fingers on a black mouse as she looked at her computer screen. She was in civies: a blue polo and blue jeans. As she clicked her mouse, I stared at the tattoo on her wrist: "Live by it, Die by it."

I was going home in a week.

On her desk were two things: a piece of carbon-copied paper (my pre-discharge summary). And a manila folder.

She clicked once more and, satisfied, asked, "How do you feel about discharge?"

"Free me, Lincoln," I said.

Elise frowned and clasped her hands in front of her.

"It was a joke," I said.

She looked into her hands and a melancholic smirk crossed her face. From the two windows, the shadows of leaves wavered as the sun splattered in. I could see the back of the elementary school playground through the window. A few red, white, and blue pinwheels spun in the wind. A little boy, by himself, kicked at one of them with his hands in his pockets. I could hear the other kids scream and holler joyfully, but he looked heavy and thoughtful; too heavy for his age.

Elise unclasped her hands and laid one on the manila folder.

"I have something to show you, Thom," Elise said.

I shrunk, slightly. The leather in my chair squeaked.

"We never talked about your shame, Thom."

I looked into my hands. They were softer now. No more brick dust. Labor-less awaiting freedom.

"I can't," I said.

She sighed and leaned forward on her elbows. Her lavender perfume was fragrant.

"Recess is over!" a teacher yelled. Her voice penetrated the windows. I looked out the window, the kid didn't move. He kept kicking at the pinwheel.

"Thom," Elise said. I took my eyes off the kid and looked at her. She bit her bottom lip. "You understand you're leaving next week, right?"

"It is what it is."

I massaged my knuckles.

"It doesn't matter to you?"

My vision blurred. "My family knows me longer as this than they have as Thomas Middlecamp. You think they'll miss him if he's gone? They barely know him." I drew in a breath, letting it all out of me, "And, as for Mom, I'm surprised she's still willing to pick me up. It's within her right to never talk to me again for the shit I've pulled."

I didn't feel self-pity; It was the hard rock of truth.

"What about your life? Your future?" Elise asked.

I looked out the window. The kid kicked the pinwheel as his teacher walked over to him and put her hand on his shoulder. He shrugged her hand off angrily. He kicked at the pinwheel with rage, kicking up clod after clod of dirt until the pinwheel flew free. It floated in the air and glimmered in the sun. And then, it disappeared.

"My future's up my arms," I said.

I looked at Elise and her eyes reddened. Her porcelain cheeks flushed like a Russian doll.

"I have something to show you," she said.

She opened the manila folder and pulled out a floppy, glossy piece of film. Her hands shook as she looked at it.

She turned the glossy film to me.

"You know what this is?" she asked.

She pointed to a white globular accumulation on a film, it looked like a massive drop of water on an oil slick: swirling and amorphous.

"No," I said.

"It's my daughter."

She shook it at me.

"That was my future. And I gave it up. And not only that, I gave up having children, too. Yup, had that taken from me. That's my shame and I carried it for years. I carried it like a soldier carries his pain: all self-loathing; all rage. I wouldn't allow myself to be happy because of it. It was my karma. My punishment. It was exactly what I thought I deserved."

"Why are you showing me this?" I asked.

She sighed, and her eyes grew melancholy.

"To be honest, in some ways, you remind me of her father."

I couldn't imagine having kids.

"And, you're still here. I'm still here," she shook the floppy film gently, "And she's not...I say all that to say, Thom, that no matter what the past looks like, no matter the things that you didn't get to be before, you have an opportunity now. You get to see yourself again. I get to live as the woman my daughter should have had as a mother. And for you, you have to confront that shame that kept you away from your family. Whether it's here, when you go home, or ten years from now. But if you don't make a plan to confront it, it will corrupt everything. Your present and future will be poisoned."

I nodded.

"So, before discharge, I not only want a plan, I need one. Give me something. Even if it's just a sentence. You gotta start somewhere," she said.

CHAPTER 11:
1, 6, 12, 60…

"You look so much healthier than you did when you first got here," Elise said.

It was the day before discharge.

Elise and I sat on the sofas facing each other in her office. She wore a long-sleeve that covered every one of her tattoos. Her hair was glossed and permed. She had a sparkling rosy shade of lipstick. And her name badge shined glossily.

She crossed her legs and tapped her pen on a yellow notepad. She smiled.

I was back in my old uniform: tattered black Nirvana T-shirt and the jeans I came in with. They were crusted at the hem with a fine white powder, and the A/C crept in through holes in the knees.

I held my notepad in my lap. I'd written one-month, six-month, one year, and five-year plan headings on my notepad. I stared at the notepad at my desk in my room the night before. I'd managed two sentences: *Get a job. Don't hang out around Lamar.*

Elise leaned forward, crossing her arms over her notepad and twirling her pencil like a propeller.

"So, what you got for me?" she asked.

I looked down at the scribble and the cubes on my notepad.

"It's not much," I said.

"Whatever you've got," she said.

"You're gonna knock my head in!"

I turned the notepad to her.

She read it out loud. "Get a job; don't hang out around Lamar."

Her eyes narrowed as she looked at it. She sat back and un-crossed her legs.

"You know the odds are stacked against you?" she said.

"I know."

"Out of the six of you that came in, half of you survive in five years."

I laid the notepad in my lap.

"We're not talking staying clean, Thom. We're talking staying alive."

I sketched a cube at the top of the page.

"You want to be a ghost?" she asked.

"Of course not."

She leaned forward.

"What about the shame, Thom? What are you hiding?" she asked pointedly.

I swallowed.

I drew shadows in the cube.

"I worry about seeing my mom again."

My eyes burned. I wiped the useless tears away. A waft of stale BO hit my nose from the armpit of my shirt. It had been washed, but the stank remained.

Elise put her notepad and pen down on the table and pushed herself up, circling the coffee table to me. Her perfume hit me first, and then I felt a soft hand on my knee.

"What else?" she asked. She was soft. She didn't sound angry, not even disappointed. Just worried.

"I've been thinking about my dad...and boxing."

"Not painting?"

I stopped shading the cube and let my pen drop.

"It's just not there anymore. The most I can do is this. Anything more is impossible," I said.

She patted my knee.

"Thom, I can't force you to follow the program. I've had to come to terms with the fact that it all won't happen in this building. There's no magic therapy or way to circumvent the chasm that is getting clean. You have to cross it. And you'll cross it without me. But," she drew a breath in, "I need you to promise me something."

I touched up a shadow, digging the edge of my pen into the notepad.

"Thom. Look at me," she said.

The growing film of tears in my eyes made her a blur, all blonded. Orbs of sunlight covered her face, and her lips shimmered in blurry rosy pearls.

"I need you to find something everyday that you can forgive. Forgive getting cut in line at H-E-B. Forgive the old lady who doesn't use her blinker. Forgive a fender bender. Forgive a co-worker. Everyday, forgive. The more you build that muscle, the more you can forgive yourself and the closer you get to true recovery. The closer you get to up-rooting the shame, because that's all shame is; it's the belief that there are things about ourselves that we can't forgive or change. That's the root of all of this."

She patted my knee slowly and handed me a tissue.

CHAPTER 12:
MOM STILL LOVED ME

July 4, 2015

Somewhere, a grill smoked. The smell of charred burgers filled the air. Firecrackers sizzled, popped, and hissed. The sun blitzed off the limestone. Elise and I stood outside waiting for Mom to pick me up. She took her hands out of her pockets and wiped her brow with her sleeve.

"Gonna have to put some more cake on," she mourned as Mom pulled up smoothly in the Ranger. The tires were covered in specks of dirt and a few mud splatters painted the skirt.

"She picked up the manny," Elise pondered.

"My dad would probably kill her if he saw that dirt on the skirt."

Mom waved through the window. She had a red, white, and blue streamer tied in her hair and wore a white T-shirt with an American flag in the middle of it.

I waved back and hiked Dad's duffle bag higher on my shoulder. A firecracker screamed.

"So, Thom," Elise said.

I turned to her. "Yea?"

"The moment you step foot off this property, it's up to you to do the work."

"I know."

She put her hand on my shoulder and squeezed gently. Sweat rolled down her face in beige droplets, picking up tiny clumps of makeup.

"Don't let the shame become your ghost," she said.

"I'll work on it."

She let go of my shoulder and stepped back.

"I also had an idea," she said and smiled broadly.

"What's that?" .

"Boxing," she said.

"Yea? What about it?"

"I know you've got your past with it, but I've had a few guys stay clean and they said it was all because of boxing."

A kid screeched gleefully from a backyard close by. A dog barked. A mother shouted, "Cochino." A dad laughed, booming. The kid cackled like a hyena.

"I don't know," I said.

She touched my arm for the last time.

"Give it a shot. It could help you fight more demons than one."

I glanced at Mom in the car. She bit her fingernail.

The strap of the duffel burned on my shoulder.

"Win the war, Thom," Elise said, "and then, give it peace."

"And I'll give you a call about the gyms."

I nodded, and turned to the Ranger, walking toward Mom and not looking back.

Mom hopped out of the Ranger chewing gum and beaming as she circled to me. I tossed Dad's duffel in the bed and wiped a smudge off the passenger side window.

She opened her arms wide like wings.

"My big chunky," Mom said.

She grabbed me around my neck and kissed my cheek in bursts. I shrunk in her arms. It wasn't the hello I'd expected.

I thought she'd be yelling or cold as ice.

"You've been eating good," she said, as she stepped back and held my shoulders looking at me.

I'd almost forgotten how light, sweet, and energetic her voice could be.

"I thought you were going to hate me," I said.

"Oh, baby, no," Mom said. "I mean, I've had a few nights where I cursed your name," she said, chuckling. Her brown eyes filled with tears and she smiled softly.

She clutched me around the neck again and kissed my cheek as her body shook and we wept, sweating in the relentless Austin sun.

"I'm just glad you gained weight. You looked like a scarecrow when I dropped you off," Mom said.

It was my first sober Fourth of July in ten years.

I hopped in the car and at my feet was a Starbucks graveyard. Mom's pocket mirror sat on the dash with an assortment of makeup cases. On Mom's side, tucked into the edge of the windshield, was a white envelope.

Mom's work badge sat in the center console in between empty packages of Nicorette gum. She shifted the manual easily as we coasted from the curb.

I looked out the sideview as the rehab and Elise disappeared from the mirror. After a quick turn, Elise was a memory, just like that.

"You've picked up the manny pretty well," I said.

The windows were rolled down and the wind lifted and blew Mom's hair around her face.

"Your Dad always tried to teach me. And call me girly, but I used to think it looked a little too masculine for a woman to drive a manual transmission. I just liked watching your dad do it. But, yea, I've picked it up," Mom said.

The envelope fluttered against the windshield as we picked up speed.

Mom looked over at me, chewing hard on a piece of gum, her eyes cheeky.

"Won't be doing it for much longer, Praise God," she said.

"Why not?"

"It's yours, Go'bay."

"Dad's gonna dig himself out of the grave if he hears you say that."

She clenched her teeth around the wad of gum. She stared past the window and into the horizon, past the Whataburger and the Mopac overpass. She squinted at her tears. "I fucking hope so."

She downshifted and we slowed to a stop gently at a red light.

She put her hands in her lap and looked over at me. Her eyes darkened.

"Your dad left it in the will. He wanted you to have this," she said. She slapped the steering wheel lightly with both hands. Then she turned to me, and her brown eyes became shadows, "and his forgiveness."

I turned away and looked out the window. Lamar was one street over. I shivered and my stomach writhed. Mom chewed her gum loudly, her jaw clicking.

"And anyways, I don't like being in this truck," she said.

I looked at her as she flicked a laminated picture hanging from the rearview.

She smiled. "You remember this?"

It was the beach picture: All of us, standing in the sun at Port A. Dad had his hands on me and Dewey's shoulders. We held our cherry ice-pops up to the camera with red-stained lips and smiled like champions. Mom stood on her toes to kiss Dad on the cheek as the waves lapped at our feet.

"The good ol' days," Mom mused, chewing.

I looked at the gear shift, then to Mom. "So, you quit smoking?"

"You gave up something that was killing you. I thought I should at least try to."

She smiled as the light turned green. The sun danced off of the streamers in her hair as the cabin lit up in shimmering vibrant rays. We drove towards Mopac, and as I looked out my window, I caught more glimpses of Lamar. I felt the weight of shame with each light we passed. The envelope fluttered in the wind and with the effect of the sun bouncing off the streamers in Mom's hair, it looked like it was burning.

CHAPTER 13:
SHAME

May 4, 2015

It was the day I'd gotten discharged after my O/D.

The day before I went to rehab.

Mom and I sat in her car. She looked through my ICU discharge papers in her lap and already had a cigarette between her lips. The A/C was on blast. Austin burned like a raisin in the sun. We sat near the top of the parking deck facing the glass cube of the hospital. I had two pairs of jewelry on: An ID wristband and a yellow bracelet that read in bolded black letters: FALL RISK. I wrapped my fingers around both and tried ripping them off. Mom cracked the window and tapped the ash off the end of her cigarette.

"How does it feel?" she asked.

"How does what feel?" I asked.

She turned to me and her eyes flashed. She put her cigarette back in her mouth and bit down on the filter.

"To be alive, Thom."

I breathed out deeply and looked away from her at the glass cube. As we sat in the car, they were cleaning out my room; clearing out the cannisters of almost a month's worth of my bodily fluids. Any pictures that had been left behind were being tossed in the garbage. I wasn't a memory to anyone in that hospital. Just a wristband. I didn't want to look at Mom. It'd confirm that something was different; that I was different. And if I looked at her, it'd mean that I'd have to change. It'd mean that this really was it.

Mom's phone rattled in the cup holder. She picked it up quickly. "Hello?" she asked.

A pause.

She sucked on her cigarette.

"Yes, he's doing fine. Just got discharged."

She exhaled and rubbed her forehead.

"Tonight?" she asked.

I looked at her. She looked at me.

"Ya'll offering a bonus?" she asked.

I pulled my phone out of my pocket and laid it on my lap. I blew white brick residue off of it, like dusting off a fossil.

I cleared out her calls and her voicemails. I wasn't going to listen to them.

I needed to call Ball, but even his name sounded different in my head.

"See you tonight," she said as she hung up.

A cold pit opened in my belly as I imagined rehab. I closed my eyes and drew in a deep breath through my nose.

Hell was on the way.

I breathed out deeply through my lips and opened my eyes. I could see the helipad on the top of the hospital.

Rehab was an inevitability.

But, fuck, the urge throttled me and struck chord after chord in all the old pathways in my veins.

I looked over at Mom. Her cigarette dangled by the skin of her lips as she stared at me.

"You've got to be fucking kidding me," she said.

"What, Mom?"

The cigarette in her mouth danced precariously as she talked.

"You have got to be fucking kidding me, Thomas."

"What do you mean, Mom?"

"You can't do fucking drugs, Thom." She pointed at the hospital. "You just got out of the fucking hospital."

My phone lay in my lap.

"I was just checking my messages," I said.

A rumbling, melodic thwacking sound like a giant bee buzzed in through Mom's cracked open window.

She pulled her lips close around her cigarette, sucked in, and put her right hand in her lap. She used her left hand to roll the window down. She breathed out deeply exhaling a massive plume, then, her shoulder shivered and she shot her right hand to my lap. She grabbed the phone and tossed it out her window at a concrete pylon.

It smashed against the cement into glittering, reflectant pieces.

"What the fuck, Mom?"

"Give me your hand, Thom," Mom said as she tossed her cigarette out the window.

"Fuck no. You're going to chop it off."

She grabbed my hand and put her pointer and middle finger on my wrist.

"Put two fingers there," she said.

Her eyes were urgent. The thwacking echoed deeply in the air, coming closer.

I put my two fingers beside hers.

A rhythmic whoosh like waves coming in and out thrummed beneath.

"Three weeks. Just for that to keep going," she said, tapping her pointer finger rapidly. "That's the only reason I've gotten maybe two hours of sleep a night. Just so you could leave the hospital with that. I didn't even care if you were a vegetable. Do you know how fucked up that it is for a mother to think? Do you give a shit that I had to think that?"

She shook with tears and put her hands in her lap. Moaning. "Please. God. Please."

She rocked back and forth, shaking her head from side to side.

"Mom, please," I said.

I wanted to nod into amnesia.

"I'm sorry, Mom. I really am. I just can't do this."

She breathed in through her teeth and put her hand on her chest. "Your ass is gonna give me a coronary."

"I'm sorry," I said, but it was an empty song. I'd sung it too many times to her.

She shook her head.

"There isn't a sorry left in the world that you actually mean."

"You have no clue what this is like. You don't know what kind of nightmare it is. You know what it's like for something in your life to walk you like a dog?"

"The fuck do you think motherhood is, Thom?"

Mom grabbed her pack of Newports and pulled out another cigarette as her hands trembled. She lit it and the flame flared as she drew a deep breath in. It illuminated all the new lines in her face. She blew out and turned to me.

"It's either now or never, Thom. For both of us. It kills me just as much as it does you. You've got no fucking idea."

"I want it to be now," I said, "I really do."

"But?"

But, it felt like I was born with a rope around my waist. I could get some slack every now and again but eventually the monkey was at the other end. Eventually he'd get to yanking.

Mom turned to the window.

"I picked up tonight," she said looking at the concrete pillar.

I wiped my eyes.

"So you have to stay with your brother," she said, pulling on her cigarette deeply.

The thwacking thundered, getting louder.

Ash lifted from Mom's cigarette and drifted out the window. The sun glowed in orange slices on the very top windows of the hospital.

The thwacking howled and then receded as a chopper the color of a banana descended to the roof slowly.

As soon as its feet touched, a group of nurses rushed towards it with a rolling gurney. Their scrub tops whipped in the wind. Their hair flew wild and chaotic.

"Ashes to ashes, dust to dust, Thom."

Mom looked over quickly. Her eyes were sharp. Her lips: tight.

I stared into her eyes and couldn't lie. I couldn't go in completely clean. I just couldn't. My skin was already starting to crawl.

"I can't go in their clean, Mom. I'm already starting to feel it. It'll only get worse."

The chopper wound down as its blades lowered like wilting

roses.

"It's one day, Thom."

"One day is hell, Mom."

She stared at the helicopter and bit down hard on the filter, her jaw clenching.

"That shit off the street will kill you," she said, gritted.

"It's the only thing I can get, Mom," I said.

Mom shook her head slowly.

The next morning, Dewey clinked in the kitchen as he finished making breakfast: turkey bacon, boiled eggs, and oatmeal.

I stood in the living room looking over pictures on the mantle.

It was still dark: 6:15 a.m. by the gilded clock above the mantle. Mom was clocking out soon. I looked over at the big double-paned window near the front door. The lamp on the windowsill illuminated Dewey's brown leather couch. On it was a pile of blankets and a pillow. Right beside it, by the front door, sat his ostrich-hide boots. His lab coat hung on his coat rack: white and pristine.

He'd slept on the sofa. I'd slept in his bed. He'd offered it to me and said, "One night of comfort." But, really, he just didn't want me tip-toeing out the front door and disappearing. I spent the night biting my nails down to the cuticles, and then worked the skin around them. I laid down. The sweats came. I got up. Laid down. Got up again. Two of his neighbors left at around 11:30 and came back at 11:58. A spider made her web outside his window. I closed my eyes for thirty minutes and woke up crying in a puddle.

The first photo on the mantle: All of us. Me, Dew, Mom, and Dad in the brown waters of Port A. Dew and I had on matching floral print swim trunks. We were maybe five and seven. We held up red ice-pops to the camera like trophies and smiled with red-stained teeth. Dad was burned to a Snipes-ian shade. His hands rested on our shoulders. He wore a boonie hat, aviators, and his bushy, black mustache curled up as he smiled broadly. Mom was in a pink bikini and a cowboy hat over a tight bun of hair dyed blue. She was as red as a lobster as she stood on her tiptoes and kissed Dad's cheek.

The second photo: Dew on his graduation day, Mom and Dad leaning into him, smiling with tears running down their faces. Mom was in a red sun-dress and wide-brimmed straw hat, her hair was thinner and blonde. Dad had his arm around Dew's shoulder. Dad wore a powder blue paisley long-sleeve that didn't hide his paunch, but his ostrich-hide boots were shined to a new polish. His Long-horns hat bathed his mahogany face in shadow, except for his big white teeth and silverish bushy mustache.

The third photo sat in a gold, glided frame: Dad and Dewey stood on a boat dock. Behind them were the blue-green seas of the Gulf of Mexico. Dewey wore a pair of Ray-Bans, a baby blue Billabong shirt and board shorts. He had a broad, ecstatic smile on his face. Dad was on the other side of the photo in a white tank top, board shorts, and his faded Longhorns hat. He saluted the photographer with a Shiner in his hand and a wide, buzzed smile. Between them, a massive, glittering swordfish dangled from a gleaming hook, blood streaming from its mouth.

"I called you," Dewey said behind me.

He leaned on the doorway between the dining room and kitchen holding two plates. He set them down on the table and walked over. He was already dressed for work: a pressed blue paisley long-sleeve shirt, khaki pants with a sharp pleat, and argyle socks.

"What do you mean?"

His gold Timex glinted in the lamplight as he got closer and pointed at the picture.

"That was last year. In Port A. It was Dad's birthday. I called you to come with us...but, you know how things go."

Dewey's eyes grew dark, and then he chuckled. "They thought me and Dad were in two different parties. Took them a second to catch on, I was a little too light to be believable."

I looked back down at the picture.

"Heroin killed my time," I said.

I wiped sweat from my brow.

Dewey put his hands in his pockets and shrugged.

"You're making the right choice now," Dewey said.

"Do I have any other?"

"It's a shot, Go'bay," he said, "that's all you ever needed."

I put the picture back on the mantle.

Dewey looked down at his watch and said, "Let's eat. Your ride'll be here soon."

We stood out front, waiting in the blue dawn. The oak trees moved like banshees swaying and whispering in the wind.

I tugged hard on a Marlboro.

Dewey had already gotten two phone calls, both ended with him shaking his head slowly with a sympathetic smile.

"Residents are fucking stupid," he said laughing. He hiked up his satchel bag, his lab coat was slung over his arm.

"I wouldn't know. I didn't go to med school. I went to Lamar University."

I smiled; Dewey's smile faded.

A few cars glided by as quiet as ghosts.

"You worried?" he asked.

"About med school?" I said, "nah, not in the least."

Dewey shook his head as his phone dinged again and his eyes lingered on me.

"I'm gonna be fine, Dew."

But, the sick was coming. Each car that passed had a skeleton driving it. The nausea was rolling in as the sun crept up the horizon.

Dewey looked down at his phone.

"She's right around the corner," he said.

His shoulders dropped and, in the glow of his screen, his eyes took on a watery film.

He trudged over to me and stuck out a limp hand. I took a pull on my Marlboro and grasped his hand firmly. He pulled me in and shook against me as we embraced.

"I fucked up back then," he said.

My cigarette ashed on his shoulder. A tiny ember burned an

even tinier hole in his shirt.

"We were kids, Dew."

He spoke in tight breaths in my ear.

"Still, I was a bad brother back then," he said.

He gripped me closer. It jarred more ash loose from my cigarette.

The groan of an agitated clutch screeched as Mom pulled into the parking lot.

I took the Marlboro from my mouth and let it drop to the earth, as a pair of headlights x-rayed me and Dewey.

The Ranger groaned as Mom put it in park.

"I've gotta go, Dew."

He held me tightly. His lab coat slipped out of his arm and his satchel slunk down his shoulder to his elbow like he was just a kid running late for the school bus.

I plopped into the front seat. Mom was still in her scrubs. Her work badge lay in the center cup holder and her scrub jacket laid in the backseat. I clocked the pockets of her jacket in the rearview. They looked empty. She smoked a cigarette through clenched lips.

"Hey," she said.

"Hey," I said.

Dewey waved at us limply as we lurched backwards.

"Fucking stick shift," Mom spat.

We drove in silence for five minutes. The rehab was only fifteen minutes away. It was 6:35. Showtime was at 7:00.

Mom bit down on her filter and I bit my fingernails as she hit a straightaway and could finally let go of her white-knuckled grip of the gearshift. My heart rocketed. We were only getting closer.

"So, were you able to do it?" I asked.

Mom cut her eyes at me and shifted down jerkily as we came to a halt at a red light.

"You know I won't make it," I said. "You know that."

She took a hard drag in hard silence. Cars marched across the intersection in front of us. She turned the lever and rolled the window down in jerking, angry motions.

"Nothing in this fucking thing is automatic."

She tossed her cigarette out the window and reached for her pack in the cupholder. The plastic still clung to the package; half the pack was gone already.

"Mom?"

My skin was really starting to crawl. Half-nerves, half-sick: Wholly rattled.

The light turned green as Mom lit a second cigarette.

A car behind us honked.

"Fuck off," she said through gritted teeth and took a deep pull.

The car behind us honked again. Mom gave them the finger out the window.

"Fuck off!" she said.

She jimmied with the gear shift and we lurched forward.

I shrank down and tried to settle myself. It'd be okay. They had methadone, but that felt as horrible as oil sludge on my skin. I sweated like a beached whale thinking about it.

"It's under my jacket," Mom whispered as she bumped over a pothole.

It felt like someone had lifted my flipper.

"Huh?" I asked, but I eyeballed the backseat in the rearview.

"You heard me," she said.

I sat up quickly, undid my seatbelt, and turned around to the backseat, lifting up her jacket.

Underneath it: My True Religion bag.

"Thank you," I breathed out heavily.

"How about you thank God? It'll take a miracle for me to not lose my license."

She had poison on her lips. We came to a jerking stop.

I rifled around in her jacket pocket and dug deep. My whole body tingled. But, I couldn't find a thing in her pockets.

"Where the fuck is it?"

"Dig deeper," Mom said.

The truck lurched again as we started moving forward.

I could feel her watching me like someone watches a mangy dog going through a garbage can. I felt her pity. But also, I knew she wanted revenge on me. She was being a cunt.

"It isn't in here. What the fuck? This funny to you?" I asked, turning to her.

Mom flinched.

I wanted her to feel my words like blades.

"It's in there," Mom said.

I dug one last time, clawing, and, finally, I felt it: a square package with two circular protuberances. I pulled it out of the pocket: two Percs. I melted and felt a sick, oily joy. I sank down into the front seat, the package had a massive gravity that felt life-giving, like it had stars trapped inside it.

And suddenly, I wanted to hurl. The slime in that moment was so strong, I could barely breathe. I'd gotten exactly what I'd wanted, just to survive, and put my mother through terror for it, but there was no way I was going in clean.

A tear rolled down Mom's cheek, and her lips quivered and flushed with blood.

"I'm sorry."

"Again?" she said. She took a tearful, trembling drag on her cig- arette as she slowed to a lurching stop at a red light.

"Where we going?" she asked, wiping her cheek.

"There's a park near here. It's got single-person bathrooms," I said.

She nodded.

"I'm sorry, Mom, really. You just don't know how it is."

She shook her head.

"Mom..." I reached out to touch her hand. The light turned green.

She yanked her hand away.

"Don't fucking touch me."

She upshifted, the truck lurched.

The wind bellowed through her open window.

"Take a left at the next light," I said.

I unzipped my bag and looked inside. The only things left were a crumpled square of foil, a lighter, and a pipe.

"Where's my rig?"

She gave me a hard, sawing head shake.

"I'm not letting you shoot it. Snort it or smoke it. That's your two options"

Snorting Percs was ass, but this was the limit for her. I knew it. Any more and I knew she'd crack.

I tapped the Percs against my leg.

"I really appreciate this," I said.

"Appreciate my ass," she moaned. "I'll be in prison by the time you get out of rehab."

Mom pulled to a stop in front of a group of grey stone bathrooms at the park. An empty swing set drifted in the morning wind. The sun rose and turned the canopy of the oak trees into flame. It was 6:45. A cordon of police tape covered the bathrooms, but, beside them, a strand of port-a-johns.

"Looks like you're smoking that in the shitters," Mom said and she looked down at her watch. "Make it quick."

I put the Percs in my bag and zipped it up. I opened the door to the blue sky and flaming leaves and stepped out, closing the door behind me.

I turned back to Mom and leaned in the window. She took a deep, long drag of her cigarette as crow's feet dragged across the side's of her eyes.

"You're wasting time staring at me," she said.

"Mom, I'm really sorry."

She put her hand up. "Give it up, Thom," she said. "I'm all the way fucked because of you. So do what you need to do and take me off the list of people who still believe your shit."

I turned and walked quickly to the port-a-johns. When I put my hand on the door, I turned around to look at Mom. She watched me with stricken eyes and soul-crushing fatigue. She bowed her head as she leaned over the steering wheel. Her body shuddered and convulsed as she cried. The sun caught her blonde hair and she looked like an angel with a crown of fire.

It was getting close to showtime.

I crept into the porta-a-john and closed the door to the smell of stagnant shit.

PART 2: FAMILY TIME

CHAPTER 14:
IT ALWAYS GOES DOWN AT CHILI'S

April 28, 2025

I rolled the window down and let my arm hang out the window. The engine cooled and ticked down like a clock. The parking lot lights flickered on as the clouds billowed in the orange-ish glow of sunset. The air was fragrant with lavender. A few purple petals danced on my hood.

The Chili's sign buzzed on and glowed a stop-sign red.

I pulled down the visor and looked at my face in the red-green glow. I had a good amount of swelling under the right eye, a scratch on the nose, and I nursed a throbbing, nauseating head-ache that I wasn't going to take ibuprofen for. It's just what came with the territory.

My phone buzzed, and I pulled it out, expecting more of the kindof texts I'd been getting all day:

Dewey: *Happy 40th butt crust!!! Sorry, I can't make it. You know how it is.*

Mom: *Happy birthday, son* 🤍 🤍 *Can't wait to see my chunky too* 🤍 🤍 🤍

Megan: *Happy Birthday.*

This time it was Frank: *Keep your mom on a leash.*

Also Frank: *Remember No cake. No fries. No junk. Salad and protein. That's it.*

Me: *What are you going to get?*

Frank: *Steak and potatoes.*

A semi without a load rolled by on Lamar. It was as black as oil.

Me: *You ever heard of the proximity principle?*

Frank: *Praise God I'm your trainer and not your sponsor.*

Turning forty and being clean for ten years was a marathon. It was about the mile markers along the way. Staying clean the first year. The second. The third. The fifth. The tenth. In those ten years I'd gotten the chance to soak up life again. The good, the bad, and the ugly.

I looked in the rearview. My gym bag lay open in the backseat and my soggy hand-wraps crawled out of it like tapeworms. Tiny smears of blood speckled the collar of my tank top. I had scratches on my arm from the clench during sparring, but when I looked down at my arms there was barely a track mark, just a tiny whitish bubble of scar tissue, a deceptively small reminder of how close Hell really is. It was also a reminder that time was catching up, and there was more to lose in the future than gain. I had to get doctors to sign waivers just so I could box; the waiver sat in the pocket of my hoodie folded four ways.

It was waiting for one. single. signature.

A pair of LED headlights flashed in my periphery. Mom rolled into the parking lot in a new white Mercedes. A Tesla followed close behind her. I turned around, grabbed my bag, and shoved it under the passenger seat. I tucked in the tongues of my hand-wraps.

I pulled my hoodie over my head, sank back down into my seat, and flashed my lights. She stopped to back in to the spot beside me. The Tesla behind her laid on the horn. Mom rolled her window down and waved them around.

They beeped again. She stuck her hand out and produced a taut, tight middle finger.

The car zoomed around her.

She backed in beside me and rolled down her passenger window, tobacco and Chanel wafted over to me.

"You trying to have the O.K. Corral at Chili's?" I said.

I shot two finger guns at the ceiling.

Mom's eyes narrowed.

"Looks like you already did," she said dimly.

Her eyes ran over the cut on my nose and the swelling on my eye.

"You doing an assessment on me?" I said.

"You sparring again?"

"Light work."

"Doesn't look light," she said.

I pointed at one of the flickering parking lot lights.

"It's the shadows. This place is old, you know that?"

She blew a raspberry stiffly.

"We're all old." She flipped down her visor, and continued, "Is Frank coming?" She stenciled her makeup underneath her eyes as she talked.

"Yup," I said.

She smirked. Then she stopped mid-stencil and turned to me. "Is Megan bringing Faith?"

"Yea," I said.

"Is Megan staying?"

"I don't know, Mom."

She sighed, shrugged, and then started rolling her window up again.

She'd had the Mercedes one month and there were empty Starbucks containers everywhere. Honey butter biscuit wrappers from Whataburger were crushed and crumpled into her cupholder. She'd probably cleaned her car once, if at all.

But, the paint job still gleamed.

An engine click-clacked somewhere close.

Frank: *Here.*

Me: *Where?*

Frank: *Pulling in.*

His gold, decaying Oldsmobile turned into the lot, clacking along.

Mom put the finishing touches on her makeup, snapped the visor shut, lit a cigarette, and hopped out of her car.

She slammed her door as Frank crawled into the parking spot in front of me.

Frank put the Olds in park as Mom strode by and rapped his hood. "Frank, your car's a piece of shit."

Frank pushed the creaking door open and shot back, "Your car's a piece of shit too, Deb. Just got a newer paint job."

Mom kept her stride and gave him the finger.

"Damn right, Frank," She said, "2025. Newest piece of shit on the block."

"She won't let an old horse die will she?" Frank said, as he chewed on an ashed cigar and wheezed heavily.

We were all getting old. Frank's once jet-black hair was all salt now. His brown skin was beige and covered in tiny holes and heavy wrinkles. His jowls hung low and he had permanent bags under his eye. But through it all, his pupils still burned. He still had some of the spirit saved from the first day I'd met him.

"You know you're not supposed to be smoking anymore," I said.

"It's my cigars, Thom, come on." He tapped his back pocket. "I've got my inhaler. I'm covered. Grab my cane out the backseat, will you?"

Frank leaned heavily on his cane as he lifted one foot and then the other over the curb as we got to the entrance. He panted and bent over, tripoding. Mom held the door open and looked at Frank with bored pity.

"Frank, they unclogged how many vessels?" she said.

Frank put up four weak fingers.

"Right, so you need to take it easy. You been doing the PT, like I told you?" she said.

"It's just a curb, Deb," Frank said.

"Yea, well if you actually did your PT, a curb wouldn't be kicking your ass."

"For the love of God, Deb."

"Whatever. Next one is the widow maker. I hope you know that."

"Good, I don't have any widows to make," Frank said.

A flash of lights illuminated us as another car turned in: a black Mazda hatchback.

Mom perked up.

"There goes my chunky," she said cheerily.

Frank hobbled forward as Mom let the door close. She stepped to the curb and rubbed her hands excitedly.

I put my hands in my pockets and looked at my reflection in the door. The collar of my tank top peaked out of the neck of my hoodie. A small spot of blood splatter showed. I pushed it back down quickly. And, then, in the red glow of the Chili's, I saw my age: a couple creek lines of worry on my forehead. A grey tint in my thin beard. My eyes looked more worn down and drooped. Not many turning points left in life. From here, it was nearly a straight shot to the finish. And it scared me in that moment. I wanted to cling to life. I wanted to cling to risk. I wanted all of life, even if it meant disaster. Frank cleared his throat and we looked at each other. He pursed his lips to breathe and then spoke.

"C'mon, Deb. Let's go in," he said to Mom.

"You giving out orders now, Frank?" Mom said, her back to him.

"Deb." Frank took a deep gulp and stood tall, straight and painful. "Be reasonable. It's his wife and kid, leave 'em be."

Mom turned and glanced at Frank and then at me.

"Let him talk to his wife," Frank said softly.

"We're separated," I said.

"She's still got your last name. Still got your kid. That's as still married as it gets," Frank said.

The Mazda crunched on the asphalt, crawling over tiny black pebbles as it inched toward the curb.

"She's got a boyfriend," I said.

"Whatever he is, he isn't you," Frank said.

Megan pulled to a stop.

Mom peered inside through the backseat window. She waved excitedly.

"Deb," Frank said, his glassy eyes glowed.

"Mom, I really would rather see them on my own. It's my birthday."

"Fine..." Mom relented and walked to Frank.

She patted his shoulder as they walked in.

"All right peg leg, in we go."

The doors closed in a blaring whoosh behind Mom and Frank. I wiped my eyes and turned to the Mazda; I was a dark reflection in Megan's tinted windows.

I stepped over a message on the curb written in bold yellow lettering: WARNING. WATCH YOUR STEP. My shoes hit asphalt and the remains of a broken bottle. I looked through the rear windshield as I circled the car. The cabin light was on and Megan dug a pencil of eyeliner in. Faith made her plushy Pikachu dance on her lap in the backseat.

Megan turned to me and rolled down the window. Her perfume was peachy. She moved one of her black curls behind her ear, exposing her porcelain neck.

"Hey," I said.

"Hey," she said, scanning my face quickly.

"Happy Birthday, Daddy!" Faith said. She waved her Pikachu at me excitedly.

"Well, thank you, baby!" I said.

Megan drew in a breath and her cheeks ballooned. "Can you get her?" she asked wearily. Megan was still in her scrubs and still had her work badge on.

"Yea, I got her," I said.

I stepped to walk around the car, but Megan piped up as I turned. "What happened to your face?" she asked.

"Sparring," I said.

"Seriously, Thom?" she said. Her face instantly twisted.

The heat of her engine hit me in waves.

"Megan, it's nothing serious, relax."

Megan took off her badge and tossed it into the center console.

"I can't fucking believe you," she hissed. Her eyes sparked.

"Megan, let it go," I said, trying to cool the flames. "It's my birthday."

Megan's face was leather tight.

She shook her head, rolled her eyes, and got back to dusting her face.

"You know they ask about her at the gym?" I said.

Megan dusted. "They miss the smell of shitty diapers?"

"Cheaper than daycare."

"I can't believe I let you bring her there."

"COVID," I said.

Megan paused and sat back with her sponge in her lap. "Don't remind me."

She stared through the windshield. Olive Garden glowed across the parking lot. Above the Olive Garden, the city rose and glittered in the vacuum of the massive Texas sky, but her eyes looked beyond. All the way South. To San Antonio. North to Lubbock. West to El Paso. Her bottom lip trembled.

I put my hand on the windowsill. The A/C chilled the hairs on my arm.

"El Paso was hell," she said.

"It's okay, Meg."

I reached in to put my hand on her shoulder. She dipped away and started dusting her face again.

"I wanted to take her to the gym this weekend," I said.

Megan grimaced. "I don't want her seeing you get beat up. It's not healthy." Her cheek twitched as she continued, "Your last fight was hell."

"It wasn't that bad, Meg."

Megan put her finger to her eyelid and dug more eyeliner in.

"You didn't have front row seats to it," she said and stopped. She held her pencil in her hand. "But we did," she said, pointing at herself and Faith.

"It must not've been that bad. You had time for a husband and a boyfriend."

Megan's mouth hung ready to argue. A bat squeaked above us as I looked in the backseat. Faith cowered and held the Pikachu in her lap like a shield.

"You need to chill," she said tightly.

She glanced in the rearview. "For her."

I put my hands in the front pocket of my hoodie and the paper crinkled.

"You gonna get her?" Megan said, finishing her liner with a trembling hand.

"Yea."

I circled the car breathing deeply and kept my hands in my pockets to keep them from shaking. My ears burned and at the back of my throat I had an unholy argument for Megan. But, it was my birthday. And Megan was right, not in front of Faith. So, I gulped down and suffocated as much of it as I could.

"Daddy!" Faith hollered. "Look at Pikachu fight." She took his plushy arms and threw two straight punches.

"Good job, baby!" I said, unbuckling Faith.

"Daddy, why's Mommy crying?" Faith asked, pointing to the front seat.

Black tears streamed down Megan's face. The anger in me was smushed to a slime.

"She's not, it's just hot out, baby."

"I'm fine, baby. Too much heat for Mommy," Megan said, blotting her face with a piece of gauze.

"Fuck," Megan whispered to herself in the visor.

I bounced Faith in my arms as Megan trailed behind us. Faith bounced her Pikachu on my shoulder.

"Pikachu wants to give you a birthday kiss, Daddy," she said. She shoved the fabric into my cheek.

Frank and Mom sat across from each other at a round, table in the back. It was close to the bathroom and the kitchen. Frank had his hands clasped on the table and stared into them while Mom laid it on him. Mom's face was tight with a mix of concern and condescension. She was the color of a strawberry.

"Frank, I told you the damn pills only work if you take them as scheduled. I told you this in the hospital. A year ago," she said.

I cleared my throat, and Mom sat back. Frank worked his bulbous knuckles.

Mom turned to me and Megan. "It's like talking to a turtle." She tossed her hands up in resignation, "I'm done with him." And then, her eyes hit Faith and she sprung up. "There's my chunky monkey!" she crooned sweetly as she swooped Faith from me.

The waitress appeared and put a margarita at Mom's seat. Frank shook his head as we all sat down. He didn't look at Mom until she'd finished her margarita.

CHAPTER 15:
POTTY BREAK

Mom had just drained her second margarita when Faith barked at Megan mid-chew, "Mommy, I have to go potty."

A fry dangled from Faith's mouth like a tentacle.

Megan finished her own fry and cut her eyes. "Baby, we just went."

Faith reached for another fry.

"Which one is it, Faith? You gotta go, or you want to eat more fries?" Megan said.

Faith smiled, chewing. "Both."

"You want me to take her?" Mom piped up. Her chair screeched as she pushed herself from the table.

Megan put her hand up.

"Who's the mom here, *Deb*?"

Mom tossed her hands up.

The waitress returned quietly.

"No need to get the knives out, *Meg*," Mom said. "Just trying to help."

"You're always trying to help, *Deb*," Megan said. "It's called, 'doing too much.'"

Mom's eyes darkened and her lips parted like the opening of a cannon.

"Mommy, please!" Faith hollered.

"Megan," Mom bristled. "It's either I help her or you help him eat his veggies." Mom nodded at Frank.

Frank poked at a piece of asparagus on his plate.

"You mind you, I'll mind me," he grumbled.

Mom glared at him and then turned back to Megan. "So any-ways..." she said.

"Will all of ya'll chill out?" I said. I sat up straight and clasped my hands on the table.

The waitress stared at the ground holding her notepad in two hands.

"Meg, please take her so we can eat in peace?"

"We. Just. Went. Thom." Megan zeroed in on me.

C'mon, I mouthed.

"I'll come back in a minute," the waitress said, and drifted away.

Megan shook her head and grabbed another fry, stabbing it into her ketchup. Mom was on the edge of her seat.

"This thing is under-cooked," Frank mused as he lifted the soggy asparagus.

"Mommy!" Faith pleaded, "I really gotta go." Faith curled over miserably on the table, chewing another French fry.

Megan pushed herself up. "Ok! We're going."

She plucked Faith up from the seat.

"I'm gonna squeeze all the poop out of you so Mimi can take a chill pill!" Megan bounced Faith on her hip as Faith flapped her hand at us. They disappeared into the bathroom near the kitchen.

Mom sat forward in her seat, a relieved smirk on her face. She grabbed the Margarita by the stem and lifted it to her lips.

"Oh!" a couple of UT students yelled. The Rockets were playing the Warriors.

I caught a glimpse of Steph missing a three. He had a wrap on his thumb.

Mom slurped her second margarita to a loud finish. She glanced at the bathroom and then narrowed her eyes at Frank. Then me. Frank tapped his cane and shook his head.

Mom leaned towards me. Her breath licorice.

"So, you fighting again?" she asked.

Steph missed another three.

"Nobody's fighting," Frank said, a finger of asparagus hanging from his mouth.

Mom glared at Frank, then slowly turned back to me. "*So, any-*

ways, when's the fight?"

I glanced at the bathroom.

"They'll be a while. You know my baby's a slow mover," Mom said. "So, when's the fight?"

I locked my eyes on her, forced myself not to blink, not to waver. We were six weeks out.

"No fighting, Mom, just light sparring."

She pointed at my eye with a lazy finger. "You don't get bruised up like that from light sparring."

"It gets rough sometimes," Frank interjected. He swallowed the asparagus and muttered, "Disgusting."

Mom held her empty margarita by the stem and rolled it around its axis.

"Does he know?" Mom said as she twirled her glass.

"Know what?" Frank jabbed another soggy piece of asparagus. "You gonna give me a sleeping pill, Deb? Put me out of my misery?"

He held the asparagus in front of his face like it was a dead snake.

"Mom, chill."

"'I'm done lying for you, Thom," she said.

She put two fingers up.

"Mom. Don't."

Frank looked over his asparagus at Mom and then me.

"Fuck's going on?" he said.

Mom bounced her two fingers like bunny ears.

"He's had a pair of pretty bad concussions, Frank."

"I know," Frank said, "he had that one after the first fight."

Mom wiggled her middle finger.

"You got no clue how bad the second was," she said. "You were in the hospital, remember, Frank?"

Frank's hand trembled. The asparagus wriggled free of his fork and fell limply to his plate.

Mom sported a Cheshire smile.

"Didn't know that. He looks fine now." He stabbed his asparagus.

"Can we talk about this any other time?" I asked.

Mom held her two fingers up tightly like poles for war flags, not bending for shit.

"Oh, you haven't seen it, Frank."

"Seen what, Deb?"

Megan pushed the bathroom door open with her back. Faith and I made eye contact. Her cheeks lifted like balloons, almost to her eyes, and as she waved wildly at me, her brown, curly hair bounced in its bun. The exit sign beside the bathroom showered her and Megan in crimson neon.

"Mom," I said, "that's enough. They're coming back."

Mom put her two fingers down as Megan put Faith back in her booster seat.

"How'd it go?" Mom asked.

"How you think?" Megan said, staring at Mom's two fingers as she curled them back into her fist.

Faith put up two fingers. "We did two, Mimi."

Mom rubbed the stem of her glass with a thoughtful poison, "Two is the word of the day, baby," she said.

"Mom," I said.

Megan glanced at me and Mom before putting another fry in her mouth. She looked over my bruises as she chewed slowly.

"What about cake, everybody?" Mom said, staring at Frank. Frank didn't take the bait.

Megan shrugged. Faith clapped her hands gleefully, her Pikachu bounced in her lap. Frank glanced at me, then reduced himself to his glass of water. He lifted it to his lips and took a slow sip and mouthed, *Don't fall for it.*

I looked back at Mom.

"I can't, Mom."

"Why not?" she said. "Isn't it your birthday?"

"C'mon." I nodded at Faith.

Mom ran her fingers around the rim of the margarita glass. The corners of her mouth twitched as she focused on the orbit of her fingertips.

"Mimi, what is it?" Faith peeped.

As her fingers circled, the glass rang clear as a bell.

"Mom, please," I said. "Why you doing this on my birthday?"

Mom looked at me sharply and said, "Because I'm the only one that seems to care if you see the next." Her finger slipped from the rim, her glass wobbled, and her lip trembled as she sat back and stared at her hands in her lap.

"What's wrong, Mimi?" Faith asked.

Mom looked up with red, glinting eyes and an awful, drunk sadness.

"It's nothing Chunk," she said.

"But, Mimi, Pika wants some cake!"

"Of course, baby. It's Daddy's birthday," Mom said.

Mom pushed herself away from the table and stood up as she wobbled slightly. She walked over to me, trailing her hand along the table. Once she reached me, she dropped her weight against me and hugged me around my neck. She kissed the top of my head. Her tears fell hot and large on my scalp.

"I'm sorry, Go'bay," she whispered. "I'm just tired."

"It's okay, Mom."

"Why's Mimi crying?"

"I'm just happy that Daddy made it to forty years, baby," Mom said, "He's come a long way."

Mom rubbed my neck, her nails catching my skin as she turned and wobbled back to her chair, plopping down with a depleted sigh.

The waitress returned, with a bright smile.

"Cake for the birthday boy?" she asked.

"Yes!" Faith screamed. "Big piece for me and Daddy." Faith bounced in her seat.

Megan smiled.

Mom did too.

"And how old is your daddy?" the waitress asked.

"Forty," I said.

"Yes, four teeth," Faith said, smiling widely.

"Aren't you the cutest thing," the waitress said, putting her hands on her hips. "And you have the cutest little curly hair."

The waitress made her way towards Faith, giving Faith's hair jealous eyes.

Mom sat up straight, split-second sober.

The waitress tucked her notepad in her apron and reached out to Faith's head.

"Excuse me, what are you about to do?" Mom asked sharply. It cut through the din of the game, the guys at the bar, and even the sounds of the kitchen dimmed. It was like a gunshot in the woods.

The waitress turned and looked at Mom. "I'm sorry, I just—" she said.

Mom laughed.

"Bless your heart," Mom said, and then her face got tight. "But the only white women touching that baby's hair are me," she pointed at Megan, "and her."

The waitress pulled her hand back quickly. "I'm so sorry, I don't' know what I was thinking."

She looked at Megan for rescue.

Megan shook her head quickly.

The waitress looked at me.

I glanced at the bar as Steph missed again, he grimaced as the ball clanked off the rim.

"I'm sorry," the waitress said.

Mom glowered and pushed her chair out.

The waitress stepped back and away from the table and her eyes widened.

"Ain't nobody gonna hurt you, girl," Mom said. She swiped her glass off the table. "'I'm not the fighter here," Mom's eyes shot at me, then back to the waitress, "And I need a refill."

"I can get that," the waitress pleaded.

"I'll get it myself," Mom said.

Mom sauntered off.

"Give us a minute," I said.

The waitress nodded and wandered away back to the kitchen, slack-shouldered.

"We gotta tip her well," I said.

Faith sat back and crossed her arms, smiling,

"I know why Mimi's mad," Faith said, sing-song.

Megan grabbed a fry, inspected it halfheartedly, and asked absently, "Why's that baby?"

Faith pointed at me. "Daddy's fighting again! That's why!"

Faith smiled brightly. She was pleased as they come with herself. She looked almost like Dad.

A few heartbeats climbed the rope of my trachea and pounded

in my head, but I kept silent. Anything that came out of my mouth would be an incrimination.

Megan shook her head tightly.

She looked down at her plate and chewed her fry viciously as Mom sauntered back with her glass in hand. Frank stared at the last of the asparagus on his.

Thankfully, it was the last margarita for Mom. She chased it with three glasses of water and took her gun sights off of me. On their way to the front door, she bounced Faith on her hip and they sung, "The Wheels on the Bus."

Frank ambled ahead of Megan and me through the dining room to the entrance. His cane tacked against the linoleum.

Megan stood beside me, gripping her elbows. She wore a nicely furnished frown with the curtain of a scowl.

We stood underneath the exit sign in between the bathrooms and the double doors that led to the kitchen. Waiters ran in and out with sizzling plates balanced precariously in their palms.

"I can't believe it," Megan hissed. "You know how many kids I see come through the ER with life-changing concussions?"

"It's just one. Then, I'm done. It's been a year, Meg."

"You know what could happen. I was the one who showed you Prichard after your first concussion. He's just now putting sounds together. Not words. *Sounds*, Thom."

A couple sat a table near us, eating in increasing silence and smaller bites.

Faith stopped singing at the entrance. And looked at the both of us.

"Lower your voice," I said. The couple had slowed their eating to a crawl.

"*You've had two. Fucking. Concussions. Thom,*" Megan hissed, jabbing two fingers into my shoulder. "*Two!*"

When she jabbed me, I remembered a wound.

"Did *the doctor* help you out with those fucked up kids?" I said. I let the wound breathe.

Megan cocked her head.

"First of all, he's a PA," she said. "Second, are you fucking dehydrated?"

I breathed out heavily. A waitress zipped by us staring down at the linoleum.

"I'll be fine. I'm in the best shape I've ever been."

I put my hands in the front pocket of my hoodie.

"You need to see your brother," Megan said. "You need to hear a professional opinion."

The waiver tickled my palm, and I boiled, quickly. "Did he send the video to Frank?"

Megan bit her lip.

"No, Thom," Megan said. "No he fucking didn't. He should have."

"Did Mom?"

Megan stayed silent, her arms crossed and her lips battened down into a brutal pinch.

Mom stood at the entrance holding Faith and staring at us. A severe look crossed her eyes.

Frank was having trouble at the hostess podium and draped himself over it. He breathed heavily as the muscles in his neck contracted.

"Look at this," I waved at him and turned back to Megan. "You want to send him over the edge?"

"You two are co-dependent."

Her eyes flashed, capturing the glow of the neon.

"You gonna throw that in my face now?" I said.

I turned to walk away, towards Frank. The couple had stopped eating. But, they gave us the grace to stare at their plates.

"It's not always gonna be the needle or the pills, Thom," Megan walked close beside me, bumping my shoulder. "I can't keep watching you kill yourself...It was hell last time."

I stopped before I hit the separation of the linoleum and the carpet of the dining room.

Frank wheezed like a pricked balloon.

"It was hell for both of us, remember?" I said.

I took my hands out of my pockets and crossed my arms.

"Stop it, Thom," Megan said sharply. "I'm talking about something bigger than that."

Megan tapped her stained white shoes. They were a colored patchwork of pee, feces, mucus, and blood mixed into an oily brownish film.

"Thom, I have to think about my health. Faith's too...if you don't stop this, I have to do something."

Plates crashed in the kitchen. Then a hush.

"What do you mean?" I asked.

"I mean, I'm gonna have them draw up the papers."

I swallowed a knot of mucus in my throat and it went down like it was sucked through a vacuum.

"Well, I'm not signing them," I said.

The words came out but didn't have a thing to prop them up with.

"Thom, I'm serious," Megan said.

"So am I."

I walked up to Frank and put my hand on his shoulder.

"Which pocket?" I said.

"Left."

"You peed today?" I said.

Frank pinched the air.

"A little."

The hostess twirled her black curls, absently, as she stared at Frank heaving. "Do I need to call the manager?" she asked.

"He's okay," Megan said as she came up behind us. She put her hand on the girl's shoulder congenially. "Just get us a glass of water for his pill."

I fished his pill bottle and his inhaler out of his back pocket and shook the bottle: a solitary pill rattled.

"Goddamit, Frank. That's exactly what I mean: *non-compliant*," Mom barked.

"Mimi, language!" Faith said, bouncing Pikachu in Mom's face.

"If...I...was...non-compliant...the bottle...would be...full," Frank rasped.

Mom snorted.

"Well, you need to get a refill then. Don't your kids *ever* look after you?" Mom said, a note of sympathy in her voice.

"Mom, ease up."

I hooked my arm underneath Frank's armpit as he draped his arm around my shoulders. I held the inhaler to his sweating mouth. I clenched him to help him stand.

"That's a good clench," he said.

"Worry about breathing in, coach."

Mom shook her head; Mom hated nursing off the clock.

Frank was four puffs in, when Mom chimed, "Give him eight," then she looked at Faith in her arms, "Okay, we're rolling baby." They danced out the double doors singing "The Wheels on the Bus."

Megan appeared at my side with a glass of water. "Here you go Frank," she said. "Thom, you got his pill?"

"Got it," I said.

Frank gulped down his pill quickly as Megan smiled feebly at me.

"I got him, Meg."

She nodded.

"I'm going to grab Faith before your mom kidnaps her." Megan nodded cheerfully at Frank and then she turned to walk away, but as she did, her phone dinged and she pulled it out of her pocket. I knew who it was. The inferno came and then the icy rage behind it. I wanted to go to her ER and rip his head off.

She was out the door and into the purple dark and fluorescence of the parking lot. Mom turned around with Faith in her arms. Megan pulled Faith from Mom; Mom was hurt by the crime.

Frank coughed into a napkin and then crumpled it quickly.

But, I saw a speck of bright blood on it.

"What's that?" I asked.

"Nothing. Bit my tongue when I was trying to chew that rubbery-ass asparagus," he said quickly. He dropped his hand to his side, with the crumpled napkin squeezed into his fist. His eyes zoomed to the door. "So, she's texting the other guy, huh?"

"Call it a birthday present," I said, looking at the napkin.

Frank shoved it into his pocket. The hostess filed her nails.

"She still came," Frank said and cleared his throat. "I gotta take a piss before we go. You got the waiver for your brother tomorrow, right?"

"Yup." I tapped my pocket.

"He gonna sign it?"

"Praying on it, coach."

Frank grunted.

"There's always Juarez," he said, coughing into his sleeve.

I shuddered as the thought of it rolled over me like a tide, then drew itself back out.

"I know, but I'd rather it be here. I want everybody there.".

"Then make sure he signs the waiver, Tommy."

Frank patted my shoulder and took his cane as it hung on the podium. He planted it on the ground.

"You gonna be okay?" I asked.

"You worry about you," he said.

He tacked away towards the bathroom.

I turned to the entrance as Mom took a cigarette out of her pocket and glanced back at me through the windows. She lit her cigarette and pulled in as the flame danced near her face. Mom stood away from Faith and Megan and blew her smoke into the wind. It lifted with a thin body and then disappeared like a wraith. Megan was busy texting with one hand and bouncing Faith in her other arm. Faith waved at me.

I waved back, but I felt useless. My family was separating itself from me. There was a new life on the horizon, but to me it didn't feel like a new beginning. Just a hollow end. My wife would soon be an ex. She'd marry another man. My daughter, how soon would it be before she saw what a fuck up I was? How soon before she was just another part of my collateral damage?

CHAPTER 16:
INDEPENDENCE DAY

July 4, 2015

The day I got discharged from Rehab, and after Mom had picked me up, we pulled into the short downward sloping hill of our driveway and parked beside the house. Mom turned off the Ranger and patted the gearshift twice. "That's the last time I'm ever doing that, thank God." She tossed the keys into my lap. "Your problem now," she said smacking on a wad of Nicorette.

The envelope on the dash glimmered in the sun as the cabin started to simmer.

"What's that?" I asked, pointing to the envelope.

Mom didn't look at. She just chewed her gum as it made tacky sounds in her teeth.

"I still can't get used to this shit," she said. "It's just a paste after a few chews."

"Mom," I asked, again. "Is that mail for me?"

"No," she said. She waved her hand at it. "It's one of those damn toll bills. I just don't want to know the damage. Unless you want to pay it for me?"

She turned and reached towards it.

"I've got enough debts," I said.

Mom opened the door and grabbed the letter quickly. She stuffed it into her purse as she got out of the car, but I caught a glimpse of the front of the envelope. There was a name on it. It looked like mine, but I couldn't be certain.

I drummed my fingers on the steering wheel as I drove down Lamar for the first time in over two months. The city was sizzling.

The first week, I cleaned the Ranger fastidiously. I rid the truck of every smashed packet of Nicorette carcasses and lipsticked Starbucks lids. I'd vacuumed and shampooed the upholstery until the wash lines stood up on ridges. I'd cleaned the windshield to near invisible. Polished the wheels. Sparkled the chrome. Waxed the white to near bleach. Changed the black oil, the transmission fluid, the radiator fluid. Installed a new alternator. There was nothing left to be done. I was at the end of my rope. I started taking it for long drives. Cruising around the city, making it a point to avoid Lamar.

"Wait a little while before you jump back into working," Mom had said. "Stay busy. Stay away from Lamar."

But, Austin is a body, and Lamar is the main vein travelling back to the heart. It'd be hard not to find yourself back on it. No matter how much you avoid it, it carries the pulse of the city.

So, one morning, I took a drive to take a drive. There was nothing left to do but enjoy the smooth throttle and slippery shift, until I found myself back again, sitting at a light staring down the barrel of Lamar as the skyscrapers of the city towered in a hot, hazy distance and blank faces walked the streets. I don't know what I expected, that the world would be different because I was?

I tore a fingernail off and my cuticle bled.

Or was I still the same and the world was just waiting for me to catch up to the lie?

There was the old Shell station. The same crew hung out front. The picture of my family at the beach danced as it hung from the mirror and I pulled in to the Shell Station next to the dumpster. I ripped the picture from the rearview and opened the glovebox. I tossed the picture back as far as it could go and snapped the glovebox shut. When I sat up, I was greeted by the eyes of a few old faces as they took long swigs of their tall boys. There was a mix of recognition and confusion in their eyes. In the rearview, my face was rounder. My skin was clearer, back to a goldish hue.

A car rolled by in the rearview. It crawled out from a street that led to a small neighborhood. The houses had brownish lawns the color of rust and curtains of all colors covering the windows. Some windows were broken. Some houses still had their Christmas decorations out. But, at one of those houses, not even a block into the neighborhood, a jet ski sat on on mildewed concrete blocks in the driveway. There was an open garage cluttered to the gills with all things humanity. The curtains were always closed in the living room window. The doorbell hung by an entrail of wires. But, nobody ever rung it. Knock twice. Wait. Then knock once again. Somebody'd crack the door and let you in. It'd be too easy. Their shit wasn't the half-second ecstasy of Ball's shit, but it had a trickle that you could nod off to. I looked at the boys sipping their tall boys. Their eyes were jaundiced and opening wide to me. They were starting to put it together again: the return of a comrade.

My phone buzzed on my hip and then stopped.

One of the guys ambled over to the dumpster. A pack of Newports lay propped against it. He wore a frayed straw hat and faded, cracking cowboy boots nearly white with overuse.

My phone buzzed again and I pulled it out of my pocket.

The caller ID read "New Life Counselling, LLC."

My heart beat loosely inside my chest as it thrummed my aorta.

Mr. Straw Hat bent down to the pack of cigarettes.

I answered the phone.

"Thom," Elise said.

"Yea?"

"It's Elise."

"I know."

The man stood up straight and turned facing me, a Port dangled from his lips.

"How's the outside world?" Elise asked.

I ran my fingers around the newly smooth steering wheel. It gleamed with wax, but even with Dad's fastidiousness, the cracks were evident. The truck was close to twenty years old.

"Just watching the wildlife on Coney Island."

Mr. Straw Hat nodded at me and mouthed, *You got something for me?*

His eyes were bulbous and orange.

I shook my head.

I'm clean.

He shook his head mournfully and took a puff of his cigarette and stepped off the curb, glassing the truck as he passed.

"This is the hard part, Thom. Living those first few days of freedom without crutches."

My heart raced like a beaten horse and worked up a metal taste in my mouth.

"So, I got in touch with one of the guys at the boxing gym I was talking about," Elise said. "Ironically, it's on Lamar," she chuckled. She sounded far away.

The horse inside me thundered. Spit flew from its mouth. Eyes wide and white.

I looked in the rearview and followed the path of Mr. Straw Hat as he turned and disappeared down the road to the neighborhood. In the distance, a sign rose from Lamar: it had a faded Lion on it.

I breathed out deeply. I could taste the mud and grit as the horse beat the track inside me.

"Thom, you there?" Elise asked.

I breathed out heavily through my nose. "Yea."

There was a pause on the other end. A siren wailed on Lamar.

"Thom," Elise asked, "where are you?"

On the curb beside the dumpster, broken glass glittered in the sunlight like stars sending their light from the past.

"Lamar."

I breathed in; the horse thrashed inside me. It was exhausting: the euphoria and catastrophe.

I was so close to the finish I deserved, the finish I craved. A finish that I knew, deeper than a horse knows its track, would kill me.

"Thom," Elise said, "you have to choose. Right now. Where do you want to be ten years from now? Five years? One year? One month? One day? This is the war, Thom. It never goes away. Ever."

The guys on the corner stared at me as I breathed in through my nose and out my mouth. I looked in the rearview. The Lion loomed in the distance.

"Will you just go, Thom?"

"What's the name of the gym?"

"Lion's Boxing Club."

CHAPTER 17:
TURN AND RUN. FUCK IT

July 2015

I pulled into the parking lot shaking. I put the truck in park and clasped my hands tightly as I worked my knuckles into a painful pressure.

When I walked in, massive fans whirred above me lazily, emitting a soft whine. Boxers thundered in the ring shooting hissing jabs at each other. A coach leaned on the ropes and barked, "More than just one jab! Two, three, four at a time!"

Yellowed, faded pictures of old boxers covered the walls from floor to ceiling. Hand-wraps lay on the floor like snake skins. Speed bags dun-duh-dun'd. A boxer skipped rope in the back by himself. An assortment of heavy bags hung like uvula from the ceiling in the back part of the gym, but also, a serene amber glow worked its way through the back windows and the boxer in the back looked meditative as he jumped.

"Can I help you?" a gruff voice called.

Just turn and walk out the door, I heard an old voice say. *Say you were lost, you can turn and walk out that door. You got the pink slip. Sell the Ranger. Be doped in an hour.*

"Ay, you good?" the voice called again.

I turned and saw a man seated at a desk in an office crowded with bills and carbon copy paper. He sported a silver buzzcut, and his gold-rimmed glasses slid down the bridge of his nose as he stared up at me. He wore a silver goatee. He had a lithe frame and corded forearms.

"Yes." I walked into his office and crossed my hands behind my back so that he wouldn't see the scar tissue. The office was a punchy smell of old leather and wood polish.

"I heard about this gym and just wanted to come try it out," I said.

"What's your name?" he asked.

"Thom."

"You ever boxed before?" He surveyed me from behind his glasses.

"I went to a boxing gym once," I said.

"And?"

"once and never again."

He put his glasses down and clasped his hands over his stack of papers. "What made you stop?"

I felt the sting of Dad's slap on my cheek again. I remembered the disappointment on Dad's face. Then, the anger.

I uncrossed my arms from behind my back and laid two fingers on the scar tissue on my arm.

"I got high instead."

"And never looked back, huh?" he asked.

"Not until I was forced to."

He nodded somberly. Behind him, the wall was cluttered with yellowed photograph after yellowed photograph of different boxers. One of them was of a man in a tuxedo and a woman in a wedding dress standing right beside the ring.

I rubbed my arm. I felt like a kid in the principal's office, waiting to hear he'd gotten expelled. No way he wasn't going to send me packing.

They don't want none of that mess in here.

"We've had a few guys like that," he mused after a while.

He narrowed his eyes thoughtfully. Then snorted. Then smirked. Then shook his head, "We'll set you up with Frank...And tell *him* that Greg told *you* to tell *him* to put that *fucking* cigar out."

CHAPTER 18:
FRANK

"My goal today is to make you throw up. Then we'll see if you come back," Frank said with a sadistic smile. He puffed on his cigar at the back of the gym as I stood before a heavy bag.

"Put that goddamned cigar out, Frank!" Greg hollered from the doorway of his office.

"It's out!" Frank hollered back.

Frank was about 175 back then. In his mid-fifties. He had a lively, lithe body with thin lightly weathered arms and rigid muscles. He had a permanent sun-dried brown complexion. He had a thick nose with big nostrils and large, black eyes. He had thin lips and a manicured salt-and-pepper goatee. His black hair was crew cut at the time and greased up. He didn't need a cane. Didn't need an inhaler. He had a spiritual air. He growled when he spoke and talked like he didn't care if he ever saw me again. He could ash me out of his memory with one swipe of his cigar on his sole.

He'd set me up with some hand-wraps and old, worn-down gloves. The stuffing worked its way in between my knuckles and felt like soggy rice Krispies; nearly the same as when I'd tried to box the first time.

"You just want me to punch the bag?" I asked.

"For a full round," Frank said, smiling. The smoke from the cigar in his teeth danced with ever word.

"Frank, the goddamned cigar!" Greg hollered.

"Aay, I got it Greg, just taking some victory laps with it!"

Frank bent his foot and rubbed his cigar out on his sole. He laid it on a wood beam; it still smoked slightly.

"How will I know when it's over?" I asked.

He pointed up at the clock tacked to the wall above the heavy bag. It ticked down in red numerals. A red bulb, yellow bulb, and green bulb were fixed to the top of it. The red bulb glowed.

"You'll hear the bell. And see the red light," Frank said.

"Now?"

"Not yet," Frank said. He beamed like a kid about to light an ant on fire with a magnifying glass.

The bell rang. The red light turned green. The clock started at 3:00

"Now!"

I started punching the bag, didn't have a shadow of a clue what I was doing. I just threw my hands at the bag. Within a few seconds, I was gassed. My arms felt like sandbags. I sweated like a pig. I breathed through a straw. I looked up at the clock, heaving and salivating.

Through the blur, it read 2:45.

Frank smiled from ear to ear. "Don't stop now," he said, "you *chose* to come here."

I kept going. But, I was treading water, and bile had started to burn its way up my throat.

"You stop now, and I won't train you. You get the fuck out and never come back again. You want to go back to where you came from?" Frank said.

Black spots popped in my vision, and each one was a blinking invitation: *Just quit*. But I kept going. It was either that or go right back down the street. I could call Ball. I knew his number by heart. One hour and I could scoop up a package.

"Keep going!" Frank bellowed.

I burped bile and threw punches a toddler could walk through. Sweat howled out of my pores. Breathing felt like it was being erased from my genetic code; every breath was an exercise in futility.

"Exhaustion is temporary kid. You throw up. You get back to the bag. You pass out. We've got smelling salts. You'll wake up. It's not about being perfect. Perfect is a fucking delusion." He looked around the gym to see if the owner was looking, then quickly grabbed his cigar from the beam and flicked a zippo, taking a deep pull.

I threw up on the worn-down mats.

"That's what the fuck I'm talking about," Frank said, blowing out a veil.

I put my hands on my knees and bent over as every muscle in my stomach tensed.

"Back to it!" Frank yelled. "Round ain't over goddammit!"

I kept going. Fist after fist. Second after second. Breaths in nightmares.

"There's an old saying," Frank continued. I didn't see him anymore. Didn't see the bag. The taste of iron painted the inside of my mouth. "'Dog ain't built, Dog is found.' Either you is or you ain't," Frank said.

The bell rang.

"Through the bell!"

I punched until the bell stopped dinging. The ding was eternal.

Frank paused and took a deep puff as I slumped to the floor, rolled over on my back, and looked up at the ceiling. The fans whirred. The sheet metal was rusted in spots and nails poked through it, as if they'd been hammered by God. I lay there, a lump. For the first time in my life, every stitch of my body was focused on breathing. No hurt. No anger. No shame. No need to numb all those things. There was the gentle whine of the fans and the excruciating work of the diaphragm.

Frank chuckled. But, I couldn't see him. Just the nails in the tin roof and the hush that comes over a gym in between rounds: The humbling silence.

Frank appeared over me, and with a puff said, "Okay, first lesson, we're not trying to break the stuffing out of the bag. Your punches should be fluid, and relaxing, like prayer."

I nodded at the ceiling.

"Lesson number two is this: don't worry about numbers. How much time is left in the round; how many rounds are left; how many days you've been boxing; how many days you've been sober. We don't do numbers here. Counting numbers always leads to failure. Effort's the only measure here."

Frank extended a hand and helped me to my feet.

"So how did I do?" I asked.

"Good enough," Frank said.

Frank looked over his shoulder, and puffed on his cigar. He had his arms crossed, and looked at me with a clenched jaw.

"But, you didn't quit," he said, "Matter of fact, never met an addict who did."

He pointed to a mop laying on a wall near a rusted stationary bike and a deflated speedbag hanging from a wood plank jutting out of the wall.

"Get to work," Frank said, "I've gotta go."

I nodded and started walking towards it.

"Keep your phone on. I'll call you bright and early tomorrow. Gonna get a run in," he said. His voice echoed throughout the gym and then the bell rang and drowned him out.

Mom sauteed some onions on the stove that night for dinner. I'd put a few burgers on the grill. The smoke wafted in through the screen door. Crickets chirped outside frantically.

"So, you went to a boxing gym?" Mom asked, her back to me, as she pushed the onions around.

"Yea," I said.

Smoke drifted from the pan.

"You're gonna burn them," I said.

"And your trainer's name was what?" she asked. Someone laid on their car horn in the neighborhood.

"Frank," I said.

Mom clicked her teeth and turned to me, holding the spatula like a yardstick.

"Go'bay, boxing ain't a safe sport," she said and then she squinted. "Your dad told me something once...what was it?" Her lips tightened and she stared at the floor. She held the spatula at her side and put a finger to her lips.

The onions sizzled and smoked. She snapped her fingers and snatched at the air like she'd snared a fly. "He said, 'You can play any other sport, but you don't play boxing.'"

"Onion's are burning," I said.

Mom turned back quickly. "Shit!" She pulled the onions from the stove. And cut the eye. An owl hooted outside.

"I'm just saying, Go'bay." She ladled the onions onto a plate, "it's a dangerous sport. I didn't like it for Dewey. I don't like it for you. I mean, *you are in your thirties*."

I rolled over the next morning, churned awake by a dream that I couldn't remember, but I was sweating and my skin crawled with a haunting despair.

I sat up and the clock on my bedside table read 4:07. I grabbed a shirt from the floor and wiped my face, then laid back and stared at the popcorn ceiling. The streetlight flickered outside my window. My easel sat beside the window and speckled shadows of oak leaves danced on it. Mom had left most of my paintings hanging. A lot of Kandinsky copies and the crude *Starry Night* I still hadn't finished. Dewey's painting was my first original, and the only thing I'd ever truly finished. But, God knows where it was.

A flash of light erupted in the darkness. My phone buzzed on my bedside table. I grabbed the phone and answered. "Hello?" I said.

"Wake up," Frank grumbled.

Been up.

"I'm up."

"You got running shoes?"

I had one pair of Asics that were worn down so thin that the soles were basically toilet paper.

"I got some," I said.

Frank coughed.

"Run a mile," he said, "I kicked your ass yesterday, get a little win for yourself."

I'd never run more than 100 feet.

"Don't be roadkill," he grunted, "meet me at the gym at 7."

Click.

CHAPTER 19:
MOM'S IN YOUR CORNER, JUST NOT THAT ONE

Mom cooked her breakfast in the kitchen. She had two eyes going. Eggs bubbled in a small pan on one and bacon sizzled and popped in a skillet on the other. She stood over the stovetop with a cigarette in her mouth as she scrambled the eggs.

She whipped around when she heard my shoes squeak on the linoleum.

"What are you doing up? Only vampires and nurses are up this early," she said.

"Going for a run."

"Mm hmm," she said, blowing out a plume.

She turned around and scrambled the eggs absently.

"Run where? To Rapeville?" Smoke drifted up from her bacon. She dashed a tail of ash in the sink beside the stove.

"A mile."

The dryer buzzed.

"Stir those eggs for me," she said and handed me the spatula.

The clock on the stove read 5:00. Mom yanked the dryer open and closed the laundry room door nearly completely but left a small amber crack as she pulled her scrubs on.

"What's the name of your trainer again?"

"I told you, Mom, Frank," I said, stirring.

She pulled the door open and glowed in her navy scrubs. She leaned against the wall and crossed her arms and her feet. The shadows on her face tightened and the bags under her eyes were as large as blowfish.

"I was looking it up, last night," Mom said, biting her bottom lip. "You know how many people a year die from boxing?"

"I'm not going to be Evander Holyfield, Mom," I said, stirring. "And I need to do something. I sit around here any longer and it'll be a disaster. I don't want to be forty and still circling the drain."

She frowned. She turned and looked at her reflection in the dark glass of the back door. She tapped her heel to her toe.

"Damn, I'm getting old."

I stirred the eggs.

"Like I said last night, Go'bay, boxing's dangerous enough when you're young; in your thirties it's a loaded gun."

The bacon popped. A hot splatter stung my cheek.

"I'm just giving it a try, Mom."

A charred smoke rose from the skillet of bacon.

I turned off the eye.

"No sir," Mom said, as she rushed over. "What do you think you're doing?" She bumped me away with her hip. "You know I like my bacon crisp."

"You mean charcoal."

"I mean well-done. Get it straight."

She smiled at me.

But since I'd been home, I couldn't look at her for too long.

I went to the sink and ran a glass of water.

"I'm heading out," I said.

I downed the water looking at my own reflection in the window above the sink.

"Sounds good," Mom said, watching her bacon smoke.

I tightened the drawstring around my sweatpants.

"You want some of this for breakfast when you get back?" she asked.

The bacon popped again and splashed against her cheek. She barely flinched.

"Yes, please."

She wiped her cheek with her arm.

"Well, you'll have it how I eat it: burnt."

I danced on my toes and limbered up as Mom rounded the corner of the house twirling her keys in her hand. The security lights flashed on, illuminating her. I stretched using the Ranger's fender. I'd never stretched in my life. Everything was a strain.

"Breakfast is on the table," Mom said, walking up to me. She tapped the hood of the Ranger and cocked her head in the low darkness. "Burnt as fuck."

"Thanks," I said.

She hugged me and kissed me on the cheek. Her makeup rubbed off on my face.

"Glad you're home, baby."

"Me too."

She smiled.

"You'll find a job," Mom said.

A cold nerve shivered down my spine.

"Hope so."

She rubbed my shoulder and held her hand there. In the blue light of dawn, her lips quivered tightly and her eyes drew down heavy. Her hand trembled against me, and then, she patted me and turned. She strode by the Ranger without even glancing at it and pressed the keys to her Lexus. Her car squeaked and blinked its headlights. Mom opened the door and the cabin light flashed on. She plopped down in her seat, and before turning her key, she looked at me. She looked like a caged lion: angry at the cage but scared of freedom. I jumped on my toes. I couldn't stop her from remembering who I was, and the cage I'd put her in. Two weeks before, I'd been in rehab trying to come up with a plan for now. I'd held my family hostage for years; it'd be a while before any of them could feel comfortable feeling free from me.

I walked up the driveway as Mom backed out. She came to a stop in the street and waved at me before she pulled away; two red eyes disappearing into the blue dawn.

I put one foot in front of the other and started my run.

When I finished my run, I stopped at the top of the driveway and dry-heaved. My knees stung and my lungs burned. I put my hands on my head and breathed in deeply. The sun was a silver outline over the trees and the sky above still gave way to stars. A chilly breeze sifted through the leaves. A mockingbird woke up and rang in the thick canopy of the oaks sloping down to the front yard. The house was silent and peaceful. And I was clear.

I warmed my breakfast in the microwave and sat outside on the back porch and ate. I watched a few deer graze. The sun cracked over the horizon and yolk flowed through the trees like gold.

CHAPTER 20:
I LOOKED LIKE HAMMERED DOG SHIT

Dog days of September 2015

"Got a smoker this Saturday," Frank said as he chewed on his cigar.

"Yea?" I said. I worked my way around the ring. "What's a smoker?"

It was an early morning training session. We were almost two months in and I could shadowbox for three rounds. I had the fluidity of an orangutan but it was progress.

Frank chuckled. "A smoker is a hard spar. All out blitz. Closest thing to a real fight as you can get."

I nodded and shot some jabs.

"I signed you up," Frank said. I stutter-stepped. The bones in my legs liquified.

"I'm not ready, Frank,"

"Stay on your toes," Frank said. "You're heel-stepping."

I put the pressure on my toes.

"And," Frank chomped, "*ready* is for people that don't ever do anything."

I still stung behind the ear from a crushing overhand right I'd taken sparring the night before. It was my third time sparring. It broke the dream. Boxing wasn't play-play. It was cause and effect and full of consequence. Can't be foolish. Can't be careless. Ain't ducking shit in the ring.

"You really think I'm good enough?" I said.

I circled on my toes.

"Better," Frank said, nodding at my feet. "Your guy will be Jerrick, It's the guy you sparred last night."

I stumbled. The canvas rumbled.

"Keep your footing," Frank noted.

My chest fluttered as I thought about two things simultaneously. Jerrick's right hand and his girlfriend with the emerald eyes.

"His girl is something else," I said.

"This ain't *Love Connection*, Tommy."

"I know."

"On your toes, stay focused," Frank said.

I circled remembering the dose of pain Jerrick handed me, and, also, the flutter in my ribs when I'd seen his girl.

It was a hot Saturday. The bay doors were open, and by 8:00 am, the sun already had the asphalt rotten with heat. The fans whirred against it, but all they did was turn the gym into an oven. Within minutes of walking in, I was a pool.

I sat on the bench beside the ring. A few guys already bounced around in the ring. The smoker had begun. Greg hung over the ropes and turned to look at Frank and I. He nodded at me and grunted at Frank. Then turned back as one of the fighter's shot a missile of a jab through the defense of his opponent. His opponent took an awkward step back, shook his head inside his headgear in a quick twitch, then breathed out, spit hanging in laces from his lips, and stepped forward again.

I unpacked my bag and started wrapping my hands.

Frank pulled out a cigar and stuck it in his mouth. Greg glanced over. Frank chewed on the end but didn't light it. The clock ticked down to one minute left in the round.

I looked outside through the open bay doors as a car pulled into the parking lot: A blacked-out Hellcat that purred as it parked. The ring thundered as the two boxers danced around each other. Going shot for shot. Hard and punishing.

The Hellcat rumbled in idle, like a burping giant.

The boxers circled each other, closer and closer. Frank chewed his cigar down, working his jaw muscles around it as he watched. The sun burst over the top of the Walmart across the street, obscuring the Hellcat as the engine cut off.

The two boxers came together, like two atoms, fusing in power and violence. They locked a set of arms, leaving one arm free. Their hands were javelins sending hooks and uppercuts and looping overhands to each other's heads, ribs, solar plexuses. Both fighter's headgear twisted and lurched with the impact of each punch, but, they didn't let go.

"Good clench work!" Greg urged. "As long as you got a hand free, you can fight!"

Frank chewed his cigar down; little specks of tobacco spackled his lips. A grin inched across his face.

Jerrick walked in as the bell rung and the fighters returned to their corners, slumping in their stools. Clear mucus dripped from their mouths and they heaved like Derby horses.

Jerrick held his chin high and clutched his gym bag with a loose grip. His flip flops skidded on the concrete. He wore a clean, gray Nike Tech suit.

One of his buddies ringside turned and dapped him up. He nodded at me and said to Jerrick, "Walk in the park, easy work."

But, behind Jerrick, as he made his rounds, was his girl. I'd caught a glimpse of her the last time. As she walked behind him, I finally got a full look. She had porcelain skin that looked as soft as ice cream, black curly hair that ran down her shoulders to the small of her back, and sharp green eyes. She had thick, full lips and wore a smile like she could eviscerate you and heal you in the same breath. She had maroon scrubs on and walked behind Jerrick with folded arms.

But, Jerrick's buddy was right.

No matter how much I wanted to impress his girl, I was easy work.

From the ring of the bell to the end of the round, he dog-walked me. The beautiful thing about boxing is that you get used to getting dog-walked in the beginning. It's liberating, in a way. It's the crucible. And Jerrick was a smelter. He had jabs that came from the fucking ether. Crushing overhands. And then, he hit me with a buckling liver shot.

The thing about liver shots is that you see it happening in slow motion. The sweep of the arm. The arc of the fist. The nearly indefensible accuracy of it. It touches. You feel fine for a brief moment, then your diaphragm shrivels, you can't breathe, and you're forced by the laws of nature go to a knee. The seconds stretch like the worst kind of purgatory; you don't care if you got to Hell or Heaven.

"Thom, you gotta shoot the jab!" Frank hollered from the corner as saliva dripped out of my mouth and I tried to catch hold of a breath.

The canvas was worn down to frayed ends. Greg counted over me.

"One...two...three..."

"In through your nose, out through your mouth!" Frank said.

I was in the wrong place.

"Four...five...six..."

Why the fuck did I choose this?

The canvas echoed as Jerrick hopped lightly on his feet in his corner.

"Seven...eight...nine..."

I wasn't shit and wasn't going to be shit.

"Quit the fucking pity party, Thom! Get your fucking ass up!" Frank hollered.

I got up from my knees just as Greg's fingers flashed ten in front of my face.

He tapped my gloves together.

"You good?" Greg asked. His glasses caught slices of the sunlight coming in through the bay doors.

"Good," I mumbled through my mouthpiece.

The bell rang and I was saved.

I trudged back to the corner. I focused on every muscle in my legs just to keep myself upright. Once I saw the stool, I sunk into it.

I put my arms on either side of the ropes and breathed deeply.

"Fuck me!" I said.

Three minutes of actually fighting, not just sparring, but fighting, and I realized why boxing was an Olympic sport: It's a marathon at full sprint.

Frank squeezed a wet towel over my headgear; Heaven dripped in cold orbs through the leather as it ran down my face. It was more refreshing than dope.

"You gotta shoot the jab, Thom! Amd not just one, but give me two, three, four, five, at a time!" Frank said, as he jot the jabs with a water bottle in his hand. "Drink some water!"

I opened my mouth. Water splashed my tongue. I glanced to the edge of the ring; Mom and Jerrick's girlfriend talked closely. Mom had snuck in right after the bell had rung. She was still in her scrubs; she'd worked the nightshift.

"Snap out of it, Thom!" Frank rumbled. "Thom, you gotta give me everything. We're building habits right now. This may just be a smoker, but we're building habits. And the main habit has to be effort. You gotta go further and dig deeper than you ever have. These last two rounds, you go in there and you claw it out. I want you empty. I want it all out there on that canvas. You hear me?"

"I'm fucking dying in there coach."

"Well, fucking good then!" Frank said. He tapped the top of my headgear, "Use whatever the fuck you got left!"

The bell rang. And I pushed myself up. Every movement felt like pushing against two atmospheres.

"Empty, Thom!" Frank said. "Empty!"

For those last two rounds, I emptied myself. I emptied it all. I sweat to tears. I couldn't see at the end. I dragged myself through Jerrick's barrages. I tunneled down a barrel of focus so narrow, all I could see and feel was leather and agony and exhaustion. I got obliterated, but I didn't go down again. The final bell rang. And my marrow moaned just holding me up.

Mucus dripped from my nose as I went to the corner and slumped in the stool. Frank took off my headgear, as the sun blitzed the open bay and landed on my head. Frank's face glowed in the sun as he smiled and put his fingers in my mouth and pulled out my mouthpiece.

"How you feeling?"

"Like hammered dog shit," I stammered.

Frank laughed and tapped the back of my neck.

Salt, iron, and bile welled up into my mouth. I looked up at Frank, and his eyes blossomed as he reached to the corner and grabbed a bucket and put it in front of my face.

I hurled.

"Now, I can teach you something," Frank growled.

I held the bucket with gloved hands.

CHAPTER 21:
BENCHMATE

I climbed down the stairs after the fight and walked to the back of the gym where a bay door opened to the back parking lot. It was full of old tires and sprouts of grass that shot out of the asphalt like an old man's scalp.

My head buzzed and my hands shook. An ass-beating is a painfully purifying thing. I stood in the shadows as Greg yelled from the ring: "Last two!"

Feet thundered up the stairs to the ring.

I took a breath and looked up at the ceiling and the dug-in nails. The rust crawled over the tin in a mosaic of holes like blisters spreading over skin. And through them, the sun glowed down in patches. The bags hung listless and opaque. A fog clung around the patches of sunlight. The bell rang. And the fighters circled around the singularity of the middle of the ring.

I stepped into the sun and my head exploded with fiery pins.

I squinted and ducked back into the shade. I closed my eyes quickly and sat down on a stool as the pins cooled. I pinched my eyes closed and waited until the pain finally relented.

When I could open my eyes again, I moved slowly and sat on the bench beside the ring and watched the last round. Mom sat beside me with her legs crossed and bounced her feet. She clapped lightly as the bell rung and the fighters retreated to their corners.

Frank stood ringside and talked to a few of the coaches. A pool of sweat accumulated at my feet, but I felt good, because even though I'd been beaten like a bait dog, I didn't quit.

I started to undo my hand wraps, but my hands shook.

"Give me your hands," Mom said softly and reached for me.

I pulled away quickly.

"Mom don't."

"Your hands are shaking," she said.

"If you do it for me now, I'll never be able to show my face in here again."

Mom sat back with her hands in her lap.

"Where's Dew?"

"You boys don't talk?"

"Been busy lately," I said.

Mom continued with melancholy, "He's on day six of seven."

"He's a worker," I said.

"Just like Dad," Mom said.

The bell rang and the pair returned to the middle, immediately clenching and tussling for position.

Mom blew out through her teeth and then, she nudged me. Jerrick and his girlfriend made their way towards us. I sat up straight and clasped my hands tightly. My wraps were undone halfway and hung limply from my wrists to the floor.

"Good work bro," he said and extended a fist.

"You too," I said. I did my best to clench every single muscle in my hand.

He turned and walked away.

"It was nice meeting you, Megan," Mom said, extending a hand to Megan. "I'll text you about ACC!"

"Thank you so much," Megan replied. She brushed her hair behind her ear and looked at me. "You fought well," she said. Her voice was soft, intelligent, and twangy. Her emerald eyes were shocking.

"Thank you," I said. Zaps of electricity shot through me just looking at her.

Frank sauntered over. Megan turned and followed her boyfriend out the door with crossed arms.

"Well, I got some good news," Mom said cheerily. She waited until the Hellcat purred itself down the street.

"What's that?" I asked, after I'd finally finished unwrapping my hands. The cloth lay soggy on the cement.

Mom waved her phone at me. "I got her phone number. She wants to go to nursing school."

"That's cool," I said.

I grabbed my wraps in a ball.

"Also," Mom said, grinning, "they're gonna break up."

I zapped with hope.

"And?" I said.

"And, she's a nice girl. Good girl."

"How can you tell?"

"Thom, I've been your mother a long time. But, I've been a woman forever. I know."

The canvas thundered as the fighters tussled.

"Well, she's with him," I said.

"With who?" Frank chimed in with his hands in his pockets. He rocked back and forth on his heels.

"This is between me and my son."

"Okay," Frank said. He took his chewed-down cigar out of his mouth and pointed at Mom. "Do we have a problem?"

"There's better things he can do than boxing," Mom said.

"He ain't a baby. He can decide. Doesn't need his mommy telling him what to do anymore." I glanced at Frank. He put his hands up. "Respectfully."

Mom glared at him, then turned to me,

"*So anyways,* you gonna call her?"

The ball of fabric in my hand dripped like a wet snake-skin. The inside of my mouth bled; I got sips of blood every time I swallowed. Even though the headache was slowly easing, my face still throbbed.

"Her boyfriend just whipped my ass, Mom. She's not going to go for it. They call it losing for a reason: you don't get anything out of it."

"She doesn't give a shit, Thom. She said you fought well!" Mom patted my leg. "Trust me. Text her."

"Distraction," Frank whistled.

"Oh, hush," Mom said and then looked at me, "Text her."

I got to the Ranger and turned the engine over and rolled down my window. I cocked my arm on the windowsill and opened my phone as a bus drove by, roaring like a dragon. I stared at Megan's number. Megan. I had a name.

I laid in bed that night and stared at the spackle. Jerrick's jabs were javelins.

Then, I remembered Megan's eyes. The warmth in them, the intelligence, the playfulness.

Then, the liver shot that brought the forces of gravity with it.

Then, Megan's voice. "You fought well." Three words that defied gravity.

I closed my eyes and rubbed my eyelids.

She'd seen that I hadn't gone down again. I hadn't quit.

But, no way a girl like that was going to go for a former junkie. She'd hear that and be out the door.

Still, there was something about her.

I was staring at her number before I knew it.

I made a promise to myself: I wasn't going to lie when the time came.

I texted her at 2:33 A.M.

Me: *Hey, it's your boyfriend's punching bag.*

I hit send and then went down a wormhole of regret. I stayed awake for hours. I stared at the ceiling. I went to the window and contemplated doom while I looked at the silent street. I went to bed and closed my eyes and tried to force myself to sleep. I hadn't been nervous like it in years. It'd been ten years—a lifetime--since I'd experienced anxiety soberly.

She texted me at 8:30 that morning.

I broke the stratosphere getting out of bed. I grabbed my phone off the floor.

Megan: *Glad you've still got some stuffing.*

PART 3: FRANK'S TIME

CHAPTER 22:
THE STAIRS OF BONNELL

Frank texted me the next morning.

I got one day off, and then it was back to it. I was expecting it to be a "get your ass out of bed and go run" text.

Frank: *Change of plans. Meet me at Mt. Bonnel*

Me: *Got it.*

Mount Bonnell is just a hill masquerading as a mountain. It overlooks a bend in Lady Bird Lake that arcs its way back to the city. Along this curve, houses worth millions crawl along the shoreline, mostly boxes of glass, or the old Conquistador style.

It was a cool morning. I put on a long-sleeve. I pulled to a stop at the bottom of the hill and got out and looked around; the parking lot was nearly empty. Frank's gold Olds sat a few lengths down from me, pulled in deeply to the curb. A lizard took its time getting across the pavement. I took in a few breathfuls of the cool, refreshing air.

My phone buzzed.

Frank: *Meet me at the top. Run.*

Me: *Omw.*

Mt. Bonnell has a set of stairs to the top, limestone quarried from somewhere nearby and lined with Junipers and Live Oaks. It's hard not to find a home in Austin that doesn't have some vein of this soft rock in its foundation or its façade.

I started up. The stairs aren't set at equal spaces. Some require a long jump. Others just a hop or a skip. Some of them, you have to run a few steps before the next stair. I made it to the top and Frank stood huddled under the large trestle overlooking Lady Bird Lake and the homes below. His hands were shoved into the pockets of his windbreaker and he had his face buried in it, his collar zipped up.

He turned to me and nodded. I walked up beside him as I caught my breath.

"It ain't even that cold," I said.

Frank turned. "You ever seen a Mexican in Minnesota?"

"I guess not."

"My people are tropical. Key word, tropic," Frank grumbled.

I looked down on the houses as a woman passed by walking her dog.

"So, how'd it feel to get your ass kicked?"

I was still finding new pockets of soreness.

"Like I said, hammered dog shit."

Frank nodded.

"You know why you got your ass kicked?"

"He was better than me." It was a simple truth.

Frank chuckled and burrowed his face deeper into his collar as a gust of wind picked up and made his windbreaker flap. I crossed my arms. Frank nodded to the houses below. There blue pools rippled in the wind.

"Are those people better than you?" Frank said.

In their driveways sat cars worth more money than I would ever make even if I was reincarnated.

"They're smarter," I said.

Frank laughed loudly and said, "Those are the same type of people who invested in Enron. They ain't smarter." He punched my shoulder and his eyes sharpened into pickaxes. "They just planned better than anybody else. And they trusted that plan."

"Plans have never been my strong point."

"Even so, I didn't think you'd make it this far. Jerrick's a good fighter, and despite what you think, you did fight well. But, smokers and competitively fighting are two different animals. You gotta have a plan."

I shrugged. "I've tried plans before, Frank. It never sinks in."

"You're sober aren't you?"

"Barely."

Frank shook his head gravely and fumbled in his pocket. He

pulled out his cigar and nodded to a clearing surrounded by squat oaks where a limestone picnic table sat.

"Let's talk, I've got something to show you," he said.

We sat down and Frank lit his cigar. He pulled a piece of folded, looseleaf paper out of his pocket. He slid it across to me and lifted his hand from it. The wind gusted. The piece of paper lifted off of the table quickly. I reached for it as it danced higher. I missed. It drifted further out of my reach,

"It's gonna fly away. I ain't make no copies," Frank murmured, taking a puff in thoughtfully.

It flew higher and I stood up to grab it. I closed my fist and the paper fluttered inside my hand like a trapped bird.

Frank blew out a wraith.

I sat down and un-crumpled the piece of paper. Frank had scribbled across the top: JAB, CLENCH, BRAWL.

I looked at him.

"Read," he said.

Jab—it'd be nice to win a fight with it, but only one man has ever done that, and that's Larry Holmes. So, we ain't getting that. So you're gonna have to use it and lose by it for a bit. But, you've gotta get it down. The jab is resilience. It says I'm here and I'm not going anywhere. You open a guy's door with it.

Clench—It's working in the vice. You got one hand free, and that's it. Your job is to make your one hand a battering ram and buzz saw. You gotta put pressure on the body and try to hit all the vital organs. Try to cave in his aorta. Try to crush his floating ribs. Try to carve out every air sac in his lungs.

Get. Him. Hurt.

Brawl—The last round. It's always a brawl. Always at the end of your breath. Always churning up blood, spit and thick mucus. It's the very expression of your inner soul. It's all up for grabs in the last round, so you have to put it all on the line. It comes down to who wants it more. Who's willing to give more of their all. How vulnerable you willing to get to pull out a victory?

I looked up at Frank. He smiled and bit down on his cigar.

"That's it," he said. "That's the plan."

"For what?"

"That's going to be our gameplan going into fights. We're going to work on it bit by bit. And I'm not going to lie to you, Thom. You're going to suffer like a half run-over skunk."

I looked back down at the crudely written list; there were tiny holes burned into it.

"But," Frank continued, "this isn't just a rubric for winning. It's what God put me here to give my fighters. It's a rubric for life, Thom. Boxing is the game of life."

CHAPTER 23:
THE JAB

The next morning, we met in the gym. I pulled into the parking lot, and there was a work truck already there. Stenciled in cursive on the quarter-panel was: *Encarnacion's Mobile Mechanic.*

Frank stood in front of me as we stood in the middle of the ring. He had one mitt held up high. The fluorescent lights buzzed above, pale-green. In the corner, near the rusty stationary bike, was an older Mexican man with a mop of hair covered with flakes of white and gray. He had a paunchy body and spindly legs.

He hit the oldest heavy bag in the gym. It hung by a rusty chain and was mummified with duct tape. He didn't have much snap but there was a full-body torque to his punches, and a deep thud emanated from the bag when he hit it.

"Throw a jab," Frank said.

I shot one at his mitt. It was the one punch I felt slightly confident about. Straight down the middle. Simple.

The bell rang. We continued.

"Again!"

I shot another.

Frank's weathered face lifted into a wide, sadistic grin. He spoke in a hushed tone.

"Again."

My arm felt as loose as an oiled piston.

"Now, to the bag," Frank said.

The sun snuck in through the cutout windows in the back of the gym. They functioned more like lungs than windows: sweaty, exhausted air out; fresh, warm, oxygenated air in.

"All right," Frank said. "You're gonna throw the jab for an en-tire round."

Frank turned and looked at the clock. Then at the entrance. The parking lot was still empty save our cars and the work truck. Greg didn't usually come in until 8:00.

Frank pulled a cigar out of his pocket and lit it with a zippo.

I could run two miles easy now. I could spar three rounds and finish a sentence. I could jump rope for five minutes straight.

One round of one punch? Easy work.

A minute in and my shoulder melted. It was a ball of burning jelly in the socket.

Frank chuckled, "Keep going," and took a deep pull. He was a voice behind a smoke screen.

"You thought this was going to be easy work?" the voice behind the veil said.

He choked and coughed.

By the time the round was over, I couldn't hold up my arm. I slumped against the wall and slid down to the floor. I took every breath coming in through the gills of the gym. The bell dinged like an alarm.

"And that's just one round!" Frank said, emerging from the veil. "We got eight more rounds to go through."

Frank got into his stance and crouched in front of the bag, his cigar clenched in his teeth.

"You got the body jab."

He shot a jab to the body of the bag. The chain tinkled.

"You got the up-jab."

Frank looked upwards, still crouched, and shot a lancing shot to the upper portion of the bag, like a spartan shooting a spear into the head of his enemy.

"You got the flick jab."

Frank stood slightly higher and flicked his jab at the top portion of the bag. "Just to lift their hands up. Lift the gate of their defense."

I nodded.

"You got the power jab."

Frank stood in a neutral stance and launched, using his toe to generate power through his legs, through his core, out through his arm as his fist cork-screwed on impact. The leather sunk under his fist and left an impression like laying a finger on a water-filled limb.

Frank returned to a neutral position and tapped his right fist to his cheek and shook his left fist out in front of him.

"The jab is your lock-pick. You get in the front door with it. You get *real* honest with your intentions with this punch." Frank tapped his cheek again with his right hand. "But remember, you open that door, and there's always somebody on the other side of it. And you got no clue how he's gonna respond. Go in smart, keep your guard up, but keep your shotgun—" Frank flashed his right hand clenched in a fist, "loaded."

Frank stood straight and pulled his cigar out of his mouth.

"But, you have to open the door," he said. "Stand outside scared all day and you gain an ass-whooping. You cross that threshold and you stand to win the whole house."

CHAPTER 24:
FIRST DATE, I KNEW THE GUILLOTINE WAS COMING. SECOND DATE, I FELT IT

Halloween's right around the corner, 2015

We played putt-putt. I spent most of the time trying not to talk. They'd covered the lighthouses in cobwebs and put up glowing inflatable monsters and witches. We walked up toward one of the windmills that was covered in wispy fake cobwebs with a massive black spider poised over the green. I stepped across the moat, passing the lighthouse and Megan stuck her golf club out and tripped me. I fell onto the grass, and blurted, "You little shit." It came out effortlessly, like the kid of me spoke it. She looked at me wide-eyed. That was it. Fatal error. I didn't mean anything by it. "I'm sorry—" I said, fumbling.

Megan burst out laughing. And it was a smooth swim after that. We sat outside her apartment in the Ranger at the end of the date. The truck idled smoothly. Megan chose the playlist for the drive home and *Scar Tissue* came on.

She crossed her leg over and leaned towards me. She planted her elbow on the center console and laid her chin on her palm.

"That was fun, baldy."

"Thanks, hairy."

She reached up and turned the volume down until Anthony sounded like a mosquito.

"So, when are we going out again?" she asked, confidently.

"You want to go out again?"

She nodded her head.

"Where do you want to go next time?" I asked.

"You said you used to work at the P. Terry's off Lamar."

My heart jumped.

"Ain't been there in years," I said, "But, yea, I did."

"Let's go there. I love their milkshakes. And then we can just sit and talk to each other."

Her eyes glowed and I was senseless. I should've kept my mouth shut.

She blinked and I felt the guillotine coming down on my neck.

The day we went to P. Terry's I ate with a pin cushion in my throat and the dry mouth made it hard to get my burger down. I took small bites and no matter how many sips of water I took, the cheese was as hard as concrete. I looked over at Megan and smiled with a mouthful. She took a monstrous bite of her burger and asked me with a bulging pocket in her mouth: "Are you okay?"

The cars rolled by on Lamar. An 18-wheeler downshifted, sounding like the drumming of a speedbag.

"I'm fine," I said with a mouthful of paste.

She looked down and laid her burger in the wrapping paper in her lap. She swallowed a pocket of food and said, "Can I ask you something?"

I bounced my leg. We had the windows open, and the bats skittered and clicked as they got their night started. The streetlights flickered on in ones and twos and the moths swarmed them. I dropped my arm out the window and tapped my fist quickly against the door. And waited.

"Is there something you're hiding from me?"

Megan's voice was soft when she asked it. Just like I guessed she'd be.

"Why you say that?"

The pin cushion in my throat expanded.

"Well, we were talking just fine until we got here—" she twirled her finger in the air—"and then you clammed up in the drive-through."

As we had pulled up to the window, I half-expected to see Cruz. I'd have to explain how we weren't just coworkers and how he used to be my drug dealer. She'd pick up on the vibe somehow, but, luckily, it was just a kid at the window: pimple-faced and perfect. I'd made a promise to myself that I wouldn't lie to her, but standing on the precipice of it was another story.

I grabbed my cup of water out of the holder and took a sip.

"I just don't want to say anything wrong," I said.

I chewed the watery paste into a sludge of cement.

I smiled at her and felt the chunks of meat in between my teeth.

She frowned, looked down, and took the burger in its wrapper and laid it on the dash. She turned to me and crossed her legs as she leaned in. Her black curls fell forward, and her voice was urgent. "Thom, if you start lying to me now, we need to just cut our losses and keep it pushing."

"I'm not lying."

"Then what is it?"

I pulled my arm inside the window and looked at the moths blackened in the glow of the light as they swarmed. The bats swooped in on them from the dark periphery. Shadows chasing shadows. I put my hands on the steering wheel. A man trudged by on the side-walk. A cigarette dangled from his lips and he stared at the cracks in the pavement. He was rail thin with a massive head. He caught me looking at him and nodded.

My heart dangled on a string, swaying side to side inside me. This was it. This was the guillotine, but, I couldn't lie. I had to take what was coming. Win or lose.

I laid my right hand, palm up, on the gearshift and exposed my arm. I laid my left pointer on the raised spots of scar tissue in the crook of my elbow. And tapped them.

I held my finger pointer there and looked up at Megan, waiting for the slice.

She bit her lip and her cheeks quivered.

I breathed in deeply through my nose.

She sighed and gently laid her hand on top of my pointer. She spread her fingers so that my pointer fit right between her ring finger and her middle finger.

The chop was coming.

"If you want to end it, I get it. I don't want you to feel hand-cuffed to me," I said, just shooting it out there. "It's a big bomb to drop, I know."

Megan sighed. I took my pointer away. She rubbed my scar tissue with her fingertip like it was a rose petal.

"Why didn't you tell me earlier?" she said as she stared at the tissue thoughtfully.

"It's a lot for one person to take in. I mean, seriously, who wants to date a former junkie?"

She shook her head slowly. Her fingers were soft and slow-moving.

"How long have you been clean?"

"Going on four months."

She ran her hand down my arm and interlaced her fingers in between my own.

Her eyes softened and she smiled at me.

"I'm proud of you," she said softly, "and it's nothing to be ashamed of, Thom."

She shook my hand gently. The moths danced in the light. The bats careened.

"We're just dumb monkeys at the end of the day; you just like the bananas too much," she said and laughed.

I laughed, too. It felt like freedom.

I turned from her and leaned on the windowsill and rubbed my lips. I blew out deeply. An openness bloomed inside me. I had to keep opening the door.

"I missed my dad's funeral because I'd OD'd," I said. "I was stuck in the hospital. I didn't *even fucking know.*"

"Thom," she said, "look at me."

I turned to her and stared into her eyes. There was no evil. No judgment. No criticism. Just empathy.

She pushed herself closer to me and kissed me on the cheek. The pin cushion in my throat evaporated.

CHAPTER 25:
THE FIRST FIGHT

November 8, 2015

"Okay, give me a one-two," Frank said.

He held the mitts at chest level. I shot a jab at his left mitt, it popped. Then, a right, that popped too. They felt snappy; I felt snappy.

"Good!" Frank said.

We stood ringside in the arena. The crowd was lively and talked excitedly amongst themselves. The PA blared bass-heavy music. The smell of popcorn was everywhere. It was my first fight and I was just about to go on. To the right of us was a table where the judges sat and held notepads and pens close like they were the nuclear codes. In front of us were the stairs to the ring. And to the left, the swath of the crowd. All told, there were probably about 100 people in the complex.

A blue-shirted announcer stood in the middle of the ring as the music quieted. His grey, greasy hair shined in the glare of the ring-lights.

"Ladies and gentlemen..."

I glanced at the crowd. Frank jabbed me.

"Focus!" Frank said. His eyes were sharp and his lips tight. "Come on, remember, gameplan, jab, jab, jab until you can open the door."

"Up next," the announcer rumbled, "in the blue corner, Thomasss Middlecammppp!!!"

I hopped up the stairs to the ring. I swung one leg and then the other under the ropes. I was in.

As I hopped around the ring, I looked out at the crowd. I chewed my mouthpiece as I looked for Megan. Through the sea of glittering phones, I saw her sitting two rows back from the front. She had blue jeans on and a salmon-colored polo. Her black hair was curled and her lips a rosy sheen. She tapped her foot nervously but her mouth bloomed when we caught each other's eyes. I tapped my gloves together and circled back to my corner where Frank stood with a water bottle in his hand and a towel over his shoulder.

"Remember the gameplan," Frank muttered, pumping his lead shoulder a few times. "Jab him till he throws up."

The ref stepped into the center of the ring and ushered me and my opponent forward.

"Touch gloves," he said.

I looked my opponent in the eyes; I'd told myself I wouldn't. I didn't want to see that he was an actual wolf and I was just a dog limping into the arena off the street. But, I couldn't help myself. I had to know.

I was surprised with what I saw. Not fear, not worry, just unknowing. I knew it, because I felt the same thing.

We touched gloves and I went back to my corner.

Frank said, "There is no magic eight-ball in boxing. No pre-cognition. The rounds determine everything. One's will. One's resolve. One's belief."

Jab, jab, jab.

The bell rang and my opponent and I both immediately rushed the center of the ring.

I caught two hard jabs, immediately. Blood pooled in the back of my throat. All I could taste was iron. My opponent was a ghost. Shot after shot, lesson after lesson. But, I felt something at the end of my fists every now and again. My hands impacted flesh. They touched something soft and giving. I heard some grunts. Everything else was a flash.

The bell rang and I marched back to my corner, gassed.

Two minutes of an amateur fight is a reckoning.

My saliva was jelly in my mouth. I spit out a wad and slumped down on my stool. Frank said something. Bell rang again.

I was back up. Back fighting. The punches became less fist and more image and feeling. The shots I took bloomed in my vision in painful blood-red splotches. We swung around the canvas, two stars orbiting each other closely.

The bell rang.

Frank hollered something.

Bell rang again.

I was just swinging and breathing the last round.

Bell rang.

I slumped down. Spat out the mouthpiece. Took a sip of water. Ref raised opponent's hand. Said all the pleasantries.

"Good fight."

"You fought hard."

Stepped down the ladder of the ring. Got to see the physician. Said, "yes, I'm fine. I remember everything."

Boom, that's it.

That was losing.

I sat on a bench behind the curtain as the PA boomed and the next fighters were announced.

Losing tastes like shit. There's the metallic flavor of blood enhanced by the artificial flavor of cheap leather and a chewed-down mouthpiece. Mom found me first and gave me a hug. I kissed her cheek with the lingered flavor.

"You should be proud of yourself, Go'bay," she said.

And then, Frank cut off my hand-wraps as the crowd roared. He did his work in silence. A gentle wheeze came from his nose.

In the waiting area with us, a pee-wee fighter in tiny trunks hit the mitts with his father. His dad worked his defense with him. His father smiled as he playfully smacked a mitt against his son's right glove.

"Hands up, kid," he said, and then, he beamed at his son and shot a playful jab at him. The kid smiled wide and slipped it fluidly.

I leaned forward, suddenly weak, and put my face in my palm

and closed my eyes as tears rushed out.

Frank stayed quiet and undid the wrap on my free hand. It was all so quick. And I'd suffered just to get my foot over the rope and into the ring. Early, early mornings. Late, late nights. Two sparse meals, every fucking day. Water and only that. Sparring. Hours and hours of sparring. Round after round. Aches echoing in every joint. The cleansing feeling after a good spar, not empty, just clean. The pain of long-suffering. The joy of long-suffering. It didn't feel like nothing. But, I'd lost. And losing meant I had nothing to show for the work I'd done.

"That zero doesn't mean a thing," Frank said softly, "You stood in the fire. You may not have won, but you fought 'till the end."

He pulled my wraps from my hands.

Then, I felt her. Just her hand on my shoulder, softly caressing. Her perfume washed the metallic taste from my teeth with gentle peach.

The bell rang. After that, I didn't remember a thing until I woke up at Megan's place later that night.

I woke up to a blistering headache. The curtains were shut and the light was dim. Megan's desk lamp was set to low and she had her school books open. The headache drummed like a war machine. Megan had called out of work the day before to take care of me after the fight. She also had a research paper for her A&P class. A bag of frozen peas thawed on my head.

I groaned and she turned from her desk.

"You're up?"

"What time is it?"

"Nine," she said glumly.

My fight had been at one.

Megan got up from the chair and walked to me.

"I've been asleep for seven hours?"

She sat down on the edge of the bed with her hands in her lap.

"You don't remember?" she asked.

"No."

She unfolded her hands and lay a hand on my leg.

"I'll get you some ibuprofen."

She stood up and walked out of the room to her kitchen. Cabinets opened and closed. The faucet hushed on and then off.

I closed my eyes. My head throbbed to a nauseating beat.

"Here you go, baby," she said. "Ibuprofen, 800."

I felt for her hand and took the pills and the glass of water.

"Thanks, baby," I said.

I washed them down and she sat back down on the bed, her body against my legs.

I opened my eyes slightly and squinted at her.

"How's studying?" I asked.

Megan fidgeted with her hands. She looked at her books on the desk and then at me.

"Can I ask you something?" she said.

"Sure," I said.

She pulled her phone from her back pocket and turned it on. She looked intently at the screen.

"Did you hear about this kid named...um," she scrolled. I shifted the peas. "Prichard Colon?" She glanced up at me. Her eyes flashed from the glow of her phone.

"The one who had to go to the hospital?" I asked.

"Yea," she said.

"Yea, that's a tough break."

Megan sucked in against her teeth.

The light, as dim as it was, still caused pulsing nausea.

"Can you turn off the light, babe?" I grumbled.

Megan got up quickly and flicked the light off.

Her bodyweight pressed hard against my leg when she sat back down on the bed. She spoke from a shadow. "But, Thom, this is a concussion that you have, right?"

"I don't know, Meg."

She was silent. An owl hooted outside.

"If you took a hard enough shot, could you end up like Prichard?"

I could've lied. But I didn't. I didn't want to break that promise to myself. To Megan.

"It's possible," I said. "But Prichard was getting hit with illegal punches. That's why they have referees."

"Thom, but if that could happen to you, then why continue? Couldn't you lose your life?"

She rubbed my leg.

The grind of training camp for two months had sanded down my soul. Sanded it down so that the only thing left was boxing. The supreme focus of it was the closest thing to euphoria. The sacrifice of it, euphoric. The hunger, euphoric. The sparring sessions, painfully euphoric. All of it for six minutes I barely remembered, but it wasn't the fight that had seeped into me, it was everything else that orbited it.

Frank had a mantra that rang in my ear the whole time: "Salvation ain't no walk in the park." And that's what it felt like, salvation.

I sat up as much as I could and looked into the shadow of Megan. I didn't want her to miss any of what I was saying. She was the one person in the world who I wanted to hear what was on my heart.

"Because there's freedom in it. I struggled for two months of training camp. It was fucking hell...but for those six minutes I was Thomas Middlecamp. I was a first name and a last name and proud of both. I was beyond a junkie. I was beyond a disappointment. I was beyond everything I am."

CHAPTER 26:
THE BEACH TRIP

Megan and I laid naked under the covers in her bed a few days later. It was early morning and I felt good, finally. Megan felt it too.

Her legs lay over the top of mine. She massaged my shins gently with her feet. Every now and again her toe would curl against my leg. Her head laid on my chest and she twirled the hair on my nipple absently with her finger. The headache had finally laid down its spear, but, getting in and out of bed was still a prayer. I stroked her hair gently and painlessly.

"We should go to the beach," she said softly.

"This time of year?" I said. "Water's gonna be cold."

"We don't have to swim. Just dip our feet in."

"When?" I asked.

"This weekend."

She looked up at me and rested her chin on my sternum. Her eyes were soft and satisfied. A burst of sunlight flew in through the window in a single ray and landed on the wall right beside us. Tiny sprites danced and moved from the visible to the invisible and Megan licked her full lips and drummed her fingers on my ribs. A curl of black hair fell across her face.

"I got Walmart money to make."

"Fuck that place," she said confidently.

"That's 11.25 an hour we're talking. And a shitty healthcare plan."

"I'm serious," Megan said. I moved the curl from her face with my finger.

I had two call-outs already for the quarter. A third one was a write-up. Most of my managers were under the age of twenty-five and new to power. They wielded it like formerly bullied kids.

Megan kissed my nipple.

"Fuck it," I said.

"South Padre?" she said, smiling.

I grumbled.

South Padre was a nightmare: Golfcarts with morbidly obese mothers and their morbidly obese children zinging through the streets. Cutting in and out of traffic hopped up on Dr. Pepper and snow cones. The water was the color of oil with a hint of sea.

"Not a fan?" she smirked.

I shook my head.

"What about Port A?" I said.

Megan blinked at me and then laid her head back down on my chest heavily.

Now, Port A, was beautiful. You could drive on the beach and truck camp. The only thing you'd hear were fishing lines being pulled in by the shore fisherman and the crackle and ripple of kites flying in the wind. They had an ice cream shop that served sundaes with brownies the size of cinderblocks.

"I don't know." She breathed in deeply and held it.

"We don't have to...Bad memories?" I thought she'd gone down there with Jerrick.

"Kind of."

Outside, a school bus wheezed to a stop.

"We can have the beach here," I said. "I'll get a kiddie pool from Wally World and fill it with water. Grab some sandbags and dump them out all over the lawn. You just get into a bikini and let me watch you dip your feet in."

Megan chuckled. She slapped my sternum gently. My solar plexus tingled.

"Nah, fuck it. Let's go," she said.

"It's shoulder season," I said. "We can get a nice Airbnb for cheap or we can camp in the back of the Ranger."

The Ranger settled smoothly into fifth as we made our way to Port A. It was warm out still, but not oven-hot. The sun glowed opaque behind a thin sheet of tombstone grey clouds. We zoomed down 361. A green placard rose up out of the horizon on the right, and as we got closer, it said: Port A, 20 miles. There was a ferry we had to take to get to the island. We'd gotten a bungalow in the historic part of Port A.

"Almost there," I said, cheerfully. I was blooming with joy just being on the road with her. We had the windows cracked and the cabin was a gentle murmur. It was hitting me that this was our first trip. I looked over at Megan.

Megan nodded as her hair danced around her face.

"Aren't you excited?" I said.

"Yea," she said, trailing off and laying her cheek against the glass. "I'm a little tired. I'm gonna take a nap."

She closed her eyes as the sign flew by us.

We pulled to a stop behind a beat-up gold Chevy. The line to get the ferry was backed up all the way to the refinery.

"I guess everybody's dipping their feet in," I laughed.

Megan didn't say a word.

I tapped my fingers on the steering wheel and looked out the sideview; we were in the belly of the snake. A trail of cars arced all the way to the horizon and disappeared. I looked over at Megan.

"We're going to be here for hours," I said.

With her head still glued to the glass, Megan nodded with her eyes closed.

The sky was the color of a bruise. The sun, a pink dot on the horizon. The clouds were puffy and peach with a purple hint of doom. The refinery loomed on our right. The spires rose like stalactites and the massive, squat cisterns wore a crimson apron of rust. Rust was everywhere. On the worker's trucks. On the bulldozers. On the cranes. Even the workers, in their hardhats and safety vests, couldn't stop the rust in their worn faces. They filtered out to the parking lot with their lunchboxes in their hands and cigarettes in their mouths. Many of them limped on wobbly knees and bad hips and the smoke curled out of their mouths quickly and disappeared like the memories of their younger years.

"You hungry?" I asked Megan, as we inched forward. I just wanted to make anything light of conversation.

She sighed, opened her eyes, and sat up slowly. She put her hands in her lap and wrung them, looking at the refinery. "My uncle used to work at a refinery like this on the other side of Corpus," she said, her voice muffled. Her chin twitched.

"Oh yeah?"

"Yeah," she laughed darkly. "He kept six beers under his bed to wake up in the morning. His breath always smelled like Coors and Marlboros."

An older man with a bushy mustache and weathered skin the color of oil reached into a cooler in the bed of his truck and produced a bottle of Corona. He thumbed a lighter from his pocket and knocked the top off.

"My dad's side of the family is all like that. My mom's, too." She nodded at him.

Megan began to shake and knocked her head softly against the window as a flood of tears ran down her cheeks. She gripped and wrung her hands in her lap intensely like she was trying to strain out every molecule of human waste she'd ever touched.

"Baby, what's wrong?" I asked.

The brake lights in front of us flickered, and the Chevy moved, again.

"The line's moving, Thom."

I pulled forward a few feet. The brake lights flicked on again, and we were at a stand-still. The sun dropped off the face of the earth and the sky took on its beat-down color. Heavy and purple.

Megan breathed out deeply, in sniffling, coughing breaths. She was a crying shadow. The Chevy's brake lights were dim and hard to discern.

"Can I tell you something, baby?" she said.

She sucked in deeply.

"Of course, baby," I said.

"Something happened to me."

My skull thundered with the echoes of my heartbeat. An old slime rose in me so cold that I couldn't gulp.

"I was six when it happened," she said.

The lights on the refinery flickered on brightly. A million stars and galaxies erupted in green, yellow, red, and blue. The car was illuminated like we were being abducted. Megan's skin was ghostly and pale. She ran her finger through her hair and tucked it behind her ear.

"I just remember the lights, Thom. He had a bright light right beside his bed. It was this amber color. And I thought, if I just stare at it long enough, time will speed up. So that's what I did. I just stared at that light until my eyes burned..."

I wanted to pull the pain out of her. I wanted to hold it. Make it my own. I didn't want her to carry any more of it, but it wasn't mine. It had to emerge from its cocoon in its own time. With its own shivering wings. And I knew if I said a single word, I'd suffocate the emergence.

So, I swallowed a slimy bit of spit, as the engine of fear revved. Megan's tears glittered as they ran down her face reflecting the lights of the refinery.

She shrunk against the window. Shaking and crying.

"Meg, come here baby."

"Not...now, Thom."

She shook.

She held her hands in her lap like vices, but I couldn't leave her stranded. Not out there, beyond the lights.

I had to reach out; I had to do it.

I reached towards her, refusing every impulse of gravity and fear. Slowly as an owl flies, I put my hand gently over top of her shaking knuckles.

She flinched.

I wrapped my fingers gently around the tightly clenched ball of her hand.

She was as stiff as concrete.

I snuck my fingers in between her fingers and opened the smallest gill in her clenched fingers.

A car honked behind us. The Chevy was two car lengths ahead.

I worked my fingers deeper. Her clenched hands slowly opened like the mouth of a clam.

The car honked again.

I worked my fingers deeper, trying to find the pearl, the parasite that had lodged itself with a damaged beauty inside of Megan.

The car behind us honked.

"Oh, fuck off!" I yelled.

I hugged the wheel and screwed my left hand across my body to shift. I could barely see above the dash. We lurched and stopped. I craned to see how close we were to the Chevy's bumper. I slammed the brakes as the Chevy's dim lights glowed brightly on my hood. We were maybe an inch short of him. My lungs burned. I sat up and breathed out.

But, I still had her hand.

Megan stared at me, smirking and crying.

"What is wrong with you?"

"Just let me hold your hand and not crash us at the same time, lady."

She rolled her eyes, and smiled, wiping her face.

"Come here baby," I said.

Megan scooted to the edge of her seat and leaned over the center console and laid her head on my bare shoulder as we clasped hands tightly.

I kissed the top of her head and cleared my throat. I'd been a lot of things in my life: a bad son. A drug addict. Homeless. A liar. A manipulator. I'd never felt pure in any of those things. Not once. But, as I held Megan against me, I felt pure. For the first time. Pure. Comfortable. Unafraid.

"It happened to me, too." It lifted gently from my lips. No weight. No fear of saying it.

Megan sniffed and looked up at me. The men at the refinery turned on their trucks. Their headlights flashed into a gallery of white eyes.

Megan lifted herself up and held my cheeks as she kissed my face, my neck, my ears.

It felt like her lips were opening old locks. I just wanted to be open with her.

"I'm so sorry that happened baby," she said. Her voice was a warmth growing. Relief washed through me until the pain of what happened felt so innocuous and distant that it swept me to a new island. A place of gentle palms and un-diseased sand. The place where certain phrases felt true.

"I love you," I said.

Megan ran her hands back and forth across my shoulders gently. They felt like feathers.

"I love you too," she said.

I kept going. I had footing on this island. The gallery of headlights to the right of us disappeared as the men in their work trucks pulled out of the refinery.

"I want to be with you the rest of my life. I know it's early and I'm supposed to talk to your dad and all, but it's how I feel and I'm not saying we get married now or have to get engaged right away. I'm just being honest. It's how I feel."

Megan laughed. "You know my dad's a drunk. He wouldn't care if a horse asked him."

"I'll put a saddle on, I don't give a fuck."

Megan laughed, and almost immediately began weeping again.

I shifted into first and we moved forward smoothly as the lights of the Ferry glowed misty and soft in the spray of the bay.

"Thom," Megan said, "boxing really scares me."

"Why baby?"

"Prichard," she said.

"That's a million to one shot, babe."

"It's always a million to one, until it happens. Then it's one of one."

I inched us forward, and then we came to a halt again.

Megan interlaced her fingers between mine as I shifted. She clenched me gently.

CHAPTER 27:
IT'S A LITTLE THING CALLED LOVE

February 14, 2016

Megan clenched my hand as we got closer and closer. Her fingers became tiny vices. My knuckles popped. Since it was Valentine's Day, everybody had the same bright idea we did.

We stood in line for a long time.

Anybody that was even thinking about getting cold feet, you saw it.

Maybe they got caught up in the idea of getting married on Valentine's Day. Maybe somebody got coerced into it. Maybe somebody's pregnant. I assume if it's not right, you get an ominous feeling right away.

"You scared?" I asked her.

She looked ahead, her eyes sharp. She had a white magnolia tucked into the curling waves in her hair, its petals were wide and its fragrance sweet. She looked up at me quickly. "No," she said, as she yanked me closer. "I'm just not letting you run out of here."

I gripped her hand tighter, as the couple ahead of us bowed their heads. They were next up. They whispered something quickly to each other, nodded, and then turned and walked out of the courtroom briskly.

We stepped forward, closer than atoms.

"So, you still want to do it?" she asked. Shaking my hand. The great seal of Texas hung behind the judge at the podium like the door to a vault. Behind it was either treasure or tragedy.

I shook her hand and whispered, "We're at the judge, babe. It's too late for me to get cold feet, now."

"I'm not talking about that," she said, nudging me. "I meant about the tattoos."

"Branded for life, huh?" I asked.

The judge looked up from behind his glasses and his mustache curled into a smile. I wonder if he could see it. He'd seen enough faces. Signed enough documents. Did he get a feel for who'd make it and who wouldn't? His smile seemed sincere enough, but his pale blue eyes were impassable.

Megan tugged against me. "Breathe baby," she said.

I exhaled and the tightness in my chess released like a coil, and in its place, stillness.

"Marriage is an institution, a commitment..." the judge began.

Me and Megan, that was the clench. And in the clench, you live in the eye of the storm.

We were in our thirties. And before we'd even gotten married, we'd been trying for a baby and had nothing, so, we went to a fertility specialist—on Mom's dollar. I told her no. She still did it—and started the process. First the injections. And the cabinet full of fertility pills and gummies and solutions. Megan hated it. She'd get hellishly sick: bursting migraines; waking up just to throw up in the middle of the night. It got to the point where I could fall asleep to her moaning.

I was still working at Walmart. Megan was a CNA but nursing school started in the fall. For extra money, Greg let me train some of the idiots who'd walk in off the street. Guys with no serious dream, they just wanted to do a few sessions, hit some mitts, and go tell their friends they were boxers. It was rare those guys ever came back after they'd scratched the itch. I picked up overnight shifts at Walmart, too. I cut grass on my days off.

We had to sell the Ranger.

It was a few weeks before my birthday.

I signed the pink slip at the Credit Union and after the banker handed it to the buyer we stood and faced each other.

"Pleasure," he said.

"No problem," I said.

He was a white-haired cowboy who kept a pack of Marlboros in the breast pocket of his plaid long-sleeve and had a snow-white mustache that was thick enough to droop over his lips. He needed something that he could tow around his ranch.

"I'll put it to good use," he said gruffly.

I laid in bed that night as Megan showered after work. I kept thinking about it. *Put it to good use.* The bathroom door opened and light filled the room. I closed my eyes and turned to my edge of the bed and lay my head on my hands. Megan hopped in and cuddled up beside me. She snuck her hand around me and rubbed my belly. Her arms were still moist and she smelled like watermelon. She kissed me on the back of my head.

"I don't feel like shit yet," she mumbled, putting soft kisses on my occiput. "I'm starting to think this is some bullshit. A placebo or something."

A hot air balloon expanded in me as I thought about it. *Put it to good use.* Would he put cigarette holes in the upholstery? Would little tumbleweeds of dirt and cow-patties roll around the dash?

I turned to face Megan. She opened her eyes slowly. "Hey baby," she said softly.

"I feel like crying," I said.

I swallowed, trying to hold down the burning feeling that was creeping into my eyes.

"What's wrong?" She put her hand on my cheek, her palm cool and wet. "You're worried about your fight?"

"No, it's not that," I said.

She sighed. "Oh, the *Ranger*."

"Yea."

The ventilation fan clicked off in the bathroom. It'd been shutting off lately. I had to fix it; the switch was broken. Our landlord's favorite hobby was dodging calls. I'd fixed most of the house for them.

"Fuck me," I said.

I started to get up.

Megan put her hand on my shoulder.

"No, Thom," she said. "Come here. It's fine."

I laid back down.

"I didn't realize how much it'd affect me," I said. My eyes burned.

Megan pulled me close and I nestled between her breasts. They were warm on my cheek, and I wrapped my arms around her, gripping her back.

"Remember why we're doing this," Megan said softly.

"I know," I said.

She kissed the top of my head gently.

I could hear every step of her heart beat: the soft drum. The gentle whoosh. The open and close of her valves.

"Go ahead and cry, baby," she said.

CHAPTER 28:
IT GETS GRITTY

I held my gym bag low on my shoulder and pushed open the door to Lion's. My liver quivered like a fish with a spear through it. There wasn't a stitch of muscle on my body that wasn't sore. The guy really took it out on me. My jabs were tighter, but I lost points in all the exchanges. It was my third loss. The guy knew how to work the inside. I looked up at the yellowed pictures of former champions taped to the walls, glorious smiles on their faces.

"Heard you lost again," Greg barked form his office. It was a little past 7:00. Greg had a swath of papers in front of him. His glasses hung low to the brim of his nose.

"You're early" I said, putting my bag down and walking to his door.

"Books," Greg grumbled.

I nodded.

Greg sat back and shook his hand free of a cramp. He crossed his hands behind his head. A smirk crossed his face. "Hurts doesn't it?"

"It ain't pleasant." But it was more than unpleasant. It was a bitter pill in my throat. It's the worst honor in a gym to be the best loser. A guy who fights with his heart but loses again and again.

"Hmm," he said, thoughtfully.

"What?"

He sat forward and pointed to a trash bin near the door. Inside of it I saw the burnt carcasses of Frank's cigars.

"You know how many of Frank's fucking cigars I have to pick up, a week?"

"I don't know."

He put both hands up and wagged all of his fingers. "At least ten of those fuckers," he laughed brutally.

I looked above Greg at the fighters on the wall behind him.

"But I'll never kick him out for good," he said. His voice was final.

"Why?"

"Because he does something most trainers can't," Greg worked his knuckles, "he prepares you for more than the ring. It ain't bull-shit. That Jab, Clench, Brawl; it's a philosophy."

"What philosophy is that?"

"Keep showing up," Greg said.

"You mean keep losing?"

Greg chuckled. "Frank's guys always lose in the amateur circuit. He had a guy go 0-20 before turning pro."

"What happened after he turned pro?"

Greg shook his head and looked at me with beams. "Fucking guy rattled off five straight wins."

I looked out the window of Greg's office as Frank's Olds pulled into the parking lot.

"Weather the storm," Greg said.

Frank got out of his car with a cigar smoking in his mouth.

Greg grumbled.

"I'll make sure he puts it out," I said.

Greg waved me off.

"Let him have it. He sees me," he said.

Frank looked at Greg the way a kid with no money stares at the ice cream man. He threw his cigar into the asphalt and stuck the toe of his shoe on it and ground it into smithereens.

CHAPTER 29:
FAIRY TALES DON'T DO IT JUSTICE

Early 2017

We finally had something viable. But, viable brought new worries, new fears to cripple the new dreams.

Megan had nightmares.

She'd wake up, pulling the sheets back like she felt a wave rushing out of her. One night, the wave was real.

I thought hell was what I'd seen in rehab.

But that night, the night that Megan woke up bleeding; that was it.

I flicked on the lamp on her desk: Her face as pale as a stone and her eyes were a green doom.

It was 1:55 in the morning. I hit ninety as we sped to the ER (we didn't have insurance nor the money for an ambulance). Megan sat on a towel as blood poured from her pelvis. She kept looking down at it, as I sped through light after light.

"Baby, don't look!" I said.

"What if she comes, and I miss it?" she said, her face pale and her eyes manic.

I hit a curb, looking at her. There was a singular horror inside me.

"Baby," I said, trembling, the ER glowed dimly in the distance, "please. Don't look."

They wheeled her in on a gurney as blood continued spewing. The doctors and nurses swarmed around her. "You have to stay in the waiting room, sir," a nurse said, pushing me back. Megan's foot dangled off the gurney as they had her legs wide open, she'd gotten her toenails painted an opaque purple. I pushed forward. The nurse yelled.

"I'm not leaving my wife!" I said.

"Let him be," the doctor said to the nurse. And then, he spoke sharply to me, "just, stay out of her way."

I followed them as they wheeled her to the massive trauma bay. "Stick to the wall!" the nurse said, ushering me against the wall.

I got small. Megan sweat through her gown, and I patted her head with a cool towel. "It's going to be okay, baby," I said.

Her head rolled back and her eyes moved loosely. "Why the fuck is this happening? We had something, didn't we?" Megan asked.

"We just had a bump in the road, baby," I said. "What's going on?" I asked the nurses.

The nurses moved around her with bags of blood and didn't look up. A doctor worked under a drape, pushing package after package of gauze into Megan's pelvis. He emerged and spoke quickly to another doctor who stood with his finger to his lips in the doorway. "We need to get her to the OR."

The other doctor nodded somberly.

Machines, and nurses and doctors emerged out of the ether and the room was a swirling chaos.

"Baby, they have to take you to the OR," I said.

Megan's cheeks trembled and the sweat on her ashen forehead wobbled. Tiny droplets from the cold towel rolled down to her lips. She wept. I was useless.

They took her back.

And delivered our baby

Megan held her.

Nineteen weeks.

They said we could have her hand print.

Megan couldn't do it.

I couldn't.

We couldn't.

We got home two days later around 9:00 p.m.

Megan pushed the back-door open and flicked the lights on in the kitchen. She had her pink robe cinched on loosely. She tossed her purse down on the floor.

"I'm taking a shower," she said.

Every word between us felt like a eulogy. She stumbled to the corner and howled once in the darkness. It was piercing and crackling like a glacier breaking. Her slippers swished on the carpet as she made her way to our bedroom.

"I'll make you something to eat," I called out to her. "Something light, oatmeal."

"Whatever," she said, her voice was an abyss.

I carried the warm bowl down the hallway. The smell of cinnamon and honey felt alien. I'd smelled only sterile hospital cleaning products and body fluids for three days. A tiny sliver of amber light escaped under the crack of our bedroom door. I pushed it open slowly. Megan lay over the covers in her robe, shaking. The shower was still running. A trail of water made its way darkly from the bathroom to the bed. Megan's hair was soggy and she still had her slippers on. I put the oatmeal down on our nightstand. A picture of the ultrasound still lay tucked underneath the lamp. I pulled it out slowly.

"Don't throw it away," she said.

"I won't."

I opened the drawer and laid it down gently. No longer it, at nineteen weeks. It was a She; she had been a living possibility.

"Thom," Megan said, "it's never going to happen."

I crawled into bed and laid down beside her. I kissed her cheek. She wiped her eyes and sniffed. She still had her wristband on from the hospital.

"You gotta have faith, Meg," I said.

Megan's school books lay open on her desk in the corner and her pen sat on her notebook. The lamp was still on from three nights ago. It glowed low, the filament was dying.

Megan sniffed again. I wrapped my arms around her. Her eyes

shivered in micro-movements. She seemed to be searching me. She searched for a while, and then, she drew in a deep breath through pursed lips.

"Thom," she said. She ran her tongue quickly over her lips. "I want you to find someone to have kids with."

"You don't want to have kids?" I asked.

Her eyes shook, but she didn't blink.

"I do...but it's not gonna happen with me, Tommy. My body is broken."

It felt like every word was a dark certainty to her.

I pulled her close.

I'd made it past thirty. I'd caused suffering and suffered for it. I wasn't supposed to be in that house, with that woman, at that age. There was a tombstone and a grave somewhere laying empty, waiting. So, every moment I got of life was a cherry. Megan was the biggest part of that cherry. I knew who she was. I knew who I was when I was with her. I'd never known myself sober with anyone. I'd never given a stringless love.

"Baby, you're more than an incubator to me. If you don't want to go through this again, I get it. It's hell. But, I'm not going anywhere."

Megan searched for the lie. I brushed the strands of soggy hair from her face.

She looked down at my chest and laughed. She laid her hand on the skin right above my right pectoral:

T ♥ M

We got the tattoos right after we saw the judge. It was corny, but I felt like a twenty-year old again when we did it. It felt like a reclamation.

"I still can't believe we did that," she said.

"Branded for life, Meg."

The lamp gave on last flicker, and died. We were bathed in darkness. The shower ran in a hush.

"Fuck me, I've got a test tomorrow," she sighed.

She started to roll over to get up and go to her desk.

I pulled her back to me.

"Baby, come here," I said. "What'd you say to me once, baby? We can cry together."

We cried in each other's arms until the sun came up.
We waited another year to try again.

CHAPTER 30:
LOSS

October 2018

Megan cooked our breakfast on a hot plate when I walked in sweating from a three miler. We were still in the same shitty-ass house.

The stove had stopped working. The landlords hadn't answered my last three calls. They were either dead or on the event horizon of a black hole.

"They're seriously not gonna fix this?" she said as she kicked the oven. It clanged back.

"C'mon," I said. "I'll be the one fixing it."

I went to the counter opposite the stove where we kept our phones in a wicker basket. A bag of red delicious apples sat beside it. Meg hated apples. I grabbed one. I looked out the back window. The yard was overgrown. Sunflowers grew in groves at the back lot, towering and drooping at their necks, but the lot was decently large enough to put something other than weeds and sunflowers and the landlords didn't even answer calls, they wouldn't mind if I added some things.

Hope fluttered delicately inside my chest, like clasping two hands over a butterfly. I took a bite of the apple.

"What do you think, Meg, a swing set?"

She turned and put her hand on her hip. Her belly had gotten big. We were more than a bump; we were twenty-six weeks.

Number two. If we lost this one, we weren't trying again.

Her eyes darkened.

"Let's get out of the woods first," she said.

She rubbed her belly lightly, like it was spring-loaded.

I felt the hands closing in on a delicate dream; it was foolish.

The eggs popped on the hot plate.

There was a knock at the front door.

"I got it," I said.

"We're not supposed to be buying things," Megan said as she rubbed her belly gently.

"I didn't," I said.

Megan moved the eggs around the skillet with the spatula and sighed deeply.

I could see through the plate glass door a blurry box. I turned and walked through the foyer to the front door as I heard the grating noise of Megan taking the skillet off.

Megan started chopping something. It crunched when she split it and crunched again.

I opened the door. The morning air was fresh and the sunlight stippled through the oak trees. I pulled the box in quickly and put it at the bottom of the stairs. I dragged it up the stairs and stashed it in the closet.

I walked back through the foyer, and said, "Just a door-to-door salesman."

A strong smell of burning cinnamon hit me as I stood at the edge of the kitchen. Megan pushed around some apples in the skillet. And her shoulders shook. The sun shone opaquely through the window and landed on her face. Her cheeks rolled with orbs of light as she cried. She turned and looked at me and started laughing.

"I think she likes apples."

She had a taste for apples, and I'd bought a crib.

The hope fluttered inside me.

December 29, 2018

Nothing in my life happened on time or at the right moment.

We were at a Whataburger when it happened. One of the employees was taking down the ornamental Christmas Trees at the entrance. Megan was on her second piece of fried apple pie.

I gave myself permission to have a single piece of fried chicken.

I'd picked her up after she got off work. She'd been a nurse in the ER for three months and was wearing her navy-blue pregnancy scrubs. I'd just gotten done sparring and had on my sauna suit. A bulge of a bruise sprouted over my right eye.

"Does everything have to be about your weight?" Megan asked with a mouthful, holding the biscuit in one hand and rubbing her belly with the other.

"I'm a mid-thirties boxer, everything is most definitely about my weight—"

Her eyes ballooned.

"What is it?" I asked, my heart narrowed into a focus of fear.

"We gotta go. Now!" she said. She chewed the last of her biscuit in her mouth. A small stain bloomed at the crotch of her scrubs. I wanted to drive off a cliff. We were so close. Too close for tragedy.

"God, please," I moaned. It just came out of me. The moon was the color of a ghoul. I felt every hair on my arms. And my heart clenched and dispersed: into my ears, into my mouth, into my tongue. A million beats all through my body, echoing and bouncing. I moved my hand through space and placed it on Megan's belly and closed my eyes.

I was going to hold her this time. I was going to see it through. I was going to hold my baby for the first and last time, it's just, we'd made it so far. So. Fucking. Far. She was almost here. Why, now? Why, God, why?

Megan's hand landed on top of mine, gently rubbing.

I opened my eyes and looked at her as tears ran down her face and pooled in her smile.

She chewed once more.

"Thom," she said, "it's okay. It's my water."

"What water?" I asked.

"Baby," she said. She rubbed my arm gently.

And, then, it hit me like a shot to the plexus; I'd forgotten to do the most important thing: the brown box in the back of the closet.

Megan chewed the last of her pie.

"I didn't set up the crib," I said.

She patted my hand, softly urgent.

"It's a tragedy, I know," she said, "but please fucking drive us to the hospital."

"Yup."

I clenched the wheel and drove like a maniac to the hospital while Megan searched the bottom of the bag for any last pieces of her pie.

December 30, 2018

The delivery room was a swarm. The fluorescent lights above Megan's bed glowed bright and pale green, like the lights of a UFO. The nurses rolled in tables full of metal tools, bent in all manner of medieval curves and sharpened points: scissors that could swim through steel; metal hooks and clamps that looked more useful for extracting the xenomorph than a baby.

"Here, put this on!" one of the nurses said as she shoved a gown and mask at me.

The flu had been bad the year before. They were already on high alert.

They pushed me towards the head of the bed, beside Megan's shoulder. I bumped into a suction canister and it howled like the vacuum of space. A nurse reached around me, bumped my head with her elbow, and turned the howling off. "Stay small, Dad," she said curtly.

They threw a drape over Megan's legs as they worked her feet into the stirrups.

"Thom," Mom said as she stood on the other side of the bed over Megan's shoulder, "put this on her head."

Mom thrust a cool, wet towel at me.

"Push, mama!" a voice bellowed from beneath the drape.

Megan sat up, squeezed and screamed: a guttural release.

I put the towel to her head. She laid back in exhaustion.

She closed her eyes and breathed out through pursed lips.

"Don't let them bathe her," she said.

"I won't, baby."

"And give me your hand."

I gave her my free hand as I patted her head, and she clenched.

The drape danced like something unholy was underneath it.

"Push! MAMA! PUSH!" the voice from the drape said.

Megan squeezed, her face contorted in the wrinkles of agony and pressure as she squeezed my hand; she could've ground my knuckles to dust.

"No more towel, baby," she said, as she laid back and breathed out heavily.

I took the towel off.

Mom rubbed Megan's shoulder. "You got this Megan," she said gently, but confident. "Faith's coming out healthy and strong."

Megan turned and looked up at Mom.

"This is hell, Deb," Megan moaned. "Epidural ain't doing shit."

Mom glanced at the nurses and lowered her mask quickly. "Can she get a bolus!" She said. She kissed Megan on the top of her head, and through the noise, Mom's voice cut clear as a bell.

"Motherhood's a beautiful hell, Megan, and this is the worst part, but, it's worth it."

The doctor beneath the drape bellowed.

"PUSH! MAMA! PUSH!"

Megan's eyes flashed as wide and open as a hooked fish. She clenched down on my hand and pushed. She Pushed; she shitted; she pissed. Pushed. Shitted. Pissed.

"LAST ONE! MAMA! SHE'S ALMOST HERE!"

"YOU GOT THIS, MEGAN!" Mom roared.

"Baby, you can do this!" I whispered into her ear.

"Oh my God! Oh my God!" Megan cried as she pushed, digging her feet into the stirrups.

The drape settled as the swarming team came to a halt and then moved magnetically to the drape.

From beneath the drape, something howled; it was the first time I'd ever heard that sound. There wasn't any placing it: it was lively, hungry, throaty, piercing.

Megan let go of her grip of my hand and closed her eyes, exhaling deeply.

I kissed her head; her hair was sticky with sweat.

I kissed her cheeks; they were a cold porcelain.

"I think the epidural's finally kicking in," Megan said. And almost immediately, she began snoring.

"Is she okay?" I asked.

The monitor behind my head beeped rhythmically like a sleigh bell

No one answered. They were too busy pulling something from beneath the drape.

A nurse walked over and hit a button to silence the monitor behind me.

"That's labor for you," the nurse said matter-of-factly, "she's just very tired. And the epidural kicked in. But she's fine."

Her eyes were focused and sharp, but, she must've seen the look on my face, because she lowered her tone.

"We're just going to weigh her very quickly," she said, and patted my shoulder gently.

"Who?" I asked.

She looked at me quizzically and said,

"Your baby."

There she was: naked, kicking and screaming. Her tiny feet and arms writhed as they lowered her to a plastic scale at the foot of the bed. Mom stood watch with her hands on her hips.

"Should I wake her up?" I said and looked down at Megan.

"No," the nurse said. "Now, take off your shirt."

"Huh?"

She looked at me like she was having to try to explain math to a chimpanzee. "Skin to skin contact, it's good for the baby."

They carried the squirming body towards me.

I pulled the gown and my shirt off quickly and held out my arms like they were going to toss it to me.

"Take your mask down," Mom whispered.

They put her in my arms.

"Put her on your skin," Mom said, softly.

I pulled her squirming sticky body to me. She kicked and howled in my arms. I tried to tense every molecule in my body to hold her.

This tiny thing moved its body against me. Its tiny chest rolled against my belly. And I then I felt it, the tiny fluttering: a heartbeat like a hummingbird.

"We never made it this far," I said as an upwelling of joy and pain mixed in my throat. It burned like hot oil. "I didn't think I'd ever see her."

The nurse's eyes broke. And her mask quivered.

"Well," she said, "she's here, Dad."

Faith's head lay at the crook of my arm, right on top of the tiny bulge of my scar tissue.

Mom rubbed my shoulders.

"Relax, Thom," Mom said. She looked at me deeply. "Everything else will come. Just be present."

I tried to relax, but:

What if I dropped her?

Or she got some of my residue on her?

What if I could never rub the junkie away?

What if it passed on to her?

"Megan said not to bathe her," I blurted.

"I didn't let them," Mom said. She lifted up on her toes to kiss my cheek. "Going for a smoke. I'll be back."

Mom was gone before I could ask what to do next.

I looked down at her as she laid against my skin. She'd quieted and gone to sleep. Her tiny neck moved with every breath. Her skin was pink and moist, covered in a ghost-white, sticky film and chunky white globules. And her hair was an auburn sheen. But, I didn't feel the thing I'd thought I'd feel. The closeness. The angel of fatherhood. The whiplash of self-sacrifice. Almost none of it.

And, also, I didn't want to say a single thing.

She was so small.

The one thing I knew for sure was that I wanted to be harmless.

To her.

To Faith.

Born December 30, 2018. 2:00 A.M. On the dot.

Six lbs. seven ounces.

6:04 A.M.

My phone buzzed under my ear as I lay on the couch. I wiped my eyes in the darkness, and sat up, yawning. I grabbed my phone and looked at it.

Mom: *be back in a bit. Just going out for another pack. We'll bathe her when I get back.*

I put the phone down and let my eyes adjust. The room was dim. The window shade was pulled down. The city was shut out.

Everything was a hovering shadow around Faith's baby warmer. She lay in the gold glow of its tiny, overhead light, swaddled and cooing.

Beside the warmer, Megan lay in her bed, the covers pulled up and over her head. I hadn't seen her face since Faith was born. When the nurses came in to get her vitals, she stuck her arm out of the covers and nothing else.

"She's tired. It's a dog-fight having a baby," Mom had said.

The thin, vertical strip of glass in the door looked out onto a lifeless hallway.

I sat back in the sofa. The warmer glowed like treasure.

She'd made it. Made it to this point. It was a frightening joy. And I was alone in it. I didn't know what to do. I didn't want to wash her by myself. I didn't want to hold her too tightly. Or kiss her too rough. Or even look at her for too long. If I looked too long, maybe karma would come calling. Maybe it'd open its mouth and swallow her. It'd rip her from me for even thinking that I deserved the joy that was blooming in my chest. It was hard to even think of that word: joy. It was anomalous. Wasn't meant for me, but, I'd been a part of it. There was no denying it. And joy was covered in slime at six pounds seven ounces.

Mom pushed the door open slowly, a cup of coffee in her hand and a smile that drooped slightly when she looked at Megan huddled under the sheets. She tip-toed in and moved through the amber glow of the soft overhead light, past the large-basin sink near the foot of the bed, to the set of couch and chairs where I sat. She put her coffee down on the small table in front of the couch. She walked over to Faith's warmer and leaned over. She whispered to her, "my lil chunky monkey." She leaned down and kissed Faith's head gently, and sighed.

She turned back to me and walked over to the clump of chairs.

She slumped down into the recliner beside me. She crossed her legs and whispered.

"Has Megan been up?"

The monitor beeped. A dark figure hovered at the slitted glass of the door, peering in.

"Not once," I said. I nodded at the door, and the shadow disappeared. "They come in and take vitals and all she does is stick her hand out."

Mom sipped her coffee tightly in the dim light.

Faith began to whine and punched against the swaddle.

"She needs a bath, Thom," Mom said.

"Me and Megan were supposed to do that—together."

Mom shook her head slowly. "Megan needs time. This was a longer time coming for her than it was for you."

"Mom," I said. "This ain't been a walk in the park for me either."

Mom sat forward and put her coffee down on the table. She laid her hand on my knee.

"I'm not saying that to beat you up, Thom," she whispered. "I just meant that giving birth is a whole-body sacrifice, for nine months. And being a dad, in the beginning, kindof means you're a bench-warmer. You shore her up when she needs you. And right now, she needs you."

I breathed in deeply. I settled onto a stone inside myself. Megan needed me and I'd be an animal if I didn't at least try.

"How?" I asked.

"I'll go get her," Mom said, slapping my knee softly. "Go get the water running. Make it warm, but not hot, you should be able to leave your arm under it. Use one of the hand towels to wipe her down."

Mom pushed herself up confidently and glided over to the warmer. Her blonde hair glowed like a halo in the soft light.

The light above the sink was green as a morgue. The stainless-steel spigot looked cold and sterile. I pushed myself up slowly. I crossed the void as Mom gathered Faith. Faith squalled with annoyance. Megan was still a huddled bundle. The monitor began to beep rapidly. Mom stepped up with Faith in one hand and tapped the monitor to silence the alarm with the other. She stood with the posture of a ballerina.

The two levers for the sink were blue and red. I gripped the red and turned it slowly. It whooshed on like a flood. Loud and horrid. It sucked out any confidence I'd been able to muster. But, I kept turning. I had to do it. Megan wasn't moving. Faith needed a bath. I adjusted the nobs and put my arm under the water. It was scalding and I pulled my arm away quickly. Mom's footsteps echoed like drum beats. I put my hand on the cold knob and turned it slowly and put my arm underneath it until a warm rush splashed over my wrist.

Mom bumped me with her shoulder. She bounced Faith and sung gently "The Wheels on the Bus" in a near whisper.

Faith was naked, pink, and a squiggly mass.

"Good?" Mom asked, pausing her song.

"Good," I choked out.

Mom chuckled and whispered to me

"You know your Daddy wouldn't let them bathe you or Dewey." Mom's eyes glistened, but her voice didn't break, "He wouldn't let them touch you. It had to be me and him, first. I missed him today. You reminded me of him, a little."

She bounced Faith one more time and kissed her curly, brown head, and then handed her to me. My heart jumped into my throat, in an instant.

"Where you going?" I asked.

"She needs to feed, Thom," Mom said certainly.

"What if something happens?"

Mom cocked her head in the darkness. "Whatchu think's gonna happen, Thom? She gonna grow wings and fly away?"

I shook my head as I held Faith underneath her arms. Her skin was dry with tiny balls of mucus and she kicked and cried at me. Her toothless mouth howled widely.

"It ain't rocket science," Mom said. "I need to talk to Megan. She needs to breast feed her."

Mom kissed my cheek.

She walked over to Megan, disappearing into the darkness.

I held Faith in front of me. She was so small, so fragile. I felt like I was going to break her no matter how much I tried not to, and that scared me.

Mom whispered to Megan in urgent, confident tones.

Faith's whining lowered to a coo as I held her close. The water running softened to a hush. A tiny sliver of sunlight emerged under the window shade. The overhead light felt less alien, more useful. As I looked at her, I saw that Faith's tiny lips puckered like Megan's plump and sinless. Her ears, like Megan's, were pointed. But her nose was puggy, like mine and it wrinkled when she whined. The tiny furrow in her brow was just like Dad's when he fell asleep watching the Longhorns play on TV.

She snuggled closer to me and shot a tiny hand up and gripped my pointer finger. Her fingers clenched around it. All of the blood in my body rushed to that point. And returned to my heart with joy.

Her nose was my nose. Her fingers were my fingers. Her heartbeat was my heartbeat.

I lowered her slowly, gently, to the basin. I cupped the water with my hand and began to wash off the tiny balls of mucus.

I felt a presence behind me, and a hand travelled down my arm: thin, porcelain.

I turned, holding Faith gently, as Megan stood beside me. Her face was drawn and exhausted, but she smiled weakly and lowered her head to my shoulder, as we washed Faith, together.

PART 4: BRAWL

CHAPTER 31:
SHE'S HOME. WE'RE HOME. NOW IT BEGINS

We got Faith home two days later, on a Tuesday.

I woke up early the next morning to Megan's shadow hovering over Faith's crib.

"Meg, she okay?"

The shadow was rigid.

I sat up on the edge of the bed waiting for her response. She was a nurse, I wasn't. She'd told me about some of the people she'd seen die already. Their eyes were empty and pale and their faces dusted of all color. Snap of the fingers and that was it, lights out.

"They don't even look like people, just husks."

I couldn't see Faith if she looked like that. I gripped the edge of the bed. I'd make myself a statue until EMS came.

"She's fine," Megan said curtly.

I pushed myself up and wobbled at the top.

"Baby, you okay?" I asked the darkness.

I walked up to Megan and held her from behind. I wrapped my hands around her waist. I kissed her cheek. She didn't move. Faith turned over on her side.

"She could fall asleep and die. You know that?" Megan said. Her voice was morbid and matter-of-fact.

She put her finger to her mouth and bit down on her nail.

"Don't let her fall asleep on her face," she said, chewing.

I kissed her again. Faith tensed. Megan tensed. I tensed.

Then, Faith threw her right hand out in relief and stuck her thumb in her mouth as a tiny fart tooted out of her.

"I'll change her," I said. "Try to get some sleep."

Megan pulled away quickly and walked briskly to the bathroom. "I need to pump."

"Okay," I said.

Megan had a force field around her since we'd gotten home. She felt impenetrable.

"I'll change her," I said again, "and then I'm going to head to the gym for exactly an hour. When I come back, I'll watch her. You need to get some sleep."

"Yea. Fine," Megan said from the bathroom.

"How's Megan?" Frank asked as we sat on the bench by the ring.

"I don't know, she's acting a little funny."

Frank frowned and then patted me on the shoulder. His face wrinkled, and his eyes searched. He kept patting my shoulder and kept searching.

"You don't have to say anything, Frank," I said.

Frank shook his head; his eyes were solemn and lonely. "I don't know what it's like to be there during those times," he said. He coughed and wheezed. "I wasn't there when any of my kids were born. Wasn't there for much of anything."

Frank's brown face was paler than usual.

He took his hand off my shoulder and looked down at the mitts at his feet.. The wind blew in through the gills of the gym. It was blue-dark outside. The clock above the bell read 6:00 A.M.

"I got thirty minutes, Frankie."

Frank bent down quickly and grabbed the mitts.

"All right, let's get up to the ring," he said, pushing himself up gingerly, "We'll get started on the brawl."

We stood in the middle of the ring and Frank slapped his mitts together.

"The brawl is nothing but pain and pressure. Ain't nobody getting out scot-free. You kill yourself in the process. Men live shorter lives than women, and here is where you'll probably be shaving off a few of those months. In a true brawl, you etch a part of his tombstone. He etches a part of yours."

A semi roared by on the street outside, like a lion coming home.

"The brawl is when you give all of you. All heart. All mind. All soul."

Frank tapped my chest with a mitt.

"Use too much heart, you leave yourself vulnerable. Vulnerable to the knockout because you don't give a shit about defense when you're fighting with heart. Yea, it'll give you all the power in the world, but you get wild. Your opponent can see your every move from a mile away."

He tapped my navel.

"Soul is the strongest part. You know why?"

I shook my head.

"That's where faith lives. Faith ain't meant for the first few rounds. It's meant for the last. It's the deepest reservoir, but, you've gotta go through the battles first. Soul wins wars, but you gotta use your heart and head to win the battles to get there."

Frank lifted his mitt towards my head. And then, immediately dropped and clutched his chest as he started hacking. He stumbled over to the corner and spat into a plastic bucket under the ropes. He hacked hard as the bell rang. His face started to get ashen, the veins in his neck pulsed with the pressure. I rushed over and put my hand on his back; my heart swung in a vacuum of fear. I felt weightless and helpless. I didn't know shit about medicine. If he fell right there, I'd have to stand and watch him take his last breaths.

"Frank," I said, trying to keep my voice straight. "You okay?"

"It's all right," Frank said in between breaths, pulling in through pursed lips. "I've got an appointment with a doc today. Let's keep going. Just give me a minute. It's getting better."

Frank held the ropes as I stood over him and patted his back. Through is shirt, I could see his ribs as they poked at his skin and the muscles in his neck tensed and relaxed as his heaving began to relent.

"I'm good," he said, standing. "Just kind of came over me."

"You good?" I asked.

"I'm good."

The bell rang.

I got Frank a bottle of water and we sat on the stairs of the ring. The muscles in his neck still rippled when he breathed.

"Ok," he said, taking a gulp. He tapped my head with his hand. "Lastly, the head, you fight with just that, and you won't risk enough. You'll quit. Take a few hard hits during a brawl, and your head will tell you the only thing you were ever meant for was losing, that you're a failure. You'll forget that you're more than that."

Frank stopped to take a few pursed breaths, a sip of water, and continued with sweat rolling down his face. "Crack a champion open and you won't see guts or brains or muscle, you'll see a willing mind, a tireless heart, and a dog-ass soul." Frank shook a dusky finger. "Brawl don't mean you get to be a berserker. It means fight with all three components, head, heart, and soul until there's not a tooth or nail left, on him or you, to fight with."

Satisfied, Frank sat back against the stairs and fished in his pocket for his cigar.

CHAPTER 32:
AND THEY'RE PAYING HOW MUCH?

March 2020

Almost two years came and went. Since Megan was a new-grad, she was stuck on nightshift, praying for a dayshift slot to open.

Mom was a huge help: we'd developed a system. Mom worked days and stayed to help out most nights—or just to be there—while Megan worked. Megan was the breadwinner, and we were barely scraping by. I quit Walmart and stayed home as Daddy Daycare, to help out with that bill. I'd saved up a little bit of money from Walmart, we called it our "rainiest" day money. We were getting close to having to use it.

And then, COVID happened.

We sat at the table in the kitchen one morning having breakfast after Megan got home from work.

Megan held her phone close to my face and tapped the screen urgently with her finger.

A hot bowl of oatmeal sat half-eaten in front of me, along with some cut-up apples for Faith and scrambled eggs.

Megan hadn't touched her eggs or bacon.

The sun rose in the fog and the first rays came in heavily through the window above the sink.

I bounced Faith on my shoulder as she finally started to sleep on the dome of my deltoid. She'd thrown up twice that morning.

Megan was still in her scrubs staring at me with wide, blood-shot eyes. Mom jammed her feet into her shoes as she stood near the front door. Out of the corner of my eye, a massive roach crawled from underneath the sink, crossed the heavy sunray on the floor, and strutted across the linoleum, casually lowering its feelers as it crawled underneath the oven.

"When's the last time they sprayed?" Mom asked. She pulled her scrub jacket on and fished in her pockets for her cigarettes.

"Never," Megan said bluntly, still facing me.

"Where the fuck are my cigarettes?"

On Megan's phone screen was a blurb: Critical Staffing, hiring, $135/hr for ER nurses. Dayshift. More than two year's experience preferred, but not required.

Faith cooed in my ear, blinking slowly.

Mom found her cigarettes and sighed deeply. She looked at her watch and walked over to me.

"Bye baby," she said, kissing Faith's head.

Mom patted me on the head and paused looking at Megan's phone screen. "Damn, that's good money. You better take that."

"Mom," I said, "it's a discussion."

"What?" Mom asked. "I'm just saying. Be foolish not to, and, it's *days*."

"Thank you, Deb—*foolish*, Thom," Megan said.

"Megan, Faith's just over a year old and you want to leave?" I said.

Megan sat up straight and glanced at Mom.

Mom looked down at her watch.

"See ya'll tonight," she said, and strode out of the dining room and through the living room. She put a cigarette in her mouth before she reached the front door.

"Thom," she said, looking at her screen, "how many times have you had to fix things around the house?"

"I'm keeping up," I said.

Megan put her phone down on the table. She leaned toward me and put her hand on my knee. "You shouldn't have to. *We* shouldn't have to. This isn't even *our* house. We got roaches crawling all over this place. I've seen mouse turds in the other bedroom and in the pantry, where Faith's food is. The A/C's always going. The heat ain't shit. We deserve better." She pointed at Faith. "She *deserves* better.

This place is probably why she gets these random stomach bugs"

I couldn't argue with her, but I felt a pang, deep down: I wasn't man enough to provide the kind of life my own family deserved. The kind of life my father gave his family.

"I'm tired of my husband doing somebody else's job in someone else's home. You want to build that swing set?" Megan pointed at her phone. "With this kind of money, we can get a nice down payment on a house. At the very least a rental that doesn't stink like cockroach shit. One with a garage, maybe? You can put in a home gym? Everybody's doing that now."

I'd gained fifteen pounds since COVID had started. I'd run sparingly and seen Frank twice. The gyms were closed. And we didn't have the money for home equipment. I was reduced to shadow-boxing in the driveway and three mile runs whenever I could squeeze out the time. Just the thought of getting real work in was a carrot worth diamonds.

"How long is the contract?" I asked.

Faith snuggled against my neck. Her tiny eyelashes tickled my carotid.

September 2020

Megan was in El Paso. I trained in the home gym. Mom basically lived with us. Faith was getting bigger by the day. We all had our own rhythms.

The COVID money allowed us to get a house with a garage, where I scrounged together a boxing gym with the rainy day money I had left from Walmart.

It was mostly stuff I found on Offerup: a rusty heavy bag covered in duct tape, a double-end bag that was just a soccer ball taped to two bungee cords, a speedbag that constantly deflated. It was a hack job, but it at least kept the training within arm's reach. Frank crawled out of his hole, finally. It was a sunny morning when we got the call that changed everything.

Faith wailed in her playpen as the bell clamored on my phone.

I dripped buckets, and a large slick of sweat bloomed on the cement around the heavy bag. Frank sat on a milk crate smoking his cigar, his mask pulled down low as he chewed the end of his cigar. He pulled it from his mouth and spat out pieces of tobacco onto the garage floor. There was already a brownish nest surrounding his feet.

"Coach, you're cleaning that later," I said circling the bag. Shooting jabs and straight rights.

I caught Frank's incredulous eye as I circled. He threw his cigar down and ground it into smithereens. "And, you're still dropping that right hand, dammit."

He pushed himself up from his knees and walked slowly over to the broom wheezing like a train. He grabbed the broom off the wall and said, "And fully rotate that hip."

A car rolled by. The driver and passenger peered into the garage with masks on and the windows up. Their eyes were delirious with fear.

Frank coughed and swept the pile out the garage door and onto the lawn.

"And your COVID test was negative?" I said.

Frank pulled his mask halfway up as he lumbered back with the broom.

Faith made hissing sounds in her playpen. She shot tiny little jabs into the air.

"Weren't no COVID," Frank coughed, and spat. "Just a head cold."

The bell on my phone dinged loudly. Frank sat back down heavily on the crate and breathed with his hand on his knee.

One of my neighbors jogged by with a mask on and waved. I waved back. It was as close as I got to anyone else other than Frank, Megan, and Mom. I hadn't seen the inside of a ring in over six months. I missed the give and take of canvas. The shock and fluid of a good exchange: slipping a jab, shooting a hook to the body, rolling the counter, shooting an uppercut on the way up. I missed the feeling of taking a good punch: the ring in the ears, the pang of pain that could wake you up more than smelling salts, the focus of all focus, it was fucking sublime.

Frank's phone rang.

He fumbled at his pockets and pulled his phone out.

Faith let out a short howl and then frowned.

Frank nodded at her as he took a few gulps of breath in.

"Frown means brown," Frank said. He flipped his phone and put it to his ear. "Yea?"

Faith started pulling at her pants, and before I could stop her, she squeezed it out.

"Too late," Frank said quickly. Then back to his conversation

It was a raw green mix.

I picked Faith up under her arms and held her at arm's length to go to the bathroom. She'd just started potty training.

She put both hands on the side of my face. And a soft sound like a hoot came from her lips.

"What's that baby?"

"I poo," she said. She pushed it out of her mouth like she was blowing out a candle. Her eyes widened.

Another car rolled by. Frank talked on the phone. His voice, was a murmur. The garage glowed golden. Faith stared up at me, her eyes glorious. A wide smile on her lips. A trail of wet poo ran down her leg.

I took a small sip of air and said, as gently as I'd ever said any words in my life, "Say it again baby, please. For Dada?"

She pointed down at her work. "I, poo."

It was her first sentence. I hugged her and squeezed her against my sternum, right above the solar plexus, the throne of the heart, and felt joy.

I looked at Frank.

His eyes were wide too.

"Can you fucking believe it!?" I asked him. "My baby said her first sentence!"

Frank held his phone out like he was showing me a brick of gold.

"Gym's back open," he said, slack-jawed.

My heart fluttered.

Faith breathed against my chest.

"What about Faith?"

Frank leaned forward and sighed out heavily.

"Ask him in person."

"Eye Cream!" Faith screamed as we passed McDonald's.

"Later, baby," I said, chewing my fingernail. I didn't know if I'd get a hard no or a soft no. I didn't know what I'd do if it was either. I had to spar. And Lion's was the only gym in town that was allowing it.

When we walked in, the gym was empty. A sanctified quiet lay over it. The lights lit up the ring in a holy glow. The frayed canvas lifted in praying fingers. The wall of yellowed pictures of old boxers were like hallowed relics. The old, dusty championship belts hanging around the tops of the walls were the cloths of saints. The ceiling was still a patchwork of rust. The heavy bags hung from the ceiling from still-rusted chains and were still covered in duct tape. The benches where I'd done and un-done my hand-wraps more times than I could remember sat as still as confessionals. The bag in the corner where Frank and I first started working was a battered jewel. It was all intact; the cathedral remained even after the apocalypse.

I knocked on Greg's door. Faith stumbled around the edge of the ring.

Greg had his mask on and put his hand up as he signed a statement on his desk. "Six feet."

His glasses slid down the bridge of his nose. He'd grown out a silver beard and was a little pudgier in the cheeks. But his bulldog eyes were still sharp.

"You brought your daughter in?" he asked.

"Yea."

My heart skipped as I heard Faith climbing up the stairs to the ring. I could just go back to my home gym. I could train there. It'd be fine. Me and Frank and Faith. We could make it work in the garage.

But it wasn't the same.

I swallowed a ball of spit and licked the crust off of my lips. I pulled my voice out of my belly and tried to say it deep and convicted, but it came out like a squeak. "Can I ask a favor?"

Greg sat back in his chair and crossed his arms over his belly. "What?"

"So, Megan's travel-nursing in El Paso, and up to this point, it's been fine training in the home gym. But..."

"Keep going."

"But I know you're letting guys spar again, and you're the only gym opening its doors again in Austin. So, I just wanted to know if I could bring Faith with me. We'll stay out of the way, I promise. Back corner."

The canvas rumbled as Faith bounced around on it.

Greg looked around me and chuckled. "People used to bring their kids here all the time. COVID ain't changing that."

Faith made hissing noises.

"Yea, I know. But, we'd be here a lot," I said.

"How many times a week?" Greg asked.

"Four or five."

Greg sat forward and crossed his hands on his desk. He looked around me to the ring. I hadn't heard Faith in a few moments. The ring hadn't thundered. It was silent as the eye of a hurricane. Greg's brow furrowed. I turned around quickly. Faith had dropped her pants and was shitting in the middle of the ring.

"Faith!" I yelled. I turned to go.

"Let her go!" Greg yelled. "Keep going baby! Good job!" Greg put up two thumbs. Faith cracked a wide, snaggle-toothed smile. "Just started potty training?" Greg asked softly.

"Today, actually," I said.

"Fun times," he said.

Faith cooed. "I, Pooooooo."

Greg became gruff again. "You're cleaning it up. I don't want a single speck of shit on that canvas. Got it?"

"Got it."

"And she does it again, that's it. Back to the home gym."

"Got it."

"This ain't a day care. Got it?"

"Got it."

"Back corner."

"Got it."

The week of Halloween, October 28th, I got a fight in.

Everybody was itching to start fighting again, so the matches got made quickly.

Unlucky me, I was rusty as shit. I got caught with hook after hook after hook. I'd let my right hand drop constantly. The last one nearly dropped me, but I managed to suffer through the final round and save it from being a complete ass-kicking.

Frank undid my hand-wraps in silence after the fight was over. It was a unanimous decision.

"Take a week off. Meet me in the gym next week," he grumbled.

He left the arena with his hands in his pockets and a wheeze on his breath.

A week later we were back in the gym and doing heavy bag work.

Frank hugged the heavy bag with one hand and held a mitt in his other. In the middle of the round, I dropped my right hand and he slapped me in the face, as hard as he could.

"I told you to keep your fucking hands up!"

I hadn't been slapped in a boxing gym like that in over fifteen years, since Dad, but the moment Frank's mitt hit my face, I felt as useless as I had at sixteen. I wanted to knock Frank's head in. I glanced around the gym and caught a few other boxers glancing back at me. A blow to the ego is hell at sixteen, but in my mid-thirties it was something else.

Frank's eyes burned ridiculous with frustration. He pointed at the clock. "Keep fucking going! Round's not over!"

The bag in front of me swung like a duct-taped metronome.

"And don't worry about them!" Frank hollered, sweeping his mitted hand around the gym, "so, I slapped you in the face, keep your fucking hands up!"

Frank's eyes were furious, but I wanted to slug him. I put my hands up. I wasn't some dopey college student; I was a father with a kid. It was nearly a war crime to hit a man like that. I wanted to unleash it on him.

But then, Faith's voice cut through the fury, sharp as a warm knife.

"Daddy, go!" Faith squeaked as she sat on a broken heavy bag laying behind me. She pointed at the clock; thirty seconds left in the round.

"Work, Daddy! Work!"

Frank shook his head and slapped the bag with his mitt. "Let's fucking go, Thom!"

And the anger went from wildfire to focused flame. I shot an arcing left hook to the upper portion of the bag. Then the lower. Then the upper again, finishing it off. I kept my right hand glued to the side of my face.

"Good!" Frank said. "Work that again. Head-body-head."

I whipped shot after shot, forging fury into fortitude.

"This is how we win the next one. Simple shit. Good fundamentals!" Frank hollered.

CHAPTER 33:
THE SWING SET STORY

May 2021

I stared at the lumber, lost.

Megan was home from the road, finally, after three contracts in El Paso. We slept on opposite sides of the bed and there was a gulf between us, but, we'd paid off the cars. And the icing on the cake, we'd got Faith a pressure-treated wood swing set. It was my job to put it together, in mid-May. Austin was ablaze.

We hadn't smelled rain in months.

But I needed to lose the water, about ten pounds of it. I pulled the drenched towel out of my back pocket and crouched over the 4x4's. Megan had bought me a new DeWalt; it glowed school-bus yellow in the sun. I picked it up and hit the trigger to cut another 4x4 as the patio door slid open. I let the saw whine its way to a metallic quiet as Faith ran past the grill towards me holding a splashing cup of lemonade in her hands.

"Daddy, I made you lemonade!" she yelled as the lemonade splashed over her wrists and arms.

She stopped in front of me smiling and held it up with both hands. She had a few suds in her curls; it smelled watermelon-y. She handed the cup to me as her hands shook. I put it to my lips and swallowed. The unmixed crystals were sharp and there was so much sugar in it that it burned my tongue.

"Is it good?" she asked.

Like horse piss.

"Best thing I've ever tasted," I said.

I saw every single tooth in her mouth as she smiled and put her hands in her pockets. She poked out her belly and rocked back and forth on her toes.

"Is it done *yet*, daddy?"

"Not yet, baby," I said.

"But, *When*, daddy?"

"Soon, baby."

"Well, Bob, how's it coming?" Megan sauntered up to me with her hands in her pockets. She looked at the wreckage in front of me: the pile of lumber and my saw. I hadn't even finished cutting the main beam yet and I'd been at it for almost two days: cut after misjudged cut.

The grill smoked as the charcoals warmed.

All of this felt so different. Megan being home. Sleeping in the same bed. Grilling for more than two. For months, it had been mostly just me and Faith:

One piece of chicken: for me. A hot dog: for Faith.

An ear of corn and some aparagus tucked in tinfoil: for me.

A cut-up apple wrapped in tinfoil with butter and cinnamon: for Faith.

"It's coming," I said, "how's corn shucking?"

"You want to show Daddy?" Megan said to Faith.

Faith held up her wrists. The tiny blonde strands from the ears of corn glowed on her caramel skin.

"Well look at you, baby!" I said. Faith smiled toothily.

"You got more cinnamon when you went to the store?" I asked.

"Yea, Faith reminded me."

Faith ran around the lumber as Megan got closer to me. The suds in Faith's hair bounced in a myriad of color.

"What shampoo did you use?" I asked Megan.

"The watermelon one," Megan said, raising an eyebrow.

"That one is hard to wash out of her hair. I told Mom to toss it. It gets all sudsy."

"Oh."

"But, I can take her to wash it out. Don't worry about it," I said.

I started to take my tool belt off. The lawnmower sputtered to a start at our neighbor, Bob's house. I needed to cut ours, too.

Megan put her hand on my shoulder. Her fingers felt alien. We hadn't touched much since she'd been home. She was preoccupied, somewhere else.

"I got her," she said, with a put-on softness.

"You sure?"

"Yea, I'll wash it out. I just—forgot."

I nodded.

"You'll pick it back up."

Faith had the end of an extension cord in her hand. She held the three pongs between her fingertips and made a hissing sound towards me and Megan.

"I'm a snake, Mommy," Faith said.

She hissed at Megan.

"Come here, baby," Megan said, "I'm going to wash the suds out of your hair."

Faith pulled away and hissed again at Megan.

"No! Daddy!"

Megan turned to me, defeated.

"Baby, you want Daddy to finish the swing set so you can swing on it right?" I said.

Faith let the head of the snake go limp.

"*Yesss*," Faith said.

"So, Daddy needs to stay outside and finish. You see all the work I have to do?" I said.

Faith dropped the head of the snake into the grass and dropped her shoulders.

"But Mommy doesn't do it right."

"Faith. That's enough. Mommy's going to do it right this time, I promise," I said.

Megan picked Faith up quickly, and one of Faith's long curls got caught in her armpit and got pulled.

"Oww! Mommy."

"Sorry, baby."

Megan walked past the grill, holding Faith tightly with two hands as Faith made a hissing noise at me and mimed her hand to look like a snake.

I looked back down at the pile at my feet. I still had to spar that night. I was sweating. That was good, but I couldn't lose too much and spar dehydrated; it was a tightrope walk. I took the jug of water beside the lumber to my lips and swigged down what I imagined half an ounce was. The water was hot. The jug had sat in the sun for too long. I'd wasted a lot of time, cut after misjudged cut.

We had two steaks. A hot dog. Three ears of corn. And an apple.

We ate and then posted up on the back porch. We had a set of lawn furniture that Megan had just bought. The cushions were taut and uncomfortable.

It was getting close to dark, and a humid breeze blew through Austin. The sky was purple and gentle. The clouds peach and popcorn. I'd strung up a line of amber-glowing globe lights from the edge of the house to the oak tree in the back. It bathed the pile of lumber in an amber glow.

I'd managed to get the main beam cut, and a few more.

I held a cold glass bottle of Topo in my hand and had the chair reclined to the back as Faith laid on my belly.

I took a sip as Megan pulled the sliding glass door open softly.

Faith shifted in her little ball on my stomach.

I put my finger to my lips.

Megan nodded and sat down in the chair right beside me. She was in shorts and a tank top and held a Whiteclaw in her hand. She'd just taken a shower and her jet-black hair was pulled into a bun. Since she'd been home she'd been running more. Her arms and legs were more defined, and I could see the muscles in her quads and calves now.

"Starting to look like a boxer," I said.

She took a sip and looked down at her legs, sighing out deeply, and then she started sobbing.

"Meg?"

"I've been gone too long."

"What do you mean?" I asked.

"I missed out. Faith's running around the house now. She's talking in sentences. What the fuck was I doing in El Paso?"

"You were working," I said.

Megan sniffed. She'd put cocoa butter all over her body, and her skin glistened in the amber glow of the globe lights. Her tears glittered.

"We haven't gotten any time to be a family, Thom."

"Have you seen the families around here?" I said, "all locked in; they fucking hate each other. I'm surprised nobody on our block isn't on *The First 48.*"

Megan smirked. Faith shifted.

"It feels like we're arguing," Megan said quietly, and took a long sip of her Whiteclaw.

I didn't say anything.

We stared at the swing set, unfinished, but not in shambles; the bones were there.

"Are we okay?" she asked.

I took a sip of my Topo.

"We're okay, Meg."

My throat burned with the fizz.

She put her hand on my shoulder. I looked at her. She looked at me. It felt different. Her eyes didn't have the same magic they used to. Faith shivered.

"I'm sorry, baby," Megan said.

"Hopefully there's not another wave." I sipped and looked back at the pile of lumber. I muscled my next words over a burning ball of fizz going down my throat, "Would you go back out there?"

Megan brought the can to her lips where it lingered as a crowd of grackles screeched across the sky.

"Maybe."

The grackles circled in the darkening sky and then, they moved upwards like shards of black glass thrown high. They lifted higher and higher until gravity grabbed them and they came crashing towards the earth in the terror of weight.

My phone vibrated on the tiny glass table between our two chairs. It was 8:30.

"I gotta go," I said.

"Where?"

"Sparring,"

"Thom, no."

She lifted her foot and crossed the gap between our chairs to touch my leg with her big toe.

"I wanted to spend time together."

Her toenail clipped a splinter I'd gotten that day.

"Fight's almost here."

I pulled my leg away, out of her reach.

She lifted her toe away, crossed her feet, and downed her White-claw completely.

"You have to take her," I said, looking down at Faith.

She'd put her thumb in her mouth, and as she slept, she frowned.

CHAPTER 33:
THE HARD LOSS

July 2021

Megan hit the road again in late May.

It was a unanimous decision.

And my fight came quicker than I'd expected.

My body was fluid. In my mind, I was going in as fresh as I'd ever been. I was getting closer to forty but my legs felt spry. I bounced up the stairs to the ring.

It was a back-and-forth fight. First round, I was a shark. Second round, I floundered. The bell rang at the end of the second, and I slumped into the stool. Frank was in my face like a hound.

"All right, that's one to one. You let up in there, what the fuck happened!?" he barked through his black cloth mask.

"I lost my wind, coach," I said. My mouthpiece was full of bloody saliva.

"Find it!" Frank rubbed my headgear and lowered his mask slightly. He put his thumb to his nose—Frank always tucked a pocket of Vaseline up there before every fight—and then wiped it around the circumference of my headgear. "Look, you're keeping your guard, well. We're not gonna lose because we're sloppy, but, you're gonna have to be fucking dog-ass this round, Thom," he said.

"Go, Daddy, Go!" Faith hollered, bouncing on Mom's knee in a chair ringside. Megan wouldn't make it back in time. She'd started another contract in Amarillo. It was a long drive.

"You know what dog-ass means?" Frank said, his brown eyes

urgent. "Spit!"

He held a red plastic bucket in front of my face. I spat out bloody mucus.

"I don't know, coach."

He got down on a knee. It popped. He wheezed. "It means you can't just win this round, Thom. You're gonna have to eat him alive. Leave nothing! Head-body-head!"

The crowd clapped and whistled. The ref motioned us out of our corners.

Faith howled.

I pushed myself to my feet.

Frank's voice cut through all the noise,

"Dog-ass, Thom. Dog!"

I stepped forward out of the corner and bounced on my toes. My legs felt like concrete, my feet felt like stones. The bounce had been sucked out of them. I turned to Frank, but he'd disappeared down the stairs already. My heart beat like a throttled child. I didn't have anything left. That dog-ass spirit in me felt like a puppy. I turned back to the ref. He stared at the clock. I'd have to brawl this guy. I'd have to. My opponent looked at me. He had a cut on his nose that glistened as it dripped on the canvas. His black jersey was soppy and stuck to his body. My skull pulsed in my headgear. I'm sure his did, too. We were both exhausted. The bell cranked up to a shrill ding.

"Last round," the ref said. "Touch gloves."

We touched our gloves quickly.

The white glow of lights above the ring erased the small, socially distanced crowd, but the last thing I saw was Faith. A tiny mickey mouse mask covered her mouth but her eyes were wide and excited. She clapped her hands wildly as Mom held her perched on her knee. But there was no Megan. She hadn't been to a single fight of mine during COVID. But, for the first time, it was noticeable. Megan had gotten the time off to come home for it.

Megan got home thirty minutes after my fight ended.

Faith stayed at Mom's after the fight. I wasn't beat up too bad, but when the garage door opened and I pulled in beside Megan's Mazda I got nauseous and my heart skipped a few beats.

I walked into the kitchen and she was cutting onions and crying.

"So, you're still alive?" she said: sharp, sarcastic, mirthful.

She'd missed a fight that I'd been close to winning. And she didn't give a shit about it. The best thing she could come up with for a greeting was to try to chop me down. And I wasn't going to feed it. It had gotten to be a habit of hers, to come home with a sour attitude and an axe to grind.

"Seriously, Megan?" I dropped my bags and turned upstairs.

"Thom," she said, dropping the knife and rushing over to me, putting her arm on my shoulder. "I'm just kidding."

The only real thing she had for me was sarcasm.

Frank and I sat on a bench in the back of the gym a few mornings later. Frank chewed on a cigar. In the corner, the old Mexican, Edwin, worked at a bag by himself.

I wrapped my hands as Faith ran around the outside of the ring, waving at me as she circled.

"How's things at home?" Frank asked, fishing for a cigar. "Where the hell is it?" he said, searching his pockets.

"I don't know," I said. I took a deep breath in as Faith circled. And circled.

Frank's zippo clicked loudly as he lit his cigar.

"We argue, but it's not even an argument, it's just distance," I said.

The bell rang. And the old man found a tire in the corner and dropped to it.

"You and Megan?" Frank spat out a piece of his cigar into a trashcan filled with crumpled water bottles.

"Three days straight, we barely talked. I slept on the couch." I said as Faith stopped at the edge of the ring on the other side. She put her hands on the stairs and started to climb. "Faith, you know that's a no," I said.

"I want to go!"

"What did I say!"

She shrunk and climbed back down.

I felt stretched.

"She's gone now, right?" Frank said, staring at the man in the corner. The bell rang. Edwin rose slowly and moved grimly back to the bag and began again. He threw plodding, thudding punches. Sweat flung from his head, shoulders, and hands. His silverish mop swung water-logged in the coarse light.

"Left this morning," I said.

Frank clasped his hands in front of him and clucked.

He turned to me, a wheeze on his lips. "What do you think it is?"

"She probably wants me to stop fighting."

"I've stared down that barrel before," Frank said.

"But, the thing that pisses me off, she said she'd be there. The fuck. And then, she's all jokey when I come inside.

"I mean, I know she just wants me to go to school and get a better job than just being Mr. Mom, but she doesn't get it. And maybe I'm delusional, but, it's more than just a routine or a hobby for me. She doesn't understand how much I love this shit. She never has."

Faith ran to a heavy bag, smacking it with her fists. Her wrists bent as she punched.

I put my hands out. "Straight hands, baby. No bend."

Frank held his cigar out in front of him, staring at the burnt end.

"Time waits on no man, Thom. Look at him." He pointed at Edwin in the corner.

The bell rang.

The round over, Edwin retreated to his corner and sat on a tire. He dripped in rivers. He stared hollowly at the cement.

"You know his story?" Frank said.

"Nope," I said.

"Edwin was an amateur when I was. I sparred him a few times. He fought at 166. Had a few fights...you know what his record was?"

"No."

Frank made an "O" with his hand.

"Never?"

"Not one win. 0-5."

"So, he stopped competing?"

Frank shook his head. "That ain't the point."

The bell rung.

Edwin got up and stepped back to the bag and began throwing punches like a buffalo pushing against a fence.

"What is it then?"

The heavy bag echoed: *Doosh. Doosh. doosh.*

"He kept coming here."

"And?"

"That's it." Frank frowned at me, pity in his eyes. "Get it?"

"So the lesson is do what I love and lose my wife? Or lose what I love and keep my wife?"

Frank shook his head. "No. The Lesson is, if you can do something you love, do it. But don't forget that life ain't just one thing," He nodded at Edwin. "He had a wife and a kid, too, just like you do."

"And?"

"Gone. Both of them. Hit by a drunk driver. Baby hadn't even walked yet."

The bell rang. Edwin retreated back to his tire. The bag swung like a lynched body.

"The clock's always ticking, Thom. Life ain't about *what* you choose, it's about *why* you choose. You have to know *why* you're choosing things, and the things you stand to lose *when* you choose things. Because you always lose *something*. Even if you make the exact right decision, something else has gotta go."

Faith ran over and tapped my leg, pointing at the clock.

"Daddy, work?"

"A little longer, baby," I said. "Time to rest."

"And then ring?" She pointed at the ring.

"Yes, baby. Daddy's got to shadowbox."

I pulled her in close to me and hugged her. I kissed the top of her head and got a whiff of the kiwi-smelling shampoo in her curls.

I looked at Edwin.

He nodded at me, his eyes as black as caskets.

Then, the bell rung.

CHAPTER 34:
FRANKIE'S GOT A BOO-BOO

October 2023

It was 2:17 in the morning—a few weeks before my ninth fight. I'd had a long layover between fights, but I didn't feel rusty.

Faith and Megan snored beside me and I heard a whirring sound like a tattoo gun. I rolled over as my phone vibrated across the bedside table. Faith snorted and cuddled up to my back, draping her arm over my ribs. Megan snored with her back to us. She'd finally come home from the road for good. And we slept in the same bed, but, Faith was always the island between us.

I picked the phone up as it buzzed in my hands. The caller ID said: Mom.

I got a dark feeling.

I rolled back over, pushing Faith gently to her side, and tapped Megan on the shoulder. She shrugged me off and murmured, "Maybe in the morning."

I pushed her slightly harder.

She rolled over quickly and hissed, "What?!"

It felt like a knife.

"Mom's calling me," I said.

Megan sighed deeply. Faith snuggled closer to me.

"What is it?" Megan asked.

"I don't know."

I got up slowly, but Faith grumbled.

"Thom don't wake her, please," Megan whispered.

"What do you want me to do? I gotta get up. Who knows why she's calling?"

"Goddammit," Megan whispered. "I've got to get up in two hours."

"I don't know what to tell you."

"Just go."

I closed the door behind me as Faith started wailing.

"Hey Mom, what's up?"

"Why's she crying?" Mom asked.

"I had to go out of the room to talk to you."

"Tell Megan to give her some warm milk with a little bit of vanilla. I left some in the fridge," Mom said.

"I don't think Megan would take a gold bar from me right now."

"Ya'll arguing?"

"It is what it is."

Mom sighed. "So anyways, you won't believe who I'm looking at."

"Who?" I asked.

"Frank," Mom said.

"The fuck?"

Mom sighed again. "I'm not supposed to tell you this, but he's got some heart problems."

"I'm coming up there," I said.

Mom relayed the message to Frank. "He's coming up here," she said, her voice far-away.

"No the hell he isn't!" Frank barked.

"Why not?" Mom barked back.

"Because I said so!" Frank said.

"You're a goddamn mule," Mom said.

"Just tell him," Frank said, "I'll see him when all of this is over with."

A bell dinged in the ER somewhere.

"Frank, you idiot," Mom said, "you're not walking out of here tomorrow. You're getting surgery and then rehab."

"I'll see him after rehab, Deb."

"That'll be weeks, Frank. Don't act like that."

"I'm not kidding, Deb."

Mom returned. "You hear that, Go'bay?"

Faith wailed in the bedroom.

"Yeah, I heard it," I said. "So, what happened?"

"Well, they did an EKG and found something. Then they took him to the Cath lab and found something else."

My heart felt like a wind-tossed butterfly.

Faith howled.

"What else?" I asked.

I took a deep breath in through my nose and held it at the top.

Mom sighed on the other end. "I really shouldn't be telling you this, but," Mom paused, and then said, "four blockages."

My heart pinched my trachea. I had to force the words out.

"Like Dad," I said.

Mom sniffed.

"Yes."

I pictured Frank crawling in his apartment. Pulling himself across the moldy linoleum of his bathroom. Grabbing the door jamb. Taking a moment to take some rattling breaths in through his nose. Sweat dripping like he was in the heat of the twelfth round. Down the homestretch and barely able to catch his breath. The black curtains closing in on either side. His heart pumping like a plugged firehose. Frank looking into the darkness of his small living room. The worn-down recliner. The couch from Goodwill that smelled like cat piss. The picture that sat near his door on the countertop of his kitchen of him with the only son that still called him. Both of them smiling at an amateur tournament years ago in El Paso.

"Put me on speaker," I said.

"I'm putting him on speaker," Mom said to Frank.

"Goddammit—" Frank barked.

An alarm blared in the ER and a voice came over the PA: "*Trauma one, ETA five minutes.*"

"Gotta go, Go'bay," Mom said. "I'm giving Frank my phone so ya'll can talk."

In the background, alarms dinged and whistled. Frank breathed in raspily. Doctors dictated nearby in sharp murmurs.

Frank's breathing paused.

A frantic bell rang out, suffocating all sound. It was high-pitched. Musical. And bloated with anxiety. I knew it. I'd heard it before. The intercom rang again: *Code Blue, ED, Bed three. Code blue, ED, Bed three.*

I shook as I held the phone. An orb of chilled sweat rolled down my temple touching every pore.

"Frank, you there?"

"Yea. Still here," he rasped.

"I'm coming up there."

"No, Tommy...stay at home."

Faith banged on the door. Screaming for me.

"I gotta come see you."

Megan's voice was sharp and barely controlled behind the door. "Do you want a spanking?"

The code blue bell rang loudly in my ear.

Faith wailed louder and banged harder. I held the door shut, as she yanked and kicked. Her feet echoed throughout the dark hallway as I listened to the ringing note of death.

CHAPTER 35:
SILENCE

I drove in silence to the hospital. I felt like gravity was starting to let me go. I felt too light. Too scared. Too alone. I had to open the windows. The air was heavy with mesquite; smoky and thick. When I pulled into the parking garage, I found a parking spot and shut the car off. I sat in my car and closed my eyes. I hadn't seen what it'd looked like when Dad died. I didn't know what a man's face looked like close to death. I wanted to nod off; I wanted to feel that cleansing, euphoric hug.

By the time I got inside, they'd already moved Frank to his bed in the ICU.

"Hey honey," Mom said, walking out of the double doors of the ICU still in her navy scrubs. She lifted her hands out wide. I embraced her as a man walked quickly behind her. His skin was just a shade darker than Frank's, but his eyebrows were just as bushy and he had Frank's large nose. He had a salt and pepper crew cut and tattoos spanning the length of both arms. He strode by with his hands in his pockets and glared at mom.

I let her go and turned and looked at him.

He stopped; his eyes were sharp as bore sights. He took one hand out of his pocket and pointed at her.

"You've got no right!"

Mom stepped around me. "It wasn't my fucking choice!" Mom said, pointing back.

He stepped toward her. I stepped up and put my right foot back, just off center, and bladed my body as much as I could.

He stopped and dropped his arms at his sides. A mix of frustration and resignation.

"You've got no fucking clue who he is," he said. He stared at me and Mom like we were just two dumb cows walking our way to slaughter.

"Fuck it. Have him," he said. "We were all done a long time ago. I came here. I saw him. I did as much as he deserves." He turned on his heels and walked out of the waiting room.

I turned to Mom. "What the hell?"

"Well—"

A nurse appeared from the double doors. "Deb?" she said.

Mom whipped around. "Yea?"

"He's rolling back in 15 minutes."

Mom reached her hand back and tugged my shirt. "Let's go."

Frank's room smelled strongly of bleach. The wall was an assortment of cannisters and tubing neatly arranged. The monitor above his bed was black and blank. A metal pole stood with tiny pumps arrayed all over. Bags of fluid hung from the top of it. The middle of the room was a wide, empty space waiting for Frank to arrive.

Mom stood near the doorway and leaned on a large, rolling chest full of drawers. She talked to Frank's nurse congenially.

"So, as you know, as his MPOA we'll need consents to give him blood—" She looked at Mom.

Mom twirled her finger. "I know the drill, Lex."

"Deb, you know I have to read this to you."

"I know, I know."

I sat in a chair near the window and looked at the floor as they continued. The linoleum had tiny dark veins running through it. Like the memory of all the blood that had dripped out of patients, onto the floor, and had become part of the hospital itself. I looked past Mom and Alexis, and into the hallway. A pair of nurses walked by laughing.

My phone vibrated in my pocket.

Megan: *How's he doing?*

Me: *He's not out yet.*

She didn't respond.

"So, in case he needs another transfusion, we'll need your signature," Alexis said to Mom, as she read a piece of paper.

Mom took the pen, swiped her signature, and handed the clipboard back to Alexis. Alexis patted Mom on the shoulder and said lowly, "I gotta go. Haven't charted shit all day. He should be back any minute."

"Okay, girl," Mom said.

Alexis gave me a professional smile and left.

"So he made you his medical power of attorney?"

Mom pushed herself off the rolling chest. "Yea," she sighed. "Few months ago. He's been getting sicker. I'm sure you've noticed."

"Yea."

Mom walked over to me; she smelled like a mix of musk and perfume. Her eyes were bloodshot and her makeup was doing overtime.

"I gotta get some sleep," she said.

She put her hand on my shoulder, and a cascade of hot fear rushed through me like an overwhelmed electrical socket.

"Go home, Ma," I said. "I'm here."

It was all the effort I could give to sandbag my tears.

Mom looked at me pitifully. "I'll stay 'till he gets settled in."

She wrapped her arms around my head and hugged me close

"He's going to be fine, Go'bay."

The door opened. I peeked around Mom. She turned her head. I felt her stomach shaking against my cheek.

"Just going to turn on the monitor," Alexis said. She tiptoed in, pressed a screen, and the monitor flashed on.

The room was empty and quiet one moment. And then, it was a sprawl of people, machines, and finally a bed. Frank lay motionless as they wheeled him in. Then, there were the sounds. The nurses and doctors stood around the bed chirping quickly. A tiny monitor beeped in his bed. There were miles and miles of lines and cords all over his body. He had a tube jutting out of his mouth and his eyes were taped shut. He had tubes coming out of his chest with bursts of blood flowing out and up to cannisters on the walls. And in the middle of his chest, running from the top of his sternum down to his plexus, a weeping incision. It glistened with fluid.

"How were his gases?" A nurse.

"How's his urine output been?" Another.

"He lost a lot of blood," one of the doctors said.

"What's his last blood pressure?" a nurse.

"We gave a few units." Another doctor.

Mom piped up. "How much?"

The doctor turned and nodded at her.

"Hey Deb—" he put his hand to his scrub cap— "we had to give him seven units."

For the first time, Mom's face slackened. She lost the professional mask. Her mouth dropped slightly, and I could see her teeth.

"Oh," Mom said.

The doctor nodded gravely.

Everyone nodded gravely.

I felt a bird in my throat. Kicking and scratching and flapping. "Is that bad?" I blurted.

The doctor turned to me.

"That's my son," Mom said. "He's one of Frank's fighters."

The doctor paused. "It's not good." He turned back to Mom and started talking.

"We'll have to do H&H's every thirty," the doctor continued.

My phone vibrated in my pocket. "For what?" I piped up again.

"More bleeding," the doctor said shortly.

They kept talking as I stood up and looked at Frank's feet and hands, which didn't twitch or move unless someone hit the bed. A car revved on the street below: low, long, and horrible. Like it was giving its last breaths at the end of a bloody brawl.

The room finally cleared and it was just me, Mom, Alexis, and Frank.

The monitor above his bed was a moving rainbow of different squiggly lines. Each with its own rhythm of squiggles: some tall and spiking, some short and square. The one in the middle was red and spiked with every heartbeat. I looked at the numbers: 109/60.

"Is that good?" I asked Alexis. I held Frank's hand. A small pink probe with a red light on the end of it was wrapped around his finger. It felt like a BandAid in my grasp. I gripped his hand, tightly.

She turned around from her computer. "It's fine," she said. She ran her hand through her hair. A massive tower stood beside her. They'd come in and out with bags of blood since he'd gotten there. Nurse after nurse. Doctor after doctor. A small pocket of bright red blood bloomed from one of the tubes coming out of Frank's chest.

My phone buzzed. I took it out of my pocket with my free hand and looked.

Megan: *When are you coming home?*

Me: *We're not out of the storm yet.*

Megan: *She's losing her shit. I need you.*

Me: *I want to be here when his eyes open.*

She didn't respond. I turned and looked at Mom as she sat in the sofa near the window; she shook her head and crossed her legs.

"You need to go home," she said.

I grasped Frank's hand tighter.

"But, aren't they waking him up soon?" I said. I looked over at Alexis. "Right?"

She gave me a pitying smile. "Well, the doctor has to come assess him first."

Frank's face twitched.

"Hey coach, it's me," I said. As I leaned closer I could still smell the faint smoke of his cigar on his skin. Steam appeared and disappeared in his tube. His mouth curled.

My pocket buzzed; I didn't look.

"What's that?" Mom said, urgently. Her voice sharp.

The monitor behind me rang loudly and rapidly.

Frank wretched forward and started coughing. Bells dinged and howled. Frank clenched my hand tightly. His eyes opened wide.

Mom rushed to the side of the bed, pushing up against me, and then something popped in his chest. I looked down at his tubes and bright red blood gushed from the tube that had been bleeding from his wound. I turned to the monitor. A phantom sun ray zoomed in through the window, and I had to squint.

And then I saw it, on the monitor, the red number: 50/30.

"I need a crash cart!" his nurse yelled out.

"Uh." It was all I had in my mouth. My heart froze like it'd lost all voltage. I couldn't breathe. A sudden block of concrete slammed over my vocal cords. Every pore opened and let loose an ocean of sweat. An engine roared in my ears. I gripped Frank's hand.

Mom grabbed some gauze and pressed them hard against Frank's open wound. Bright red blood streamed over her porcelain hand as it seemed like Frank's chest was going to crack open. The tubing shook. Alexis hit a button at the back of the bed. More dinging. Nurses rushed in, Doctors, too. A massive grey cart the color of a tombstone with an assortment of drawers was rolled into the room.

I got pushed out of the way.

"We gotta get him to OR," a doctor said.

The room became a chaotic menagerie. I stood there as they unplugged tube after tube from the wall and then attached those tubes to other tubes. The tube that connected to his ventilator flopped like a slug. The monitor above his head went blank as the nurses wrenched it from the wall and put it on the bed. Other things were tossed all over Frank: Charts. Cords. Monitors. A rainbow of scrubbed people flooded the room and situated themselves around different parts of the bed.

Someone pushed the tower of blood.

Someone, the ventilator.

Someone, a pole of IVs.

Someone, the bed itself: Frank.

And out the door they went in a gaggle of sharp, chirpy speech and Frank disappeared out of sight. As he moved down the hall and disappeared, he became the sound of a bell.

We waited in Frank's empty room as Mom rubbed my back.

I sat and picked my fingernails.

The door to Frank's room opened and Alexis stepped in and closed the door softly behind her.

It was dark outside and the only light in the room came from the dim overhead light where Frank's bed had been.

"So," she said, breathing out heavily, "he's in the OR. Should be back soon."

"He's alive?" I asked.

Alexis sighed, "Yes," she said, "he's alive, but he had to get another surgery."

Mom patted my back.

"Thank you, Alexis," she said.

Alexis nodded. She pulled the massive cart that looked like a tombstone out of the room and the door closed in a hush behind her.

Mom shook me.

"Your fight's Friday, right?"

My phone buzzed.

I looked up at her and was ashamed of myself. All that commotion and the only thing I could do for Frank was stand in the way. I wasn't a nurse, but damn I could've done something.

"Two days," I said.

I had weigh-ins the next morning.

I drove up North Lamar with my shirt off and the wind blowing into the cabin. My sauna suit lay limply in the back seat. The last droplets of sweat were finally evaporating.

I'd made weight.

My phone buzzed in the cup holder; it was Mom. I crossed two lanes of traffic and turned into the parking lot of the Chinatown strip mall. I pulled into a spot facing the street and took a deep breath in before I answered.

"How's he doing?"

"Good," Mom said, "recovering fine."

"How much blood did he lose?"

"Well," Mom said, sighing deeply, "a lot."

I put my hand on the steering wheel and tucked my phone against my shoulder, bending my ear to it, so I could pick at my nail beds.

"But, he's okay?"

"He'll be fine," she said.

I worked a piece of skin free.

"How'd weigh-in go?" Mom asked.

"Fine. 176. Like always."

A frantic beep pulsed on Mom's end.

"Hold on," Mom said, "I gotta talk to his nurse."

I bit my pinky nail and pulled it, ripping it off down to the quick.

Across the street at a BP, there was a familiar gaggle. Men and women with ashen faces smoking thin cigarettes with thin fingers and pale, haunted eyes. One guy was wearing a Billabong shirt tattered with holes. His jeans were covered in grease and ripped at the knees. His skin was a golden-ish color, like mine, but he was much older. The dead on him looked much more refined.

Mom hopped back on. "So, you still going to fight?" she asked.

The frantic beeping continued.

"Everything all right?" I asked.

"Yea, his IV is done," Mom said.

"Oh," I said.

"Who's gonna corner you?"

"I don't know," I said. "I'm gonna ask Greg."

I gulped.

"So there's no way Frank's gonna be able to make it?" I felt childish asking it. I knew the answer. I just wanted to hear it differently.

"Oh, Go'bay," Mom said sadly, "no, this is gonna take a long time."

Across the street, the troop dispersed. A single struggle on their minds; for them, the weight of the world boiled down to one animal urge, one vice.

I bent over the steering wheel and closed my eyes, thinking of Dad.

"Go'bay, you still there?" Mom asked.

Her voice crackled in my ear.

Another monitor beeped frantically on the other end, manic as the final bell.

CHAPTER 36:
TIME TO TAKE A SEAT, KID

November 2023

I stumbled back to the corner. My legs were all fluid, no bones. I made it to the ropes and grabbed them. I took deep breaths in through my nose as I tried to open up the tiny air sacs in my lungs, but it felt like the air I breathed in was bursting with needles.

"Turn around kid," a voice said.

A stool slid in front of me and I turned around and slumped down into it. My mouthpiece was a river.

"Spit out your mouthpiece," a gloved hand said. It extended its palm out to me and I did as I was told.

It came out of my mouth a glob.

Greg couldn't corner me. He had two other fighters fighting at the same time, so one of the officials put out a call to the coaches.

"It's 1-1," my coach said. He was a middle school English teacher in Austin. He had thick, wide-rimmed spectacles and a white bushy mustache. His face was a permanent shade of alcoholic red. He was USA-boxing licensed and all of his fighters had already lost.

So, he was my cornerman. He'd told me his name, but I'd forgotten it in the flurry, so I just called him coach.

"Got it, coach,"

I looked at the crowd and saw Megan bouncing Faith on her knee. Megan had her phone out, and she smiled at the screen.

Coach got down in front of me.

"Hey!" he said. He slapped my knee. "You listening?"

"Yes, coach," I said.

"It's going to be a brawl this last round," he said. "Pick your spots, but give it your all!"

"Yes, coach."

The bell dinged.

"Give him hell!" coach said.

The bell rang and there was no jab from either of us; no knocking on the front door: We rushed each other. The lights were bright and brilliant above us. I threw a hard uppercut, and his nose erupted in blood. He threw a hook. It caught me square in the temple of my headgear. My ear stung and vibrated like a cymbal and the wobble in my knees shook my DNA. The dark spots jumped in my eyes. But, I didn't go down. I saw a sliver of unprotected fabric on the right side of his abdomen, shot a hook at it. He grunted through his mouthpiece. I felt a rain of spit on my face. I shot another hook. Caught an uppercut. Shot a jab. Felt a thud. The sound of the crowd dulled. The referee became a shadow on the periphery. The lights dimmed. It was just me and him. Shot after shot. Blow after blow. Thudding. Hurting. Crunching. An engine revved in the distance. A monitor beeped. A mallet crashed against the side of my head. My knuckle touched something soft like a soul. The engine revved. I saw myself in the hospital bed, tube wriggling like a slug, choking me. My knuckle hit a hard surface, a chin maybe. Maybe an eye socket. All I saw was red. I closed my eyes. I didn't have enough breath to keep them open. Just enough to keep the heart beating. Start throwing. The brawl is within. The engine revved closer. Frank's blood spewed out of his chest. Dad lay dead on a gear shift. I drifted in and out.

Faith shrieked, "Go, Daddy, go!"

And then, black.

The smell of vomit was everywhere.

Bob Ross talked softly. I tried opening my eyes, but a sliver of light led to a splintering headache. I shut my eyes and covered my face.

"Fuck!"

"Thom?" Megan called from somewhere close. In the darkness I felt her sit down close to me and rub my leg.

"Keep your eyes closed, Thom."

"Ok."

"*Try not to paint with a heavy brush,*" Bob droned. "*Keep it light. Relaxed.*"

Bile rushed up and I rolled over and threw up whatever I had left in my stomach. Not much of anything. Just a corrosive acid pushing itself past my teeth, the taste of it lingered on my tongue like I had licked a cracked open battery.

"What the fuck happened?" I asked.

Megan stopped rubbing me and let her hand lay there like I was a patient: lightly, tenderly professional.

"You don't remember?" she asked.

"No.".

"You seemed fine when you stepped out of the ring. A little dazed, but nothing crazy. But then," Megan sniffed, "you got home and started throwing up. You wouldn't stop."

The thud, crunch, and crack of my opponent's punches came back in shards. "That guy was a fucking elephant."

"It was hard to watch."

I opened my eyes just enough to see an ugly shiver in her shadow

"Did I throw up all night or something?"

"Thom," Megan said, "it's been a whole day."

The drone of the TV bounced around my skull. Heavy, throbbing, and painful.

I closed my eyes.

"Can you turn the TV off?" I asked.

The light and sound from the TV vanished. Megan spoke from the darkness. "I can't do that again," she said.

"I can't talk about this now, Meg."

Megan started weeping. "Thom, do you know how hard that was for your daughter to see?"

"My head's about to split open."

"It fucking should, Thom!" Megan hissed. "Your daughter had to see that. You getting sick like that after a fight. It's traumatizing."

"Where is she?"

The pressure of her body against my leg released as she got up. Her voice came from above. "She's at your mom's. Dewey just left. He said you're probably out of the woods. It's a miracle he didn't have to take you in."

"Who stopped him?"

"I did," she said.

"Why?"

"I don't know. I should've let him take you in. But I got scared."

"Of what?"

"Prichard, Thom," she said. "If I took you in and they found something, there'd be no going back. I had it all mapped out, down to how big of a shift you'd have. I imagined you like Prichard: with a trach. Barely alive. I'd rather you die at home than rot in some hospital bed. So, I told Dewey unless you looked like you were going to die, you had to stay here."

"Well, I'm fine."

"Your mom did something, too."

"What?" I asked.

"She took a video."

"Of what?"

"Of you, Thom," Megan said, "the way you were."

"What for?"

"I don't know," Megan said, her voice was low.

Megan put a cold hand on my shoulder.

"I'm not going through that again, Thom. I can't. It'd kill me. It'd kill your daughter. Don't you get that? You've got two concussions now."

"Is Frank out of the hospital?"

"Did you hear me, Thom?" her voice was sharp.

"Yea, I fucking heard you. Where's Frank?"

"He got extubated yesterday."

"He's fine?"

A phone dinged.

I opened my eyes. A small, bright light appeared.

Megan walked quickly to the counter and grabbed her phone.

"Who's that?"

"Work," she said.

"Is Frank fine?"
"Yea, he's fine." The words sprinted out of her mouth.
The punches knocked around in my head for a long time.

CHAPTER 37:
THE WORST LOSS

Megan showered upstairs. Against the rhythmic swish of water, *With or Without You* played on repeat on a speaker in the bathroom.

I rolled over to the edge of the sofa. The living room was quiet. I opened my eyes slowly trying to ease off the pressure. I licked the vomit off my lips. I sat up and waited for the throbbing, and then the nausea, then the dizziness. I held my breath in a silent prayer. After a few moments of waiting for the storm, I pushed myself up to my feet, slowly. The blood in my skull swished around. The throbbing pain came in, but didn't crack me. I had enough equilibrium to stand. I stumbled forward and nearly fell, but I put my hands out, grabbed the counter, and kept myself from toppling. I took baby steps around to the kitchen as I gripped every edge of the counter I could. I just needed a glass of water and four ibuprofen. I stepped off the carpet onto the tile, and immediately a spike of pain shot up my foot. Followed by a recorded roar. I pulled my foot up quickly, and beneath it, a plastic dinosaur howled at me.

"Thom?" Megan called down.

I kicked Faith's toy away. It squealed like a beacon. "Fine," I called back. But, it was barely above I whisper. I didn't want to raise my voice. I'd made it this far without getting nauseous. I ambled to the cabinets by the sink. The light on the stove was set to low and cast a gentle glow. Coffee whistled in a pot on the stove and Megan's mug sat right beside it with the bag of turbinado and Oatmilk creamer standing like sentries. Her work badge laid on the counter, catching a glimmer. She was picking up night shifts again.

My stomach bubbled. I dove for the sink and spat yellow, acidic bile into some dirty cups and bowls of half-empty oatmeal. As I wiped my mouth and looked at my reflection in the window, something flashed in my periphery: bright and white. I looked down and saw Megan's phone on the counter.

Megan cut the water. I wiped my mouth and reached for her phone.

Her feet thudded on the floor upstairs.

She got a message: *Hey* 😊 *Is everything okay?*

And then a second one: *Get back to me when you can love* 😊

From: *Richie*.

I didn't know a Richie.

The glow from her phone made the blood in my head throb in waves. I didn't have a single thing left to throw up, but I got an ocean of saliva in my throat.

Who the fuck was Richie?

I stumbled out of the kitchen to the bottom of the stairs.

I started hoarse: "Megan?"

She was brushing her teeth.

"Megan!"

"Thom?" she called down.

Megan cut the music off.

White veins crackled across my vision like lightning. I dropped Megan's phone and crumbled at the foot of the stairs.

Megan came down the stairs two at a time and flicked the light on when she got to the top of the landing. I opened my eyes and looked up at her. Her hair was still stringy and wet, and she had a stain of toothpaste on the corner of her lips.

I pushed myself up and grabbed her phone, pushing it towards her: "Who the fuck is this? Richie?"

"He's a PA. I work with him."

"Is this who you were texting at the fight?".

"He's just a guy from work. I was asking him about you."

I looked down at the texts. A fire burned on my face. "He didn't text about me."

She stared at me. The muscles in her neck tight, her jaw clenched, her eyes: set.

We were two fighters in the middle of the ring. Holding our gloves at our sides, breathing in the air before catastrophe. It was a game of whoever flinched.

She looked away. A millisecond. That was it.

"You've got to be fucking kidding, Megan."

"He's a friend."

"He know you're married? Got a kid?"

"He knows."

'How fucking long, Megan?"

"He's just someone to talk to."

"Megan. You'd flip your shit if a woman texted me like that."

"You're a fucking asshole. You think I'd be fucking one of my coworkers?"

"You're married, Megan. This is our marriage. Not you, me, and fucking Richie. Fuck is wrong with you?" I pushed myself up on the stairs, every move was brutal.

I grabbed the banister and pulled myself up. I didn't care if I hurled all over the carpet. A deep craving rushed up my arm: warm, sweet, and soothing. I turned to the kitchen and stumbled to the counter and doubled over. Megan bound down the steps. She put her wet hands on my shoulders. Her fingers were as slimy as slugs.

"Fuck off me."

I shook her off.

The veins of lightning still crackled in my vision, but I could see through the storm.

Through the thundering pain, the keys glinted on the key ring beside the glow of the stove light. I stumbled to them.

"Thom, you can't fucking drive."

"I gotta go see Frank."

She grabbed my wrists, her hair swinging madly and her eyes wild as a banshee's.

"Thom! You have a fucking wife! Frank's fine!"

"And you've got a fucking husband!"

My head throbbed and rolled.

I shook her free and stumbled over to the cabinet beside the sink. I caught myself in the window. My face was covered in dark bruises. My eyelids were heavy and swollen, round as pregnant bellies.

I opened the cabinet, grabbed the bottle of ibuprofen, and dumped out four pills. I turned on the faucet and cupped some water in my hand. I tossed them back, and as I swallowed, tiny cuts on my lips and the inside of my cheeks stung.

"I'm going to the hospital."

"No, you're not," she said as she stood in front of me, her arms crossed.

"Meg, get out of my way," I said. The adrenaline started kicking in. The white veins in my vision started dissipating. The pot of coffee screamed. "I always promised you I'd never hit you, and I never will, but I swear to God, move."

Megan's lips trembled as she stepped to the side.

"Thom, I know where you want to go. Please baby. Don't."

My arm hummed with an old energy, a drive, a hunger.

"You going to call the cops?" I asked.

"If you drive, I will," she said.

"I'm walking then."

"Thom. Please. Baby."

"Don't you have work to go to? Can't fucking believe you."

I walked past her and turned the corner to the back door. I shoved my feet in my shoes with no socks on. In the window in the backdoor, I saw myself wearing a blood-stained tank top and shorts. In my bruised eyes, I saw it. I felt it. It was back again. The rope around my waist tugged me towards the door, towards euphoria.

Megan appeared behind me, her reflection shimmered.

"All the fucking shit we've been through," she said through defeated breaths.

I turned on her.

"I never cheated once. Raised our fucking daughter while you were off fucking God knows who."

"You always think it's easier out there! Don't you care what I went through? What I did for this family? You don't think about the terror I go through every time you step in the ring?"

"Fucking coworker," I said.

"It's not like that, Thom. We're just friends."

"You're fucking married, Megan. What kind of male friends you got that call you love and send you fucking smiley-faces?"

"I need a goddamn husband, Thom," Megan said, "not a little boy chasing his boxing dreams. At this rate, your daughter's gonna learn how to feed you through a G-Tube before she learns how to spell."

Megan burst into tears in the dim light. Her hands to her face. Her skin white as ash. She didn't look like a banshee anymore. She looked like she'd drowned.

"Fuck this," I said.

I pushed out the door, and the humidity hugged me.

I slammed the door behind me. The floodlight blazed on. Bats chattered above as I stumbled onto the back lawn. Faith's swing set was a dark monolith. I bent over as my stomach surged and washed out of my mouth. The four pills came rolling out still housed in their orange casing, slightly pinkened with saliva. The back door opened. I turned slowly. Tiny jewels of tears ran down Megan's cheeks. She held her arms at her sides and looked at me, without love and without hate. Just like a patient she couldn't save.

PART 5: FAITH

CHAPTER 38:
DEWEY THE "DARK CLOUD" MIDDLECAMP

April 29, 2025

The morning after my fortieth birthday, I was in a sterile room getting dressed. A hospital gown lay at my feet, and I was surrounded by anatomical pictures of the brain and skull. One poster that hung up near the door stated:

Suffering from Intractable Migraines?

Tried everything?

And beneath it a woman's face screwed in pain: Her brow corded, her jaw rippling, and her eyes shuttered.

Low-dose ketamine may be the answer to all of your problems! Ask your physician about it today!

There was a knock at the door.

"Thom?" a low, feminine voice asked.

"Yes."

Elena opened the door. She was in her mid-thirties. She had skin the color of Werther's, a bright smile, warm, green eyes and high, taut cheekbones. Her lips were the color of pink carnations. And her black hair curled down the span of her back.

"Your brother's ready to see you."

"Be out in a minute. Thanks, Elena."

"Take your time," she said gently.

I pulled my sweatpants up over my sore knees. My elbows

popped when I tied my drawstring. I had to sit in a chair to put on my shoes. I stood up and walked to the door, looking at the woman's face on the poster before I opened it. I'd have scored her pain an eight out of ten the way she looked. My migraines were usually a seven. If I was hard sparring, it'd jump to a nine.

"Hey, Dew," I said as I closed the door to his office behind me.

He smiled as he talked on the phone with his boots kicked up on his desk.

One second, he mouthed and put his finger up.

He laughed and put his hand behind his head. A gold Rolex glinted on his wrist in the sunlight coming in from the massive, single-paned window behind his desk.

"You owe me two, fucker," he said to whoever.

I put my hands in my pockets.

Dewey had just moved to this office. He wanted the ability to do CT on-site, which his last office didn't have.

The smell of paint was still the major flavor in the room.

The walls were an eggshell white. He'd hung up some pictures. A few still laid staged at different places on the polished teak flooring waiting to be hung. A canvas photo of Pennybacker near the door. A photo of a massive Longhorn with a dangling penis on the wall on the right side of his desk. In the middle of the room, in front of Dewey's desk, was a stained mahogany coffee table that shined as glossy as a pearl. Two white ivory leather couches sat facing each other on either side of it. A box of tissues stood like a mourner's sentry in the middle of the table. To the immediate left of the door, tucked into a corner, was a bookshelf without books, just pictures.

On the top shelf: a picture of Dewey in a cowboy hat arm-in-arm with a couple of old leathery cowboys.

Mid-shelf, another picture: a silver badge inside a glass case with a commemorative certificate: "Honorary Texas Ranger."

Under that: a picture of Dewey beside a white stallion, his beige hand on its white neck and a blonde mane flowing down its back like it'd been permed.

"All right, I'll catch you later," Dewey said.

He hung up the phone, and sat forward.

I looked at the picture of the stallion. The horse had wild blue eyes, like he'd rear up any moment and kick Dewey in the face.

"Just lucked up on a pair of seats at the 50 yard-line to the Red River Rivalry," Dewey said, chuckling. "Dad would've lost his shit if he was still here."

He pushed himself up from his leather-backed chair and walked around his desk towards me.

I took my hands out of my pockets and picked up the photo of him with the Rangers and held it out to him.

"You a Ranger now?" I said.

Dewey smoothed out his lab coat as he walked over to me. He smiled sadly.

"One of the Ranger's got ALS," he said.

"What's that?"

"It's a neurologic disease. Starts with weakness. Maybe you trip over your feet a little more often than you used to. Maybe you drop your fork while you're eating. Then, boom, you can't wag your finger and have to blink to a computer screen to communicate."

"Fuck. How'd he get it?" I asked.

Dewey took the photo from me and stared into it. "Rode bulls when he was younger. Got bucked a few too many times."

I put my hands back in my pockets.

"Imagine you're still alive but can't move a thing. Can't even itch your nose," Dewey said. Dewey looked up and stared at me darkly.

"Sound likes hell," I said.

Dewey put the photo down and opened his arms wide.

"Been a while since I seen you," he said, and smiled.

"You know how life is," I said.

"Yea," Dewey said, clenching his jaw.

We embraced in the cloud of his Aqua Di Gio.

"Still laying that shit on strong?" I asked after we stepped apart.

Dewey glanced down at my hands before he responded. "Dad had taste," he said.

I shrugged.

"No pictures of the family, though," I said, thumbing at the bookshelf.

"Motherfucker, did you look at my table?" he pointed to his desk.

Lined up in a row were the three pictures he'd had on his mantle before I'd gone to rehab. The desk was a mahogany color and varnished so purely that it looked like marble.

He stepped back and shucked his wrists out. "Got a new watch, too. Take a look." He held out his wrist.

"Nice."

He grabbed my wrist and pulled me close to him "Take a look," he said.

My hand tremored as he held my wrist and I looked over the watch. I tried tensing but the tremors wouldn't stop.

I looked up at Dewey. His brow narrowed. He studied my hand and moved his lips as if he was counting.

I pulled my hand back and shoved it back in my pocket and felt the paper of the waiver. The edges were sharp.

"You got something in your pocket?" Dewey asked. His eyes curious.

"Nah."

The bell dinged as a patient entered the waiting room out front.

"How much was that?" I asked, nodding at the watch.

He beamed. "Enough to make a nigga shine."

He patted me on the shoulder. "Come on," he said. He held his hand out to the ivory sofas.

I plopped down and put my hands on my knees. Some of the wrapping plastic was still on one of the armrests.

Dewey stood behind the sofa on his side and smiled broadly at me. He clapped his hands once.

"I got something for you," he smiled, and rubbed his hands together peevishly.

"What?"

"You're gonna lose your shit," he said. He bent down and stood up holding a square the size of his torso wrapped in brown paper. "Guess."

It was thin and wide. Dewey had to hold it with two hands.

"I don't know."

"C'mon nigga."

"I don't know, Dew."

Dewey chuckled.

"Mom had it in storage," he said. "I couldn't let it stay there. It's heritage stuff."

He took off the brown paper wrapping and turned the canvas to me. The sun caught it and I saw the image: The hands raised. The gloved fists. The stark blue and the contrast of the dark background. Dewey's eyes painted bright as beacons. A championship belt around his waist.

"No fuckin' way," I said.

"Yup," Dewey grinned. "Dad saved it."

He laid it on the couch and then circled around and sat beside it, staring at it.

"So what you got for me?" I asked.

He turned and sat forward resting his elbows on his knees and clasped his hands in front of him. He looked at me like he hadn't heard.

"How was the party?" he asked.

I shifted. My back hurt. "It was all right. Megan came."

"Hey, that's improvement." He clapped his hands gently.

"She's still dating that *doctor*."

Dewey shook his head, and turned back to the painting. "You were a great artist, Go'bay," he said. He turned back to me. "Why don't you give it a shot again?

"It's just not there anymore, Dew."

"Could've been Van Gogh."

"Waste of time. Dad thought it was a pipe dream."

"I never heard him say that," Dew said.

"He didn't have to," I said, "didn't want me using his last name."

"Thom, come on. We were all wrong that night. Everybody."

"I know."

Dewey sat forward and clasped his hands, working his knuckles as his Rolex rolled down to the bottom of his wrist.

"It was my fault anyways," he muttered. "My big fucking mouth."

There was a knock at the door. Dew sat up straight and looked over.

"Come in," he said.

Elena peered in.

She waved a CD in a jewel case.

"Results are in," she said.

"Bring it over."

Dewey pushed himself up quickly and strode briskly to his desk where a monitor and a small CPU sat and plopped in his chair. Elena gave me a glancing smile as she walked by.

Dewey took the CD from her hands. "Thanks, and draw up some ketamine for Mrs. Stevens, will you?"

She put her hand on her hip. "I will," Elena said, "How much does she weigh?"

Dewey put his finger to his lip and said, "Eighty-two kilos."

She nodded.

"So I'm going to lunch. You want anything?" she asked Dewey, pushing her hair behind her neck.

"Nope."

She turned to me. "Thom?"

I shook my head. "No, I'm cutting."

"What're you weighing?" Dewey asked sharply.

"177. Weighed myself this morning."

Dewey sat back, tented his fingers, and stared into his computer screen.

Elena laid her hand on Dewey's shoulder. "Be back around two?"

"Yea," Dewey said, nodding his head, still contemplating the computer. He raised his eyebrow the way Dad used to when he was focused.

Elena hovered at the door before leaving and said, "Remember you've got to sign the DEA form since it's a Schedule One."

"Got it," Dewey said.

The door closed in a hush.

Dewey sat forward.

I thumbed at the door. "You should ask her out."

He looked up confused as a stung scorpion. "Huh?"

"Elena."

Dewey waved it off. And showed me the back of his hand and wiggled his ringless finger.

"You don't get a new practice and a new wife. One will eat the other."

"She's nice."

"It's always nice. Then you get married. Start having trouble having kids. Start arguing about who's a better parent. Better partner. It's a war, right?" Dewey glanced at me, then sunk into his screen. "This shit always takes forever to load."

CHAPTER 39:
THE RESULTS ARE IN

"Got it!" Dewey blew a raspberry.

I had my hands on my knees as I bounced my feet quickly in the leather chair facing Dewey's desk.

A stinging shot sprung up behind my ear. I had to close my eyes. I'd sparred the day before and got caught with an overhand right. I was a half-second late getting my guard up. All I'd thought about during sparring was the waiver. It was a loaded barrel aimed straight at my dreams.

The pain slowly dissipated. I exhaled and opened my eyes slowly.

Dewey's eyes rolled down the screen. His face went from hopeful to tight.

"Bad news?" I asked.

Dewey clicked his teeth and sat back in his chair. He pulled his phone out of his pocket and started texting feverishly.

"Yo, Dewey."

"One second."

My heart beat quickly.

"Bad or good, Dew?"

He kept typing.

I put my hands on my knees and leaned forward, my heart rattled. Pins and needles swept through me. I reached into my pocket and pulled the waiver out with trembling hands.

"DEW!"

He tossed his phone on the table with a bitter disappointment. He tented his hands, rested his chin on his fingertips, and murmured, "Clean."

"Excuse me?"

"I said it was *clean*," he said.

"Nothing?" I said.

"Not a goddamn thing," he said and bit down on his lower lip.

"Damn right," I said.

"So, you're still going to fight, Go'bay?"

"Clean is clean, Dewey."

"You're walking the tight-rope over CTE. Chronic. Traumatic. Encephalopathy. You got any clue what that's like?"

"CT's clean ain't it?" I said.

"Clean for now, yea."

"So, sign it," I said.

I pulled the crumpled waiver out and slapped it on the table.

Dewey didn't make a move, just stared at it.

"Two concussions and still engaging in a combat sport is a full-stop." Dewey flicked his hand at the screen. "Changes or not."

I sat back. He didn't get it. It was hard for any of them to understand. Why do it to myself? To Megan? To Faith? To Mom? They all thought I had Peter Pan syndrome. Maybe I did. But, I'd lived on the island of abuse for a long time. And boxing was the only island I'd lived on where I felt any sense of hope.

I turned and pointed at the painting on the sofa.

"You know I was doing pills back then?"

Dewey shook his head.

"I was already on coke, and starting Percs when Dad kicked me out."

Dewey sat forward, his eyes mournful. "Thom," he pleaded, "he didn't have a choice."

"I know he didn't. He should've kicked me out. It was the right thing to do. I made my bed, so I had to sleep in it."

"Yea," Dewey said.

"Coming up on ten years, Dew." I put both hands up. "Ten. You ever think you'd see that. Back then?"

"To be honest," he said and shook his head, "I thought you'd be dead."

"Exactly. And you know why I'm still here?"

Dewey rocked back and forth in his chair.

"Boxing gave that to me. I learned a lot in rehab, but it didn't really click until I started boxing."

"What about self-preservation, Go'bay? When to stop?"

"I wouldn't have a thing to preserve if it weren't for boxing. It's not just some sport to me, Dew."

Dewey sighed and looked behind me to the painting. "I understand that, Go'bay."

"So sign it."

It lay on the table, four creases in it as it moved like a flag in the ventilated breeze on his desk. Dewey looked at it like it was infectious, something to be cured.

"You know the clinical trials for Ketamine treatments for PTSD have been more than promising," he said after a pause.

I laid my arm on his desk, pulled my sleeve up, put my fingers on my vein and held them against it. The scar tissue was a fossil.

"Drug addict, remember?"

Dewey shook his head slowly, "It's controlled."

"Fuck are we talking about here?" I picked up the waiver and tossed it at him. "The CT's clean. Just do me a favor and sign it."

"No."

"Dew, I'm two weeks out. They need this form yesterday. CT's clean. Even if you weren't my brother, any neurologist with two marbles would sign it."

Dewey sat forward and tented his fingers. He rested his teeth on his knuckles. "Ain't doing it."

I sat back and crossed my feet and put my hands behind my head. An old rhythm percolated in my brain. "You don't want to sign it, fine. I can go to Juarez. They don't make you jump through hoops down there."

Dewey clenched his jaw and a sliver of light entered his eyes. "Don't fucking game me," he said. "You used to pull that shit with Mom. Ain't gonna work on me."

My heart beat faster and travelled up my throat, like a lit fuse. I sat forward.

"Dew, you're not leaving me an option," I said. "I'm fucking serious." And I stared at him, at the ridges on his forehead.

"You're not," he said.

"Try me."

At once, we were teenagers again. I was talking him into something all over. Walking him down the road, walking him down it just to break his character, break his resolve. I may not have ever sparred Dewey, but he was still my older brother. And at the end of the day, I knew I could play him. He'd rather me die in front of his face than hear about it through Frank's crappy cellphone from a hospital in Jaurez.

"You're a fucking burden, you know that!" Dewey hissed, reaching quickly for the waiver. He picked it up and read it, then threw it back down. "You're risking your life for this shit!"

Dewey's Rolex glimmered as the sun touched it.

"We can't all shine like you!"

Dewey shook his head and massaged his knuckles.

"You talk all this shit about how boxing saved you. But what about your family? How hard was it to get that? You willing to stake all of that on boxing?" He glowered, staring at the waiver.

It lay unsigned between us.

"Just sign the waiver, Dew."

Some of us burn just enough to keep the lights on.

CHAPTER 40:
BATS AND OWLS, OWLS AND BATS

A week later, I made my way to Megan's after the gym to go pick up Faith, and I couldn't stop the thoughts coming. Training was as good as meditation, but it was my first pro fight. Anything could happen. Or couldn't.

Dew still hadn't signed the waiver. It was a massive craw. The kind of craw that invaded my dreams: dreams of getting turned away at the ring, dreams of getting knocked out, the ref counting down, and then the loss getting waived because I wasn't supposed to be fighting in the first place: Fighting for nothing.

Thankfully, I also caught a case of some of the good jitters: the electric joy of upcoming competition.

It had finally start to settle in: I was fighting in my first pro fight the next week.

I pulled up to the curb of Megan's house. My back and knees felt good.

My jabs were snappy and the combinations flowed free and loose.

I was fluid in the ring. Brutal fluid.

Frank's only comment was to watch my jab placement.

The good feeling got washed away the moment I put the car in park. I hated coming back to the house. I didn't want to see her boyfriend: Fuckface Richie. Sometimes he'd be there when I came to pick up Faith but he never showed his face.

"He's not confrontational," Megan would say.

"Richie the pussy."

"No, Thom. It's just not everything has to be a fight," she'd say.

"You sure? You damn sure had enough for me."

And then, we'd both stop talking and contemplate the pebbles on the welcome mat.

But, this time, I didn't see his Tesla in the driveway. My home gym had been liquidated and there was enough space for one car in the garage. Two, maybe.

I cut the lights and cracked the windows. An orange glow burned softly through the sky. There was a myriad of clouds; some wispy, peach, and smeared pastel, and then others tall, purple, and billowing. A single flash of lightning ran like an excited vein from a strand of dark clouds. A horde of bats darted by as the streetlights flickered on in white orbs. I put my fingernail in my mouth. And chewed off a piece. My phone jingled. I looked down: Megan. I slid the cursor with a wet thumb and chewed.

"Hey." My nail popped in my teeth.

"Seriously, still biting your fingernails?"

"Just to keep them from getting too long," I said.

"It doesn't make a difference, Thom."

"It's the pros, Meg. You don't miss by inches. You miss by a centimeter and get knocked out by a millimeter. Everything matters."

"Dewey send in the waiver?" she asked.

"Not yet."

Megan coughed. "Be right back," she said. She started yelling on the other end: "Quit shoving their heads in the toilets!"

Faith cried. "But I like how they move when I flush!"

"Put it down! Get your bookbag, now!"

Megan picked up the phone again. "You coming in?"

"What'd she do?"

"Twisting off Barbie heads and putting them in the toilets again. You coming in?"

"Is he there?"

"Is who here?"

"Don't play," I said.

"We're separated. Remember?"

"Doesn't mean I want to see him."

Megan breathed in deeply but didn't say a thing.

Another spit of lightning shot between two towering thunderheads. A few drops of rain splattered down on the windshield.

Finally, Megan sighed, exhausted and sounding frustrated.

"Are you coming in or do I need to bring her out…? I really need you to come in because I've got a lot of stuff and I can't bring it out all at once."

"Yea, coming."

She hung up.

I put my hands in my pockets and walked the driveway to our front door. Our yard looked like a rat's nest. Fescue climbed the oak trees. The rose bushes grew wild and covered our bedroom windows. I nearly tripped on Faith's Fisher-Price trike. I looked at our neighbor's place, Bob and Terry; their lawn was immaculate. Every blade accounted for. Every thorn on his bushes smoothed. A nice setup of accent lights lined the walkway to his front door. Ours were black, the bulbs burned out many moons ago.

The porch light flicked on as a strand of lightning illuminated the sky, thunder crackled, and over at Bob and Terry's a bat and an owl met in the glare.

The owl swooped in silently with death on its talons. It grasped the bat in its claws as the bat screeched mid-air, it's tiny body writhing for life against the laws of nature: Some things live. Some things die. Some things are meant to be eaten. Some things are meant to be the eaters. You are what you are in this world.

Megan opened the door. She had her hair down in bouncy, shining black curls. A light sheen of lip gloss on her plump lips. Her emerald eyes glowed. Her face was lightly powdered, but Megan didn't need it. It was like seeing her for the first time again; seeing her as a woman. She was thirty-nine and still gorgeous. Her face was a little more rounded, and she had tiny riverbeds of crow's feet, but they lifted when she smiled, like dragonfly wings.

Faith held Megan's finger. Megan leaned on one hip and held the door open with her free hand. She had on a pair of black cowhide boots, blue jeans, and a black tank-top that dipped and showed the creamy porcelain of her cleavage.

"Daddy!" Faith screeched.

I bent down and gave Faith a kiss on the cheek as she hugged me around my neck. I went to stand, but Faith's grip was small and sure. I placed my hands on her wrists, "I have to talk to Mommy real quick."

Faith held tight.

"Let go, baby," I said.

"Faith," Megan urged.

Faith held tight, but I imagined where Megan would be that night. What she'd be doing. Who she'd be doing it with.

"Let me go!" I snapped.

Faith's arms dropped from my neck loosely and she cowered from me, hiding behind Megan, bitten.

An oily shame washed over me, seeping into every vessel of my heart. It felt like a genetic ugliness; something that was just a part of who I was. I could never get rid of it.

"I'm sorry, Faithy. Daddy's just tired," I said quickly. "He's got a fight coming up, remember?"

Faith's lip trembled as Megan rubbed her head. Megan burned and her eyes shook: incredulous and angry. She bent down to Faith. "Daddy's just tired, babe," she said, kissing the crown of Faith's head. "Go get your bookbag."

Faith put her finger in her mouth and sucked. "I'm sorry, Daddy," she said. I held my arms out to her as she turned and ran inside to get her bookbag.

"What the fuck, Thom?" Megan hissed. A firefly burst and then dimmed near her face.

"What?"

"Don't ever talk to her like that. Apologize when she gets back."

"I will," I said.

Megan stared at me with her hand on her hip, self-righteous and beautiful.

The hurt boiled up, and I spoke from it. "Date tonight?"

"That's none of your business."

"Still my wife."

"Name only."

We glared at each other as Faith trudged towards us.

"She's coming. Put a smile on, Dad."

I stared at Megan's neck. I used to kiss her right above her clavicle. I'd run my hands down to her pelvis as she moaned and melted into me. Her body would become a fountain and ruin the bedsheets. It was a spot I held secret. And then, a painful anger bloomed in spikes of imagination: I saw his lips touching the skin on Megan's neck. Richie, making my wife wet. And then, him chasing Faith around the swing set I'd built. Her slipping up, calling him Daddy. The surprise on her face, and his. The dissolution of me into memory as he took hold of that name and I became a relic.

"Thom," Megan sapped her fingers.

Faith held her bookbag by a strap and dragged it on the ground behind her with her thumb in her mouth.

"Daddy, that was really mean," she said.

She looked puzzled and hurt. I'd raised my voice before, but I was never angry. At least I tried my best not to be. But I couldn't lie to her. If I had to be honest with anyone, it was her. I bent down, and looked at her in the eyes. I wanted her to see it all. "Daddy's just a little scared, baby."

Megan tapped her foot. Faith took her finger out of her mouth and spoke with clarity.

"It's okay to be scared. Fighting is scary."

I pulled her to me. Faith let go of her bookbag and nuzzled me as I smelled artificial kiwi. She planted a tiny kiss on my cheek and her lips were a soft redemption.

"New shampoo?" I said, clutching Faith and looking up at Megan.

"Yea?" Megan asked quizzically.

"Did you check the chemicals? Some of those dyes make her break out."

"I checked. We're good," Megan said, smirking.

I stood up with Faith in my arms. Megan bent down to grab Faith's bag and her shirt rode up the small of her back. In the glow of the foyer, I saw on the valley of her back a grey, faded tattoo: M♥T. She still hadn't gotten it removed. Over a year later and I was still an ever-present part of her body. Megan stood up holding the bag in one hand. She pulled her shirt down.

"What?" she asked, cocking her head as she handed me the bag and I slung it over my shoulder.

"You still haven't gotten it removed?"

She blushed and leaned in to kiss Faith. "Be good for Daddy."

"You didn't answer my question."

"Faith," Megan said, "headgear."

Faith quickly put her hands to her ears and laid her head on my clavicle.

Megan licked her lips and shoved her hands in her back pockets, kicking at a pebble on the doorstep, before looking up at me.

"Well, they said it'd take a fortune to get it removed. It's either that or get the D-I-V-O-R-C-E."

It wasn't a real weight without words. She'd said papers. But not the word. And hearing it now, in the shadow of my old home, with Faith in my arms and taking her somewhere else, it hit me. The life I'd lived was trying to leave me. Trying to separate itself. Unclenching itself from me. Ending the brawl. Jabbing out and stepping away into the darkness.

"You're serious," I said.

"Yes, Thom," she said. "I told you what I'd have to do if you went through with this."

"I didn't break the vows, Megan. You did."

"What do you mean?" she said.

"You were the one that said you weren't fucking your coworkers."

"Thom, stop it!" Megan hissed.

Faith shoved her face deeper into my clavicle. "I don't like this."

I ground my molars.

A few bats chased frenetic moths above us and a Charger opened up, groaning on the highway.

Megan's perfume wafted out to me. Peach, spicy, and fragrant. Her eyes grew dark like a widower's; like she was looking at a ghost who used to hold her world in its palm, and, yet, now, it couldn't hold a pebble.

"I still remember the day you started the swing set," she said, tears in her eyes. Her phone vibrated in her front pocket. "I watched you from the kitchen, and for just a moment, I wasn't a nurse. I was just a wife getting dinner ready and you were a husband building a swing set. Just one fucking moment, Thom. And then, it got dark again. You remember that?"

CHAPTER 41:
CHICKENS ROOST

We were back at my apartment after I'd picked up Faith.

She laid beside me curled up into a ball.

Megan's boyfriend had probably crawled out of his hole right after we'd left.

It was a little after 11:00.

I had an earbud shoved into my ear as deeply as I could and had the volume down to near silent as I watched some of my sparring of footage. I caught a glimpse of Faith at ringside, playing with her black Barbie that Mom got her.

Me and my sparring partner circled.

Our feet thundered as I slipped, dug, and caught him with a left hook to the body, but he caught me with a check hook to the head on my way back up.

Frank hung over the ropes shouting, "Hands up, Tommy. Keep to your sequences." I was still dropping my hands, and with ten seconds left, I took another macabre hook. The sweat jumped from my head as it sprayed across the ring. The bell rang. My sparring partner and I tapped gloves as Faith's voice, tiny and sweet, rang out, "Hands up, Daddy!" I walked back to the corner and Frank's grimace. "This guy is not going to let you escape, Thom," Frank echoed. "We're going pro, Thom. You won't be able to slip a single. Fucking. Atom. Every punch coming at you is gonna be the definition of precision. You gotta be sharper."

As I watched the video and Frank squirted water in my mouth, I looked away from my phone and into the darkness.

D-I-V-O-R-C-E.

The way Megan had said every single letter.

Faith snorted, then yawned, and then dropped back into snoring. Her breath smelling like Spaghetti-O's and Colgate. I turned my volume to silent just as a message came in. It was Frank.

Frank: *We need to meet.*

Me: *it's 11:30.*

Frank: *It's urgent.*

Me: *You call 911?*

Frank: *It's not that.*

Me: *I've got Faith.*

Frank: *Deb's on the way over to yours. I already told her.*

Me: *What's going on?*

Frank: *I just gotta see you.*

My heart beat rapidly. Dewey hadn't sent in the waiver. That had to be it.

Me: *I gotta call mom.*

Frank: *I told you, she's on the way.*

CHAPTER 42:
MOM ON GRANDMA DUTY

There was a knock at my front door. I slid my arm out from underneath Faith's ear and let her head drop gently down on the pillow. She opened her eyes in the darkness as I stood over the bed. "Where you going, Daddy?"

I bent down and kissed her head. "Go back to sleep, baby," I said. The smell of kiwi in her hair was still thick. "Mimi came for a visit."

Faith nodded and closed her eyes.

I stood up over her; the streetlight outside filtered through the blinds and landed on Faith in pale green slits and black bars. She looked imprisoned in it. I walked to the window to turn the blinds down, and the bed creaked as Faith turned. My shadow covered her.

"Daddy, can you leave the blinds open?"

"Why, baby?"

"I have bad dreams."

Her voice was full of heartbreak, too much. I walked over to her, my shadow growing and expanding in the darkness until I blotted out the light. I sat down beside her and stroked the top of her head.

"What kind of dreams, baby?"

Faith shivered and turned away from me.

Mom knocked at the door a little louder.

"What dreams, baby?"

"I can't tell you, *Daddy*," Faith said, sniffing into the comforter.

Faith felt far from me. Far away where I couldn't reach her. In a place where kids bury things that they dig up later as adults.

My phone buzzed on the end table.

I kissed Faith's head one last time, letting my lips linger in her hair, and she didn't say a word, just laid on her stomach, sniffing.

I left the door open as I went to the living room, and left Faith there covered in slitted fluorescence.

I slid the lock and put my finger to my lips. Mom crept in yawning. She smelled skunky.

"She's sleeping," I whispered.

Mom pointed to the bedroom. "In there?"

"Yea."

She nodded at me and started tiptoeing to the room. I grasped her arm.

"What's going on?"

Mom turned on me.

"You smoking weed?" I asked.

"And, if I was?"

"The fuck is going on? Aren't you the grandparent here?"

"I'm being one. I'm going to go put my baby to sleep."

"What the hell is going on, Mom?"

"Frank needs to see you," she said.

"He having an exacerbation?"

Mom shook her arm loose. "Son," she said, her voice cracking, "you need to go see him."

"Mom, tell me you didn't send it to him."

Mom shook her head, and in the pale light, her eyes glimmered.

She turned away quickly and sniffed as she marched quietly to the bedroom. Faith whined at her.

"Where's Daddy going?" Faith asked.

Mom bent down and lifted Faith from the bed and started humming and dancing gently. Faith laid her head on mom's shoulder and her eyes sparkled in tears as they danced in the barred light.

Frank and I sat in his Olds in an HEB parking lot facing Lamar. The fluorescent lights burned above us and the glow crept into the car like a greenish slime.

Frank was in a small slice of shadow and wheezed in the darkness. The prongs of his cannula sat in his nose travelling in a long plastic cord to his oxygen tank in the back seat. A cigar smoked in the ashtray. "For the aroma". I had my window open, just to let the smoke escape. Frank tapped his phone nervously in his lap and looked over at me. I couldn't see his eyes, but he had a deep seriousness to him.

"I'll always be thankful to your mom," he said. "She was a huge help to me when I was in the hospital. But me and her never really got along, for one reason and one reason alone."

"Why's that?"

"I represent the voice in your head that tells her no."

"I don't always listen to you, Frank. We argue all the time."

"It's not about the day to day. Whether or not you'll be her DD to some wine festival or when she needs you to change her oil. It's about the big things. When it's her no, versus my yes, she's always felt like there's a battle to be lost there. And the longer I've been around, the more I've represented an opposition within her own family. To her own voice. No mother likes the idea that anybody has more say in her child's mind than she does. No mother."

Frank looked down at the smoking cigar. He shuffled in his seat slightly. The Texas state perfume wafted in: mesquite. I took a breath. Frank took a breath. A car pulled in front of us with the lights on. Frank put his hand up to cover his face.

"We tempt ourselves," he said, nodding at the cigar.

"Put it out then," I said.

He laughed. A smile swept across his face and in its ashes he became morose. "It came in."

"The waiver?"

"Yup," Frank said.

"Thank God."

Frank looked at me and his nostrils flared as he took deep breaths in. The car in front of us still had its headlights on; it illuminated every pore on Frank's face. He was haggard as ever. His skin a lifeless caramel. His salt and pepper hair thin. His cheeks losing fat by the day. He was gaunt. Stricken.

He sighed and said, "Fuck it." He reached for the cigar and took a deep pull. He slid down in his seat as he blew out a fog. "Been almost two weeks."

I rolled the window down and hung my arm out the side as a bus wheezed on its brakes. It was just outside the reach of the parking lot and didn't get any of the glow of the light. The people got off like shuffling wraiths. The car in front of us cut its light. The driver got out, glanced at us, hit the lock button on his keys twice, and went inside.

"Your mom, she's one of those," Frank said, taking a puff, "one of those *so-anyways* women."

He wheezed deeply.

"*So-anyways* women?" I asked.

"You know, you say something they don't like, and they go, '*so, anyways*'..." he mused with the wand of his cigar, casting a spell lazily in the air with the tail of his smoke. "It's dismissive."

Frank looked down at the phone in his lap nervously. With his free hand, he tapped the screen. It opened in fragments.

"Frank, why am I here?"

He turned to me quickly; he was a ghost with a burning ruby in his mouth.

"Your mom never showed it to me," Frank said woefully. He tapped his fragmented screen. "She said it had to be nuclear."

He tossed his phone in my lap.

"Hit play."

It was all black at first, but I could tell the videotaper was moving and breathing. The fragmented screen shook slightly as they approached what appeared to be a door. Then the flash came on. The door had the faint marks of crayon near the bottom where two stick-figure boxers fought each other. A decapitated Barbie lay on the floor. It was a door I knew well. It was our bedroom in Megan's house.

A hand wrinkled by years of overusing hand sanitizer turned the knob and pushed the door open. The light travelled from a bloodied boxing jersey to a pair of boxing shoes to the foot of a bed as the sound of retching and dry heaving became more prominent. The camera panned to a window with blackout curtains pulled tightly shut and then back towards the bed, where the first thing the camera's light flashed on was a small garbage can.

I looked over at Frank; he furrowed his brow as he puffed on his cigar.

I looked back down at the screen as the light landed upon its subjects: Megan holding my head as I puked into the garbage can over the edge of the bed.. She looked up quickly at the light. "Deb, are you fucking recording this?" she hissed.

"Yes, I am."

"Who's looking after Faith?" Megan asked, her eyes widening to the door.

"Dewey's here now," Mom said. "He's watching her."

I looked up at the camera; I looked ghostly as fuck. I was pale and my eyes were bloodshot. I had bruises all over my face. And dried blood crusted on my nose and upper lip. And a rope of spit hung from my mouth to the trash can.

"What the h—," I went to say and retched, heaving again. My ribs poked out with each retch. It was all mucus at that point.

"It's okay, baby," Megan said, stroking my head.

"Megan, there's barely a photo him of when he was on drugs. He's been sober so long, that time made us forget. You want to know what it looked like when he got junk sick? When he'd show up to our house at two in the morning sick as a dog? This is it. This is what it looks like."

"Later, Deb," Megan growled. "This isn't the time or the place."

"It's always later with him, right? That's what he tells you. This is what later gets, Megan."

Mom turned the camera to her face and put up two fingers. "This is the second one," she whispered. Her voice cracked. "Not gonna be your accomplice again, Go'bay. If you try to get back in the ring, Imma show this to Frank. Imma show this to the Commission. Imma show this to goddam Trump if I have to."

The camera cut off.

The fragmented screen went blank.

I looked over at Frank. He held the cigar in between his teeth. He chewed on the end of it. The mesquite wrapping paper became black with saliva. We both sweated. Even at night the heat was relentless. The sky was dark as a bruise again.

CHAPTER 43:
LOOK AT US

"I can't help but think, Thom, is she right?" Frank asked.

"What do you mean?" I said.

"About all of it." Frank looked down at his cigar. "I can't put this shit down to save my own damn life."

He looked at me with wide, yellowed eyes.

"Frank, we've prepared."

"Yea, but what are we really up against?" he asked.

"I know what I'm up against."

Frank took a puff. "What if I've done to you what you've been doing your best to be sober from for all these years?"

"Frank, I haven't touched a single drug in ten years."

"It's not about the drugs, Thom."

"What is it, Frank? What the fuck is it?"

"Frankly, it's about putting you in a situation where your wants and needs have become the same again. You make anything you desire into a God and that's got nothing do with healing; that's an addiction. And that's the deadliest thing a man can have happen to him. It has nothing to do with the ring. It's the mindset. Because you've got the animal. I know we'll get a win. But then it's back to the old demon. Chasing. Chasing. Chasing."

Frank took his eyes off me and stared straight ahead.

He was a burning cherry in the darkness. And I had to come up with something, because the next time he took a puff, the cherry would light and illuminate the both of us. I felt the game inside me again. The game of saying what I needed to get where I wanted to go.

"I'm quitting after this," I said.

Frank took a massive puff and the cherry at the end of his cigar nearly lit on fire as he looked at me with bulbous eyes and pulled in cheeks. He took a jabby sniff of oxygen through the prongs in his nose and chuckled through his teeth as he blew out a brawling exhaust of smoke.

"That's a smoke-shade, Thom," he said.

"You know what, Frank. Where's the ethos? We're at the finish line here."

Frank tossed the cigar out the window and started coughing. It was hacking, wet and loose. He pulled a handkerchief from his pocket as he leaned over the steering wheel. "Get my inhaler," he said. "It's in the console."

I opened the center console, reached in and pulled out the inhaler as he coughed and coughed.

The car in front of us flashed it's lights on as Frank's eyes bulged with each cough and the vein in his neck grew like a fat snake. He took one final massive hack and coughed out a wad into his handkerchief, quickly closing it on itself. He handed me his handkerchief, and I handed him the inhaler. I held the handkerchief in my lap as I spoke.

"I get to choose how I live my life, Frank. That's what sobriety is. I took the choices of life away from myself for years, and being sober, I got those choices back. This sport has given me everything. I wouldn't have met Megan without it. I wouldn't have met you. Wouldn't have Faith. All of those are cherries in my life, because otherwise I'd be dead a long time ago, grave dug and everything. I'm not doing this because I need to get the O off. Or I want to. I owe this sport a debt, because it taught me the two most important things I never once had in my life." I put up two fingers in the darkness. "How to find purpose in sobriety. And how to be sober enough to be a father. I don't have a fucking win to my name except my daughter. So, when she sees her daddy step in that ring and fight for his life, she'll know something about me. She'll know her daddy was a man of honor and duty. Above everything. That's what matters. Boxing's given me a legacy to show my daughter. And for that, I owe it everything."

I tossed the phone back to Frank. He jumped as it fell into his lap, taking another puff on the inhaler. His breathing settled.

"So, you can take that. You, mom, Megan, and Dewey. I love you all. But, I'm telling you, when I step foot in the ring, it's for my baby. She has to see that a man stands for something. He commits to what he says and follows it through with every ounce of his energy. It's either that or I step back out on the street. There's only two options for me and for her. I've chosen already."

I opened the door and stepped out of his car. The air was hot, and the bats echo-locating above sounded like trains screeching on their brakes.

In the glare of the parking lot lights, I felt hot and clenched. I closed my fists closed against my sides and felt a fabric: I was still holding Frank's handkerchief. I opened my fist and it unfolded. There was a flower of bright red blood on it.

CHAPTER 44:
GRACKLES NEVER DIE

The morning of the fight, I wasn't hungry. Didn't want a damn thing. I forced myself to eat a little bit of oatmeal. I stared out the window while I ate. I watched the grackles in the parking lot below. The parking lot was full. My neighbors had had a party the night before. They'd left a box of pizza out there and the grackles were fighting over the last piece. I took a sip of my gallon of water. My pee was as clear as glacial runoff. Frank was on the way over. Last minute game plans. This was it. The moment that bell went off, that was it, no more game planning. I had to bang down the front door. I had to be sharp. Focused. But, I'd be lying if I didn't say the butterflies weren't buzzing. They flew through my arteries.

My opponent was one of those old school Mexican fighters; all-brawl-no-brakes type fighters.

I chewed on my oatmeal. But it was tasteless, bland, and the texture of cardboard. I tossed it in the sink and planted my hands on the counter. One grackle fought off two at a time; a third circled and ripped out his tail feathers. He kept fighting. Hell, who knew? If it went well, I'd go for another. One thing I did know, getting that zero off was going to be euphoric. That feeling lifted me to the ceiling as I watched the mob. And then, my stomach shrunk to the size of a raisin. The mob of grackles tore at the grounded grackle. Picked at him. Ripped his feathers. They cackled joyously. But still he fought. It was a screeching, squawking brawl. Feathers. Beaks. Claws. Yellow eyes ragged with hunger. Inside of that brawl, I pictured myself. Fighting with ferocious intensity. To the very end. But, I would be victorious. Every jab quicker. Every hook harder. Every parry and return a crime and a punishment. I had to visualize myself winning. I had to visualize that the risk being taken within that all-out brawl was worth every single feather on my body.

The brawl ended and the downed grackle lay flapping what was left of itself on the cardboard.

I sat in my car at the Arena watching the fighters walk in with their families. Girlfriends rubbed their boyfriend's backs. Mothers looked worried. Fathers looked tense. Children were in awe.

The fighters wore their family's faces, and their own.

I could smell the buttery grease of popcorn cooking inside.

One of the fighters walking in had Adidas nearly like mine; his wife held his hand and his daughter jumped at his side.

I had my jug of water in the passenger seat and my gym bag in the backseat.

My bag was lighter than usual. It wasn't weighed down by head-gear: just a cup, mouthpiece, and stuff for Frank to wrap my hands.

I checked my phone again.

It was 7:30.

I was on the undercards. I'd be fighting as soon as the clock struck 8:00. I grabbed my gallon and took another sip.

Megan had parked two spaces behind me. I craned as I looked in the rearview; I couldn't see Faith in the backseat. Maybe she was slumped over sleeping. My ears drummed as I looked back at the entrance and watched more of the crowd filter in. The butterflies were all over me.

I closed my eyes and envisioned the first step: swinging my feet underneath the ropes and slipping my head underneath. I'd stand in my corner shooting my arms out to keep them loose as I hopped on two feet. I'd look out on the crowd and see Megan, and Faith, Mom, and Dewey, Frank. I could feel Dad urging me on. I could feel his pride in the fact that I'd come this far. That above all else his son could be a professional at something. I'd be more than he'd ever dreamed. He'd have a son who crawled out of a hole and found freedom in the ring.

I'd paint the ring with my victory. I opened my eyes and looked in the rearview one more time. I still couldn't see Faith, but I did see Megan, doing her makeup, her eyes were hard; metallic.

She'd see my hand getting raised and hear her last name being announced. I'd be able to look at her in the eyes again. She'd see that it wasn't all for nothing. I could go into coaching. It'd be better than advertising. I could say that I was not only a pro, but I was a winning pro. I got out of my car and entered the last burn of the central Texas sun.

As I walked up to Megan's car, a grackle hobbled out from the car in front of hers. It's tail feathers were ragged and the feathers on its wings were akimbo. It couldn't lift from the earth if it wanted to. As it hobbled quickly across the asphalt to disappear underneath another car, it gave me a yellow-eyed, fearful glare.

As I got closer to Megan's car, I caught a final blast of sunlight. It blinded me and I put my hand up. It disappeared behind a building as I got to Faith's side of the backseat and looked in through the window.

Her car seat was empty, just the glimmer of her seat buckle and an empty McDonald's kid's meal.

I opened Megan's passenger door quickly and looked in. "Where's Faith?"

Megan was on the phone. "I'm on the phone with my mom."

"Where's Faith?" I asked, louder.

"I'll call you back in a second." She hung up and turned to me.

I tossed my bag and jug into the back and slid into the front seat. I turned around and looked behind the driver's seat; maybe she was crawling around looking for a fry.

Nothing.

"Where's she at, Megan?"

Megan looked at me, her makeup half-done. She had two spots of blush not brushed in and her lips were rouged, but her eyes hung low with a mix of anger and despair. "I didn't bring her."

I shook. "Megan, why?"

She cocked her head at me and a tear ran down the right side of her face carrying a black trail of eyeliner.

"You fucking kidding me?" she asked and shook her head.

She turned and wiped away her black tear in the visor mirror.

"What?" I asked.

"I didn't want her to be here for it, Thom," Megan said. "You got no clue what last night was like."

"What happened?"

Frank's gold Oldsmobile pulled past the front door and slid into a parking spot at the far end of the lot.

"She had nightmares last night. She dreamt you got hit and didn't get up."

"Megan, for God's sake, why do you tell her about this stuff?"

"I didn't, Thom!"

"Who, then!?"

"Nobody, Thom. Faith's seen more of your fights than I have. I was travelling. It was you, her, and Mommy Mimi remember?" Megan slapped the visor shut. Her makeup done and her lips trembled.

"You were fucking somebody else, that's what I remember."

"Oh, shut the fuck up," Megan said.

"She's never seen me get hurt."

Megan's neck was reddening by the second and she shook so much her body vibrated. Her jet-black hair was a permed sheen, the oily texture of the broken grackle I'd seen. She turned to the center console, opened it and pulled out an envelope. She slammed the console, turned to me with poison in her eyes, and tossed the envelope in my lap. "No, Thom," she said, sniffling. "She saw much worse."

I glanced down at the envelope. It was a creamy color, like eggnog, and there was printed cursive on the mailing address: Hammers and Hammerstein, LLC.

"I had to do it," she said.

"Do what?" I said.

My heart was a booming drum: Boom. Boom. Boom. Boom. Boom. A surge of ice and fear rushed through my body so quickly, I nearly threw up. I looked out the window. This was reality.

Divorce attorneys.

"Why, Meg?"

"Why what?" Megan said.

"Why this?" I asked. I held the letter and shook it at her.

"You stopped making me feel safe."

"No matter how fucked up I was, I'd never hit you, Meg. You know that."

"I'm not talking about that."

"Then, what the fuck do you mean?"

"How many times did I tell you I was scared and it was killing me every time you stepped in the ring?"

I ran my fingers over the envelope. My phone buzzed in my pocket. "You weren't even there half the time," I said.

Megan eyes were two green beacons on fire.

"That's not the fucking point! I was your wife and I was telling you that what you were doing was hurting me. Hurting our family. And what did you do? You kept going. Told me we'd talk about it later. You know why I took that sixth contract?"

"Why, Megan?"

"I felt like throwing up sleeping next to you. I'd stay awake all night looking for new contracts. Just to get away from you."

A cauldron of anger erupted inside me. "You're a horrible mother."

"Fuck you," she said.

"What about me, Megan? You think it made me feel safe to know my wife was talking about our marriage with another man? God knows if you were fucking him or not?"

"I wasn't!"

She stopped and breathed in as she turned to me.

"We had a chance at being a family. Don't you remember, Thom? I came home from the road. I was ready to be a mother again. I was ready to settle in, but you couldn't be present. You were seeking something outside our home. Me and Faith weren't enough for you. After all of it. The nightmares. The miscarriages. All those fucking nights in the hospital. The postpartum I went through. All of it. I still couldn't satisfy you. We couldn't. You still needed something outside of yourself to chase because you still hadn't solved the problem of Thom."

The hurt within me softened. The anger became a smoothed blade. The shame nearly evaporated. And then, I saw a grackle. It hopped and skittered and flapped beside Megan's car as it was chased by a mob. His eyes were wild with pain and fear. And rage. He turned on them, nipping and biting and screeching. He fought a few off and dashed away.

I turned to Megan.

"What about you, Megan? Running away every chance you could get? Searching for contracts the moment you got home? What about that, huh? You said you couldn't stand being home. Couldn't stand being near me. What about your fucking presence? Fucking mom of the year over here?"

"You've got no fucking clue!" she shouted.

"You've got no fucking clue!" I shouted.

Megan sniffed horribly and turned away, her jaw clenched as her cheeks rippled with corded muscles. She spoke and it felt like she was finally releasing a horrible sadness. "I couldn't fucking believe our daughter survived my body! Do you know I thought that? For years. I couldn't stand being home because I thought that she'd die if I was too close to her for too long. For years my womb was a fucking morgue, Thom! Do you fucking get that!"

Megan sank low and laid against her window, sniffing. "I am a horrible mother," she said, and looked over at me, weeping. "Thom, you have no idea the choices we make for you. The things we all do. For you." She stared out her window, both hands on the wheel. The grackle fought for its life somewhere.

"Thom, I need you to go," Megan said quietly, wiping away her tears, "I need to fix my makeup."

I took the envelope out of my lap and put it on top of the center console. I grabbed my bag and jug out of the back, and opened the door to the heat. The sun was on its final burn. Frank made his way to the front with his cane and small training bag. His cigar smoked in his mouth and his oxygen tubing wrapped from his nose to a small saddlebag slung on his shoulder. He puffed and nodded at me, then went inside.

I turned to Megan.

"You coming?"

"Close the door, Thom."

I slammed the door and stood with my bag and jug looking at the entrance. Frank stood behind the glass, breathing in through his nose and taking puffs of his inhaler. He nodded at me and then glanced to his left. Mom and Dewey walked up to the entrance slowly talking together. Dewey looked down at his phone. He had on a sweatshirt and sweatpants and his lab coat slung over his shoulder. Mom was in jeans and an ER Nurses Rock T-shirt, and she had her arms crossed tightly as she talked to Dewey. Dewey showed Mom his phone and they both shook their heads. As I looked at them, I thought of all the reasons why I chose boxing over almost everything. And one thing came to mind: *Live By it, Die By it.*

Mom and Dewey stopped at the entrance and looked at me.

CHAPTER 45:
ROUND ROCK IS 4 SWEATY HUGS

Frank stood sentry behind the glass double doors as I walked up to the gaggle of my family. Megan trailed far behind me. Frank sucked in deeply through the prongs in his nose. He had both hands gripped around the door handle.

Mom and Dewey stood closely, shoulder to shoulder, just to the left of the doorway. Mom didn't even look back at Frank; she just tapped her foot and smoked a cigarette with her arms crossed. Mom's hair was shiny like wax, and just as immovable.

I pulled my bag up higher on my shoulder as I made my way to the curb. The parking lot lights flickered on and the moths started to swarm them. The sun was giving way to a purple twilight.

Mom took a deep and final pull of her cigarette. Dewey kicked some pebbles in the asphalt. Mom's cheeks got tight and she really did look old. Mom was in her early sixties now. No matter how much makeup she put on, the wrinkles showed at the corners of her eyes and the worry lines lay etched deep into her tanned forehead. Her brown eyes were starting to grow dim. She stooped a little. Mom nudged Dew. He looked up and smiled, but his eyes were impenetrable glass; the glass of a doctor.

"What you two conspiring?" I said, as I stopped in front of them.

"Your victory party," Mom said. Her voice was tight.

"What's your problem?" I asked Dewey.

"Perks of being a doctor," he said, "Had to go to the hospital for a consult."

"Why the sweatsuit?"

"I was at a yoga class, fuckwad. Any more questions?"

Mom glanced at Dewey, and said, clipped, "Both of you, chill."

Dewey turned to Mom. "You're too soft on him."

Mom opened her mouth to speak, and then closed it.

The lights in the arena glimmered behind the glass panes of the door.

I thought of Faith and turned to Megan.

"Tell me your mom is bringing Faith," I said. "Tell me you called her and said you didn't know what you were thinking."

"No, Thom," she said, coldly, "I didn't."

"How could you do this to me, Megan?"

She tapped her finger on my chest. I had a black tank-top on, the side of my pec was exposed.

"How could you do this to us, Thom?" she said.

Her finger lingered on my skin.

I looked down: T ♥ M

Dew and Mom whispered something to each other as my heart thrummed like a guitar.

"We going in?" Mom asked with sudden impatience, her voice cutting.

Megan stepped back and looked away, biting her lip.

Dewey reached into the pocket of his lab coat and pulled something out quickly and shoved it into his sweatpants pocket.

"What you got in there?" I pointed.

"It's a present for your fight, Thom," Mom said cheerily, her eyes covered in a glossy film.

She uncrossed her arms, walked over to me and kissed me on the cheek. "It's something from all of us. Because we love you." Mom wrapped her arms around my neck. The parking lot was quiet. The PA rumbled inside. Mom held me close. Tighter. My head swelled in Mom's grip.

"Mom, I gotta go."

"Just let me hug you, Thom. It's been so long."

She smelled strongly of whiskey and tobacco.

The PA began announcing the names for the undercard.

"Ma, I gotta get wrapped and go see the officials."

"Thom, this is it, right?" Her cheek was pressed against mine. Her hair spray tasted sterile on my lips.

"This is it. Just getting that O off as a pro. It's for Faith, Ma."

The PA rumbled. I heard my name. My heart raced and echoed in my throat. The jitters ran up and down my spine. I tried to step away, but Mom's grip was sure. I put my hands on her wrists.

"Ma, I'm serious, I gotta go!"

"We're tired, Thom, don't you get that? I'm. so. Fucking. Tired." She stepped back and cupped my face.

"You remember the beach trip?" she asked.

Tears ran down her cheeks. Her lip curled and then crumpled into her teeth as she bit down.

"Yes, Ma."

She tapped her foot, biting down. Her lips engorged and her face was red as a lit wick.

"You remember Daddy?" Mom whispered.

"I do," I said.

"Now or never, Ma," Dewey said.

In a flash, Mom side-stepped to my left and grabbed my arm. Megan rushed me and grabbed me from the right. They locked their arms and hugged me tightly, in a vice. My gym bag squeezed against my side. The toe of my boxing shoes nudged my ribs hard.

Dewey tossed off his lab coat and pulled out a plastic cylinder. He ripped a pink sticker off of it. I saw some of the lettering on it before he tossed it.

Three letters: KET.

I struggled, trying to push them off, but they had their hands locked in and pushed towards my center. My heart raced.

Frank stood in the window breathing in and out through his nose. His face was stricken and his jaw muscles rippled as he struggled with every breath.

"Meg, the fuck is this. Quit playing. I have to fucking go!"

"Thom, why can't you let it all go?" Megan said, crying against me. She struggled as I tried to shake her and Mom free, but she didn't budge. Mom and Megan clasped their hands together around my abdomen.

"Dew, what the fuck?"

He looked at me and I saw myself in his eyes. Saw it in the pale glow and the buzzing light. I was skinny again, gaunt. Dewey lunged for my shoulder and stuck the needle in. The parking lot was empty. The sky was empty. No stars that night. Just a curtain of black.

"What choice did we have?" he whispered somberly. "You said it yourself, Go'bay. This or Juarez. You think I'm going to let my brother die in some shithole parking lot in Mexico?"

The rumble of the PA shook the windowpanes. A sting shot up my shoulder.

I started to yell, but Dewey shoved his shoulder in my mouth, busting my lip.

Nothing to see here. Just a family hugging their fighter before his first pro fight.

"What the fuck?" I murmured into Dewey's shoulder, but my tongue was getting heavy. My head was getting heavy. The butterflies in my belly stopped fluttering and started limping through me. I tried to get out a yell one more time, but my tongue just rolled around in my mouth. My legs became liquid and weak.

Dewey garbled, "You thought you were the only asshole good with needles?"

My body slackened and then a blissful, consuming looseness, like catching a punch clean hit me.

Then, black. Black like death. I knew it all over again.

CHAPTER 46:
RING, BELL, RING

I sat on a stool at the edge of the ring with my hand over a folding chair. Frank sat facing me, running his bulbous knuckles through my hand wraps. The PA blared as they disconnected the mic for the National Anthem. A girl stepped down from the ring. She had pouty lips and caramel skin. She smiled nervously at me with glimmering hazel eyes and her brown curls bounced with each step. I nodded back at her and turned to look at the crowd; they were a sea of imperceptible faces underneath strobing green, yellow, and red lights. All except my family. The announcer droned. "Ladies and gentleman…"

Frank's cannula and oxygen tank was gone. His skin glowed with renewed color and vigor. He chewed on an unlit cigar as he wrapped my hands.

"Go, Daddy, GO!' Faith yelled, clapping her hands. Megan's mom had brought Faith at the last minute.

Megan bounced her on one knee and clapped to the music as it played the announcer off. He was morbidly obese and had buckteeth.

Mom smiled at me, her legs and arms crossed. They had good seats, on my corner, so close to the ring that they'd probably catch the spray of our blood and sweat.

"Other hand," Frank said.

I flexed my wrist and handed him my other wrist. He got to work quickly. I had a good sweat going. Frank and me had done some mitt-work a few minutes before. He was fluid. Back to a form less hobbled.

"Remember," he said, finishing up my handwrap, "first round, focus on the jab."

The door in the back of the arena swung open. I looked up, and my heart drummed; I felt each *lub-dub*.

It was Cruz. He strolled in carrying a plate of steaming hamburgers from outside. He was in his P. Terry's uniform. His hair was slickly combed back. Not a flake of pepper in it, pure black. Not a crease to his face. The light shone down on his tribal tattoo and it glowed like he'd just gotten it that day. He hadn't aged.

"Man," I said, "time is good to some people."

Frank chuckled and slapped my hands. He chewed on his cigar as pieces of the paper fell to the floor. "You're up."

The crowd roared.

But, the announcer never called my name.

JAB

The song switched as I walked to the stairs to the ring: **Right hand 2 God.** The vinyl scratched at the beginning of the song, and I put one foot on the first step. I climbed to the top and the lights dimmed. The strobe-lights cut out. The bass kicked in and the crowd disappeared. An engine revved outside. The smell of charred burgers burned in the close atmosphere. The smoke filled my nostrils. The only people I could see were Mom, Megan, Dewey, and Faith. Mom was crying, shaking her head side to side. Megan's tears showered Faith, but Faith didn't notice. Faith clapped her hands raucously. Her curls bounced as she clapped.

"GO, Daddy, Go!" she screamed.

I turned around and looked down the stairs at Frank one last time. Young as the day I'd first met him. Healthy. Cigar in his mouth, cherry burning. Skin tight to his face. Jaws clenched. Bright brown eyes and brown skin glowing with life.

Frank motioned up to the ring, the smoke of his cigar a halo around his head. The ringside judges were gone. No physician. No huddle of fighters staring at the canvas waiting their turn. All gone.

"This is it, Thom," Frank said from below.

I lifted the ropes and swung my leg under. The canvas was black and pulled taut like a drum. Not a fray on its surface.

Inside the ring, were three stenciled words arranged in a triangle: Hurt, Anger, Shame.

I bounced on my toes as Frank appeared in front of my face. He obscured my vision of the other corner, but I caught a glimpse of a leg swinging under the ropes.

A sudden veil was cast over us, it was just me and him.

"Okay," Frank said, cigar burning, "This it, Thom. Keep it simple. Jab. Clench. Brawl."

The smell of vinegar shot though the veil. A sting of pain hit me and I looked down at my right arm. My abscess was there again. Pus-filled, bulging, and weeping. I tried wiping it off with my glove, but it kept weeping.

I looked back at Frank, but he was staring at the other corner. His cigar smoke was a wall, I had to squint to make out the figures on the other side.

My opponent's trainer hopped in, and there was a break in the veil.

The fighter's trainer had a thick gray mop of peppered hair, and he held a True Religion bag in his hand. He turned to look at me. His eyes were black as caskets.

"Go! Daddy, GO!" Faith yelled. Her voice was as clear as running water.

Frank turned to me.

"He's gonna want to brawl you, Thom. Gonna come at you hard."

And I was tiny inside. Too tiny to fight. All the hurt came flooding back in waves of isolation, lovelessness, worthlessness.

Edwin shouted in the other corner in a gravelly, angry tone as he coached my opponent: "He's gonna be easy work. You know the gameplan, swing for the fences. Turn his ass into a Make-A-Wish kid."

Frank tapped the top of my head.

"Focus, Go'bay," he said.

His eyes glowed. It was the first time he'd ever called me that. All the chambers in my heart rang and clattered in my chest.

"He's gonna throw everything at you, and the kitchen sink."

Frank took a deep puff on his cigar. "So don't give him your whole heart in the first round."

The bell rung.

Frank tapped my shoulder and whispered in my ear. "You've seen him before."

The veil disappeared,

And so did Edwin.

It was just me and my opponent, facing each other. There was a single light above us, illuminating just the ring. And I did know him.

He had an abscess on his arm, painful black eyes full of malice and a curly brown afro. His cheeks were pulled in tight and he had dark ringlets around his eyes.

He was me: Twenty years old.

I put my guard up as we both rushed to the middle of the ring.

He chomped on his mouthpiece. He sported a wide grin. He wasn't going to stop until he got what he wanted. I didn't know if I could stop him. I couldn't back then.

I threw a jab immediately. His breath smelled like vinegar as he hissed and slipped and launched into me with a barrage of hooks to the head and body. My spine tingled as circuits of pain bounced back and forth from my jaw to my sacrum.

"That's what you get," he garbled through his mouthpiece. He smiled as he slipped back in front of me; his mouthpiece was all canines; stenciled on it were the letters H-U-R-T.

"I'm gonna take chunks out of you all night," he said.

I threw a jab at his face. I wanted to shatter his mouth. He slipped again and crouched low. He shot a hook to the left side of my body, landing on my spleen; then an uppercut, slicing through my guard and smashing against my chin, and then he shot a final hook to the liver. The lights above the ring dimmed. The Hurt was a blur.

"That's why I'm the hurt, Thom," he said, hissing. "I'll take everything. Jab ain't gonna do shit. You're coming back with me."

He stepped back, out of the reach of my flimsy jab. I sucked in gulps of air, but they barely reached my lungs. Each punch was pain and blood.

"I'll take them too." He pointed with a gloved hand to the

crowd, not a bead of sweat on his skin.

The lights flashed on in the arena, illuminating my family sitting in their seats at ringside.

Megan covered over her eyes as tears flooded through her porcelain hands. Mom coughed out black wads of spit. Dewey sat beside Mom, his eyes listless and vacant. I jabbed from my high-guard.

"Too fucking slow." He came back with five crunching shots.

"Gonna take your mom's savings." He licked his lips. "She's gonna die to give it to me."

Fires burned in every pore of my skin.

"You're coming with me. Where you always belonged," he said.

The shots came. The lights dimmed. He was just a voice now.

"You'll never change. You'll lose your daughter. Your family. Everything. It's who you always were. Worthless."

The canvas under my feet was soft and pliant on my soles. I could just drop my arms and fall into it. There was safety in defeat. I knew it well enough.

"Thom," Frank's voice cut in, gravelly. "You have to use your heart, kid. You're not him. You never were, but you've got to show him. You won't be able to stop him by shutting his mouth. Stop aiming for it. Take the jab to the body. Feint him. You're going to have to play your game. Not his."

Another blow. Another breath heavy as sin.

"Go! Daddy! Go!" Faith screamed. Her voice pierced the darkness, high and sweet. "You're not trying!"

I opened my eyes as an overhand right came straight for my head. I slipped and launched a jab to his body. He grunted.

"Fucker!" he said, his eyes glowed red.

"You're just hurt," I said through my blood-soaked mouthpiece. That's all he ever was: Hurt.

I feinted a jab to his head and shot another to his plexus. He grunted and stumbled back.

"You're going to ruin them," he garbled through his mouthpiece, swinging like a wolverine.

I slipped, and as I crouched low, I took a deep breath in. "No," I said, "no."

No: it was just a syllable, but it felt like the world lifting.

No was power. No was peace.

No was freedom.

I shot another jab to his plexus, a launching jab that started from the tip of my toes and travelled beautifully up the chain of my body and out of my fist like the release of an arrow. It connected flush, and his sternum caved in. He stumbled down to one knee. The blood in my mouthpiece tasted sweet, and the hell inside my lungs was like redemption. Edwin jumped into the ring as the bell rung. He hooked his arms under the closed eyes and gasping breaths of my Hurt. Edwin's pupils were a soft blackness, and his irises were as bright as white dwarfs. He nodded at me and pulled my Hurt out of the ring.

I stumbled back to the corner.

Faith screamed, "Go! Daddy! Go!"

I slumped down in the stool and Frank wiped my face.

"That's it, right?" I said.

Frank shook his head, the cigar smoke curling into the bright lights. The crowd cheered. The smell of vinegar and charred burgers was gone.

"It's a battle royale, Thom. You fight until there's nobody left."

CLENCH

Frank's cigar was halfway done. The muscles in his neck retracted and his lips were slightly bluish. He wheezed as he wiped my head and then squeezed a wet towel over my face.

"How'm I looking, though?" I asked.

He took a deep wheezing puff and turned around to look at the fighter swinging his leg underneath the ropes. All I could see were a Adidas pair of boxing shoes, a caramel leg, and blue trunks.

"Fuck!" Frank hissed. Turning to me quickly, he rubbed my face down with a glob of Vaseline. "This guy's an angry clencher. He's gonna pull you in, Thom. But you gotta stay relaxed in there. Work the angles on the inside, then get free." He put his fist to my chest softly. He laid his knuckles on my sternum and pushed in gently. "Close your eyes," he said, "breathe in deep."

I sucked in through my nose and smelled the hint of Aqua Di Gio.

"Keep your eyes closed and listen," Frank said as the music hummed on. A slow, deep beat began to play: *Blame on Me.*

"We may need to win this round on points. Won't be able to knock him out, but work the angles, get out of the clench and he's useless once you start working him from the outside. You have to be willing to let go, Thom. Let go."

The bell rung and the referee called from the center. "Let's go."

I opened my eyes as Frank's cigar left a greyish veil, and I stood within it. I tapped my gloves together and my eyes stung. I turned to catch a last glimpse of the crowd and bit down on my mouthpiece.

Megan stared into the ring, her eyes red and focused. Mom had her hands over her eyes, peeking through the slits. And Faith's brow was furrowed and her tiny mouth was cut straight as a board. She barked, "He's already hurt, Daddy!"

I stepped out of the veil, and rushing towards me was Dewey, eighteen years old with a full, curly afro and not a line on his face from reading CTs over and over again. Not a flicker of regret and despair in his face.

No, just two balls of black anger burning in his eyes and a crimson mouthpiece with the letters A-N-G-E-R stenciled across it.

"C'mon lil' bro," he said. "Imma send you back to the gutter."

He rushed onto me, the Aqua di Gio heavy on his Vaselined skin. He grabbed me underneath my arm before I could send a jab out towards him. The crowd disappeared under the lights as our bodies got close. His skin was a burning heat. And he dug uppercuts into my sternum and hooks to my liver and spleen. I swung a hook over his head, and like a dancer, he switched his feet and grabbed my other arm and got a clear line on my liver. He hurled a hook at it. And it took away my breath. I tried to go down, but he held me up.

"Fuck no, nigga," he said, his voice full of poison. "You gonna feel all of this."

He shot a ripping uppercut to my solar plexus. It was lightning in my body all the way down to my marrow.

Faith screamed from somewhere, her voice high-pitched.

"Now that I got you, I got some things I gotta say," he said. His lips were close to my ear as he clutched my arm in his arm; he had a vice stronger than Frank in his best day.

The thunder of his voice choked out all the sound of the arena. He twisted my shoulder.

The joint popped in its socket. The pain ripped through me. I was a drum for him; an echo.

"I fucking hated you. Fucking hated having to take care of you in the summer when they both had to work. Fucking hated the lecture. 'If anything happens to him it's your ass.'"

I shot my shoulder into his. But he was a block of cement. Didn't move. Didn't grunt.

"You were a burden! Fucking burden all my life. But, still, Mom coddled you. Had to coddle her hopeless fucking Go'bay."

An uppercut landed clean on my lower jaw. The shockwave was so intense, I bit down through my mouthpiece, cutting my tongue with my teeth. Blood pooled in my mouth. Spots of purple pain danced in my eyes.

"Fuck do you mean?" I garbled out with a mouthful of blood. "You were the first born!"

"First is worst."

A hook hit my liver.

"First suffers," he said.

A hook hammered my head.

"First has to be responsible for his brother's fuck ups. Always!" Dewey barked through his mouthpiece,

As he landed a final hook to my body, I would've crumpled, if I could've.

He'd broken my ribs. But, from it, a flowering anger bloomed inside me. It roared up through my throat, and whatever I had left to say in my lungs erupted. I spewed blood all over Dewey's face.

"You were supposed to be my older brother. My fucking protector. But you left me out to dry. Ratted me out. You knew Dad would banish me. You knew it, Dew. You know how fucking painful that was? To walk around Austin without a home? Without a last fucking name? I was a fucking ghost. A nothing."

"How do you think I felt?" Dewey hollered. "Dad all worried about you that night. He didn't even come with me and Mom to Chili's after. He spent the rest of the night putting your stupid fucking painting back together. Your family's better off without you anyways. Not even man enough to take care of your own damn wife and kid. Fucking pathetic."

He let go of me and I dropped to the canvas. I lay on the ground and blinked as the referee began his count. But, I was out. This was it. I couldn't beat him. He had me.

Faith needed a man that wasn't me. Megan too. They deserved better. Deserved better than a junkie. Deserved better than a Walmart employee. They deserved everything I could never be.

I closed my eyes. I could slip away. Just let it all go.

From the darkness, a faint echo, "Go! Daddy, Go!"

I opened my eyes.

A pair of fingers appeared in my vision. The walls were closing in. The darkness encroaching. The singularity closing.

"One...two....three..." the ref counted.

I closed my eyes.

I wasn't meant to survive this long anyways. Faith would be better off.

My heartbeat thrummed in my ears.

An engine revved somewhere in the distance. The sound of a Ranger at an intersection, thrown into park by a man slung over the gearshift. The sun was blinding in the cabin and the man sweat profusely. He licked his lips one last time as a blue glow oozed from the horizon, covering the road, covering the Ranger, enveloping the man.

From the blue glow, the sound of lapping waves. And from those lapping waves; a voice.

"It was a good day, Go'bay," Dad said, "that day at the beach."

He chuckled.

"Your mom tried to brush that red dye off ya'lls teeth for the rest of the night."

I opened my eyes, and breathed.

"...six...seven"

"Go'bay, here's the thing," Dad said. "You stay down, you live down. And it ain't just you that stays there. Your family gets swallowed by all that anger. It's a hungry thing. And if you let it, it will take everything."

"...eight..."

"Son, please," Dad echoed. "You gotta work the angles. That

anger ain't as strong as you. He's just ashamed. He just ain't showing it. But that's all it is. And he's gonna want to clench. Pull you into his world. And he'll beat you there if you stay. I promise you. You clench a clencher and the beating's only gonna get worse."

The blueness pulsed, and I heard in it, a softness like the feeling of waves lapping at my feet.

"Get up, Go'bay," Dad said, "let go."

"....nine..."

My diaphragm contracted and I took a deep, cleansing breath in through my nose. Dad's Aqua di Gio perfumed the ring. Not overpowering, just present. I pushed myself up as the count hit ten.

"You good?" the ref said, his face a blur.

I wiped away my tears. "I'm good," I said.

"Son, you gotta give it grace. And only thing grace is, is letting go," Dad said.

Dewey turned from his corner, his face filled with disgust and rage.

"I'm putting you down for good," Dewey smiled.

The referee motioned us forward, and as Dewey's arm went for the clench, I side-stepped and hit him with a check hook, catching the side of his face. He rushed again, his face burning in frustration, but he had a new cut above his eyebrow. And I settled into myself. Into a deeper place. Past the anger and the hurt.

"Go! Daddy! Go!" Faith screamed.

I bounced on my toes as Dewey rushed like a bull. I shot a sharp jab, and another, then rolled and switched my feet catching him with a swimming shot to the body and pivoted away. He grunted and turned back to me, but his shoulders dropped, and as he rushed, he heaved. His chest caved in and out. His smile was pathetic and weak. And his eyes lost some of the burning anger. I jumped around on my feet, my ribs still crying in pain, but I didn't focus on them. I focused on the fluid of my body, the joy of movement, the ecstasy of the kinetic chain as I shot a jab.

"Gotta let him go, son," Dad said.

I shot another jab. And then a hard right hand. It landed flushed on the cut. The blood spurted from it in droplets.

"You so often go for the bad memories," Dad said. "There's some good in there Go'bay, just dig a little deeper."

Dewey rushed me. I slipped him and shot a sweeping hook to the liver. His flesh felt sweet against the leather of my gloves.

Dewey grunted, and his eyes boiled. And then widened.

He sunk to a knee.

He breathed deeply as the ref counted, and when he looked up at me I didn't see the fighter. Didn't see the doctor.

I saw my brother. I saw his smile when we were kids. Splashing in the shore at the beach. The sunlight glittering in diamonds on the breakers. Grandma stood holding the camera on the shoreline.

"All right, here it comes," she said, her finger on the button. The wind whipped her silky reddish-blonde hair in her face. "Hurry up, ya here? Damn wind's gonna blow me to Mexico."

Before the camera flashed, I looked up at Dad and into the sun. He leaned over me and Dewey and was a gentle shadow shading us from the blinding light and the rushing wind. He smiled and a dimple showed on his cheek. Mom looked down at us, hanging over his shoulder, the wind whipped her blue hair across her face and her eyes were full of love and peace as Dad put his hands gently on me and Dewey's shoulders. "My boys," Dad said serenely. "Now, look at Grandma."

We turned to her, me and my brother, popsicles in hand, and toasted the world.

The bell rang and I turned from Dewey back to my corner. The stool appeared and Frank hobbled under the ropes to meet me. His face was wrinkled and his eyes were heavy and bloodshot. The plastic tubing of oxygen was wrapped like a noose around his neck and he took huge, sniffing breaths through his nose, but still, he clenched his cigar in his teeth. He took it out and held it as he coughed up a speck of blood in his hand and wiped it on his pants leg. I slumped down on the stool and laid my arms on the ropes. I was exhausted. Nothing crossed my mind except a prayer for the final bell. Frank produced a towel and started wiping my face. He put his cigar back in his mouth as it burned to an end.

BRAWL

The lights began to dim in the arena as I laid my arms on top of the ropes, trying to help my ribs expand. I was spent, each breath was a marathon. Spit and blood pooled in my mouthpiece. I was lucky to be there. Lucky to have made it that far.

Frank pressed the endswell against my eyebrow. I had a vicious cut that was a crimson curtain in my vision. I wanted to melt into the stool and disappear. I didn't want to push anymore. I just wanted to give in.

"I'm done, Frank," I heaved.

The lights dimmed to a faint glow. The crowd melted into the abyss.

Out of the curtain of blood, Mom disintegrated into nothing. I tasted the iron in my mouth, mixing with the salt in my tears.

Megan, disintegrated.

Frank pressed harder.

Faith waved at me. Her cheeks reddening as tears fell down her face.

"Baby, no," I said.

"Daddy, don't quit," she said softly as she disappeared. Her voice a plaintive echo.

"Frank," I said. "I can't go on without them."

He turned and stared into the abyss and bit down hard on his cigar. It was just a burnt end at this point. The abyss swallowed him as he turned back to me. He melted into a single, hovering cherry, but his voice remained.

"That's because only you can finish this thing, Thom." His fist touched my sternum. "This guy's crafty. You ain't gonna be able to just brawl him."

"Frank, I can't. My family's gone. I got nothing to fight for."

"Thom, you fight for them by fighting for yourself. That's what this is all about."

He shoved his knuckle deep against my sternum. My heart rattled against it, nearly empty, like a grackle flapping its broken wings on a piece of cardboard.

He lifted his fist from my sternum and gave my gut a soft punch.

"This right here, Thom, your soul, this is what you're fighting for. And you're gonna have to empty it out there. Goddammit if the last round ain't worse than hell. It's always that way. Ward and Gatti. Benn and Eubanks. It's all soul. They pulled it out from the same place that you'll have to if you want to have a chance at winning."

"Where's that, coach?"

"From Faith."

In the darkness, the end of his cigar blossomed like a lantern.

From the darkness, the referee spoke. "Fighters," he rumbled. "Step to the center."

Imperceptibly, I was up and at the edge of a tiny field of white light illuminating the last word on the canvas: Shame.

"Touch gloves," the ref said.

I reached out a glove.

"I ain't touching shit." It was a child's voice that spoke with the anger of a man.

I knew that voice.

I'd heard it many times. Heard him when I saw the text from Richie. Heard him when I saw Mom bent over the steering wheel as she shouldered the weight of a felony. I heard him when I walked away from my shattered canvas after Dewey's fight. Heard him when Dad slapped me. I knew him well.

A plaintive note on an electric guitar struck up in the arena: *Maggot Brain.*

"Fight!" the ref's voice urged.

And we stepped into the limelight.

There he was; there I was: Nine years old. Golden brown skin. Dark angry eyes painted in perpetual shame. And a scraggly reddish afro.

"This is it, Go'bay," Shame said, smiling. All white teeth. He didn't need a mouthpiece. He knew my counters. Knew my evasions. He had answers for all of them. He was going to leave the arena spotless. Same as he'd come in.

And from the darkness, Faith,

"Daddy! You can't just stand there!"

The first blow knocked me into the abyss.

I stumbled back, as the blows landed from every corner of space.

Dark matter exploded in my eyes. I put my hands up going through the motions of blocking, but I was fighting blind. And from the darkness, sets of eyes opened at me. Eight blinking eyes, sparkling and poisonous. The blows kept coming. I put my hands up into a high, tight guard. The cracking power of the blows nearly broke my wrists and hands. His voice pierced the darkness, a child howling: "You block me. You try to hide from me. And she gets it," Shame spat.

The constellation of eyes in the darkness blinked in twinkles of horrible joy.

The blows stopped.

I took down my hands and looked for him.

The spiders were laughing.

In the middle of the ring, the light shone down in a single ray, and Shame stood there in a near perfect stance.

His hands were in a tight high guard.

His shoulders relaxed.

His torso bladed. His breathing was soft and easy. His legs, though tiny, were muscled and electric. He balanced on the balls of his feet like he'd been born to bob and weave. And in front of him was Faith, holding her Pikachu up at him, making it dance before him.

She smiled at him.

"Daddy, I'm making Pikachu dance," she said to him.

"Imma make you let go of it," my voice came out of his lips like a poison.

Faith's eyes widened as she held up her Pikachu to shield herself. She turned to me.

"Daddy! Help! Please!" she screamed.

It was a curdling siren of fear. I'd never heard it in that register.

The blinking eyes on the periphery cackled.

Shame turned to me. "I told ya what I would do," he said, and turned back to Faith. He got into his stance and pushed off his back foot launching a jab towards her.

"No you fucking don't!" I screamed. I rushed out of the corner.

"Daddy!" Faith cried.

I howled, but the canvas grabbed me with spider legs of fabric. My ankles tickled horribly with their hairs.

I tried kicking them off.

His fist corkscrewed towards Faith.

Faith cowered.

The Pikachu exploded into a puff of yellow and white stuffing and the jab landed flush against her face. It knocked her out of the light. And he rushed towards her, disappearing into the darkness.

The spider legs let go and I rushed to the middle of the ring. But, he was gone. So was she.

"Daddy!" Faith cried from the darkness. Then, there was the horrible sound of gloves hitting flesh. Faith moaned in pain.

"Stop it, Daddy! Please." The voice was slowly losing its life.

I pushed towards the darkness, but I was trapped in the glow of the single beam of light; a blinding prism.

Shame's voice echoed with every punch.

"This is your fault!" he howled.

Thwack!

"You made me do this!"

Thwack!

I pushed against the prism, but it was useless. The hands of the canvas reached up and grabbed my arms and dragged me down. I breathed through a straw, laying there. Pressed against the canvas.

"You passed it on to her," he growled, "The germ of me."

"Please," I cried. "Why are you doing this?"

"This is where you belong, Thom. This is who you are. A shameful man. Worthless. Can't even protect your own daughter. Couldn't even protect yourself from some pedo art teacher. No wonder your wife wants to fuck another man. Go back to where you belong. Lamar ain't too far from here. Never is."

The light above shuttered off. The spiders yapped like coyotes in the darkness. Barking. Howling.

I lay on the canvas, my soul leaving my body. The spiders crawled all over my skin. Their fingers were everywhere. I closed my eyes.

"Please," I cried. "Help me."

I bit down on my mouthpiece and chewed. Chewed the blood, spit, and mucus of my soul. I had nothing left. No faith.

"Thom," a soft, feminine voice whispered in my ear, "this how you gonna leave it?"

"I don't have anything left," I said.

"Did you give everything?" the voice whispered.

"I gave it all." I spit out my mouthpiece and stared into a crawling nightmare.

A speck of light widened above.

Faith's cries echoed.

"Can't change who you are, Thom," Shame said, but his voice was growing fainter.

The light widened some more. The crawling abyss relented slightly as a figure emerged. First, it was two legs bathed in shadow, then, two arms. Then, the body of a woman. She was carrying something. I blinked and there she was.

Elise smiled at me as she cradled her daughter to her bare chest. Her baby nursed gently.

Elise's hair was strawberry. Her lips were thinner.

She chuckled. "I'm a natural red."

She looked back down at her nursing baby as she spoke to me.

"So what about the shame, Thom? You ever address it?" she said, kissing her baby's forehead.

"I thought I did."

"How?" she asked.

"I started boxing."

Elise shook her head and stroked her baby's fontanelle. Tears ran down her cheeks, down her jaw, down her clavicle, down the globe of her breast and around it to her nipple to the mouth of her baby.

"Thom, you don't address it by fighting it. The war's still going on inside of you. Look," she said.

I was able to get up and sit on my knees. Faith sat in a corner, huddled, bruised, and bleeding, rocking back and forth.

Elise floated down beside me and pointed to another corner.

Megan stood in it with bruises all over her chest and mouth and eyes and face.

Dewey was huddled in another corner rocking back and forth.

Mom was in her own corner as well, smoking a cigarette on cut lips and a bruise black as a plum on her sternum. The bruise made a sound like a ticking clock.

"The war continued, Thom. And there's always collateral

damage."

I looked over at Faith. My heart cracked.

I wanted to hug her. Hold her. Console her.

I tried get up and run to her. But I couldn't. I was held in place.

"Let me go!" I turned and yelled at Elise.

"You have to let go of the handcuffs first," Elise said softly.

I looked down at a pair of sterling silver cuffs on my wrists.

A long chain was attached to the center link and it ran to all four corners of the ring. I tried to wrench my hands free. Tried to muscle the links free, but the more I did the tighter the cuffs got around my wrists.

"Thom," she said, "You shut him out, and he ends up shackling more of you."

The chain clanged and pulled my hands high and up. I was wrenched upward to my feet.

"What do I do?" I asked.

"You have to face it," Elise said.

"I don't know how," I said.

All the shame in my life ran through my body like I was caught in a current. It whipped and tossed me as the ring filled with water up to my chin.

The only thing saving me was the chain, and I grabbed onto it as it dunked me and lifted me and I caught gulping breaths.

"Thom, you'll get battered to pieces if you hold on. You have to let go."

The waves rushed around me but I could still see Elise through the sea foam. Her baby was gone, but Elise held her arms like her daughter was still there.

Elise wept and looked down at the invisible form.

"It's the only way, Thom," she said.

"Go, Daddy, Go!" Faith's voice cut through the crashing waves around me.

As I was dunked and lifted again, I held my hands tightly to the chain, gripping it for dear life.

"I can give you the key," Elise said.

The waters receded as the chain dumped me on the canvas, and I lay there panting.

Elise bent down to me and handed me a small key.

"It's up to you, Thom," Elise said.

I held the key in my hands. It was tiny. Simple. Grey. Not much at all.

"But, you have to unshackle yourself," she said. "For her."

Elise pointed to the corner as I lifted my head and a spotlight flicked on at Faith in the corner. She was grown. She had grown into her chubby cheeks, and her nose was more angular. Her hazel eyes glowed brightly and she smiled at me, but her teeth were broken and snaggled. She was covered with bruises.

"He'll follow her too, Thom, Follow your whole family line. Until there's nothing but collateral damage."

"Daddy, please," Faith said. She was shackled, too.

I couldn't do it anymore. I just couldn't.

I fumbled with the key as the chain yanked and Faith disappeared.

"Unshackle yourself, Thom," Elise said. "Here he comes. You have to get up and face him."

From the darkness, my nine-year-old self rushed me, holding the end of the chain as I undid the shackles and pushed myself to my feet.

"What do I do?"

"Let him come." Elise said.

"I have to fight him off."

"No, you don't."

He rushed me. The spiders sat on the edge of Elise's light, eyes hungry and waiting.

"You've been fighting him your whole life. Give it a rest. Give him that peace. So you can give it to yourself."

Elise nodded at each corner where my family stood. "So you can give it to them."

Faith stood at the corner. "You can do it Daddy," she said. "Please."

I dropped my guard as he rushed me. And I didn't feel the blow. Didn't feel the pain.

I looked up, cradled by Elise.

"That's it, Thom."

The light expanded.

"What you fight, you avoid. What you face with open arms, you give peace."

I blinked, and I was standing in the middle of the ring. The light shined softly on me. I held something small in my arms. It had small arms. A small torso. And had its tiny, reddish afro buried in my chest. It sweat madly against me and cried, pitifully.

I clutched him close. His gloves laid on the canvas. His mouthpiece covered in bloody saliva lay dripping on the stenciled Shame in the center of the ring.

"It's time for both of us to let it go," I said, "I'm sorry for what happened, but you and I both know I can't keep living like this. It's time, Go'bay."

He garbled a reply. "I know, Thom," he said and looked up at me, "I just needed you to tell me that it was okay to let go."

I woke up in my bedroom and looked up at the popcorn ceiling. Half of the ceiling was smooth, the other, popcorn.

It was one of Dad's last projects, half-finished.

I turned over and saw Frank, sitting on my old painting stool near my easel by the window. A few hardened paintbrushes laid on the wood platform. Frank leaned slightly back, sitting against my desk where I'd drawn and sketched for hours.

He had his hands clasped on his cane as he looked out the window onto the street. The maple leaves filtered the glow in a golden light. It was splotchy, and wavering.

"Hey," I said.

"Hey," he said, turning to me.

His eyes were baleful and jaundiced. He sucked in deeply through the prongs in his nose. His oxygen concentrator, a wheeled box the size of a CPU, sat and hummed at his feet. I wanted to know why they did it, not because I wanted to fight or yell or control. I didn't feel that rage anymore. I just wanted to know.

"Who gave the go-ahead? Megan?" I asked.

Frank shook his head. "Nope."

"Mom?"

Again, he shook his head. "Nope"

"Dewey?"

"Nope."

Frank looked at the door. Then at his hands. He laid his cane against his leg and sat forward and rubbed his palms slowly.

"You?"

Frank nodded solemnly. Head-bobbing like a turtle.

"Why?"

"Those videos, Tommy. It was too much."

I wanted to be angry. Self-righteous. Vengeful. But the fight didn't spring up. War didn't feel natural anymore. It would've just been another prelude to lying. I had to tell him the only thing worth telling, the only thing that meant freedom:

"I relapsed a year ago. The night I found out about Richie."

"Heroin?"

"Almost, I was right off Lamar. Standing at the Shell station. I stared at my lock screen for thirty minutes. I had a few guys's numbers still memorized. Ain't that crazy? Ten years later and it came back like that." I breathed out deeply and looked up at the ceiling as I remembered that moment. My heart was a frenzied bird. Just darting back and forth. From thought to thought, trying to settle on one. I'd told myself up until that point that I was free. That freedom and boxing were synonymous. I'd told myself I wasn't an addict, but in that moment, it came back like it'd never left.

"I opened the lock screen and Faith had somehow gotten a hold of my phone and screenshotted herself giving me a kiss. Her lips were smushed to the screen."

Frank chuckled. "She's a smart one."

"I looked at her face for a while and then went to a bar and got shit-faced. Smoked a cigarette too. Woke up the next morning laying on the porch."

I'd felt like shit that morning. I opened my eyes to heat. It had been 10:00 A.M.

And when I sat up, there was a sticky note on my chest. *I love you, but I just can't do this anymore. Back door's open.*

"I could tell," Frank said.

I looked over at him. He was a dalmatian of sunlight.

"How?"

"You looked funny the next day at the gym. Your face was all bloated and red."

Frank chuckled and then stared at the easel.

A car passed on the street, bass bumping.

"I remember your dad," he said.

"You knew him?"

"I did," Frank stared at his knuckles. "He was a decent fighter. Just undisciplined. I let my guys tee off on him."

Frank shook his head woefully.

I couldn't imagine Dad leaving himself open.

"Coaches can be the worst. Sometimes we're the worst part of the sport, pushing our little marionettes out there," Frank said.

Mom rattled around in the kitchen downstairs, getting breakfast ready. Someone sshh'd her. It sounded like Faith.

The walls of my parent's house were paper thin. I don't know how I snuck out when I was a kid. I used to think that Dad knew I was leaving, and one day he'd hoped I'd leave and never come back, but maybe he knew as much as I did that it was hard raising kids. He couldn't force me to be the best version of myself. Maybe he knew I needed the crucible. Maybe the agony for him was that he couldn't protect me from it. He couldn't protect me from the losses that a man places on himself.

Frank cleared his throat. "Ya know, Thom, taking a loss doesn't make you a loser. It's a fundamental law of life: you're going to lose more than you win. But, to you, the nine losses was like 9,000,"

"Frank, I just wanted to show my family that it wasn't all smoke and mirrors. And then when I got bat-shit drunk, I was back where I'd been ten years ago. Fucked up. A loser. Square one could come back in an instant. That scared the fuck out of me."

Frank shifted on the stool. He turned from the window and faced me.. He planted his cane in front of him. He clasped his hands on it and rested his chin on his knuckles. "Losers walk out on their kids and never come back. Losers pretend like shit doesn't hurt them. They walk around thinking they're bulletproof. It's either a win or a loss for them but they never learn any of the lessons boxing is trying to teach them. They go through life with a broken mind and a broken family in the wreckage. Mindset is the determinant, not the record."

A tiny droplet of shame still lingered in me, but I knew if I kept it in me, it'd become a lake and then an ocean. The only way to stop it was to let it out and let it go.

"I'm forty and I still work at Walmart. If I have a heart attack at work, that's what they'll say about me. Died wearing a name tag unloading a pallet of frozen peas," I said.

Frank smiled, and I saw the old glimmer. The fire that only a coach has; the kind of fire that can get other men to walk through a volcano.

"Your daughter doesn't need to read your nametag to remember your name. She knows you. Not only does she know you. She saw you during COVID. All those losses. All that heartbreak. She saw her daddy fall and pick himself up each time. She knows who you are, Thom. All the way. When I went to see my kids once every two years, they needed a refresher. Now, I only talk to them at Christmas. They call me just to make sure I'm still breathing. And even that's more than I deserve." Frank laughed. "They don't even know that I've got..." he cleared his throat then stuttered, "what I've got."

"What's that mean?" I asked.

"It's hell out there, Tommy. The only way you make it through is if you start loving yourself and loving the people around you. You'll miss everything if you don't. That's where the tenth loss lives. That's where your daughter forgets you, and your wife carves your name into a tombstone and lives the rest of her life with another man."

Frank looked away. "If she'll take you. Go back, and don't look back. Forgive her for what she's done, just as much as she's got to forgive you for what you've done. And if she won't or you can't find it in your heart to reconcile, you be a man, forgive her and take it. Take it and love her as the mother of your kid. Give her some peace, so she can give it to your daughter...There's nothing worse than being barely above a nametag to your own family.

This is your crossroads, Tommy. Sometimes a man can't see it. We get so focused on the mission, we start missing things. I know the stakes you've put up. But, that doesn't mean your family doesn't put it up too. Every time you step foot in that ring, you take the punches, but it's your family that deals with the aftermath, myself included."

Frank leaned on his cane heavily, and his back quivered. He drew in a deep, expansive breath and breathed out through his nose. When he spoke, his lips trembled.

"I've got cancer, Tommy. Non-small cell carcinoma. Stage IV," Frank said. "They say chemo could give me a chance."

Frank's cane was the center of gravity.

The oak leaves danced in the window. Some of them yellow. Some green. The sunlight glowed in the yellows like a snapshot of life in decay. The shadows of the young, green leaves landed darkly on Frank's face.

Keys jingled downstairs. Faith howled joyfully.

"Where they going?" I asked

"The park," Frank murmured.

I heard the front door open. Faith sung as they made their way to the car. Mom and Megan talked as their shoes clicked on the pavement. Car doors opened and closed. The Lexus turned on, backed out, and was gone.

And then, the house was silent except for Frank's wheeze and the hum of his concentrator.

I stared at Frank. He sighed deeply.

"I'd love a cigar right now."

He cleared his throat, and sniffed.

"You know, the first and last lesson in boxing is humility, Tommy. First lesson is when you get humbled by a guy who's just better than you. Second time is when the game finally passes you. You get dog-walked for the second time in your life and that's when you have to be man enough to face it. You gotta be humble to start something, but you also gotta be humble enough to finish it. If you hold onto it, that's where the losing is. You devote yourself to the wrong things. You make the mistake of calling it nobility, but there's no nobility in devoting yourself to things that don't have your last name. Just losing."

Frank shook his head and tapped his cane. Tear ran down his cheeks like rainwater, dripping from the shadows of the young leaves on his face. He wiped his face with his sleeve and pushed himself to his feet, leaning heavily on his cane. "Your mother left a letter for you," Frank said as he nodded at my desk. He grabbed the handle of his rolling concentrator. "I've got an appointment with my on-cologist."

I sat up slowly and my head felt clear and light. I put both hands on the edge of the bed and saw the thin envelope with a yellow sticky note. "Who's going to take you?" I asked.

"Uber," He shrugged. "I couldn't expect my kids to give me that honor now. I never gave it to them."

"I can take you," I started to stand, but sat back down immediately, my head felt like a spinning top.

"No," Frank said softly, "you still need your rest."

I steadied myself with my hands on the edge of the bed and stared into the carpet, trying to keep the world from spinning. "I can help you get downstairs at least," I said, "give me a second."

"I got it, Tommy," Frank said. "I'll just take it slow."

Frank walked over to me slowly, his cannister wheels clanging as the tiny rusted screws holding the wheels together wobbled in their motion, but Frank held his shoulders back and his chin slightly tucked.. He wasn't down for the count, not by any means, but he was humbled. We both were.

He stopped in front of me and let the cannister rest on it wheels. He leaned forward holding his cane and grabbed me around the neck.

"Pray for me, Tommy," he said, "And talk to your wife."

There was a sticky note over the envelope and it read:

Go'bay,

I was supposed to give this letter to you 10 years ago, the day you got out of rehab, but I was scared. I didn't know what Daddy had said. I still don't. But it's been long enough. You get the choice now. I can't keep trying to choose your life for you. If Daddy said some mean things in it, so be it. If he said some good, so be that, too. But it was for you, and I held it. Just like I held everything else. It's time for all of us to let go. Even you.

Love always,

Mom.

I held the envelope. My heart revved. But I wasn't going to avoid it. No more avoiding. No more pretending. No more fearing. No more shaming. Just facing and forgiving. I slid my nail across the envelope and it loosened its lip easily. I pulled the letter out. It was yellowed and looseleaf. I unfolded it on my desk, smoothing it as Mom's Lexus rolled back down the driveway.

Dear Thom,

I'm writing you this because I got some news the other day. I had some wacky stuff on my EKG. So, they referred me to see a cardiologist and he says I need stents. He says I've got some pretty bad blockages. So, I've got to go under the knife and I'm scared, Go'bay. Not because of the surgery but because of the drugs. I don't want them to give me the kind of drugs that you do. It scares me shitless. It always has. I feel like I've seen it all my life; I felt like I was a casualty of it. First, it was your grandad. For him, it was the alcohol and cocaine. He took me to your uncle's house once and there was this mound of white powder on the table; I thought it was sugar. I wanted to taste it, but when I went to stick my finger in, your grandad whooped the shit out of me; only good thing he ever did. And then, it took him. Took him away from me. From your aunt. From your grandma. He was dead by the time he was 45. I've made it almost ten years longer than he did. Praise God. But I see it taking you Go'bay. And it filled me with rage for so long.

Still does. I couldn't protect you from the world, again. I'd failed you when I couldn't protect you from your art teacher. I failed you when I couldn't protect you from the drugs. I failed my father by letting that disease creep back into his family. And I took it out on you, and that's my biggest regret in life, because, above all else, I love you Go'bay. I loved you from the moment I held you in my arms. I swear, you had the most golden-brown skin I'd ever seen. When me and Mom bathed you for the first time all I could feel was your heartbeat underneath my fingers. It felt like my heartbeat. My heartbeat was a living thing. I could hold it. Feel it. Love it.

So, if something happens to me on the operating table, I want you to do something for me; I'm going to try to start doing it for me too, as long as I'm alive.

I want you to know I forgive you. I hope you can accept it. I want you to work on forgiving yourself, too. It's the only gift you'll ever give yourself that'll actually get better the more you use it. So, use it, Go'bay. Use it like water to soil.

I hope you'll start painting again.

Love always,

Dad

P.S. The Ranger's yours if I go. Mom, God bless her, would trash it in a heartbeat.

For most of my life, I'd thought of "no" all wrong. I thought "no" meant: no living, no enjoyment, no pleasure, no joy. I enjoyed "yes."

"Yes" was pleasure-seeking.

"Yes" was pain-denying.

"Yes" was getting my hands on anything I could to keep the Yes's going.

"Yes" meant I could escape myself for just a little bit longer.

Everything had to be outside of myself to make sense, because nothing inside ever did.

I never gave myself the opportunity to sit with what the Yes's were avoiding.

But as I sat at the desk with Dad's letter in front of me I realized something:

"No" didn't mean pointless suffering.

"No" didn't mean more hurt, more anger, more shame.

"No" meant discipline.

"No" meant integrity.

"No" meant peace.

Sometimes you do have to stand and fight.

And sometimes standing and fighting simply meant standing, facing, accepting—and saying no to everything else.

Sometimes fighting for peace is forgiveness, the act of giving peace even when you're not ready.

"Ready is for people who don't ever do anything. "

CHAPTER 47:
IT FEELS SO GENTLE

August 2026

I stand on the curb in the Chili's parking lot as cars roll by on Lamar. I kick a few pieces of barky, black mulch with my tennis shoes. I put my hands in my pockets. There are a couple of plastic packages on my fingertips. The sun sets in a deep peach. The wispy clouds above are filled with the final glow of the sun, a mix of purple, peach, and violet. The cars roll by in a soft hush behind me. A bus comes to a halt at a stop as its brakes wheeze gently. The tag on the back of my collar makes my neck tingle like a spider is crawling on me. As I grab it and rip it off, Megan's Mazda pulls into the parking lot.

When I see her now, I understand things a bit more. I understand why she felt like she had to choose what she chose.

I don't agree with it. And it hurts still. But, I've learned to put its anger in its place. It's a wound that I've come to understand and, on some levels, appreciate, because of the nature of the pain it caused. That pain was my crucible. And my pain was my responsibility. And to sit with it, and accept what had happened, whether I felt like it or not, was the only way I could move on. It was the only way to let the wound heal. It's the only way that I could give my daughter what she deserved: peace.

The lights in the parking lot flicker on and emit a soft buzz. Megan pulls to a stop in front of me and cuts her lights. Tiny moths begin their nightly carousel, swirling around the lights as starlings swoop in for their meal. Megan waves softly at me. I wave back.

I step off the curb and make my way to her window.

She rolls her window down and the first gush of air I get is her fruity perfume and the smell of her hair. Her hair is curled and a glossy black sheen. She has a fresh shade of makeup on, expertly done. She hangs her arm out the window. Her ring finger glimmers with a large diamond.

The rehearsal dinner is tonight.

"Well, hello, Mr. Therapist," she smiles.

"Hey Meg," I say. I shift in my scrubs. I still don't feel comfortable in them. I've just started clinicals.

"What you got in your pockets?" she motions, clicking her teeth at me.

I finger the small packages against my thigh, trying to grab a hold of them. It's embarrassing. I feel like a criminal to still have them.

I pull out two packages and open my palm: albuterol.

"Forgot to turn them back into the med storage," I say.

"I'm calling the board," Megan says, chuckling. She puts her hand on my wrist. Her diamond ring is a kaleidoscopic flash of light as it catches some of the glow of the parking lot lights. "I'm glad you're doing this, Thom."

Her eyes linger and she holds my wrist softly, not clenching. Her eyes become dark and a raven caws above.

As I look back at her I want her to feel what's inside of me:

It's okay. I'm okay. I want to be happy. I want you to be happy.

She shakes her head and smiles as she says, "Even got yourself a nametag, Thomas Middlecamp, RT Student."

"Yay, Daddy!" Faith cries from the backseat, kicking her feet.

Megan leans towards me. "I'm sorry about Frank."

"Yea," I say, "but, his family came. They at least got to speak to him before it was all over."

Megan nods as a sparkling tear rolls down her cheeks. She lets go of my wrist and crosses her arms on the windowsill. She plants her chin on top of her hands and looks up at me. "Did you finish the painting?"

I turn away looking at Lamar.

I'd be out there if it wasn't for Frank. I don't think I can ever pay him back for that. He saved my life and all I have for him is a painting of us I'd done:

Me and him. Standing ringside, his arm over my shoulder. I smiled with a cut and bruised-up face holding up my gloves. His cigar hung from his mouth and he had a smile like a kid who'd just gotten off his training wheels. It's all I have to give. It's the best I can give for what he did. Of all the people I've ever met in my life, he's been the only one who's shown me that there are lessons in the darkness. Lessons in the clench. Lessons in the brawl. I can learn from my losses. I can still get back up on my two feet. I can be more than a man who spent his entire life driving while staring into the rearview. I let my tears go as I look at Lamar unafraid of what I see in its mirror. I wipe my eyes and turn back to Megan.

"So you and Richie coming to the funeral?" I ask.

Megan's eyes grow wide. "Is that okay?"

I can't run from the future as much as I can run from the past. Running is just a way down a rabbit hole. I want life. I want peace.

Peace: It's a hard hill to climb, but I can see the arcing river of myself from it. I can look at my reflection without looking away.

"It's always gonna hurt. It shouldn't have gone down that way," I say. Megan's face turns sour. Her smile fades and her brow begins to screw. "But I can't hold onto that forever. And ever since we talked about things, I've been able to make peace with what happened between us. I have to make peace with him, too. He's going to be around our daughter. I want her to experience peace in her family, finally."

Megan's eyes soften and her lip trembles. She turns from me. Her black curls bounce and her head shakes slightly. She sniffs and looks back at me as she rubs her tears away.

"Daddy, can we go?" Faith whines.

"In a minute, baby," I say.

I take it all in. I take in Megan and Faith. I take in the Chili's. I take in Lamar. I take in Austin. And I can't help the surge of sorrow and joy I feel. I thought that school would feel like giving up on something. I thought that school and a job in a hospital was something that I'd be doing for someone else. I thought that way for years, but today at clinicals I saw a kid: 22 years old, with a tube down his throat: OD'd. And I felt something real. I felt like maybe there was a conversation to be had. Maybe the day he'd get extubated I'd be the one to do it. Maybe I could sit down and talk to him for a few minutes on my lunch break. Maybe he could finally open up the box that every addict keeps locked up; the box that seems to ever only open with the drugs; never knowing we have the key in our hands the entire time. Our hands are clenched around it, clenched so tightly because it's always easier to say yes. Maybe I could tell my story. Or maybe, I could shut up and listen and let some of those things inside his box howl. Maybe I could allow him to get some breathing room, some space with peace, because I can take it. I can face it. I can accept it.

ABOUT THE AUTHOR

Rodger Ella lives in Austin, Texas. When not writing, or hanging out with his dog, Faith, you can find him at Unity Combat Club in Austin, Texas. He is currently working on his next novel of speculative fiction. If you'd like to support his work, please consider leaving a review where you purchased this book.

"Thank you for reading Ghosts of Lamar. If you have a moment, an honest review on the platform of your choice helps other readers discover Thom's story. You can also scan below to join and be forwarded to my Substack and join the newsletter for updates about future releases.

9 798995 476504